PENGUIN BOOKS

THE PORTAB
SHERWOOD A~~NDERSON~~

Each volume in The Viking Portable Library either presents a representative selection from the works of a single outstanding writer or offers a comprehensive anthology on a special subject. Averaging 700 pages in length and designed for compactness and readability, these books fill a need not met by other compilations. All are edited by distinguished authorities, who have written introductory essays and included much other helpful material.

"The Viking Portables have done more for good reading and good writers than anything that has come along since I can remember."
—Arthur Mizener

Horace Gregory, a major poet and literary critic, is the author of many books, including *A History of American Poetry, 1900–1940*, written with his wife, Marya Zaturenska, and *The House on Jefferson Street.*

The Portable

SHERWOOD ANDERSON

Revised Edition

Edited, and with an introduction, by
HORACE GREGORY

PENGUIN BOOKS

Penguin Books Ltd, Harmondsworth,
Middlesex, England
Penguin Books, 40 West 23rd Street,
New York, New York 10010, U.S.A.
Penguin Books Australia Ltd, Ringwood,
Victoria, Australia
Penguin Books Canada Limited, 2801 John Street,
Markham, Ontario, Canada L3R 1B4
Penguin Books (N.Z.) Ltd, 182–190 Wairau Road,
Auckland 10, New Zealand

First published in the United States of America
by The Viking Press 1949
Paperbound edition published 1956
Revised edition published 1972
Reprinted 1973, 1974, 1976
Published in Penguin Books 1977
Reprinted 1979, 1981, 1983

LIBRARY OF CONGRESS CATALOGING IN PUBLICATION DATA
Anderson, Sherwood, 1876–1941.
  The portable Sherwood Anderson.
  Reprint of the ed. published in 1972 by Viking Press, New York,
in series: The Viking portable library.
  I. Title.
PS3501.N4A6   1977   813′.5′2   77-8163
ISBN 0 14 015.076 5

Printed in the United States of America by
Kingsport Press, Inc., Kingsport, Tennessee
Set in Linotype Times Roman

Acknowledgment is made to Liveright Publishing Corporation for permission to include "Death in the Woods" and "A Meeting South" from *Death
in the Woods,* "In Washington" from *Hello Towns,* and four sketches from
Sherwood Anderson's Notebook.

Contents

FROM POOR WHITE

SELECTED STORIES

MEN AND WOMEN

REPORTAGE AND EDITORIAL

A SELECTION OF LETTERS

The Portable Sherwood Anderson

Editor's Note

So as to satisfy several points I have made concerning Sherwood Anderson, I have slightly changed the Introduction. At the suggestion of Malcolm Cowley, this edition of the *Portable* differs from the first by the inclusion of the entire text of *Winesburg, Ohio*, and an editorial abridgment of *Poor White*.

Editor's Introduction:
A Historical Interpretation

When Sherwood Anderson died in 1941 the moment was not unlike that at the death of D. H. Lawrence eleven years earlier: a pause was felt, even though neither writer was then at the widest span of his reputation. Today Sherwood Anderson's reputation is more secure than it was in 1941, and his short novels, tales and stories, like the writings of D. H. Lawrence, have lived well beyond their day of being in or out of fashion. Like the legend of his life which he created in his autobiographies and memoirs, his tales and stories have independent life of their own, an existence no longer sustained and modified by that of a widely known figure on a lecture platform. The decade following a writer's death provides, often enough, the severest test of his true vitality. Even in his lifetime, his popularity, his "fame" may suffer (as Anderson's did) polar extremes of critical approval and indifference, but the years following his death are a test of his survival in the world that he has left behind him. Of American writers of the 1920s who were also "poets" (in the same sense that some European writers of prose are given that distinction), Sherwood Anderson has achieved his promise of "immortality", and it is not surprising that his place in the literature of the twentieth century is close to that of two writers for whom he felt particular kinship, Gertrude Stein and D. H. Lawrence.

The reservation of a place in the company of Gertrude Stein and D. H. Lawrence scarcely defines the singular impression that Sherwood Anderson makes upon the imagination of the reader, yet for all the particular qualities that have set him apart from other writers of the day, it is not inappropriate to think of *Winesburg, Ohio* and *Horses and Men* as placed in the same climate in which *Sons and Lovers* and *The Prussian Officer* and Gertrude Stein's *Three Lives* exist. In each, one finds something of the same temperature, the same charm, the same authentic presence of a personality.

All three writers joined in the large, and for them victorious, cause of liberating prose from a multitude of literary clichés, and thereby saving their own works from the dust that falls so thickly upon library shelves. Each gives the reader (and beyond this their kinship ends) a vision usually reserved for readers of poetry alone, a view of life, familiar to be sure in "realistic" detail, but far more "alive" than the resources of prose and of fiction commonly permit.

European readers who come to Anderson's *Winesburg, Ohio* for the first time feel the proximity of a new speech, a "new country," a fresh view of the Main Street that Sinclair Lewis had opened for them. The interrelated stories of *Winesburg, Ohio* offer something that is less foreign to them than the restless, half-satirical observant eye that guides the reader so faithfully through the pages of Lewis's realistic novel. What is felt in *Winesburg, Ohio*, felt rather than read, overheard rather than stressed, is a memory of youth, of early "joys and sorrows," and this is conveyed with the simplicity of a folk tale, a style known in all languages. To the American reader another level of almost subterranean feeling is contained in Sherwood Anderson's novels and stories. The streets and landscapes here depicted are close to the roots of an American heritage which takes its definition from the writings of Emerson, Whitman, Thoreau, Melville, and Mark Twain. Critics with as diverse opinions of Anderson as those expressed by Lionel Trilling on one hand and Van

Wyck Brooks on the other have agreed in recognizing these particular features of Anderson's "Americanism," his almost instinctive and acknowledged debt to writers who represent the Emersonian aspect of the Great Tradition in American literature. It is clear enough that Anderson's writings are of that heritage and not in the Great Tradition of Hawthorne and Henry James. But why were they "instinctively" so, why were they ranged so conclusively on the side of Thoreau and Whitman? As one reads Anderson's autobiographies and memoirs, it is absurd to think of him reading Thoreau, Emerson, and Whitman in the spirit of one determined to follow a "party line" in choosing the sources of his inspiration; it is absurd to think of him surrounded by books in order to draw "ideas" and intellectual convictions from them. He drew upon the life he saw about him, the very air he breathed on memories of a roving, outdoor childhood, on the few books loaned to him by friendly schoolteachers, and on the talk of middle-aged men in small Middle Western towns who had taken a fancy to the brilliant, sensitive, imaginative son of a Southern drifter and tall-tale teller. These were the essentials of Sherwood Anderson's early impressions; they are the actual sources of whatever Anderson thought and saw and felt; and all other experiences, whether of reading or of sensitively overhearing conversation which flowed around him, were superimposed upon them.

The impact on Anderson's imagination of Thoreau and Whitman came in later life, but the important impressions of his boyhood were the associations of what is now called a "democratic" heritage: the diluted forms of oratory at Fourth of July celebrations, the speeches made at county fairs, the talk overheard at race tracks, and through the swinging doors of the nineteenth-century, Middle Western, small-town saloon. In these surroundings, legends of Abraham Lincoln flourished, floating upward into Ohio from Illinois and Kentucky— stories pertinent to Anderson's own half-Southern, log-cabin origins. He, too, came from a "shiftless, drifting" family, and so he was particularly sympathetic to the picture of Lincoln reading books by the flickering, red glare thrown from a log-cabin hearth, to the figure of "the man of sorrows" and unrequited love, the shrewd country lawyer who told tall stories in the back rooms of general stores, the gaunt, distracted figure, clad in a nightshirt, pacing the floor of his bedroom in the White House, reading jokes aloud from an open book or periodical, and finally, the martyred President, who loved the North and South alike, the author of the Gettysburg Address—these pictures hung as icons in the mind of the impressionable boy.

Beneath the seeming contradictions of Anderson's discussions in his memoirs, novels, and topical essays of socialism, democracy, and the twentieth century "machine age," there lies a singular loyalty to the heritage of a Middle Western boyhood. It is in this connection that the year of his birth, 1876, and the place where he was born, Camden, Ohio, are of relevant meaning. Anderson grew up in a place that was permeated by that "religion of humanity" of which Emerson was the transcendental fountainhead, showering forth his concepts of the "oversoul" like rain from the clouds; across the prairies of the Middle West his name and Thoreau's represented New England "culture," and when their writings were read at all, which was only in small circles, they were tolerated with more respect than understanding. Those who lived through the post-bellum years of the Civil War in the Middle West demanded both more and less of their own priests of "humanity" than they did of the memory of Emerson.

The new priests were champions of reason and of Herbert Spencer's *First Principles*, of Henry George's *Progress and Poverty* and Edward Bellamy's *Looking Backward*, of Robert Ingersoll's lectures on the Gods ("An Honest God Is the Noblest Work of Man") and on Individuality ("Every human being should take a road of his own....Every mind.... should think, investigate and conclude for itself"). These new priests spoke in the names of "democracy," "science," "progress," and "liberty"; most of them were in revolt against the older Protestant sects and denominations of New England, against Puritan restraints and moralities, and yet the shadows of older taboos were among their obsessions. Sherwood Anderson's generation in Ohio and Illinois felt in boyhood the presence of Ingersoll's "individuality" and his faith in "science" with greater intimacy, and, perhaps, greater clarity, than Thoreau's "Civil Disobedience."

Compared with Ingersoll's rhetoric, a flamboyant language of evangelical threats and promises ("Science took a tear from the cheek of unpaid labor, converted it into steam, created a giant that turns with tireless arm, the countless wheels of toil"), Thoreau's writings seem austere, and his serene appreciation of solitude at Walden almost classic in feeling and Puritanical. But to Anderson's generation the voice of Ingersoll was the voice of "progress"; it promised the arrival of a "new day" for those who had been attracted to The Noble Order of the Knights of Labor, and yet it shouted down with equal vehemence of the totalitarian Utopia of Bellamy's *Looking Backward*. "We are believers in individual independence," said Ingersoll. "We invent . . . we enslave the winds and waves." It was through the invention of machines and the tools to control, improve, and mend them, that the "religion of humanity" offered its rewards on earth to members of its congregation; and to Sherwood Anderson the delight of invention for its own sake never lost its spell. To invent became part of his pleasure in telling a story, and the very inventions of the machine age, an age whose virtues he came to distrust and to criticize, never lost their fascination.

Although Ingersoll's attacks on Christianity had crippled his political career and had left him, scarcely content, with the office of Attorney-General for the State of Illinois, his influence on those who read him or heard him talk grew to enormous proportions. Anderson had little concern for merely rational arguments in favor of science, and no respect whatever for inflated rhetoric, yet the sentiments of Ingersoll, overheard or half-heard from the lips of talkers in small-town newspaper offices and saloons, are of the same character as those that filled the young and speculative mind of George Willard in *Winesburg, Ohio*. The sentiments of Ingersoll prepared Willard for the story of the Reverend Curtis Hartman in "'The Strength of God," and the same source of inspiration provides a logic of its own for the arrival of Hugh McVey, the inventor, the central figure, if not the "hero," of Anderson's *Poor White*.

As we speak of Anderson's heritage and his place in American letters, it is never appropriate to name too loudly other writers who directly influenced his writings; like D. H. Lawrence, Anderson is a singularly unbookish figure, an "original," a "'maker" in his own right. He is also the self-educated writer, whose brief stay at college (the college was Wittenberg at Springfield, Ohio. "Later they called me back. They gave me a degree," he wrote in his *Memoirs*) was the least memorable of his experiences. Yet like many self-taught writers, what he read for pleasure held a place more deeply rooted in his imagination than the place held by required reading in the minds of those who are "educated" by the thousands in colleges and universities. As one reads Anderson's stories and autobiographies, three older writers come to mind: one is Herman Melville, another Mark Twain, and the third George Borrow. In writing tributes to older writers for whom he felt a particular affinity, Anderson always remembered Borrow, and in doing so he showed a more profound depth of self-knowledge than many of his critics have attributed to him. Superficially, his choice of Borrow seems very far from the area of his distinctly American heritage. In the oceanic stream of nineteenth-century British prose, Borrow, the author of *The Bible in Spain, Lavengro*, and *The Romany Rye*, was a distant figure to his contemporaries. But that distance, and the failure of critics to classify Borrow's books as fiction or autobiography, as stories or novels, have their relevance to the attraction that Anderson felt to Borrow. The people about whom Borrow wrote, companions of the road and alehouse, pugilists, "bruisers," tinkers, "the Flaming Tinman," boys who loved horses and ponies, gypsies, fortune-tellers, the poverty-stricken Welsh and Irish nomadic figures, are not unlike the people that Anderson knew in the American Middle West. All of Borrow's people are tellers of stories, and whether Borrow retold these stories with respect for literal truth is of less importance than is the record he created of the essential life within and around them. His writings have the same peripatetic atmosphere that is sometimes felt in Anderson's *Horses and Men* or *A Story-Teller's Story:* his was an art of speech that wanders slightly, that seems to walk, that philosophizes gently in an almost absent-minded fashion. It is important also that Borrow, the accomplished linguist, called himself "the Word-Master," for Anderson, with far greater aesthetic discrimination than Borrow, knew himself to be a "Word-Master" of another, and American, kind.

Anderson's liking for Borrow has an instinctive rightness beyond anything he could have learned through a conventional education. Borrow showed what a writer could do while ignoring the conventional rules for writing autobiographies and novels. This was a valuable lesson that Anderson never forgot; he became, as Thomas Seccombe wrote of Borrow, not a "matter-of-fact," but a "matter-of-fiction" man. He did not allow Borrow to influence him directly, and in matters of style, in which Borrow was notoriously uneven, Anderson greatly improved upon him. The choice of Borrow as one of his models placed Anderson on the side of those who see and feel things from the ground up, from the pavement of a city street, from the grasses of a field, from the threshold of a house. This view is always an independent view that refuses to become housebroken.

Anderson's debt to Mark Twain is less veiled than that to Borrow, for Mark Twain's *Huckleberry Finn* is literally close to an American time and place that Anderson knew. In his letters to Van Wyck Brooks, Anderson speaks authoritatively on the subject of Mark Twain, whom he sees as a distinctly American phenomenon, a figure who stands in the company of and between the figures of Lincoln and Whitman: "Twain's way lies somewhere between the roads taken by the other two men"; and in respect to Twain and Borrow, Anderson wrote, "In my own mind I have always coupled Mark Twain with George Borrow. I get the same quality of honesty in them, the same wholesome disregard of literary precedent." Of the "real" Twain, Anderson wrote to Brooks, "Should not one go to Huck Finn for the real man, working out of a real people?" The people of Anderson's boyhood in the Middle West were but a single generation beyond Tom Sawyer and Huckleberry Finn, and there was an unbroken continuity between the two generations. Huckleberry Finn's skepticism concerning the virtues of church-going was of a piece with the world that Anderson knew, a world whose enjoyment was of the earth. Anderson's affinity to Mark Twain was as "natural," as unstudied, as Anderson's memories of growing up and coming of age. Equally natural was the example of perspective taken from Borrow, choosing the life of the out-of-doors as the true center of worldly experience.

With Melville, Anderson's affinities are of a far less conscious order; they belong to the inward-looking, darkened "nocturnal" aspects of Anderson's heritage. The affinities to Twain and Borrow are of daylight character; they are clear and specific and are sharply outlined within the lively scenes that Anderson created, but his kinship with Melville belongs to that diffused and shadowy area of his imagination which Paul Rosenfeld named as mysticism. As they spoke of his mysticism, even Anderson's best friends became confused because Anderson, like Borrow before him, distrusted philosophic generalities; for himself, he would have little or none of them; he would plead ignorance of large thoughts and pretensions, though he would gladly speak of how he came to write a story and, in *A Story-Teller's Story*, tell something very like another story to illustrate his point. He thought in symbols, in metaphors, in images, in turns of phrasing, in terms of a situation, or a scene of action—and in this language whatever is meant by his "mysticism" is half revealed. The friendship of Ishmael, in *Moby Dick*, with the dark-skinned savage Queequeg has a quality akin to the quality of the boy's contact with Negroes in "The Man Who Became a Woman" or the sound of Negro laughter in Anderson's *Dark Laughter*. It was once fashionable to call such "mysticism" Freudian, because it touched upon the emotions of adolescent sexual experience. In Anderson those emotions are transcended in "Death in the Woods," and whatever "mysticism" may be found within them, including the expression of mystery and awe, is of an older heritage than are the teachings of Freud in America. Ishmael's decision to share a bed with Queequeg—"Better sleep with a sober canibal than a drunken Christian"—and the horror of Queequeg's first impression upon him are closely, if broadly, allied to the mysteries, the transcendental qualities, of sexual experience in Anderson's stories, and to find that kinship one need go no further than the story "Hands" in *Winesburg, Ohio*. The diffused affinity that Anderson has to Melville is not a facile one, for Anderson made it one of his few rules to stand aside from "literary precedent," to re-create scenes of action in terms of his own experience rather than to lean upon experiences gained from reading the works of others. The kinship of Anderson's writings with *Moby Dick* embraces that side of Anderson's imagination which is "non-realistic," and which converts what is outwardly the simple telling of a story into a series of symbolic actions. The fluttering, "talking" quality of Wing Biddlebaum's "slender expressive fingers, forever active," in "Hands," is endowed with the mystery that Anderson makes his readers feel. And when the Reverend Curtis Hartman in "The Strength of God" breaks a church window with his fist, the action carries with it undertones of symbolic, almost transcendental, meaning; the impulse which drove Curtis Hartman to his action was a force greater than his will, and with appropriate irony he assigned that impulse to "the strength of God."

Throughout many of Anderson's stories and in his autobiography, *Tar: A Midwest Childhood*, the figure of the boy who is created to tell the tale bears a strong family resemblance to Melville's Ishmael, and behind this figure there is the other Ishmael, son of the bond-woman Hagar in Genesis. The figure is one who will inherit no fortune, is of nomadic character; a figure whose association with the Biblical story, half-concealed behind his obvious relationship to Huckleberry Finn, gives him a faint aura of transcendental kinship with the Old Testament. Ishmael will inherit no fortune; he is the typical nomad. Though Anderson's Ishmael, if we choose to call him so, has acquired a resemblance to Huckleberry Finn, he still retains an aura of transcendental kinship with the Old Testament. Literally, of course, the boy's mother, as she appears in *Tar*, is no Hagar, but the roving character of the family milieu is close enough to Hagar's wanderings in the desert to make explicit Waldo Frank's observations on *Winesburg, Ohio*, that Tar, growing older, is George Willard, and that "a Testamental accent and vision modulate every page of Sherwood Anderson's great story." So they do. Despite Anderson's "naturalism," despite his skepticism concerning the moralities of orthodox church-goers and the Reverend Curtis Hartman, an atmosphere of Biblical vision and semi-divine faith attends the motives and denouements of Anderson's Middle Westerners.

It may seem strange that Anderson, the maker of legends and stories, is not among the best of those who write auto-biographies as their major work of art. Anderson's gifts as "a matter-of-fiction man," like those of George Borrow, usurped his hold upon literal facts. In the writing of *Tar* he had half promised himself to write *the* autobiographical story, but in his foreword he explains his lack of interest in literal truth:

> It was only after I had created Tar Moorehead, had brought him to life in my own fancy, that I could sit down before my sheets and feel at ease. It was only then I faced myself, accepted myself. "If you are a born liar, a man of the fancy, why not be what you are," I said to myself, and having said it I at once began writing with a new feeling of comfort.

It was only when Anderson saw himself as a character that his re-creation of essential truths began to take on the air of remarkable candor; in his posthumously published *Memoirs* he is frankly bored with the chronological progress of events, and is deliberately careless in the naming of dates, as though everything he had to say about himself belonged to a single moment in the past that is called "once upon a time." In all his autobiographical books and sketches, it is the legend of his life that charmed him and charms his readers; his love of wandering, of men and women, of horses, of Midwestern landscapes, of county fairs, of small-town streets and houses, takes on the colors of a reality that is far more convincing than the figure of their author. The real Anderson is in his stories, in George Willard of Winesburg, in "The Man Who Became a Woman," in "I'm a Fool," in Tar Moorehead, and is notably less visible whenever he assumes the personal pronoun "I" in *A Story-Teller's Story* and in his *Memoirs*.

To understand the importance of his legend a few facts (over which Anderson glided in his *Memoirs*) are pertinent: Anderson was one of seven children in a family that migrated from town to town in rural Ohio; his mother was of Italian or German origin, and his father, a man of declining fortunes, came to Ohio from the Southern United States, and was consecutively a harness dealer and a house painter. As a small boy, Anderson was known as "Jobby" Anderson, the boy who did odd jobs of great variety which later formed the general background of the experiences that came to life in his stories. From this he drifted into jobs in factories, into and out of Chicago, and then enlisted as a private in the Spanish-American War, which carried him through Southern training camps and south to Cuba. Then came his short winter at a Middle Western college, and from there he went to Chicago and wrote copy in an advertising office; and shortly after this experience he went into business and ran a small paint factory in Elyria, Ohio, only to return to Chicago and an advertising office, and at last to begin in earnest a career of writing stories. These experiences were central to a culture and an environment that he shared in part with other writers of his generation, with Theodore Dreiser, who was born in Indiana, with Edgar Lee Masters, born in Garnett, Kansas, with Vachel Lindsay, of Springfield, Illinois, with Carl Sandburg of Galesburg, Illinois—and these were writers who, like Anderson, came into wide public recognition in middle age. Anderson, in his autobiographies, had much the same story to tell as his contemporaries. All had something of the same unorthodox schooling, and many of the same memories of Ingersoll, Herbert Spencer, Henry George, Edward Bellamy, and William Jennings Bryan. All carried with them a boyish admiration of Abraham Lincoln, and Masters, not unlike Anderson, had a special fondness for the writings of Mark Twain. Anderson's autobiographies cross and recross the territory also discovered in the autobiographical writings of Dreiser, Masters, and Lindsay, or the monumental biographies of Lincoln written by Carl Sandburg. These are all of one cloth, and only the particulars of Anderson's own legend weave a distinctive pattern through the fabric. Not a few of the literal facts of his life—the classless poverty of the Middle West, in which a new job, a new life, lay at the next turning of the road or the next railway station; the experiences of a short, successful Spanish-American War, which for so many young men was almost a patriotic holiday —were of the cloth, and not of the pattern. The more valuable part of what he had to say was contained in the legend of how he made up his mind not to be a business man, how he stepped out of his paint factory in Elyria, Ohio. As he began to look about him in the small town and become absorbed in the lives of the townspeople, as he began to sit at his office desk only to "lose myself in the writing of others. . . . it was all disastrous to my business," the time had arrived to pack up and go:

I resorted to slickness, to craftiness. Already I had got a reputation for a kind of queerness among my acquaintances. Men had seen me walking somewhere in the outskirts of the town and suddenly beginning to run... The impression got abroad. I perhaps encouraged it—that I was overworking, was on the point of a nervous breakdown. . . . The thought occurred to me that if men thought me a little insane they would forgive me if I lit out, left the business in which they invested their money on their hands. I did it one day —walked into my office and called the stenographer—It was a bright warm day in summer. I closed the door in my office and spoke to her. A startled look came into her eyes. "My feet are cold and wet," I said. "I have been walking too long on the bed of a river." Saying these words I walked out of the door leaving her staring after me with frightened eyes.

I walked eastward along a railroad track, toward the city of Cleveland. There were five or six dollars in my pocket.

The episode has a classic ring, and it is Anderson's contribution to the legend of how poets and novelists in the Middle West found themselves: Masters, the Chicago lawyer, giving up his practice when the notoriety of *The Spoon River Anthology* awakened distrust among his clients; Sandburg creating the impression, according to his biographer, Karl Detzer, of a "wandering minstrel with a frayed shirt-collar and an old guitar"; and Lindsay trading rhymes for bread and lodging across the United States from New York to San Francisco.

Anderson's personal decision was of more superficial likeness to the decisions made by those writers who had created the Middle Western school, "a robin's egg renaissance," as Anderson called it, in Chicago. It was consistent also with what he had to say in the novels and stories that brought him fame, and with the tradition of Ishmael, the man who walks alone, and it was finally consistent that he should be converted to socialism but then tear up the essay to which he had given the title, "Why I Am a Socialist."

II

If the "real Anderson" is seen more clearly in legendary episodes of the autobiographies than when he employs too consciously the pronoun "I," how vividly, how memorably he moves before the reader in his major novel, *Poor White.* It may seem pretentious to call so modest a book a major novel: its bulk is scarcely greater than *Winesburg, Ohio* and no greater than Anderson's *Many Marriages, Windy McPherson's Son, Marching Men, Dark Laughter,* and *Kit Brandon.* But one never measures Anderson's writings by their physical size, for he is essentially the creator of short forms in fiction, in which the short novel is included; despite his easy, deceptively rambling manner, his true concerns were for scenes and people that could be revealed in a single gesture, a single episode. When he wrote an introduction to the Modern Library edition of *Poor White*, he told his readers that the actual hero of the book was a small Ohio town, Bidwell, Ohio, and that the people of the town, even the central figure, Hugh McVey, the 'poor white" Lincolnesque inventor, were supernumeraries—they were, it is true, the life of the town, but what happened to the town was what he wished remembered. Today one reads *Poor White* almost as though it were a particular kind of historical novel; time has refreshed it and thrown into perspective the ideas, the events, the atmosphere of a late-nineteenth-century American small town that had thrust forward the fortunes of a Hugh McVey.

What values *Poor White* has gained in the years between its publication in 1920 and today are similar to those we place upon Frank Norris's *The Pit* and Dreiser's *The Titan*. The elder novels take Chicago as their center, and the scenes of the Middle Western city, with its "pioneer" competition and rapid acquisition of wealth, have now assumed, with greater force than any costume novel attempting to revive the period could have done, the character of both historical and social novels. The town of Bidwell, Ohio, and the book *Poor White* itself are parallel creations of the same period on a smaller scale. *Poor White* belongs among the few books that have restored with memorable vitality the life of an era, its hopes and desires, its conflicts between material prosperity and ethics, and its disillusionments, in a manner that stimulates the historical imagination. The book belongs to the period, those years between the middle 1870's and the first ten years of the present century, that gave Thorstein Veblen's *The Theory of the Leisure Class* (the book was first published in 1899 and it is relevant to say that its author was born in Wisconsin and taught for a number of years at the University of Chicago) its air of immediate reference. It was in *Poor White* that the ideas, the talk overheard in Anderson's boyhood, bore fruit. In the second chapter of *Poor White* we come upon the following observation:

In even the smallest of the towns [the towns of the Middle

West] inhabited only by farm laborers, a quaint interesting civilization was being developed. Men worked hard but were much in the open air and had time to think. Their minds reached out toward the solution of the mystery of existence. The schoolmaster and the country lawyer read Tom Paine's *Age of Reason* and Bellamy's *Looking Backward*. They discussed these books with their fellows. There was a feeling, ill-expressed, that America had something real and spiritual to offer to the rest of the world. . . . Long-drawn-out discussions of religious beliefs and the political destiny of America were carried on.

Anderson names some of the sources from which novelists like Dreiser and philosophic economists like Veblen drew, as he did, inspiration as if from the air, and he names the premise on which a number of their critical attitudes were founded. Anderson also described the evangelical promise of that "new force" in American life of which Ingersoll was so ardent a champion:

A new force that was being born into American life and into life everywhere all over the world was feeding on the old dying individualistic life. The new force stirred and aroused the people. It met a need that was universal. It was meant to seal men together, to wipe out national lines, to walk under seas and fly through the air, to change the entire face of the world in which men lived. Already the giant that was to be king in the place of old kings was calling his servants and his armies to serve him. He used the methods of old kings and promised his followers booty and gain . . . The Morgans, Fricks, Goulds, Carnegies, Vanderbilts, servants of the new king, princes of the new faith, merchants all, a new kind of rulers of men, defined the world-old law of class that puts the merchant below the craftsman, and added to the confusion of men by taking on the air of creators. . . .
And all over the country, in the towns, the farm houses, and the growing cities of the new country, people stirred

and awakened. Thought and poetry died or passed as a heritage to feeble fawning men who also became servants of the new order. Serious young men in Bidwell and in other American towns, whose fathers had walked together on moonlight nights along Turner's Pike to talk of God, went away to technical schools. . . . The impulse had reached back to their father's fathers on moonlit roads of England, Germany, Ireland, France, and Italy, and back of these to the moonlit hills of Judea where shepherds talked and serious young men, John and Matthew and Jesus, caught the drift of the talk and made poetry of it; but the serious-minded sons of these men in the new land were swept away from thinking and dreaming. From all sides the voice of the new age that was to do definite things shouted at them. Eagerly they took up the cry and ran with it.

In these lines Anderson conveys the emotional and speculative temper of the day and region which *Poor White* re-creates concretely in the imagination of the reader; but he also gives the scenes of his novel a historical perspective, by establishing their contemporaneous disillusionments. His position is obviously not that held by either the theorist, the reformer, the economist, or the politician, but rather the one held by the novelist, the American, non-Marxian historian, the individual who shared the hopes of those who had preached the religion of humanity.

Anderson did not reach the occomplishment of *Poor White* without preparation; in writing *Winesburg, Ohio* he had begun to discover his style, and in the last chapters of the book he had really found it. He records the importance of that discovery in his *Memoirs*, how the book came to life in a series of stories while he was living in a Chicago rooming house. But *Poor White* also has behind it his first novel, *Windy McPherson's Son*, published in 1916, and more particularly his second book, *Marching Men*, which Anderson mistakenly thought should have been a poem. *Marching Men* was a novel that failed to accomplish its intentions— yet it foreshadowed the kind of historical novel that *Poor White* eventually brought into being. At best the book was a historical tract—an outline of an idea for a novel which was to embrace the problem of labor leadership in America, and this was to be topped off by the spectacle of American workingmen marching in a huge body to correct maladjustments in our industrial and technological revolutions. Anderson's vision was prophetic as well as an inspired recreation of past events. What the book lacked—and this was also the cause of failure in the writing of *Windy McPherson's Son*—was mature understanding of human impulses and their results. Anderson's early attempts to write "a novel of ideas" quickly fell to earth. The nearest he could approach to that ambition was to write the historical parable of *Poor White*: meanwhile *Marching Men* remained too didactic, too abstract in feeling, too consciously "humanitarian" to take on the semblance of life. Its hero, "Beaut" McGregor, the tall, awkward red-haired miner's son who becomes a lawyer, and afterward a leader of workingmen, is too thinly drawn; he is an unindividualized type, whose eventual failure as a leader of men is not felt by the reader. And the entire book is punctuated by fictional clichés. Behind the obvious failure of the book, however, Anderson gives meaning even to his all-too-typical hero, for McGregor recalls the figure of General Coxey, who in the Populist movement, during the administration of Grover Cleveland, led an army of unemployed men to Washington, D. C. McGregor also resembles another Populist hero, John Peter Altgeld, Governor of Illinois, who pardoned the Haymarket anarchists and attacked Cleveland's action in sending federal troops into Illinois to break the American Railway Union. It is important that both Coxey and Altgeld were natives of Anderson's Ohio, and though the McGregor of Anderson's book was a Pennsylvania miner's son, his temperament fits the characters of the native Populist heroes of Anderson's early manhood. It is important also to remember that the living models from which the fictional McGregor was drawn received public ridicule and abuse, and that their groups of marching men, like McGregor's, met with the extremes of spectacular notoriety and failure. The only scene in *Marching Men* that comes to life is irrelevant to the historical and social themes of the book—and that is the passionate recital of trouble with women by a minor character, a barber. In the barber's speech on his unhappy marriage and his relationship to women the accents of the future Anderson are heard; the barber's theme is expanded in *Many Marriages*, and is heard with greater clarity in *Dark Laughter*. It it sounded fitfully in Anderson's first novel, *Windy McPherson's Son*.

A far too broad and loose fictional method of writing cultural history had its beginnings in *Windy McPherson's Son;* in *Marching Men* Anderson still attempted what seemed to be an impossible task; in *Poor White* his failures were followed by a unique achievement in American fiction. In this novel Hugh McVey, the self-educated "poor white" inventor of farm machinery, who turns the little town of Bidwell, Ohio, into a center of industrial "progress," with war between craftsmen and machine-workers, between workers and employers, remains unaware, until the closing pages of the book, of the evil and loss of spiritual heritage that his well-intentioned machines have brought to the people of the town. In leaving the Chicago of *Windy McPherson's Son* and of *Marching Men* for a scene not unlike that of *Winesburg, Ohio*, Anderson found the means of giving the people of his novels flesh and blood—and through their actions, their speculative thinking, their hopes, their sense of having made mistakes, we find the real Anderson.

His Hugh McVey, as he confessed in a letter to Van Wyck Brooks, was conceived in the physical image of Lincoln, and was "a Lincolnian type from Missouri." And because of this conception, the figure carries an aura of myth-making around it and is slightly larger than life-size. Hugh McVey, as one reads of him, becomes more than one man, and one associates him with other inventors of devices and machines, with Thomas Alva Edison and with Henry Ford. His belated emotional maturity, his devotion to mechanical crafts and skills, his near-blindness to issues that lie outside the province of making machines are characteristic of the scientific-inventor type and lead McVey to the disillusionments he suffers in the face of industrial troubles, of strikes and lockouts, to the scene in which he looks at a group of colored stones held loosely in his hand:

> The same light that had played over the stones in his hand began to play over his mind, and for a moment he became not an inventor but a poet. The revolution within had really begun. A new declaration of independence wrote itself within him. "The gods have thrown the towns like stones over the flat country, but the stones have no color. They do not burn and change in the light," he thought.

The scene also brings Hugh McVey close to the character of his author, the real Anderson, the man of insight, who had become weary of advancing the causes of business and salesmanship in Chicago advertising offices, had felt the emptiness behind the slogans of American prosperity and progress, and had contributed to the most extreme, most experimental of non-commercial little magazines, Margaret Anderson's *The Little Review*, then edited and published in Chicago. Like D. H. Lawrence, Anderson is frequently most successful in his fiction when one of his characters reveals some aspect of his own insight and emotion.

At Hugh McVey's side, how typical of her time and place, is Clara Butterworth! Clara, the daughter of a well-to-do farmer, had gone to college and then come back home to marry. She is one of the most convincing of Anderson's portraits of women, and she is treated by him with the chivalry which, despite his candor in talking about sexual relationships, always enters into his descriptions of girls and women. The exterior manner of Anderson's portraits of women, whether he views them working at looms in a factory or as ex-hostesses of brothels (see the portrait of Aunt Sally in "A Meeting South") is that of the shrewd American provincial—but under the surface of this half-worldly, half-boyish admiration, a deeply chivalrous attitude toward woman emerges. To unsophisticated and would-be realistic readers, Anderson's chivalry might well seem odd. By combining chivalry with sexual candor he achieved a very nearly European manner, with an air that seemed almost Italian. It is little wonder that fifty years ago American critics called him "an Ohio pagan."

Poor White, a tribute to a cultural past, does not, of course, resemble the costume historical novel in any of its features: it is as plotless as though Anderson had wisely taken to heart Mark Twain's warning to the readers of *Huckleberry Finn*—"persons attempting to find a plot in it will be shot." And he drew as much from the example of Mark Twain's kind of plotlessness (which never, however, permitted a story to lack action and incident) as from the examples provided by the stories in Gertrude Stein's *Three Lives*.

No novel of the American small town in the Middle West evokes in the minds of its readers so much of the cultural heritage of its milieu as does *Poor White*. In his later novels Anderson never recaptured the richness of associations that *Poor White* contains. Certainly no other American novel so memorably and clearly charts the course from an agrarian way of life to the discontents of technocratic—and urban—civilization.

III

One of Anderson's critics has remarked on his ability to write at his best only when the impulse to write urgently moved him, and that statement has an enlightening truth within it for anyone examining his short stories. In these he held to his position of being one whose concern for prose was like a poet's concern for the art of verse. He was the teller of stories, one who desired only to gratify his needs to talk and to charm his listeners—and all this without the thought of earning money or material rewards. But if his standards seem often those of one who perpetuates the folk tale in its original simplicity, he was also the conscious artist.

His prose is less close to poetry than one might suspect, and very like impressionistic painting. In reading his stories, one sometimes thinks of Renoir, whose style—the impress of his personality—shone in every stroke of his brush upon the canvas. At its best Anderson's prose has the same authority, and even in such brief sketches as "The American County Fair" one can discern the presence of light and air between each word in a descriptive paragraph. The same impressionistic strokes of writing introduce the reader to scenes in "The Egg" and "The Man Who Became a Woman." It is in seeming at times to wander away from his story that Anderson so often relaxes and lures his readers, and within the details of an impressionistic haze of light and color that he often creates an "artlessness" that conceals his art.

In Anderson's stories, from the early pieces which became parts of a series in *Winesburg, Ohio,* to his masterpiece "Death in the Woods," one sees the particulars of people, rather than the types that one finds in his novels. The first edition of *The Triumph of the Egg: A Book of Impressions from American Life in Tales and Poems* (its subtitle is not to be ignored) is illustrated by photographs of grotesques in clay by Tennessee Mitchell. The burlesque heads of the people in this book are in spirit with the stories told about them: their very eccentricities are carried upward into a higher register of fantasy. Since Anderson's view is always from the earth upward, in the story of "The Egg" the flight of fancy takes off from a child's-eye-view level, and we are warned early in the story that a grotesque humor will be released: we are told, "Grotesques are born out of eggs as out of people." The scene of the story is again Bidwell, Ohio, the very setting in which the events of *Poor White* took place. The story is of chicken-farming and its failure, seen through the eyes of a child whose father was an unhappy chicken-farmer, and the grotesques which come out of the eggs, the misfits, the deformed wonders of the world—the side-show of two-headed roosters and five-legged hens—are the centers of meaning in the story. The story is painful, ridiculous, naive, and ultimately terrifying—the story of the ex-chicken-farmer who becomes a restaurant-owner and a grotesque himself—but it is one that only Anderson could tell and yet create a minor masterpiece. And the sidelights of the story illuminate a burlesque of American salesmanship, for the ex-chicken-farmer and his wife, as Anderson writes, "became ambitious. The American passion for getting up in the world took possession of them." From the child's-eye-view through which Anderson presents it, the story has the authenticity of a fable, an air of candor which saves it from falling into bad taste, and the high spirit in which it is told rescues it from a mawkish concern over the spectacle of repeated failure, for the grotesque man is no more successful as a restaurant-keeper and panic-stricken salesman than he was as a chicken-farmer. It is the kind of story that, having been told once, cannot be told again; it is the story that makes the entire book, *The Triumph of the Egg*, memorable, and all the other stories and verses in the volume grow pale beside it; these others seem to have been written with less urgency of impulse and, though no less lyrical in tone, are thin and diffused. The book is in fact The Triumph of the Egg.

Anderson's ventures into the higher registers of fancy (which make it strange to think of him as a realist, as he was once classified) did not end with *The Triumph of the Egg*—the ventures had actually begun in "Hands," the first of the *Winesburg* stories, and indeed the prelude to *Winesburg* was called "The Book of the Grotesque." As the image, the theme, and the fear of being grotesque matured in Anderson's imagination, some of the most clearly inspired of his stories were possessed by it. The fears of being strange and, similarly, the painful, half-comic experiences of "growing up," pervade the stories and sketches of *Horses and Men*. The book is literally of horses and men, and no American writer of Anderson's generation or any other has caught the colors, the lights and shadows, the spirit of the race track as well as he; the race track is Anderson's milieu quite as the American county fair is, and among those who write of sports, he is in the company of Ring Lardner and Ernest Hemingway. But here also his view of the scene is a characteristic upward glance, the view of country boys in "I'm a Fool" and "The Man Who Became a Woman." The boys are grooms' helpers, "swipes," and they follow the circuit of race-track activities with the same delight with which their younger brothers would try to enter the world of the traveling Wild West show or circus. The influence of George Borrow's attraction to gypsy life is active here, but Anderson translates it wholly into American sights and scenes.

Yet all this is finally only the happy choice of a decor for what he really has to say, and in "The Man Who Became a Woman" what is said touches upon the fears, the mysteries of adolescence—the fear of the boy (now grown to a man) on discovering that he is "strange," is not wholly masculine, and, underlying this, the fear of sterility and death. With a touch as sure as that of D. H. Lawrence, and with none of the mechanical features of overt psychological fiction, Anderson uses, with deceptive simplicity, the scenes in the barroom and the hay-loft, and the incident of the boy's fall, naked, into the shell of bones which was once the carcass of a horse, as the means to tell his story. None of Anderson's stories, with the exception of "Death in the Woods," is a better example of his skill in giving the so-called common experiences of familiar, everyday life, an aura of internal meaning. In this story there is also the fear of Negro laughter, a fear which enters at extended length into two of his later novels, *Dark Laughter* and *Beyond Desire*. In "The Man Who Became a Woman," that particular fear is made more convincing, more appropriate than in the novels; the boy's innocence, his lack of experience, do much to justify his fear, and the fear properly belongs to the immature, the unpoised, the ignorant.

"I'm a Fool" is done with the same turning of light upon common experience—the telling of an awkward, grotesque, foolish lie. Again it is part of the painful experience of growing up, a boyish shrewdness that failed of its desires; it is the image of the concealed, the fatal mistake made by the glib, the young, the unworldly, who parade their candor and innocence wherever they walk and breathe.

"Death in the Woods," Anderson's masterpiece among his shorter stories, is of a different temper and key than the colorful, high-spirited narratives of *Horses and Men*. It is a story which, as Anderson realized, demanded perfection of its kind: he rewrote it several times; it had originally been an episode in *Tar*, and had continued to haunt Anderson's imagination. The strong initial impulse to write it was not enough, for the story, beyond any other story that Anderson wrote, was the summing up of a lifetime's experience, and in its final version it became Anderson's last look backward into the Middle West of his childhood. It was the last of his *Mid-American Chants*, the book of verses in prose, the last of the prose poems in *A New Testament*, and though its external form is plainly that of a story, its internal structure is that of poetry; it has the power of saying more than prose is required to say, and saying it in the fewest words. But of more importance than the phonetic art of the story is the interplay of those prose rhythms of which Anderson had become a master, and the control of its central theme. To the editors of *The Oxford Anthology of American Literature* Anderson wrote in 1937:

It seems to me that the theme of the story is the persistent animal hunger of man. There are these women who spend their whole lives, rather dumbly, feeding this hunger. For years I wanted to write this story.

As for the technique, it was quite definitely thought out. Over a period of several years I made several attempts that had to be thrown aside. For example I thought it necessary to…lift the animal hunger, I wanted to get at, out of the realm of sex. Therefore my tired-out, sexless old woman, the dogs feeding from the food attached to her body after her own death.

The story has its particular form…the young man and the German fighting over a girl in the road, the son bringing his mistress to his mother's house, the butcher, half-grudgingly and yet out of pity, giving her the meat bones, the dogs circling in the mysterious moonlit night in the forest, the men and boys of the town hurrying out of town to find the body . . . What is wanted is something beyond the horizon, to retain the sense of mystery in life while showing at the same time, at what cost our ordinary animal hungers are sometimes fed.

Anderson's explanation is like that of a poet presenting the argument of a poem; and the story contains the kind of poetry that we associated with Wordsworth—the recollection of youthful experience, the figures of common speech, the instinctive dignity and life of the poor, the moonlit rural scene—done with the simplicity that Wordsworth sought and attained. It is for this reason (among others) that the story transcends its regional atmosphere, and becomes the universal story that it is. One can think of it, and not inappropriately, as a story that applies to the years of cold and famine in postwar twentieth-century Europe; it has that kind of universality, one that makes possible analogies in life as well as literature. In writing it Anderson's transcendental note was clearly sounded. The note transcends, in more than one meaning of the verb, the writers from whom Anderson drew inspiration—his own contemporaries, Gertrude Stein, Dreiser, D. H. Lawrence, as well as the writers who came before him in revolt against the Puritan New England tradition—and places him not too far from the figures of Thoreau and Emerson.

But "Death in the Woods" has still another association with poetry that should not be ignored. And in this there is an explicit relationship between the imagery of the old women's death at night in the snow and the opening lines of Shelley's poem "Queen Mab":

> How wonderful is Death,
> Death, and his brother Sleep!
> One, pale as yonder waning moon
> With lips of lurid blue;
> The other, rosy as the morn

When throned on ocean's wave
It blushes o'er the world;
Yet both so passing wonderful!

From Anderson's story one has the following description of a miraculous metamorphosis: "Her body was frozen stiff when it was found, and the shoulders were so narrow and the body so slight that in death it looked like the body of some charming young girl. . . . It had grown dark by the time we got to where the old woman had left the road but the moon had come out. . . . 'I didn't see any wounds. She was a beautiful young girl. Her face was buried in the snow. . . .'" It was a scene of mystery and wonder and it evokes something of the same feeling that is awakened by the lines that Shelley wrote. Since the old woman had fallen asleep before she died, there is the same juxtaposition of sleep and death as in the poem—as well as the same clear hint of a metamorphosis from death to a rebirth: in the poem the figure of youth is in the reference to Aurora.

Yet these resemblances should not be read as proof that Anderson was trying to rewrite Shelley's lines, nor can one prove that Anderson had read "Queen Mab." He may have glanced at it; he may have heard a few lines read aloud by a schoolteacher, for during the years that Anderson went to school, Byron's great popularity had declined, and among the Romantic poets who were widely talked about and quoted was Shelley, a name that Anderson was certain to overhear. Shelley, the Radical, the Idol-Breaker, was also taken up by those who listened to Ingersol and talked about "free love:" "Death in the Woods" was written out of memories of early boyhood: the adolescent associations of sex, sleep, and death are contained within them; "Queen Mab" is one of youthful Shelley's early poems, so it is not too surprising that its imagery has something of the same character. In "A Meeting South" Anderson spoke of Shelley and Keats, and this was in describing a young Southern poet who seemed to be drinking himself to death.

If the preceding remarks seem to have steered too far from

Anderson to Shelley, the digression shows certain likenesses of Anderson's prose to poetry. This is among the reasons why he sometimes thought of himself as a poet. Or rather the kind of poet who drops in to talk and then begins to tell a story.

To enter that dangerous ground which lies between prose and poetry, and to emerge at last, as Anderson does in "Death in the Woods," unscarred by its pitfalls, is a considerable accomplishment, one that has been achieved by few writers in America, and of this small number most are writers whose books provide larger scenes of action than are witnessed in any of Anderson's short stories or novels. It was his contribution and perhaps his destiny, to limit the size of his canvas, to give those who read him a view whose depth, like that of a picture, is greater than the span of the frame around it, and that is one of the reasons why Anderson's best stories have the penetrating quality of Ishmael's gaze in the opening chapters of *Moby Dick*.

I V

In the years between his writing of *Windy McPherson's Son* in 1916 and his death in 1941, Anderson wrote twenty-five books, including seven novels, a half-dozen volumes of essays, and two plays, dramatizations of scenes from *Winesburg, Ohio* and *The Triumph of the Egg*. The essays were, properly speaking, editorials on the themes that entered his novels and short stories. They supplemented his lecture tours and the editing of two small-town newspapers, which occupied his time during the latter years of his life, and they were concerned with the problems of a self-consciously transitional machine age in America. Many of the subjects with which Anderson dealt, his speculations on sex, and what was spoken of as "the war of the sexes" have, at least in the terms he employed, passed out of fashion, with little likelihood of revival. Nor do such novels as *Beyond Desire, Many Marriages,* and *Dark Laughter*, bold and candid as they were at the time they were written, have much possibility of attracting the eye and ear of a later generation: they advanced themes implicit in some of the stories published in this volume, but in the novels the editorial and theoretical aspects of the "machine age" (which editorial writers now call an "atomic age") are disfigurations. And the richness, the sense of the mystery of life, which Anderson gave voice to in his stories thins to an echo of itself in the later novels.

The real Anderson of the stories, sketches, and novels collected in this volume was one who greatly enjoyed life as he found it, but his discovery of it was no easy accomplishment, and the difficulty of this discovery involves his particular genius as a writer. With the writing of the stories in *Winesburg, Ohio,* that discovery had begun, and when the book was published he was a man of forty-three, an age at which too many American writers have left their best years behind them. In Anderson the hidden riches of his personality and art had flowered late, and through them he expressed as few writers can the sensual joys of living on this earth. Much of what he had to say came from these sources, and in his writings the reader shares with him the poignancy of things seen and heard: images of the race track, the sight of moonlight in winter, the stones held in the hand of Hugh McVey, or, in the last pages of *Winesburg, Ohio,* George Willard at the station platform at seven forty-five in the morning stepping on the train. In these scenes the joy of being is almost kinetic, a joy of bodily movement, of seeing things and human beings in transit, freshly and directly, and then moving on. As the unnamed spectator in his own books, Anderson often becomes the charmed and delighted visitor on earth, and the reader shares with him the sense of discovering, under drab exteriors, the strangeness and the physical beauty in what are usually passed by as ordinary things and people.

These qualities, which are felt throughout his writings, brought him the friendship of two courageous and discerning publishers, B. W. Huebsch and Horace Liveright; and to these among many were added the friendships of Dreiser, Van Wyck Brooks, Paul Rosenfeld (whose last days in 1946 were spent editing an omnibus edition of Anderson's shorter pieces), Waldo Frank, Carl Sandburg, and Gertrude Stein. But more extraordinary than these older friendships was the admiration and affection he received from younger writers. In America literary generations are so short and their figures are so quickly discarded, that to find an older man who holds the affection of the young is to discover a rarity. In this respect Anderson's qualities did not go unrewarded, bringing him the regard of many young writers, including Hart Crane, William Faulkner, Thomas Wolfe—each of whom saw in Anderson a reflection of his own concern for the arts of prose and poetry. They and many others owe a debt to the imaginative insight Anderson possessed and to the intimate, speaking voices of his prose. He was their Ishmael, their contemporary, and their master.

At a time, today, when most of the writers of Anderson's generation are highly respected and less read, Anderson's stories hold a place that is undisputed, and each new reader, welcoming his modesty, feels no constraint in reading Anderson for pleasure. This volume is edited with Anderson's new readers kept in mind, and it contains those selections from his writings which even now seem to assure him of a life beyond the horizon, beyond the moment of his own enriched experience and ours.

HORACE GREGORY

The Chronology of Sherwood Anderson's Life and Books

1876. September 13, Sherwood Anderson born in Camden, Ohio.

1879-1897. The events of these years (without dates attached to them) are described in *Tar, A Story-Teller's Story*, and *Sherwood Anderson's Memoirs*. The picture is one of a family drifting from one small Ohio town to another: the father, a "story-teller" from the South who had served in the Union Army and who declined from the saddlery-and-harness business into odd jobs of house- and sign-painting, the mother, a woman of Italian or of German descent, who gave birth to seven children, of whom Sherwood Anderson was the third. Karl Anderson, the painter, was Sherwood Anderson's elder brother. The genius for story-telling, the eye for color, came to Sherwood Anderson within the circle of his family; his schooling was irregular, and was both accelerated and modified by his need to take many odd jobs; he sold newspapers, worked in cabbage fields and on racecourses, was a stable-boy and a factory hand.

1898-1912. Anderson volunteered for service in the U.S. Army during the Spanish-American War and on his return from Cuba spent a short time at Wittenberg College in Ohio.

Even before the war, he had begun to write, and among the jobs he had held during a stay in Chicago was one as a copy-writer in an advertising office. He resumed this position upon leaving Wittenberg. He married and returned to Ohio, this time to Elyria, where he ran a paint factory. From running a business he turned again to an advertising office in Chicago, and began to meet young writers in Chicago.

1912-1915. Anderson began to contribute essays and stories to Margaret Anderson's and Jane Heap's *The Little Review*, and in his *Memoirs* he tells of meeting Carl Sandburg, Ben Hecht, Floyd Dell, Eunice Tietjens.

1916. The chronology of Anderson's books begins with his first novel, *Windy McPherson's Son*.

1917. *Marching Men*, a novel.

1918. *Mid-American Chants*, unrhymed poems.

1919. *Winesburg, Ohio*, a group of tales of Ohio small-town life.

1920. *Poor White*, a novel.

1921. *The Triumph of the Egg*, a book of impressions of American life in tales and poems. In this year Anderson received *The Dial* award of two thousand dollars, which, with the recognition he had received as the author of *Winesburg, Ohio* and *Poor White*, gave him a sense of well-being that permitted a holiday in Europe. He had already enlarged the orbit of his travels from areas of which Chicago was the center to New York.

1922-1923. *Many Marriages*, a novel, and *Horses and Men*, tales long and short from American life, were published. Anderson spent the greater part of the year in New Orleans, where he shared an apartment with William Faulkner.

1924. *A Story-Teller's Story*, the tale of an American writer's journey through his own imaginative world and through the world of facts. From this book one learns why Anderson disregarded dates in his autobiographies; in it he wrote: "I think it was Joseph Conrad who said that a writer only began to live after he began to write. It pleased me to think I was after all but ten years old. Plenty of time ahead for such a one. Time to look about, plenty of time to look about."

1925. "The Modern Writer," an essay; *Dark Laughter*, a novel, the only novel Anderson wrote that became commercially successful. With the money earned from this book he bought a farm near Marion, Virginia, and he also purchased and edited two newspapers in Marion. *Hands and Other Stories*, selected from *Winesburg, Ohio*.

1926. *Sherwood Anderson's Notebook; Tar: A Midwest Childhood*.

1927. *A New Testament*, poems in prose. Through this period, he continued his series of lectures throughout the country, which had become one of his ways of earning a livelihood.

1929. *Hello Towns!*, selected pieces from his newspapers; "Nearer the Grass Roots," an essay; *Alice and the Lost Novel*, stories.

1930. *The American County Fair*.

1931. *Perhaps Women*, an essay on women which continued the discussions of sex that had appeared in his novels from *Marching Men* to *Dark Laughter*.

1932. *Beyond Desire*, a novel.

1933. *Death in the Woods and Other Stories*.

1934. "No Swank," an essay. In this year he dramatized *Winesburg, Ohio*, which was put on the stage by the Hedgerow Theatre Group.

1935. *Puzzled America*, an essay.

1936. *Kit Brandon*, a novel.

1937. Four plays were published: *Winesburg, Ohio, The Triumph of the Egg, Mother,* and *They Married Later.* The last three are one-act plays.

1939. *Home Town,* a book of prose sketches.

1941. Death from peritonitis on a trip to South America; he died at Cristobal, Canal Zone.

1942. *Sherwood Anderson's Memoirs.*

1947. *The Sherwood Anderson Reader,* edited by Paul Rosenfeld.

A Selected Bibliography on Sherwood Anderson

Since the publication of *Winesburg, Ohio*, in 1919, few writers of his generation have attracted more diversified critical attention than Sherwood Anderson. Today (1971) his *Winesburg, Ohio*, and *Poor White* are more widely read than ever, and in universities and colleges his writings are well known to serious students of American life and culture. Naturally enough, the literature on Anderson is greater than the volume of his best work, and is sometimes contradictory. The following short list is a highly selective bibliography, chosen with the hope of stirring further interest in Anderson rather than of being definitive. Some of the titles are out of print and must be sought out in the larger university or public libraries.

Harlan Hatcher's *Creating the Modern American Novel* (New York: Farrar & Rinehart, 1935): Hatcher's chapter on Anderson is the first in a section which carries the spectacular title of "Freudian Psychology and the Sex Age," but the chapter itself contains many sound observations on the nature of Anderson's position in American literature. Hatcher was among the first of Anderson's critics to insist that his gifts were not those of a realist, and that he was one of "the few first-rate symbolists in America." The chapter is also valuable for its appreciation of Anderson's "instincts." Of them Hatcher wrote: "He [Anderson] has always been willing to trust these instincts and let them bring into his novels the unaccountable tumult of the soul which defies all reason." Hatcher's chapter remains the best of all academic (and sympathetic) commentaries on Anderson's place in American fiction of the nineteen-twenties.

Waldo Frank's essay on *Winesburg, Ohio* (*Story*, September-October 1941) is the most penetrating of all critical observations on the book in which Anderson "found himself." Frank observed Anderson's instinctive emotional debt to the heritage of the Old Testament, and with great persuasion and imaginative insight he convinces even the most skeptical of what he believes to be the sources of Anderson's so-called mysticism. Frank is one of the few among Anderson's friends who were able to detach the value of Anderson's writings from the charms of Anderson's personality; the piece is also one of the best of Waldo Frank's critical writings.

Of short critical commentaries on Anderson, Lionel Trilling's "Sherwood Anderson" (*Kenyon Review*, Summer 1941) is the most stimulating because it opens several views toward a final evaluation of Andersons' writings. Although it is too brief to be conclusive in itself (and Trilling seems to be of two minds regarding Anderson's contribution to American literature), the essay provides the means of discussing pros and cons of Anderson's reputation in the eyes of contemporary critics. Trilling clearly states Anderson's preoccupation with the details of adolescent emotion, and raises doubts as to its moral value. In general, and not so clearly, he relates the body of Anderson's writings to the "Whitman tradition" in American letters. He repeats a brilliant but essentially unsound and ill-informed attack on Anderson made by Wyndham Lewis in *Paleface, and speculates* upon the validity of Anderson's "truth": "Anderson's truth may have become a falsehood in his hands through limitations in himself, but one has only to take it out of his hands to see again that it is still a truth. . . ." The value of Trilling's remarks lies in the effort to discuss Anderson with appropriate seriousness; but they also show Anderson's ability (which was not unlike D. H. Lawrence's) to concern and bedevil his serious critics.

The most revealing and engaging of the personal memoirs of Anderson is in Margaret Anderson's *My Thirty Years' War* (New York: Covici, Friede, Inc., 1930). Her portrait of Anderson recalls him giving her advice on the fortunes of her magazine, *The Little Review*. Another early Chicago portrait may be found in Robert Morss Lovett's tribute to Anderson in *The Virginia Quarterly Review* (Summer 1941).

Malcolm Cowley's introduction to *Winesburg, Ohio*, (New York: The Viking Press, Viking Compass edition, 1960) is a sensitive reappraisal of Anderson's gift of storytelling, with special stress upon Anderson's art in creating an "epiphany" at the climax of a story or an episode.

Walter B. Rideout is another perceptive critic of Anderson's art, particularly in his essay "The Simplicity of *Winesburg, Ohio*' (*Shenandoah*, Washington and Lee University Review, Spring 1962) and in the introduction to *Poor White* (New York: The Viking Press, Viking Compass edition, 1965).

There are also two valuable anthologies of critical writings on Anderson: *"Winesburg, Ohio," Text and Criticism*, edited by John H. Ferres, in the Viking Critical Library, General Editor, Malcolm Cowley (New York: The Viking Press, 1966) and *The Achievement of Sherwood Anderson: Essays in criticism*, edited by Ray Lewis White (Chapel Hill: University of North Carolina Press, 1966). Both books contain extensive bibliographies.

For readers who wish to study Anderson's writing at greater length, *The Sherwood Anderson Reader*, edited by Paul Rosenfeld (Boston: Houghton, Mifflin, 1947), and *The Letters of Sherwood Anderson*, edited by Howard Mumford Jones and Walter B. Rideout (Boston: Little, Brown, 1953), are recommended.

Valuable for its footnotes and its photographs of Anderson and his family is *Sherwood Anderson's Memoirs*: *A Critical Edition*, edited by Ray Lewis White (Chapel Hill: University of North Carolina Press, 1969).

WINESBURG, OHIO

Editor's Note

Winesburg, Ohio, is Sherwood Anderson's fourth book and his first collection of tales, and was published in 1919. Some of the stories had already appeared in *The Little Review,* then published in Chicago, which was the most high-spirited of the "little magazines" in the years 1914-1928. Within its pages, James Joyce's *Ulysses* as well as stories by Sherwood Anderson and poems by Hart Crane made an early appearance. Of its editor, Margaret Anderson—she was not related to the writer—Sherwood Anderson wrote in *A Story Teller's Story:* "Miss Anderson and myself had in common a fondness for rather striking clothes and for strutting a bit upon the stage of life that drew us closely together but being at bottom fellow Chicagoans we were bound not to take each other too seriously—at least not under the rose." And of him, Miss Anderson wrote in *My Thirty Years' War:* "Floyd Dell and I talked of Pater and of living with the hard gem-like flame. Sherwood Anderson used to listen to us in a certain amazement (resembling fear) and indicating clearly that nothing would induce him into such fancy realms. But I liked Sherwood—because he, too, was a talker and of a highly special type. He didn't talk ideas—he told stories. (It sounds bad but the stories were good. So was the telling.) He said to everyone: You don't mind if I use that story you've just told, do you? No one minded. Sherwood's story never bore any relation to the original. He read us the manuscript of *Windy McPherson's Son.* Floyd was passionate about it—I, a little less so. It was a new prose but I knew by Sherwood's look that he would do something even better."

In a lecture called "A Writer's Conception of Realism," published in 1939, Anderson said of *Winesburg, Ohio:* "The book was written in a crowded tenement district of Chicago. The hint for almost every character was taken from my fellow lodgers in a large rooming house, many of whom had never lived in a village....Most people are afraid to trust their imagination and the artist is not....Realism, in so far as the word means reality to life, is always bad art." These statements explain what Miss Anderson meant when she said "Sherwood's story never bore any relation to the original." They also explain why the stories of *Winesburg, Ohio,* although they are set in the remembered atmosphere of a small town in America, have a "universal" quality.

If one remembers the moment when *Winesburg, Ohio* first appeared as a book, it is little wonder that the book became a landmark in American fiction. At that moment it held the same relationship to prose as Edgar Lee Masters' *The Spoon River Anthology* held to verse. It was admired for its candor and for its realism, and for its success in shocking the sensibilities of insensible people.

The Book of the Grotesque

The writer, an old man with a white mustache, had some difficulty in getting into bed. The windows of the house in which he lived were high and he wanted to look at the trees when he awoke in the morning. A carpenter came to fix the bed so that it would be on a level with the window.

Quite a fuss was made about the matter. The carpenter, who had been a soldier in the Civil War, came into the writer's room and sat down to talk of building a platform for the purpose of raising the bed. The writer had cigars lying about and the carpenter smoked.

For a time the two men talked of the raising of the bed and then they talked of other things. The soldier got on the subject of the war. The writer, in fact, led him to that subject. The carpenter had once been a prisoner in Andersonville prison and had lost a brother. The brother had died of starvation, and whenever the carpenter got upon that subject he cried. He, like the old writer, had a white mustache, and when he cried he puckered up his lips and the mustache bobbed up and down. The weeping old man with the cigar in his mouth was ludicrous. The plan the writer had for the raising of his bed was forgotten and later the carpenter did it in his own way and the writer, who was past sixty, had to help himself with a chair when he went to bed at night.

In his bed the writer rolled over on his side and lay quite still. For years he had been beset with notions concerning his heart. He was a hard smoker and his heart fluttered. The idea had got into his mind that he would some time die unexpectedly and always when he got into bed he thought of that. It did not alarm him. The effect in fact was quite a special thing and not easily explained. It made him more alive, there in bed, than at any other time. Perfectly still he lay and his body was old and not of much use any more, but something inside him was altogether young. He was like a pregnant woman, only that the thing inside him was not a baby but a youth. No, it wasn't a youth, it was a woman, young, and wearing a coat of mail like a knight. It is absurd, you see, to try to tell what was inside the old writer as he lay on his high bed and listened to the fluttering of his heart. The thing to get at is what the writer, or the young thing within the writer, was thinking about.

The old writer, like all of the people in the world, had got, during his long life, a great many notions in his head. He had once been quite handsome and a number of women had been in love with him. And then, of course, he had known people, many people, known them in a peculiarly intimate way that was different from the way in which you and I know people. At least that is what the writer thought and the thought pleased him. Why quarrel with an old man concerning his thoughts?

In the bed the writer had a dream that was not a dream. As he grew somewhat sleepy but was still conscious, figures began to appear before his eyes. He imagined the young indescribable thing within himself was driving a long procession of figures before his eyes.

You see the interest in all this lies in the figures that went before the eyes of the writer. They were all grotesques. All of the men and women the writer had ever known had become grotesques.

The grotesques were not all horrible. Some were amusing, some almost beautiful, and one, a woman all drawn out of shape, hurt the old man by her grotesqueness. When she passed he made a noise like a small dog whimpering. Had you come into the room you might have supposed the old man had unpleasant dreams or perhaps indigestion.

For an hour the procession of grotesques passed before the eyes of the old man, and then, although it was a painful thing to do, he crept out of bed and began to write. Some one of the grotesques had made a deep impression on his mind and he wanted to describe it.

At his desk the writer worked for an hour. In the end he wrote a book which he called "The Book of the Grotesque." It was never published, but I saw it once and it made an indelible impression on my mind. The book had one central thought that is very strange and has always remained with me. By remembering it I have been able to understand many people and things that I was never able to understand before. The thought was involved but a simple statement of it would be something like this :

That in the beginning when the world was young there were a great many thoughts but no such thing as a truth. Man made the truths himself and each truth was a composite of a great many vague thoughts. All about in the world were the truths and they were all beautiful.

The old man had listed hundreds of the truths in his book. I will not try to tell you of all of them. There was the truth of virginity and the truth of passion, the truth of wealth and of poverty, of thrift and of profligacy, of carelessness and abandon. Hundreds and hundreds were the truths and they were all beautiful.

And then the people came along. Each as he appeared snatched up one of the truths and some who were quite strong snatched up a dozen of them.

It was the truths that made the people grotesques. The old man had quite an elaborate theory concerning the matter. It was his notion that the moment one of the people took one of the truths to himself, called it his truth, and tried to live his life by it, he became a grotesque and the truth he embraced became a falsehood.

You can see for yourself how the old man, who had spent

all of his life writing and was filled with words, would write hundreds of pages concerning this matter. The subject would become so big in his mind that he himself would be in danger of becoming a grotesque. He didn't, I suppose, for the same reason that he never published the book. It was the young thing inside him that saved the old man.

Concerning the old carpenter who fixed the bed for the writer, I only mentioned him because he, like many of what are called very common people, became the nearest thing to what is understandable and lovable of all the grotesques in the writer's book.

Hands

Upon the half decayed veranda of a small frame house that stood near the edge of a ravine near the town of Winesburg, Ohio, a fat little old man walked nervously up and down. Across a long field that had been seeded for clover but that had produced only a dense crop of yellow mustard weeds, he could see the public highway along which went a wagon filled with berry pickers returning from the fields. The berry pickers, youths and maidens, laughed and shouted boisterously. A boy clad in a blue shirt leaped from the wagon and attempted to drag after him one of the maidens, who screamed and protested shrilly. The feet of the boy in the road kicked up a cloud of dust that floated across the face of the departing sun. Over the long field came a thin girlish voice. "Oh, you Wing Biddlebaum, comb your hair, it's falling into your eyes," commanded the voice to the man, who was bald and whose nervous little hands fiddled about the bare white forehead as though arranging a mass of tangled locks.

Wing Biddlebaum, forever frightened and beset by a ghostly band of doubts, did not think of himself as in any way a part of the life of the town where he had lived for twenty years. Among all the people of Winesburg but one had come close to him. With George Willard, son of Tom Willard, the proprietor of the New Willard House, he had formed something like a friendship. George Willard was the reporter on the *Winesburg Eagle* and sometimes in the evenings he walked out along the highway to Wing Biddlebaum's house. Now as the old man walked up and down on the veranda, his hands moving nervously about, he was hoping that George Willard would come and spend the evening with him. After the wagon containing the berry pickers had passed, he went across the field through the tall mustard weeds and climbing a rail fence peered anxiously along the road to the town. For a moment he stood thus, rubbing his hands together and looking up and down the road, and then, fear overcoming him, ran back to walk again upon the porch on his own house.

In the presence of George Willard, Wing Biddlebaum, who for twenty years had been the town mystery, lost something of his timidity, and his shadowy personality, submerged in a sea of doubts, came forth to look at the world. With the young reporter at his side, he ventured in the light of day into Main Street or strode up and down on the rickety front porch of his own house, talking excitedly. The voice that had been low and trembling became shrill and loud. The bent figure straightened. With a kind of wriggle, like a fish returned to the brook by the fisherman, Biddlebaum the silent began to talk, striving to put into words the ideas that had been accumulated by his mind during long years of silence.

Wing Biddlebaum talked much with his hands. The slender expressive fingers, forever active, forever striving to conceal themselves in his pockets or behind his back, came forth and became the piston rods of his machinery of expression.

The story of Wing Biddlebaum is a story of hands. Their restless activity, like unto the beating of the wings of an imprisoned bird, had given him his name. Some obscure poet of the town had thought of it. The hands alarmed their owner. He wanted to keep them hidden away and looked with amazement at the quiet inexpressive hands of other men who worked beside him in the fields, or passed, driving sleepy teams on country roads.

When he talked to George Willard, Wing Biddlebaum closed

his fists and beat with them upon a table or on the walls of his house. The action made him more comfortable. If the desire to talk came to him when the two were walking in the fields, he sought out a stump or the top board of a fence and with his hands pounding busily talked with renewed ease.

The story of Wing Biddlebaum's hands is worth a book in itself. Sympathetically set forth it would tap many strange, beautiful qualities in obscure men. It is a job for a poet. In Winesburg the hands had attracted attention merely because of their activity. With them Wing Biddlebaum had picked as high as a hundred and forty quarts of strawberries in a day. They became his distinguishing feature, the source of his fame. Also they made more grotesque an already grotesque and elusive individuality. Winesburg was proud of the hands of Wing Biddlebaum in the same spirit in which it was proud of Banker White's new stone house and Wesley Moyer's bay stallion, Tony Tip, that had won the two-fifteen trot at the fall races in Cleveland.

As for George Willard, he had many times wanted to ask about the hands. At times an almost overwhelming curiosity had taken hold of him. He felt that there must be a reason for their strange activity and their inclination to keep hidden away and only a growing respect for Wing Biddlebaum kept him from blurting out the questions that were often in his mind.

Once he had been on the point of asking. The two were walking in the fields on a summer afternoon and had stopped to sit upon a grassy bank. All afternoon Wing Biddlebaum had talked as one inspired. By a fence he had stopped and beating like a giant woodpecker upon the top board had shouted at George Willard, condemning his tendency to be too much influenced by the people about him. "You are destroying yourself," he cried. "You have the inclination to be alone and to dream and you are afraid of dreams. You want to be like others in town here. You hear them talk and you try to imitate them."

On the grassy bank Wing Biddlebaum had tried again to

drive his point home. His voice became soft and reminiscent, and with a sigh of contentment he launched into a long rambling talk, speaking as one lost in a dream.

Out of the dream Wing Biddlebaum made a picture for George Willard. In the picture men lived again in a kind of pastoral golden age. Across a green open country came clean-limbed young men, some afoot, some mounted upon horses. In crowds the young men came to gather about the feet of an old man who sat beneath a tree in a tiny garden and who talked to them.

Wing Biddlebaum became wholly inspired. For once he forgot the hands. Slowly they stole forth and lay upon George Willard's shoulders. Something new and bold came into the voice that talked. "You must try to forget all you have learned," said the old man. "You must begin to dream. From this time on you must shut your ears to the roaring of the voices."

Pausing in his speech, Wing Biddlebaum looked long and earnestly at George Willard. His eyes glowed. Again he raised the hands to caress the boy and then a look of horror swept over his face.

With a convulsive movement of his body, Wing Biddlebaum sprang to his feet and thrust his hands deep into his trousers pockets. Tears came to his eyes. "I must be getting along home. I can talk no more with you," he said nervously.

Without looking back, the old man had hurried down the hillside and across a meadow, leaving George Willard perplexed and frightened upon the grassy slope. With a shiver of dread the boy arose and went along the road toward town. "I'll not ask him about his hands," he thought, touched by the memory of the terror he had seen in the man's eyes. "There's something wrong, but I don't want to know what it is. His hands have something to do with his fear of me and of everyone."

And George Willard was right. Let us look briefly into the story of the hands. Perhaps our talking of them will arouse the poet who will tell the hidden wonder story of the influence for which the hands were but fluttering penants of promise.

In his youth Wing Biddlebaum had been a school teacher in a town in Pennsylvania. He was not then known as Wing Biddlebaum, but went by the less euphonic name of Adolph Myers. As Adolph Myers he was much loved by the boys of his school.

Adolph Myers was meant by nature to be a teacher of youth. He was one of those rare, little-understood men who rule by a power so gentle that it passes as a lovable weakness. In their feeling for the boys under their charge such men are not unlike the finer sort of women in their love of men.

And yet that is but crudely stated. It needs the poet there. With the boys of his school, Adolph Myers had walked in the evening or had sat talking until dusk upon the schoolhouse steps lost in a kind of dream. Here and there went his hands, caressing the shoulders of the boys, playing about the tousled heads. As he talked his voice became soft and musical. There was a caress in that also. In a way the voice and the hands, the stroking of the shoulders and the touching of the hair were a part of the schoolmaster's effort to carry a dream into the young minds. By the caress that was in his fingers he expressed himself. He was one of those men in whom the force that creates life is diffused, not centralized. Under the caress of his hands doubt and disbelief went out of the minds of the boys and they began also to dream.

And then the tragedy. A half-witted boy of the school became enamored of the young master. In his bed at night he imagined unspeakable things and in the morning went forth to tell his dreams as facts. Strange, hideous accusations fell from his loose-hung lips. Through the Pennsylvania town went a shiver. Hidden, shadowy doubts that had been in men's minds concerning Adolph Myers were galvanized into beliefs.

The tragedy did not linger. Trembling lads were jerked out of bed and questioned. "He put his arms about me," said one. "His fingers were always playing in my hair," said another.

One afternoon a man of the town, Henry Bradford, who kept a saloon, came to the schoolhouse door. Calling Adolph

Myers into the school yard he began to beat him with his fists. As this hard knuckles beat down into the frightened face of the schoolmaster, his wrath became more and more terrible. Screaming with dismay, the children ran here and there like disturbed insects. "I'll teach you to put your hands on my boy, you beast," roared the saloon keeper, who tired of beating the master, had begun to kick him about the yard.

Adolph Myers was driven from the Pennsylvania town in the night. With lanterns in their hands a dozen men came to the door of the house where he lived alone and commanded that he dress and come forth. It was raining and one of the men had a rope in his hands. They had intended to hang the schoolmaster, but something in his figure, so small, white, and pitiful, touched their hearts and they let him escape. As he ran away into the darkness they repented of their weakness and ran after him, swearing and throwing sticks and great balls of soft mud at the figure that screamed and ran faster and faster into the darkness.

For twenty years Adolph Myers had lived alone in Winesburg. He was but forty but looked sixty-five. The name of Biddlebaum he got from a box of goods seen at a freight station as he hurried through an eastern Ohio town. He had an aunt in Winesburg, a black-toothed old woman who raised chickens, and with her he lived until she died. He had been ill for a year after the experience in Pennsylvania, and after his recovery worked as a day laborer in the fields, going timidly about and striving to conceal his hands. Although he did not understand what had happened he felt that the hands must be to blame. Again and again the fathers of the boys talked of the hands. "Keep your hands to yourself," the saloon keeper had roared, dancing with fury in the schoolhouse yard.

Upon the veranda of his house by the ravine, Wing Biddlebaum continued to walk up and down until the sun had disappeared and the road beyond the field was lost in the grey shadows. Going into his house he cut slices of bread and spread honey upon them. When the rumble of the evening train that took away the express cars loaded with the day's harvest of berries had passed and restored the silence of the summer night, he went again to walk upon the veranda. In the darkness he could not see the hands and they became quiet. Although he still hungered for the presence of the boy, who was the medium through which he expressed his love of man, the hunger became again a part of his loneliness and his waiting. Lighting a lamp, Wing Biddlebaum washed the few dishes soiled by his simple meal and, setting up a folding cot by the screen door that led to the porch, prepared to undress for the night. A few stray white bread crumbs lay on the cleanly washed floor by the table; putting the lamp upon a low stool he began to pick up the crumbs, carrying them to his mouth one by one with unbelievable rapidity. In the dense blotch of light beneath the table, the kneeling figure looked like a priest engaged in some service of his church. The nervous expressive fingers, flashing in and out of the light, might well have been mistaken for the fingers of the devotee going swiftly through decade after decade of his rosary.

Paper Pills

He was an old man with a white beard and huge nose and hands. Long before the time during which we will know him, he was a doctor and drove a jaded white horse from house to house through the streets of Winesburg. Later he married a girl who had money. She had been left a large fertile farm when her father died. The girl was quiet, tall, and dark, and to many people she seemed very beautiful. Everyone in Winesburg wondered why she married the doctor. Within a year after the marriage she died.

The knuckles of the doctor's hands were extraordinarily large. When the hands were closed they looked like clusters of unpainted wooden balls as large as walnuts fastened together by steel rods. He smoked a cob pipe and after his wife's death sat all day in his empty office close by a window that was covered with cobwebs. He never opened the window. Once on a hot day in August he tried but found it stuck fast and after that he forgot all about it.

Winesburg had forgotten the old man, but in Doctor Reefy there were the seeds of something very fine. Alone in his musty office in the Heffner Block above the Paris Dry Goods Company's store, he worked ceaselessly, building up something that he himself destroyed. Little pyramids of truth he erected and after erecting knocked them down again that he might have the truths to erect other pyramids.

Doctor Reefy was a tall man who had worn one suit of clothes for ten years. It was frayed at the sleeves and little holes had appeared at the knees and elbows. In the office he wore also a linen duster with huge pockets into which he continually stuffed scraps of paper. After some weeks the scraps of paper became little hard round balls, and when the pockets were filled he dumped them out upon the floor. For ten years he had but one friend, another old man named John Spaniard who owned a tree nursery. Sometimes, in a playful mood, old Doctor Reefy took from his pockets a handful of the paper balls and threw them at the nursery man. "That is to confound you, you blithering old sentimentalist," he cried, shaking with laughter.

The story of Doctor Reefy and his courtship of the tall dark girl who became his wife and left her money to him is a very curious story. It is delicious, like the twisted little apples that grow in the orchards of Winesburg. In the fall one walks in the orchards and the ground is hard with frost underfoot. The apples have been taken from the trees by the pickers. They have been put in barrels and shipped to the cities where they will be eaten in apartments that are filled with books, magazines, furniture, and people. On the trees are only a few gnarled apples that the pickers have rejected. They look like the knuckles of Doctor Reefy's hands. One nibbles at them and they are delicious. Into a little round place at the side of the apple has been gathered all of its sweetness. One runs from tree to tree over the frosted ground picking the gnarled, twisted apples and filling his pockets with them. Only the few know the sweetness of the twisted apples.

The girl and Doctor Reefy began their courtship on a summer afternoon. He was forty-five then and already he had begun the practice of filling his pockets with the scraps of paper that became hard balls and were thrown away. The habit had been formed as he sat in his buggy behind the jaded white horse and went slowly along country roads. On the papers were written thoughts, ends of thoughts, beginnings of thoughts.

One by one the mind of Doctor Reefy had made the thoughts. Out of many of them he formed a truth that arose gigantic in his mind. The truth clouded the world. It became terrible and then faded away and the little thoughts began again.

The tall dark girl came to see Doctor Reefy because she was in the family way and had become frightened. She was in that condition because of a series of circumstances also curious.

The death of her father and mother and the rich acres of land that had come down to her had set a train of suitors on her heels. For two years she saw suitors almost every evening. Except two they were all alike. They talked to her of passion and there was a strained eager quality in their voices and in their eyes when they looked at her. The two who were different were much unlike each other. One of them, a slender young man with white hands, the son of a jeweler in Winesburg, talked continually of virginity. When he was with her he was never off the subject. The other, a black-haired boy with large ears, said nothing at all but always managed to get her into the darkness, where he began to kiss her.

For a time the tall dark girl thought she would marry the jeweler's son. For hours she sat in silence listening as he talked to her and then she began to be afraid of something. Beneath his talk of virginity she began to think there was a lust greater than in all the others. At times it seemed to her that as he talked he was holding her body in his hands. She imagined him turning it slowly about in the white hands and staring at it. At night she dreamed that he had bitten into her body and that his jaws were dripping. She had the dream three times, then she became in the family way to the one who said nothing at all but who in the moment of his passion actually did bite her shoulder so that for days the marks of his teeth showed.

After the tall dark girl came to know Doctor Reefy it seemed to her that she never wanted to leave him again. She went into his office one morning and without her saying anything he seemed to know what had happened to her.

In the office of the doctor there was a woman, the wife of the man who kept the bookstore in Winesburg. Like all old-fashioned country practitioners, Doctor Reefy pulled teeth, and the woman who waited held a handkerchief to her teeth and groaned. Her husband was with her and when the tooth was taken out they both screamed and blood ran down on the woman's white dress. The tall dark girl did not pay any attention. When the woman and the man had gone the doctor smiled. "I will take you driving into the country with me," he said.

For several weeks the tall dark girl and the doctor were together almost every day. The condition that had brought her to him passed in an illness, but she was like one who has discovered the sweetness of the twisted apples, she could not get her mind fixed again upon the round perfect fruit that is eaten in the city apartments. In the fall after the beginning of her acquaintanceship with him she married Doctor Reefy and in the following spring she died. During the winter he read to her all of the odds and ends of thoughts he had scribbled on the bits of paper. After he had read them he laughed and stuffed them away in his pockets to become round hard balls.

Mother

Elizabeth Willard, the mother of George Willard, was tall and gaunt and her face was marked with smallpox scars. Although she was but forty-five, some obscure disease had taken the fire out of her figure. Listlessly she went about the disorderly old hotel looking at the faded wall-paper and the ragged carpets and, when she was able to be about, doing the work of a chambermaid among beds soiled by the slumbers of fat traveling men. Her husband, Tom Willard, a slender, graceful man with square shoulders, a quick military step, and a black mustache trained to turn sharply up at the ends, tried to put the wife out of his mind. The presence of the tall ghostly figure, moving slowly through the halls, he took as a reproach to himself. When he thought of her he grew angry and swore. The hotel was unprofitable and forever on the edge of failure and he wished himself out of it. He thought of the old house and the woman who lived there with him as things defeated and done for. The hotel in which he had begun life so hopefully was now a mere ghost of what a hotel should be. As he went spruce and business-like through the streets of Winesburg, he sometimes stopped and turned quickly about as though fearing that the spirit of the hotel and of the woman would follow him even into the streets. "Damn such a life, damn it!" he sputtered aimlessly.

Tom Willard had a passion for village politics and for years had been the leading Democrat in a strongly Republican community. Some day, he told himself, the tide of things political will turn in my favor and the years of ineffectual service count big in the bestowal of rewards. He dreamed of going to Congress and even of becoming governor. Once when a younger member of the party arose at a political conference and began to boast of his faithful service, Tom Willard grew white with fury. "Shut up, you," he roared, glaring about, "What do you know of service? What are you but a boy? Look at what I've done here! I was a Democrat here in Winesburg when it was a crime to be a Democrat. In the old days they fairly hunted us with guns."

Between Elizabeth and her one son George there was a deep unexpressed bond of sympathy, based on a girlhood dream that had long ago died. In the son's presence she was timid and reserved, but sometimes while he hurried about town intent upon his duties as a reporter, she went into his room and closing the door knelt by a little desk, made of a kitchen table, that sat near a window. In the room by the desk she went through a ceremony that was half a prayer, half a demand, addressed to the skies. In the boyish figure she yearned to see something half forgotten that had once been a part of herself re-created. The prayer concerned that. "Even though I die, I will in some way keep defeat from you," she cried, and so deep was her determination that her whole body shook. Her eyes glowed and she clenched her fists. "If I am dead and see him becoming a meaningless drab figure like myself, I will come back," she declared. "I ask God now to give me that privilege, I demand it. I will pay for it. God may beat me with his fists. I will take any blow that may befall if but this my boy be allowed to express something for us both." Pausing uncertainly, the woman stared about the boy's room. "And do not let him become smart and successful either," she added vaguely.

The communion between George Willard and his mother was outwardly a formal thing without meaning. When she was ill and sat by the window in her room he sometimes went in the evening to make her a visit. They sat by a window that looked over the roof of a small frame building into Main Street. By turning their heads they could see through another window, along an alleyway that ran behind the Main Street stores and into the back door of Abner Groff's bakery. Sometimes as they sat thus a picture of village life presented itself to them. At the back door of his shop appeared Abner Groff with a stick or an empty milk bottle in his hand. For a long time there was a feud between the baker and a grey cat that belonged to Sylvester West, the druggist. The boy and his mother saw the cat creep into the door of the bakery and presently emerge followed by the baker, who swore and waved his arms about. The baker's eyes were small and red and his black hair and beard were filled with flour dust. Sometimes he was so angry that, although the cat had disappeared, he hurled sticks, bits of broken glass, and even some of the tools of his trade about. Once he broke a window at the back of Sinning's Hardware Store. In the alley the grey cat crouched behind barrels filled with torn paper and broken bottles above which flew a black swarm of flies. Once when she was alone, and after watching a prolonged and ineffectual outburst on the part of the baker, Elizabeth Willard put her head down on her long white hands and wept. After that she did not look along the alleyway any more, but tried to forget the contest between the bearded man and the cat. It seemed like a rehearsal of her own life, terrible in its vividness.

In the evening when the son sat in the room with his mother, the silence made them both feel awkward. Darkness came on and the evening train came in at the station. In the street below feet tramped up and down upon a board sidewalk. In the station yard, after the evening train had gone, there was a heavy silence. Perhaps Skinner Leason, the express agent, moved a truck the length of the station platform. Over on Main Street sounded a man's voice, laughing. The door of the express office banged. George Willard arose and crossing the room fumbled for the doorknob. Sometimes he knocked against a chair, making it scrape along the floor. By the window sat the sick woman, perfectly still, listless. Her long hands, white and bloodless, could be seen drooping over the ends of the arms of the chair. "I think you had better be out among the boys. You are too much indoors," she said, striving to relieve the embarrassment of the departure. "I thought I would take a walk," replied George Willard, who felt awkward and confused.

One evening in July, when the transient guests who made the New Willard House their temporary home had become scarce, and the hallways, lighted only by kerosene lamps turned low, were plunged in gloom, Elizabeth Willard had an adventure. She had been ill in bed for several days and her son had not come to visit her. She was alarmed. The feeble blaze of life that remained in her body was blown into a flame by her anxiety and she crept out of bed, dressed and hurried along the hallway toward her son's room, shaking with exaggerated fears. As she went along she steadied herself with her hand, slipped along the papered walls of the hall and breathed with difficulty. The air whistled through her teeth. As she hurried forward she thought how foolish she was. "He is concerned with boyish affairs," she told herself. "Perhaps he has now begun to walk about in the evening with girls."

Elizabeth Willard had a dread of being seen by guests in the hotel that had once belonged to her father and the ownership of which still stood recorded in her name in the county courthouse. The hotel was continually losing patronage because of its shabbiness and she thought of herself as also shabby. Her own room was in an obscure corner and when she felt able to work she voluntarily worked among the beds, preferring the labor that could be done when the guests were abroad seeking trade among the merchants of Winesburg.

By the door of her son's room the mother knelt upon the floor and listened for some sound from within. When she heard the boy moving about and talking in low tones a smile came to her lips. George Willard had a habit of talking aloud to himself and to hear him doing so had always given his mother a peculiar pleasure. The habit in him, she felt, strengthened the secret bond that existed between them. A thousand times she had whispered to herself of the matter. "He is groping about, trying to find himself," she thought. "He is not a dull clod, all words and smartness. Within him there is a secret something that is striving to grow. It is the thing I let be killed in myself."

In the darkness in the hallway by the door the sick woman arose and started again toward her own room. She was afraid that the door would open and the boy come upon her. When she had reached a safe distance and was about to turn a corner into a second hallway she stopped and bracing herself with her hands waited, thinking to shake off a trembling fit of weakness that had come upon her. The presence of the boy in the room had made her happy. In her bed, during the long hours alone, the little fears that had visited her had become giants. Now they were all gone. "When I get back to my room I shall sleep," she murmured gratefully.

But Elizabeth Willard was not to return to her bed and to sleep. As she stood trembling in the darkness the door of her son's room opened and the boy's father, Tom Willard, stepped out. In the light that streamed out at the door he stood with the knob in his hand and talked. What he said infuriated the woman.

Tom Willard was ambitious for his son. He had always thought of himself as a successful man, although nothing he had ever done had turned out successful. However, when he was out of sight of the New Willard House and had no fear of coming upon his wife, he swaggered and began to dramatize himself as one of the chief men of the town. He wanted his son to succeed. He it was who had secured for the boy the position on the *Winesburg Eagle*. Now, with a ring of earnestness in his voice, he was advising concerning some course of conduct. "I tell you what, George, you've got to wake up," he said sharply. "Will Henderson has spoken to me three times concerning the matter. He says you go along for hours not hearing when you are spoken to and acting like a gawky girl. What ails you?" Tom Willard laughed good-naturedly. "Well, I guess you'll get over it," he said. "I told Will that. You're not a fool and you're not a woman. You're Tom Willard's son and you'll wake up. I'm not afraid. What you say clears things up. If being a newspaper man had put the notion of becoming a writer into your mind that's all right. Only I guess you'll have to wake up to do that too, eh?"

Tom Willard went briskly along the hallway and down a flight of stairs to the office. The woman in the darkness could hear him laughing and talking with a guest who was striving to wear away a dull evening by dozing in a chair by the office door. She returned to the door her son's room. The weakness had passed from her body as by a miracle and she stepped boldly along. A thousand ideas raced through her head. When she heard the scraping of a chair and the sound of a pen scratching upon paper, she again turned and went back along the hallway to her own room.

A definite determination had come into the mind of the defeated wife of the Winesburg hotel keeper. The determination was the result of long years of quiet and rather ineffectual thinking. "Now," she told herself, "I will act. There is something threatening my boy and I will ward it off." The fact that the conversation between Tom Willard and his son had been rather quiet and natural, as though an understanding existed between them, maddened her. Although for years she had hated her husband, her hatred had always before been a quite impersonal thing. He had been merely a part of something else that she hated. Now, and by the few words at the door, he had become the thing personified. In the darkness of her own room she clenched her fists and glared about. Going to a cloth bag that hung on a nail by the wall she took out a long pair of sewing scissors and held them in her hand like a dagger. "I will stab him," she said aloud. "He has chosen to be the voice of evil and I will kill him. When I have killed him something will snap within myself and I will die also. It will be a release for all of us."

In her girlhood and before her marriage with Tom Willard, Elizabeth had borne a somewhat shaky reputation in Winesburg. For years she had been what is called "stage-struck" and had paraded through the streets with traveling men guests at her father's hotel, wearing loud clothes and urging them to tell her of life in the cities out of which they had come. Once she startled the town by putting on men's clothes and riding a bicycle down Main Street.

In her own mind the tall dark girl had been in those days much confused. A great restlessness was in her and it expressed itself in two ways. First there was an uneasy desire for change, for some big definite movement to her life. It was this feeling that had turned her mind to the stage. She dreamed of joining some company and wandering over the world, seeing always new faces and giving something out of herself to all people. Sometimes at night she was quite beside herself with the thought, but when she tried to talk of the matter to the members of the theatrical companies that came to Winesburg and stopped at her father's hotel, she got nowhere. They did not seem to know what she meant, or if she did get something of her passion expressed, they only laughed. "It's not like that," they said. "It's as dull and uninteresting as this here. Nothing comes of it."

With the travelling men when she walked about with them, and later with Tom Willard, it was quite different. Always they seemed to understand and sympathize with her. On the side streets of the village, in the darkness under the trees, they took hold of her hand and she thought that something unexpressed in herself came forth and became a part of an unexpressed something in them.

And then there was the second expression of her restlessness. When that came she felt for a time released and happy. She did not blame the men who walked with her and later she did not blame Tom Willard. It was always the same, beginning with kisses and ending, after strange wild emotions, with peace and then sobbing repentance. When she sobbed she put her hand upon the face of the man and had always the same thought. Even though he were large and bearded she thought he had become suddenly a little boy. She wondered why he did not sob also.

In her room, tucked away in a corner of the old Willard House, Elizabeth Willard lighted a lamp and put it on a dressing table that stood by the door. A thought had come into her mind and she went to a closet and brought out a small square box and set it on the table. The box contained material for make-up and had been left with other things by a theatrical company that had once been stranded in Winesburg. Elizabeth Willard had decided that she would be beautiful. Her hair was still black and there was a great mass of it braided and coiled about her head. The scene that was to take place in the office below began to grow in her mind. No ghostly worn-out figure should confront Tom Willard, but something quite unexpected and startling. Tall and with dusky cheeks and hair that fell in a mass from her shoulders, a figure should come striding down the stairway before the startled loungers in the hotel office. The figure would be silent—it would be swift and terrible. As a tigress whose cub had been threatened would she appear, coming out of the shadows, stealing noiselessly along and holding the long wicked scissors in her hand.

With a little broken sob in her throat, Elizabeth Willard blew out the light that stood upon the table and stood weak and trembling in the darkness. The strength that had been as a miracle in her body left and she half reeled across the floor, clutching at the back of the chair in which she had spent so many long days staring out over the tin roofs into the main street of Winesburg. In the hallway there was the sound of footsteps and George Willard came in at the door. Sitting in a chair beside his mother he began to talk. "I'm going to get out of here," he said. "I don't know where I shall go or what I shall do but I am going away."

The woman in the chair waited and trembled. An impulse came to her. "I suppose you had better wake up," she said. "You think that? You will go to the city and make money, eh? It will be better for you, you think, to be a business man, to be brisk and smart and alive?" She waited and trembled.

The son shook his head. "I suppose I can't make you understand, but oh, I wish I could," he said earnestly. "I can't even talk to father about it. I don't try. There isn't any use. I don't know what I shall do. I just want to go away and look at people and think."

Silence fell upon the room where the boy and woman sat together. Again, as on the other evenings, they were embarrassed. After a time the boy tried again to talk. "I suppose it won't be for a year or two but I've been thinking about it," he said, rising and going toward the door. "Something father said makes it sure that I shall have to go away." He fumbled with the door knob. In the room the silence became unbearable to the woman. She wanted to cry out with joy because of the words that had come from the lips of her son, but the expression of joy had become impossible to her. "I think you had better go out among the boys. You are too much indoors," she said: "I thought I would go for a little walk," replied the son stepping akwardly out of the room and closing the door.

The Philosopher

Doctor Parcival was a large man with a drooping mouth covered by a yellow mustache. He always wore a dirty white waistcoat out of the pockets of which protruded a number of the kind of black cigars known as stogies. His teeth were black and irregular and there was something strange about his eyes. The lid of the left eye twitched; it fell down and snapped up; it was exactly as though the lid of the eye were a window shade and someone stood inside the doctor's head playing with the cord.

Doctor Parcival had a liking for the boy, George Willard. It began when George had been working for a year on the *Winesburg Eagle* and the acquaintanceship was entirely a matter of the doctor's own making.

In the late afternoon Will Henderson, owner and editor of the *Eagle,* went over to Tom Willy's saloon. Along an alleyway he went and slipping in at the back door of the saloon began drinking a drink made of a combination of sloe gin and soda water. Will Henderson was a sensualist and had reached the age of forty-five. He imagined the gin renewed the youth in him. Like most sensualists he enjoyed talking of women, and for an hour he lingered about gossiping with Tom Willy. The saloon keeper was a short, broad-shouldered man with peculiarly marked hands. That flaming kind of birthmark that sometimes paints with red the faces of men and women had touched with red Tom Willy's fingers and the backs of his hands. As he stood by the bar talking to Will Henderson he rubbed the hands together. As he grew more and more excited the red of his fingers deepened. It was as though the hands had been dipped in blood that had dried and faded.

As Will Henderson stood at the bar looking at the red hands and talking of women, his assistant, George Willard, sat in the office of the *Winesburg Eagle* and listened to the talk of Doctor Parcival.

Doctor Parcival appeared immediately after Will Henderson had disappeared. One might have supposed that the doctor had been watching from his office window and had seen the editor going along the alleyway. Coming in at the front door and finding himself a chair, he lighted one of the stogies and crossing his legs began to talk. He seemed intent upon convincing the boy of the advisability of adopting a line of conduct that he was himself unable to define.

"If you have your eyes open you will see that although I call myself a doctor I have mighty few patients," he began. "There is a reason for that. It is not an accident and it is not because I do not know as much of medicine as anyone here. I do not want patients. The reason, you see, does not appear on the surface. It lies in fact in my character, which has, if you think about it, many strange turns. Why I want to talk to you of the matter I don't know. I might keep still and get more credit in your eyes. I have a desire to make you admire me, that's a fact. I don't know why. That's why I talk. It's very amusing, eh?"

Sometimes the doctor launched into long tales concerning himself. To the boy the tales were very real and full of meaning. He began to admire the fat unclean-looking man and, in the afternoon when Will Henderson had gone, looked forward with keen interest to the doctor's coming.

Doctor Parcival had been in Winesburg about five years. He came from Chicago and when he arrived was drunk and got into a fight with Albert Longworth, the baggageman. The fight concerned a trunk and ended by the doctor's being escorted to the village lockup. When he was released he rented a room above a shoe-repairing shop at the lower end of Main Street and put out the sign that announced himself as a doctor. Although he had but few patients and these of the poorer sort who were unable to pay, he seemed to have plenty of money for his needs. He slept in the office that was unspeakably dirty and dined at Biff Carter's lunch room in a small frame building opposite the railroad station. In the summer the lunch room was filled with flies and Biff Carter's white apron was more dirty than his floor. Doctor Parcival did not mind. Into the lunch room he stalked and deposited twenty cents upon the counter. "Feed me what you wish for that," he said laughing. "Use up food that you wouldn't otherwise sell. It makes no difference to me. I am a man of distinction, you see. Why should I concern myself with what I eat."

The tales that Doctor Parcival told George Willard began nowhere and ended nowhere. Sometimes the boy thought they must all be inventions, a pack of lies. And then again he was convinced that they contained the very essence of truth.

"I was a reporter like you here," Doctor Parcival began. "It was in a town in Iowa—or was it in Illinois? I don't remember and anyway it makes no difference. Perhaps I am trying to conceal my identity and don't want to be very definite. Have you ever thought it strange that I have money for my needs although I do nothing? I may have stolen a great sum of money or been involved in a murder before I came here. There is food for thought in that, eh? If you were a really smart newspaper reporter you would look me up. In Chicago there was a Doctor Cronin who was murdered. Have you heard of that? Some men murdered him and put him in a trunk. In the early morning they hauled the trunk across the city. It sat on the back of an express wagon and they were on the seat as unconcerned as anything. Along they went through quiet streets where everyone was asleep. The sun was just coming up over the lake. Funny, eh—just to think of them smoking pipes and chattering as they drove along as unconcerned as I am now. Perhaps I was one of those men. That would be a strange turn of things, now wouldn't it, eh?"

Again Doctor Parcival began his tale: "Well, anyway there I was, a reporter on a paper just as you are here, running about and getting little items to print. My mother was poor. She took in washing. Her dream was to make me a Presbyterian minister and I was studying with that end in view.

"My father had been insane for a number of years. He was in an asylum over at Dayton, Ohio. There you see I have let it slip out! All of this took place in Ohio, right here in Ohio. There is a clew if you ever get the notion of looking me up.

"I was going to tell you of my brother. That's the object of all this. That's what I'm getting at. My brother was a railroad painter and had a job on the Big Four. You know that road runs through Ohio here. With other men he lived in a box car and away they went from town to town painting the railroad property—switches, crossing gates, bridges, and stations.

"The Big four paints its stations a nasty orange color. How I hated that color! My brother was always covered with it. On pay days he used to get drunk and come home wearing his paint-covered clothes and bringing his money with him. He did not give it to mother but laid it in a pile on our kitchen table.

"About the house he went in the clothes covered with the nasty orange colored paint. I can see the picture. My mother, who was small and had red, sad-looking eyes, would come into the house from a little shed at the back. That's where she spent her time over the washtub scrubbing people's dirty clothes. In she would come and stand by the table, rubbing her eyes with her apron that was covered with soap-suds.

" 'Don't touch it! Don't you dare touch that money,' my brother roared, and then he himself took five or ten dollars and went tramping off to the saloons. When he had spent what he had taken he came back for more. He never gave my mother any money at all but stayed about until he had spent it all, a little at a time. Then he went back to his job with the painting crew on the railroad. After he had gone things began to arrive at our house, groceries and such things.

Sometimes there would be a dress for mother or a pair of shoes for me.

"Strange, eh? My mother loved my brother much more than she did me, although he never said a kind word to either of us and always raved up and down threatening us if we dared so much as touch the money that sometimes lay on the table three days.

"We got along pretty well. I studied to be a minister and prayed. I was a regular ass about saying prayers. You should have heard me. When my father died I prayed all night, just as I did sometimes when my brother was in town drinking and going about buying the things for us. In the evening after supper I knelt by the table where the money lay and prayed for hours. When no one was looking I stole a dollar or two and put it in my pocket. That makes me laugh now but then it was terrible. It was on my mind all the time. I got six dollars a week from my job on the paper and always took it straight home to mother. The few dollars I stole from my brother's pile I spent on myself, you know, for trifles, candy and cigarettes and such things.

"When my father died at the asylum over at Dayton, I went over there. I borrowed some money from the man for whom I worked and went on the train at night. It was raining. In the asylum they treated me as though I were a king.

"The men who had jobs in the asylum had found out I was a newspaper reporter. That made them afraid. There had been some negligence, some carelessness, you see, when father was ill. They thought perhaps I would write it up in the paper and make a fuss. I never intended to do anything of the kind.

"Anyway, in I went to the room where my father lay dead and blessed the dead body. I wonder what put that notion into my head. Wouldn't my brother, the painter, have laughed, though. There I stood over the dead body and spread out my hands. The superintendent of the asylum and some of his helpers came in and stood about looking sheepish. It was very amusing. I spread out my hands and said, 'Let peace brood over this carcass.' That's what I said."

Jumping to his feet and breaking off the tale, Doctor Parcival began to walk up and down in the office of the *Winesburg Eagle* where George Willard sat listening. He was awkward and, as the office was small, continually knocked against things. "What a fool I am to be talking," he said. "That is not my object in coming here and forcing my acquaintanceship upon you. I have something else in mind. You are a reporter just as I was once and you have attracted my attention. You may end by becoming just such another fool. I want to warn you and keep on warning you. That's why I seek you out."

Doctor Parcival began talking of George Willard's attitude toward men. It seemed to the boy that the man had but one object in view, to make everyone seem despicable. "I want to fill you with hatred and contempt so that you will be a superior being," he declared. "Look at my brother. There was a fellow, eh? He despised everyone, you see. You have no idea with what contempt he looked upon mother and me. And was he not our superior? You know he was. You have not seen him and yet I have made you feel that. I have given you a sense of it. He is dead. Once when he was drunk he lay down on the tracks and the car in which he lived with the other painters ran over him."

One day in August Doctor Parcival had an adventure in Winesburg. For a month George Willard had been going each morning to spend an hour in the doctor's office. The visits came about through a desire on the part of the doctor to read to the boy from the pages of a book he was in the process of writing. To write the book Doctor Parcival declared was the object of his coming to Winesburg to live.

On the morning in August before the coming of the boy, an incident had happened in the doctor's office. There had been an accident on Main Street. A team of horses had been frightened by a train and had run away. A little girl, the daughter of a farmer, had been thrown from a buggy and killed.

On Main Street everyone had become excited and a cry

for doctors had gone up. All three of the active practitioners of the town had come quickly but had found the child dead. From the crowd someone had run to the office of Doctor Parcival who had bluntly refused to go down out of his office to the dead child. The useless cruelty of his refusal had passed unnoticed. Indeed, the man who had come up the stairway to summon him had hurried away without hearing the refusal.

All of this, Doctor Parcival did not know and when George Willard came to his office he found the man shaking with terror. "What I have done will arouse the people of this town," he declared excitedly. "Do I not know human nature? Do I not know what will happen? Word of my refusal will be whispered about. Presently men will get together in groups and talk of it. They will come here. We will quarrel and there will be talk of hanging. Then they will come again bearing a rope in their hands."

Doctor Parcival shook with fright. "I have a presentiment," he declared emphatically. "It may be that what I am talking about will not occur this morning. It may be put off until tonight but I will be hanged. Everyone will get excited. I will be hanged to a lamp-post on Main Street."

Going to the door of his dirty office, Doctor Parcival looked timidly down the stairway leading to the street. When he returned the fright that had been in his eyes was beginning to be replaced by doubt. Coming on tiptoe across the room he tapped George Willard on the shoulder. "If, not now, sometime," he whispered, shaking his head. "In the end I will be crucified, uselessly crucified."

Doctor Parcival began to plead with George Willard. "You must pay attention to me," he urged. "If something happens perhaps you will be able to write the book that I may never get written. The idea is very simple, so simple that if you are not careful you will forget it. It is this—that everyone in the world is Christ and they are all crucified. That's what I want to say. Don't you forget that. Whatever happens, don't you dare let yourself forget.'

Nobody Knows

Looking cautiously about, George Willard arose from his desk in the office of the *Winesburg Eagle* and went hurriedly out at the back door. The night was warm and cloudy and although it was not yet eight o'clock, the alleyway back of the *Eagle* Office was pitch dark. A team of horses tied to a post somewhere in the darkness stamped on the hard-baked ground. A cat sprang from under George Willard's feet and ran away into the night. The young man was nervous. All day he had gone about his work like one dazed by a blow. In the alleyway he trembled as though with fright.

In the darkness George Willard walked along the alleyway, going carefully and cautiously. The back doors of the Winesburg stores were open and he could see men sitting about under the store lamps. In Myerbaum's Notion Store Mrs. Willy the saloon keeper's wife stood by the counter with a basket on her arm. Sid Green the clerk was waiting on her. He leaned over the counter and talked earnestly.

George Willard crouched and then jumped through the path of light that came out at the door. He began to run forward in the darkness. Behind Ed Griffith's saloon old Jerry Bird the town drunkard lay asleep on the ground. The runner stumbled over the sprawling legs. He laughed brokenly.

George Willard had set forth upon an adventure. All day

he had been trying to make up his mind to go through with the adventure and now he was acting. In the office of the *Winesburg Eagle* he had been sitting since six o'clock trying to think.

There had been no decision. He had just jumped to his feet, hurried past Will Henderson who was reading proof in the printshop and started to run along the alleyway.

Through street after street went George Willard, avoiding the people who passed. He crossed and recrossed the road. When he passed a street lamp he pulled his hat down over his face. He did not dare think. In his mind there was a fear but it was a new kind of fear. He was afraid the adventure on which he had set out would be spoiled, that he would lose courage and turn back.

George Willard found Louise Trunnion in the kitchen of her father's house. She was washing dishes by the light of a kerosene lamp. There she stood behind the screen door in the little shedlike kitchen at the back of the house. George Willard stopped by a picket fence and tried to control the shaking of his body. Only a narrow potato patch separated him from the adventure. Five minutes passed before he felt sure enough of himself to call to her. "Louise! Oh, Louise!" he called. The cry stuck in his throat. His voice became a hoarse whisper.

Louise Trunnion came out across the potato patch holding the dish cloth in her hand. "How do you know I want to go out with you," she said sulkily. "What makes you so sure?"

George Willard did not answer. In silence the two stood in the darkness with the fence between them. "You go on along," she said. "Pa's in there. I'll come along. You wait by Williams' barn."

The young newspaper reporter had received a letter from Louise Trunnion. It had come that morning to the office of the *Winesburg Eagle*. The letter was brief. "I'm yours if you want me," it said. He thought it annoying that in the darkness by the fence she had pretended there was nothing between them. "She has a nerve! Well, gracious sakes, she has a nerve," he muttered as he went along the street and passed a row of vacant lots where corn grew. The corn was shoulder high and had been planted right down to the sidewalk.

When Louise Trunnion came out of the front door of her house she still wore the gingham dress in which she had been washing dishes. There was no hat on her head. The boy could see her standing with the doorknob in her hand talking to someone within, no doubt to old Jake Trunnion, her father. Old Jake was half deaf and she shouted. The door closed and everything was dark and silent in the little side street. George Willard trembled more violently than ever.

In the shadows by Williams' barn George and Louise stood, not daring to talk. She was not particularly comely and there was a black smudge on the side of her nose. George thought she must have rubbed her nose with her finger after she had been handling some of the kitchen pots.

The young man began to laugh nervously. "It's warm," he said. He wanted to touch her with his hand. "I'm not very bold," he thought. Just to touch the folds of the soiled gingham dress would, he decided, be an exquisite pleasure. She began to quibble. "You think you're better than I am. Don't tell me, I guess I know," she said drawing closer to him.

A flood of words burst from George Willard. He remembered the look that had lurked in the girl's eyes when they had met on the streets and thought of the note she had written. Doubt left him. The whispered tales concerning her that had gone about town gave him confidence. He became wholly the male, bold and aggressive. In his heart there was no sympathy for her. "Ah, come on, it'll be all right. There won't be anyone know anything. How can they know?" he urged.

They began to walk along a narrow brick sidewalk between the cracks of which tall weeds grew. Some of the bricks were missing and the sidewalk was rough and irregular. He took hold of her hand that was also rough and thought it delightfully small. "I can't go far," she said and her voice was quiet, unperturbed.

They crossed a bridge that ran over a tiny stream and passed another vacant lot in which corn grew. The street ended. In the path at the side of the road they were compelled to walk one behind the other. Will Overton's berry field lay beside the road and there was a pile of boards. "Will is going to build a shed to store berry crates here," said George and they sat down upon the boards.

When George Willard got back into Main Street it was past ten o'clock and had begun to rain. Three times he walked up and down the length of Main Street. Sylvester West's Drug Store was still open and he went in and bought a cigar. When Shorty Crandall the clerk came out at the door with him he was pleased. For five minutes the two stood in the shelter of the store awning and talked. George Willard felt satisfied. He had wanted more than anything else to talk to some man. Around a corner toward the New Willard House he went whistling softly.

On the sidewalk at the side of Winney's Dry Goods Store where there was a high board fence covered with circus pictures, he stopped whistling and stood perfectly still in the darkness, attentive, listening as though for a voice calling his name. Then again he laughed nervously. "She hasn't got anything on me. Nobody knows," he muttered doggedly and went on his way.

Godliness

There were always three or four old people sitting on the front porch of the house or puttering about the garden of the Bentley farm. Three of the old people were women and sisters to Jesse. They were a colorless, soft-voiced lot. Then there was a silent old man with thin white hair who was Jesse's uncle.

The farmhouse was built of wood, a board outer-covering over a framework of logs. It was in reality not one house but a cluster of houses joined together in a rather haphazard manner. Inside, the place was full of surprises. One went up steps from the living room into the dining room and there were always steps to be ascended or descended in passing from one room to another. At meal times the place was like a beehive. At one moment all was quiet, then doors began to open, feet clattered on stairs, a murmur of soft voices arose and people appeared from a dozen obscure corners.

Beside the old people, already mentioned, many others lived in the Bentley house. There were four hired men, a woman named Aunt Callie Beebe, who was in charge of the housekeeping, a dull-witted girl named Eliza Stoughton, who made beds and helped with the milking, a boy who worked in the stables, and Jesse Bentley himself, the owner and overlord of it all.

By the time the American Civil War had been over for twenty years, that part of Northern Ohio where the Bentley farms lay had begun to emerge from pioneer life. Jesse then owned machinery for harvesting grain. He had built modern barns and most of his land was drained with carefully laid tile drain, but in order to understand the man we will have to go back to an earlier day.

The Bentley family had been in Northern Ohio for several generations before Jesse's time. They came from New York State and took up land when the country was new and land could be had at a low price. For a long time they, in common with all the other Middle Western people, were very poor. The land they had settled upon was heavily wooded and covered with fallen logs and underbrush. After the long hard labor of clearing these away and cutting the timber, there were still the stumps to be reckoned with. Plows run through the fields caught on hidden roots, stones lay all about, on the low places water gathered, and the young corn turned yellow, sickened and died.

When Jesse Bentley's father and brothers had come into their ownership of the place, much of the harder part of the work of clearing had been done, but they clung to old traditions and worked like driven animals. They lived as practically all of the farming people of the time lived. In the spring and through most of the winter the highways leading into the town of Winesburg were a sea of mud. The four young men of the family worked hard all day in the fields, they ate heavily of coarse, greasy food, and at night slept like tired beasts on beds of straw. Into their lives came little that was not coarse and brutal and outwardly they were themselves coarse and brutal. On Saturday afternoons they hitched a team of horses to a three-seated wagon and went off to town. In town they stood about the stoves in the stores talking to other farmers or to the store keepers. They were dressed in overalls and in the winter wore heavy coats that were flecked with mud. Their hands as they stretched them out to the heat of the stoves were cracked and red. It was difficult for them to talk and so they for the most part kept silent. When they had bought meat, flour, sugar, and salt, they went into one of the Winesburg saloons and drank beer. Under the influence of drink the naturally strong lusts of their natures, kept suppressed by the heroic labor of breaking up new ground, were released. A kind of crude and animal-like poetic fervor took possession of them. On the road home they stood up on the wagon seats and shouted at the stars. Sometimes they fought long and bitterly and at other times they broke forth into songs. Once Enoch Bentley, the older one of the boys, struck his father, old Tom Bentley, with the butt of a teamster's whip, and the old man seemed likely to die. For days Enoch lay hid in the straw in the loft of the stable ready to flee if the result of his momentary passion turned out to be murder. He was kept alive with food brought by his mother, who also kept him informed of the injured man's condition. When all turned out well he emerged from his hiding place and went back to the work of clearing land as though nothing had happened.

The Civil War brought a sharp turn to the fortunes of the Bentleys and was responsible for the rise of the youngest son, Jesse. Enoch, Edward, Harry, and Will Bentley all enlisted and before the long war ended they were all killed. For a time after they went away to the South, old Tom tried to run the place, but he was not successful. When the last of the four had been killed he sent word to Jesse that he would have to come home.

Then the mother, who had not been well for a year, died suddenly, and the father became altogether discouraged. He talked of selling the farm and moving into town. All day he went about shaking his head and muttering. The work in the fields was neglected and weeds grew high in the corn. Old Tom hired men but he did not use them intelligently. When they had gone away to the fields in the morning he wandered into the the woods and sat down on a log. Sometimes he forgot to come home at night and one of the daughters had to go in search of him.

When Jesse Bentley came home to the farm and began

to take charge of things he was a slight, sensitive-looking man of twenty-two. At eighteen he had left home to go to school to become a scholar and eventually to become a minister of the Presbyterian Church. All through his boyhood he had been what in our country was called an "odd sheep" and had not got on with his brothers. Of all the family only his mother had understood him and she was now dead. When he came home to take charge of the farm, that had at that time grown to more than six hundred acres, everyone on the farms about and in the nearby town of Winesburg smiled at the idea of his trying to handle the work that had been done by his four strong brothers.

There was indeed good cause to smile. By the standards of his day Jesse did not look like a man at all. He was small and very slender and womanish of body and, true to the traditions of young ministers, wore a long black coat and a narrow black string tie. The neighbors were amused when they saw him, after the years away, and they were even more amused when they saw the woman he had married in the city.

As a matter of fact, Jesse's wife did soon go under. That was perhaps Jesse's fault. A farm in Northern Ohio in the hard years after the Civil War was no place for a delicate woman, and Katherine Bentley was delicate. Jesse was hard with her as he was with everybody about him in those days. She tried to do such work as all the neighbor women about her did and he let her go on without interference. She helped to do the milking and did part of the housework; she made the beds for the men and prepared their food. For a year she worked every day from sunrise until late at night and then after giving birth to a child she died.

As for Jesse Bentley—although he was a delicately built man there was something within him that could not easily be killed. He had brown curly hair and grey eyes that were at times hard and direct, at times wavering and uncertain. Not only was he slender but he was also short of stature. His mouth was like the mouth of a sensitive and very determined child. Jesse Bentley was a fanatic. He was a

man born out of his time and place and for this he suffered
and made others suffer. Never did he succeed in getting what
he wanted out of life and he did not know what he wanted.
Within a very short time after he came home to the Bentley
farm he made everyone there a little afraid of him, and his
wife, who should have been close to him as his mother had
been, was afraid also. At the end of two weeks after his
coming, old Tom Bentley made over to him the entire ownership of the place and retired into the background. Everyone
retired into the background. In spite of his youth and inex-
perience, Jesse had the trick of mastering the souls of his
people. He was so in earnest in everything he did and said
that no one understood him. He made everyone on the farm
work as they had never worked before and yet there was
no joy in the work. If things went well they went well for
Jesse and never for the people who were his dependents.
Like a thousand other strong men who have come into the
world here in America in these later times, Jesse was but
half strong. He could master others but he could not master
himself. The running of the farm as it had never been run
before was easy for him. When he came home from Cleveland
where he had been in school, he shut himself off from all
of his people and began to make plans. He thought about
the farm night and day and that made him successful. Other
men on the farms about him worked too hard and were too
tired to think, but to think of the farm and to be everlastingly
making plans for its success was a relief to Jesse. It partially
satisfied something in his passionate nature. Immediately after
he came home he had a wing built on to the old house and
in a large room facing the west he had windows that looked
into the barnyard and other windows that looked off across
the fields. By the window he sat down to think. Hour after
hour and day after day he sat and looked over the land
and thought out his new place in life. The passionate burning
thing in his nature flamed up and his eyes became hard.
He wanted to make the farm produce as no farm in his
state had ever produced before and then he wanted something
else. It was the indefinable hunger within that made his eyes

waver and that kept him always more and more silent before people. He would have given much to achieve peace and in him was a fear that peace was the thing he could not achieve.

All over his body Jesse Bentley was alive. In his small frame was gathered the force of a long line of strong men. He had always been extraordinarily alive when he was a small boy on the farm and later when he was a young man in school. In the school he had studied and thought of God and the Bible with his whole mind and heart. As time passed and he grew to know people better, he began to think of himself as an extraordinary man, one set apart from his fellows. He wanted terribly to make his life a thing of great importance, and as he looked about at his fellow men and saw how like clods they lived it seemed to him that he could not bear to become also such a clod. Although in his absorption in himself and in his own destiny he was blind to the fact that his young wife was doing a strong woman's work even after she had become large with child and that she was killing herself in his service, he did not intend to be unkind to her. When his father, who was old and twisted with toil, made over to him the ownership of the farm and seemed content to creep away to a corner and wait for death, he shrugged his shoulders and dismissed the old man from his mind.

In the room by the window overlooking the land that had come down to him sat Jesse thinking of his own affairs. In the stables he could hear the tramping of his horses and the restless movement of his cattle. Away in the fields he could see other cattle wandering over green hills. The voices of men, his men who worked for him, came in to him through the window. From the milkhouse there was the steady thump, thump of a churn being manipulated by the half-witted girl, Eliza Stoughton Jesse's mind went back to the men of Old Testament days who had also owned lands and herds. He remembered how God had come down out of the skies and talked to these men and he wanted God to notice and to talk to him also. A kind of feverish boyish eagerness to in some way achieve in his own life the flavor of significance that had hung over these men took possession of him. Being a prayerful man he spoke of the matter aloud to God and the sound of his own words strengthened and fed his eagerness.

"I am a new kind of man come into possession of these fields," he declared. "Look upon me, O God, and look Thou also upon my neighbors and all the men who have gone before me here! O God, create in me another Jesse, like that one of old, to rule over men and to be the father of sons who shall be rulers!" Jesse grew excited as he talked aloud and jumping to his feet walked up and down in the room. In fancy he saw himself living in old times and among old peoples. The land that lay stretched out before him became of vast significance, a place peopled by his fancy with a new race of men sprung from himself. It seemed to him that in his day as in those other and older days, kingdoms might be created and new impulses given to the lives of men by the power of God speaking through a chosen servant. He longed to be such a servant. "It is God's work I have come to the land to do," he declared in a loud voice and his short figure straightened and he thought that something like a halo of Godly approval hung over him.

It will perhaps be somewhat difficult for the men and women of a later day to understand Jesse Bentley. In the last fifty years a vast change has taken place in the lives of our people. A revolution has in fact taken place. The coming of industrialism, attended by all the roar and rattle of affairs, the shrill cries of millions of new voices that have come among us from overseas, the going and coming of trains, the growth of cities, the building of the interurban car lines that weave in and out of towns and past farm-houses, and now in these later days the coming of the automobiles has worked a tremendous change in the lives and in the habits of thought of our people of Mid-America. Books, badly imagined and written though they may be in the hurry of our times, are in every household, magazines circulate by the millions of copies, newspapers are everywhere. In our day a farmer standing by the stove in the store in his village has his mind filled to overflowing with the words of other men. The newspapers and the magazines have pumped him full. Much of the old brutal ignorance that had in it also a kind of beautiful childlike innocence is gone forever. The farmer by the stove is brother to the men of the cities, and if you listen you will find him talking as glibly and as senselessly as the best city man of us all.

In Jesse Bentley's time and in the country districts of the whole Middle West in the years after the Civil War it was not so. Men labored too hard and were too tired to read. In them was no desire for words printed upon paper. As they worked in the fields, vague, half-formed thoughts took possession of them. They believed in God and in God's power to control their lives. In the little Protestant churches they gathered on Sunday to hear of God and his works. The churches were the center of the social and intellectual life of the times. The figure of God was big in the hearts of men.

And so, having been born an imaginative child and having within him a great intellectual eagerness, Jesse Bentley had turned wholeheartedly toward God. When the war took his brothers away, he saw the hand of God in that. When his father became ill and could no longer attend to the running of the farm, he took that also as a sign from God. In the city, when the word came to him, he walked about at night through the streets thinking of the matter and when he had come home and had got the work on the farm well under way, he went again at night to walk through the forests and over the low hills and to think of God.

As he walked the importance of his own figure in some divine plan grew in his mind. He grew avaricious and was impatient that the farm contained only six hundred acres. Kneeling in a fence corner at the edge of some meadow, he sent his voice abroad into the silence and looking up he saw the stars shining down at him.

One evening, some months after his father's death, and when his wife Katherine was expecting at any moment to be laid abed of childbirth, Jesse left his house and went for a long walk. The Bentley farm was situated in a tiny valley watered by Wine Creek, and Jesse walked along the banks of the stream to the end of his own land and on through the fields of his neighbors. As he walked the valley broadened and then narrowed again. Great open stretches of field and wood lay before him. The moon came out from behind clouds, and, climbing a low hill, he sat down to think.

Jesse thought that as the true servant of God the entire stretch of country through which he had walked should have come into his possession. He thought of his dead brothers and blamed them that they had not worked harder and achieved more. Before him in the moonlight the tiny stream ran down over stones, and he began to think of the men of old times who like himself had owned flocks and lands.

A fantastic impulse, half fear, half greediness, took possession of Jesse Bentley. He remembered how in the old Bible story the Lord had appeared to that other Jesse and told him to send his son David to where Saul and the men of Israel were fighting the Philistines in the Valley of Elah. Into Jesse's mind came the conviction that all of the Ohio farmers who owned land in the valley of Wine Creek were Philistines and enemies of God. "Suppose," he whispered to himself, "there should come from among them one who, like Goliath the Philistine of Gath, could defeat me and take from me my possessions." In fancy he felt the sickening dread that he thought must have lain heavy on the heart of Saul before the coming David. Jumping to his feet, he began to run through the night. As he ran he called to God. His voice carried far over the low hills. 'Jehovah of Hosts," he cried, "send to me this night out of the womb of Katherine, a son. Let Thy grace alight upon me. Send me a son to be called David who shall help me to pluck at last all of these lands out of the hands of the Philistines and turn them to Thy service and to the building of Thy kingdom on earth."

Part II

David Hardy of Winesburg, Ohio, was the grandson of Jesse

Bentley, the owner of Bentley farms. When he was twelve years old he went to the old Bentley place to live. His mother, Louise Bentley, the girl who came into the world on that night when Jesse ran through the fields crying to God that he be given a son, had grown to womanhood on the farm and had married young John Hardy of Winesburg, who became a banker. Louise and her husband did not live happily together and everyone agreed that she was to blame. She was a small woman with sharp grey eyes and black hair. From childhood she had been inclined to fits of temper and when not angry she was often morose and silent. In Winesburg it was said that she drank. Her husband, the banker, who was a careful, shrewd man, tried hard to make her happy. When he began to make money he bought for her a large brick house on Elm Street in Winesburg and he was the first man in that town to keep a manservant to drive his wife's carriage.

But Louise could not be made happy. She flew into half insane fits of temper during which she was sometimes silent, sometimes noisy and quarrelsome. She swore and cried out in her anger. She got a knife from the kitchen and threatened her husband's life. Once she deliberately set fire to the house, and often she hid herself away for days in her own room and would see no one. Her life, lived as a half recluse, gave rise to all sorts of stories concerning her. It was said that she took drugs and that she hid herself away from people because she was often so under the influence of drink that her condition could not be concealed. Sometimes on summer afternoons she came out of the house and got into her carriage. Dismissing the driver she took the reins in her own hands and drove off at top speed through the streets. If a pedestrian got in her way she drove straight ahead and the frightened citizen had to escape as best he could. To the people of the town it seemed as though she wanted to run them down. When she had driven through several streets, tearing around corners and beating the horses with the whip, she drove off into the country. On the country roads after she had gotten out of sight of the houses she let the horses slow down to a walk and her wild, reckless mood passed. She became thoughtful and muttered words. Sometimes tears came into her eyes. And then when she came back into town she again drove furiously through the quiet streets. But for the influence of her husband and the respect he inspired in people's minds she would have been arrested more than once by the town marshal.

Young David Hardy grew up in the house with this woman and as can well be imagined there was not much joy in his childhood. He was too young then to have opinions of his own about people, but at times it was difficult for him not to have very definite opinions about the woman who was his mother. David was always a quiet, orderly boy and for a long time was thought by the people of Winesburg to be something of a dullard. His eyes were brown and as a child he had a habit of looking at things and people a long time without appearing to see what he was looking at. When he heard his mother spoken of harshly or when he overheard her berating his father, he was frightened and ran away to hide. Sometimes he could not find a hiding place and that confused him. Turning his face toward a tree or if he was indoors toward the wall, he closed his eyes and tried not to think of anything. He had a habit of talking aloud to himself, and early in life a spirit of quiet sadness often took possession of him.

On the occasions when David went to visit his grandfather on the Bentley farm, he was altogether contented and happy. Often he wished that he would never have to go back to town and once when he had come home from the farm after a long visit, something happened that had a lasting effect on his mind.

David had come back into town with one of his hired men. The man was in a hurry to go about his own affairs and left the boy at the head of the street in which the Hardy house stood. It was early dusk of a fall evening and the sky was overcast with clouds. Something happened to David. He could not bear to go into the house where his mother and father lived, and on an impulse he decided to run away from home. He intended to go back to the farm and to his grandfather, but lost his way and for hours he wandered weeping and frightened on country roads. It started to rain and lightning flashed in the sky. The boy's imagination was excited and he fancied that he could see and hear strange things in the darkness. Into his mind came the conviction that he was walking and running in some terrible void where no one had ever been before. The darkness about him seemed limitless. The sound of the wind blowing in trees was terrifying. When a team of horses approached along the road in which he walked he was frightened and climbed a fence. Through a field he ran until he came into another road and getting upon his knees felt of the soft ground with his fingers. But for the figure of his grandfather, whom he was afraid he would never find in the darkness, he thought the world must be altogether empty. When his cries were heard by a farmer who was walking home from town and he was brought back to his father's house, he was so tired and excited that he did not know what was happening to him.

By chance David's father knew that he had disappeared. On the street he had met the farm hand from the Bentley place and knew of his son's return to town. When the boy did not come home an alarm was set up and John Hardy with several men of the town went to search the country. The report that David had been kidnapped ran about through the streets of Winesburg. When he came home there were no lights in the house, but his mother appeared and clutched him eagerly in her arms. David thought she had suddenly become another woman. He could not believe that so delightful a thing had happened. With her own hands Louise Hardy bathed his tired young body and cooked him food. She would not let him go to bed but, when he had put on his nightgown, blew out the lights and sat down in a chair to hold him in her arms. For an hour the woman sat in the darkness and held her boy. All the time she kept talking in a low voice. David could not understand what had so changed her. Her habitually dissatisfied face had become, he thought, the most peaceful and lovely thing he had ever seen. When he began to weep she held him more and more tightly. On and on went her voice. It was not harsh or shrill as when she talked to her husband, but was like rain falling on trees. Presently men began coming to the door to report that he had not been found, but she made him hide and be silent until she had sent them away. He thought it must be a game his mother and the men of the town were playing with him and laughed joyously. Into his mind came the thought that his having been lost and frightened in the darkness was an altogether unimportant matter. He thought that he would have been willing to go through the frightful experience a thousand times to be sure of finding at the end of the long black road a thing so lovely as his mother had suddenly become.

During the last years of young David's boyhood he saw his mother but seldom and she became for him just a woman with whom he had once lived. Still he could not get her figure out of his mind and as he grew older it became more definite. When he was twelve years old he went to the Bentley farm to live. Old Jesse came into town and fairly demanded that he be given charge of the boy. The old man was excited and determined on having his own way. He talked to John Hardy in the office of the Winesburg Savings Bank and then the two men went to the house on Elm Street to talk with Louise. They both expected her to make trouble but were mistaken. She was very quiet and when Jesse had explained his mission and had gone on at some length about the advantages to come through having the boy out of doors and in the quiet atmosphere of the old farmhouse, she nodded her head in approval. "It is an atmosphere not corrupted by my presence," she said sharply. Her shoulders shook and she seemed about to fly into a fit of temper. "It is a place for a man child, although it was never a place for me," she went on. "You never wanted me there and of course the air of your house did me no good. It was like poison in my blood but it will be different with him."

Louise turned and went out of the room, leaving the two men to sit in embarassed silence. As very often happened she later stayed in her room for days. Even when the boy's clothes were packed and he was taken away she did not appear. The loss of her son made a sharp break in her life and she seemed less inclined to quarrel with her husband. John Hardy thought it had all turned out very well indeed.

And so young David went to live in the Bentley farmhouse with Jesse. Two of the old farmer's sisters were alive and still lived in the house. They were afraid of Jesse and rarely spoke when he was about. One of the women who had been noted for her flaming red hair when she was younger was a born mother and became the boy's caretaker. Every night when he had gone to bed she went into his room and sat on the floor until he fell asleep. When he became drowsy she became bold and whispered things that he later thought he must have dreamed.

Her soft low voice called him endearing names and he dreamed that his mother had come to him and that she had changed so that she was always as she had been that time after he ran away. He also grew bold and reaching out his hand stroked the face of the woman on the floor so that she was ecstatically happy. Everyone in the old house became happy after the boy went there. The hard insistent thing in Jesse Bentley that had kept the people in the house silent and timid and that had never been dispelled by the presence of the girl Louise was apparently swept away by the coming of the boy. It was as though God had relented and sent a son to the man.

The man who had proclaimed himself the only true servant of God in all the valley of Wine Creek, and who had wanted God to send him a sign of approval by way of a son out of the womb of Katherine, began to think that at last his prayers had been answered. Although he was at that time only fifty-five years old he looked seventy and was worn out with much thinking and scheming. The effort he had made to extend his land holdings had been successful and there were few farms in the valley that did not belong to him, but until David came he was a bitterly disappointed man.

There were two influences at work in Jesse Bentley and all his life his mind had been a battleground for these influences. First there was the old thing in him. He wanted to be a man of God and a leader among men of God. His walking in the fields and through the forests at night had brought him close to nature and there were forces in the passionately religious man that ran out to the forces in nature. The disappointment that had come to him when a daughter and not a son had been born to Katherine had fallen upon him like a blow struck by some unseen hand and the blow had somewhat softened his egotism. He still believed that God might at any moment make himself manifest out of the winds or the clouds, but he no longer demanded such recognition. Instead he prayed for it. Sometimes he was altogether doubtful and thought God had deserted the world. He regretted the fate that had not let him live in a simpler and sweeter time when at the beckoning of some strange cloud in the sky men left their lands and houses and went forth into the wilderness to create new races. While he worked night and day to make his farms more productive and to extend his holdings of land, he regretted that he could not use his own restless energy in the building of temples, the slaying of unbelievers and in general in the work of glorifying God's name on earth.

That is what Jesse hungered for and then also he hungered for something else. He had grown into maturity in America in the years after the Civil War and he, like all men of his time, had been touched by the deep influences that were at work in the country during those years when modern industrialism was being born. He began to buy machines that would permit him to do the work of the farms while employing fewer men and he sometimes thought that if he were a younger man he would give up farming altogether and start a factory in Winesburg for the making of machinery. Jesse formed the habit of reading newspapers and magazines. He invented a machine for the making of fence out of wire. Faintly he realized that the atmosphere of old times and places that he had always cultivated in his own mind was strange and foreign to the thing that was growing up in the minds of others. The beginning of the most materialistic age in the history of the world, when wars would be fought without patriotism, when men would forget God and only pay attention to moral standards, when the will to power would replace the will to serve and beauty would be well-nigh forgotten in the terrible headlong rush of mankind toward the acquiring of possessions, was telling its story to Jesse the man of God as it was to the men about him. The greedy thing in him wanted to make money faster than it could be made by tilling the land. More than once he went into Winesburg to talk with his son-in-law John Hardy about it. "You are a banker and you will have chances I never had," he said and his eyes shone. "I am thinking about it all the time. Big things are going to be done in the country and there will be more money to be made than I ever dreamed of. You get into it. I wish I were younger and had your chance." Jesse Bentley walked up and down in the bank office and grew more and more excited as he talked. At one time in his life he had been threatened with paralysis and his left side remained somewhat weakened. As he talked his left eyelid twitched. Later when he drove back home and when night came on and the stars came out it was harder to get back the old feeling of a close and personal God who lived in the sky overhead and who might at any moment reach out his hand, touch him on the shoulder, and appoint for him some heroic task to be done. Jesse's mind was fixed upon the things read in newspapers and magazines, on fortunes to be made almost without effort by shrewd men who bought and sold. For him the coming of the boy David did much to bring back with renewed force the old faith and it seemed to him that God had at last looked with favor upon him.

As for the boy on the farm, life began to reveal itself to him in a thousand new and delightful ways. The kindly attitude of all about him expanded his quiet nature and he lost the half timid, hesitating manner he had always had with his people. At night when he went to bed after a long day of adventures in the stables, in the fields, or driving about from farm to farm with his grandfather, he wanted to embrace everyone in the house. If Sherley Bentley, the woman who came each night to sit on the floor by his bedside, did not appear at once, he went to the head of the stairs and shouted, his young voice ringing through the narrow halls where for so long there had been a tradition of silence. In the morning when he awoke and lay still in bed, the sounds that came in to him through the windows filled him with delight. He thought with a shudder of the life in the house in Winesburg and of his mother's angry voice that had always made him tremble. There in the country all sounds were pleasant sounds. When he awoke at dawn the barnyard back of the house also awoke. In the house people stirred about. Eliza Stoughton the half-witted girl was poked in the ribs by a farm hand and giggled noisily, in some distant field a cow bawled and was answered by the cattle in the stables, and one of the farm hands spoke sharply to the horse he was grooming by the stable door. David leaped out of bed and ran to a window. All of the people stirring about excited his mind, and he wondered what his mother was doing in the house in town.

From the windows of his own room he could not see directly into the barnyard where the farm hands had now all assembled to do the morning chores, but he could hear the voices of the men and the neighing of the horses. When one of the men laughed, he laughed also. Leaning out at the open window, he looked into an orchard where a fat sow wandered about with a litter of tiny pigs at her heels. Every morning he counted the pigs. "Four, five, six, seven," he said slowly, wetting his finger and making straight up and down marks on the window ledge. David ran to put on his trousers and shirt. A feverish desire to get out of doors took possession of him. Every morning he made such a noise coming down stairs that Aunt Callie, the housekeeper, declared he was trying to tear the house down. When he had run through the long old house, shutting doors behind him with a bang, he came into the barnyard and looked about with an amazed air of expectancy. It seemed to him that in such a place tremendous things might have happened during the night. The farm hands looked at him and laughed. Henry Strader, an old man who had been on the farm since Jesse came into possession and who before David's time had never been known to make a joke, made the same joke every morning. It amused David so that he laughed and clapped his hands. "See, come here and look," cried the old man. "Grandfather Jesse's white mare has torn the black stocking she wears on her foot."

Day after day through the long summer, Jesse Bentley drove from farm to farm up and down the valley of Wine Creek, and his grandson went with him. They rode in a comfortable old phaeton drawn by the white horse. The old man scratched his thin white beard and talked to himself of his plans for increasing the productiveness of the fields they visited and of God's part in the plans all men made. Sometimes he looked at David and smiled happily and then for a long time he appeared to forget the boy's existence. More and more every day now his mind turned back again to the dreams that had filled his mind when he had first come out of the city to live on the land. One afternoon he startled David by letting his dreams take entire possession of him. With the boy as a witness, he went through a ceremony and brought about an accident that nearly destroyed the companionship that was growing up between them.

Jesse and his grandson were driving in a distant part of the valley some miles from home. A forest came down to the road and through the forest Wine Creek wriggled its way over stones toward a distant river. All the afternoon Jesse had been in a meditative mood and now he began to talk. His mind went back to the night when he had been frightened by thoughts of a giant that might come to rob and plunder him of his possessions, and again as on that night when he had run through the fields crying for a son, he became excited to the edge of insanity. Stopping the horse he got out of the buggy and asked David to get out also. The two climbed over a fence and walked along the bank of the stream. The boy paid no attention to the muttering of his grandfather, but ran along beside him and wondered what was going to happen. When a rabbit jumped up and ran away through the woods, he clapped his hands and danced with delight. He looked at the tall trees and was sorry that he was not a little animal to climb high in the air without being frightened. Stooping, he picked up a small stone and threw it over the head of his grandfather into a clump of bushes. "Wake up, little animal. Go and climb to the top of the trees," he shouted in a shrill voice.

Jesse Bentley went along under the trees with his head bowed and with his mind in a ferment. His earnestness affected the boy, who presently became silent and a little alarmed. Into the old man's mind had come the notion that now he could bring from God a word or a sign out of the sky, that the presence of the boy and man on their knees in some lonely spot in the forest would make the miracle he had been waiting for almost inevitable. "It was in just such a place as this that other David tended the sheep when his father came and told him to go down unto Saul," he muttered.

Taking the boy rather roughly by the shoulder, he climbed over a fallen log and when he had come to an open place among the trees he dropped upon his knees and began to pray in a loud voice.

A kind of terror he had never known before took possession of David. Crouching beneath a tree he watched the man on the ground before him and his own knees began to tremble. It seemed to him that he was in the presence not only of his grandfather but of someone else, someone who might hurt him, someone who was not kindly but dangerous and brutal. He began to cry and reaching down picked up a small stick, which he held tightly gripped in his fingers. When Jesse Bentley, absorbed in his own idea, suddenly arose and advanced toward him, his terror grew until his whole body shook. In the woods an intense silence seemed to lie over everything and suddenly out of the silence came the old man's harsh and insistent voice. Gripping the boy's shoulders, Jesse turned his face to the sky and shouted. The whole left side of his face twitched and his hand on the boy's shoulder twitched also. "Make a sign to me, God," he cried. "Here I stand with the boy David. Come down to me out of the sky and make Thy presence known to me."

With a cry of fear, David turned and, shaking himself loose from the hands that held him, ran away through the forest. He did not believe that the man who turned up his face and in a harsh voice shouted at the sky was his grandfather at all. The man did not look like his grandfather. The conviction that something strange and terrible had happened, that by some miracle a new and dangerous person had come into the body of the kindly old man, took possession of him. On and on he ran down the hillside, sobbing as he ran. When he fell over the roots of a tree and in falling struck his head, he arose and tried to run on again. His head hurt so that presently he fell down and lay still, but it was only after Jesse had carried him to the buggy and he awoke to find the old man's hand stroking his head tenderly that the terror left him. "Take me away. There is a terrible man back there in the woods," he declared firmly, while Jesse looked away over the tops of the trees and again his lips cried out to God. "What have I done that Thou dost not approve of me," he whispered softly, saying the words over and over as he drove rapidly along the road with the boy's cut and bleeding head held tenderly against his shoulder.

Part III | SURRENDER

The story of Louise Bentley, who became Mrs. John Hardy and lived with her husband in a brick house on Elm Street in Winesburg, is a story of misunderstanding.

Before such women as Louise can be understood and their lives made livable, much will have to be done. Thoughtful books will have to be written and thoughtful lives lived by people about them.

Born of a delicate and overworked mother, and an impulsive, hard, imaginative father, who did not look with favor upon her coming into the world, Louise was from childhood a neurotic, one of the race of over-sensitive women that in later days industrialism was to bring in such great numbers into the world.

During her early years she lived on the Bentley farm, a silent, moody child, wanting love more than anything else in the world and not getting it. When she was fifteen she went to live in Winesburg with the family of Albert Hardy, who had a store for the sale of buggies and wagons, and was a member of the town board of education.

Louise went into town to be a student in the Winesburg High School and she went to live at the Hardys' because Albert Hardy and her father were friends.

Hardy, the vehicle merchant of Winesburg, like thousands of other men of his times, was an enthusiast on the subject of education. He had made his own way in the world without learning got from books, but he was convinced that had he but known books things would have gone better with him. To everyone who came into his shop he talked of the matter, and in his own household he drove his family distracted by his constant harping on the subject.

He had two daughters and one son, John Hardy, and more than once the daughters threatened to leave school altogether. As a matter of principle they did just enough work in their classes to avoid punishment. "I hate books and I hate anyone who likes books," Harriet, the younger of the two girls, declared passionately.

In Winesburg as on the farm Louise was not happy. For years she had dreamed of the time when she could go forth into the world, and she looked upon the move into the Hardy household as a great step in the direction of freedom. Always when she had thought of the matter, it had seemed to her that in town all must be gaiety and life, that there men and women must live happily and freely, giving and taking friendship and affection as one takes the feel of a wind on the cheek. After the silence and the cheerlessness of life in the Bentley house, she dreamed of stepping forth into an atmosphere that was warm and pulsating with life and reality. And in the Hardy household Louise might have got something of the thing for which she so hungered but for a mistake she made when she had just come to town.

Louise won the disfavor of the two Hardy girls, Mary

and Harriet, by her application to her studies in school. She did not come to the house until the day when school was to begin and knew nothing of the feeling they had in the matter. She was timid and during the first month made no acquaintances. Every Friday afternoon one of the hired men from the farm drove into Winesburg and took her home for the week-end, so that she did not spend the Saturday holiday with the town people. Because she was embarrassed and lonely she worked constantly at her studies. To Mary and Harriet, it seemed as though she tried to make trouble for them by her proficiency. In her eagerness to appear well Louise wanted to answer every question put to the class by the teacher. She jumped up and down and her eyes flashed. Then when she had answered some question the others in the class had been unable to answer, she smiled happily. "See, I have done it for you," her eyes seemed to say. "You need not bother about the matter. I will answer all questions. For the whole class it will be easy while I am here."

In the evening after supper in the Hardy house, Albert Hardy began to praise Louise. One of the teachers had spoken highly of her and he was delighted. "Well, again I have heard of it," he began, looking hard at his daughters and then turning to smile at Louise. "Another of the teachers has told me of the good work Louise is doing. Everyone in Winesburg is telling me how smart she is. I am ashamed that they do not speak so of my own girls." Arising, the merchant marched about the room and lighted his evening cigar.

The two girls looked at each other and shook their heads wearily. Seeing their indifference the father became angry. "I tell you it is something for you two to be thinking about," he cried, glaring at them. "There is a big change coming here in America and in learning is the only hope of the coming generations. Louise is the daughter of a rich man but she is not ashamed to study. It should make you ashamed to see what she does."

The merchant took his hat from a rack by the door and

prepared to depart for the evening. At the door he stopped and glared back. So fierce was his manner that Louise was frightened and ran upstairs to her own room. The daughters began to speak of their own affairs. "Pay attention to me," roared the merchant. "Your minds are lazy. Your indifference to education is affecting your characters. You will amount to nothing. Now mark what I say—Louise will be so far ahead of you that you will never catch up."

The distracted man went out of the house and into the street shaking with wrath. He went along muttering words and swearing, but when he got into Main Street his anger passed. He stopped to talk of the weather or the crops with some other merchant or with a farmer who had come into town and forgot his daughters altogether or, if he thought of them, only shrugged his shoulders. "Oh, well, girls will be girls," he muttered philosophically.

In the house when Louise came down into the room where the two girls sat, they would have nothing to do with her. One evening after she had been there for more than six weeks and was heartbroken because of the continued air of coldness with which she was always greeted, she burst into tears. "Shut up your crying and go back to your own room and to your books," Mary Hardy said sharply.

The room occupied by Louise was on the second floor of the Hardy house, and her window looked out upon an orchard. There was a stove in the room and every evening young John Hardy carried up an armful of wood and put it in a box that stood by the wall. During the second month after she came to the house, Louise gave up all hope of getting on a friendly footing with the Hardy girls and went to her own room as soon as the evening meal was at an end.

Her mind began to play with thoughts of making friends with John Hardy. When he came into the room with the wood in his arms, she pretended to be busy with her studies but watched him eagerly. When he had put the wood in the box and turned to go out, she put down her head and blushed. She tried to make talk but could say nothing, and after he had gone she was angry at herself for her stupidity.

The mind of the country girl became filled with the idea of drawing close to the young man. She thought that in him might be found the quality she had all her life been seeking in people. It seemed to her that between herself and all the other people in the world, a wall had been built up and that she was living just on the edge of some warm inner circle of life that must be quite open and understandable to others. She became obsessed with the thought that it wanted but a courageous act on her part to make all of her association with people something quite different, and that it was possible by such an act to pass into a new life as one opens a door and goes into a room. Day and night she thought of the matter, but although the thing she wanted so earnestly was something very warm and close it had as yet no conscious connection with sex. It had not become that definite, and her mind had only alighted upon the person of John Hardy because he was at hand and unlike his sisters had not been unfriendly to her.

The Hardy sisters, Mary and Harriet, were both older than Louise. In a certain kind of knowledge of the world they were years older. They lived as all of the young women of Middle Western towns lived. In those days young women did not go out of our towns to Eastern colleges and ideas in regard to social classes had hardly begun to exist. A daughter of a laborer was in much the same social position as a daughter of a farmer or a merchant, and there were no leisure classes. A girl was "nice" or she was "not nice." If a nice girl, she had a young man who came to her house to see her on Sunday and on Wednesday evenings. Sometimes she went with her young man to a dance or a church social. At other times she received him at the house and was given the use of the parlor for that purpose. No one intruded upon her. For hours the two sat behind closed doors. Sometimes the lights were turned low and the young man and woman embraced. Cheeks became hot and hair disarranged. After a year or two, if the impulse within them became strong and insistent enough, they married.

One evening during her first winter in Winesburg, Louise had an adventure that gave a new impulse to her desire to break down the wall that she thought stood between her and John Hardy. It was Wednesday and immediately after the evening meal Albert Hardy put on his hat and went away. Young John brought the wood and put it in the box in Louise's room. "You do work hard, don't you?" he said awkwardly, and then before she could answer he also went away.

Louise heard him go out of the house and had a mad desire to run after him. Opening her window she leaned out and called softly. "John, dear John, come back, don't go away." The night was cloudy and she could not see far into the darkness, but as she waited she fancied she could hear a soft little noise as of someone going on tiptoes through the trees in the orchard. She was frightened and closed the window quickly. For an hour she moved about the room trembling with excitement and when she could not longer bear the waiting, she crept into the hall and down the stairs into a closet-like room that opened off the parlor.

Louise had decided that she would perform the courageous act that had for weeks been in her mind. She was convinced that John Hardy had concealed himself in the orchard beneath her window and she was determined to find him and tell him that she wanted him to come close to her, to hold her in his arms, to tell her of his thoughts and dreams and to listen while she told him her thoughts and dreams. "In the darkness it will be easier to say things," she whispered to herself, as she stood in the little room groping for the door.

And then suddenly Louise realized that she was not alone in the house. In the parlor on the other side of the door a man's voice spoke softly and the door opened. Louise just had time to conceal herself in a little opening beneath the stairway when Mary Hardy, accompanied by her young man, came into the little dark room.

For an hour Louise sat on the floor in the darkness and listened. Without words Mary Hardy, with the aid of the man who had come to spend the evening with her, brought to the country girl a knowledge of men and women. Putting her head down until she was curled into a little ball she lay perfectly still. It seemed to her that by some strange impulse of the gods, a great gift had been brought to Mary Hardy and she could not understand the older woman's determined protest.

The young man took Mary Hardy into his arms and kissed her. When she struggled and laughed, he but held her the more tightly. For an hour the contest between them went on and then they went back into the parlor and Louise escaped up the stairs. "I hope you were quiet out there. You must not disturb the little mouse at her studies," she heard Harriet saying to her sister as she stood by her own door in the hallway above.

Louise wrote a note to John Hardy and late that night, when all in the house were asleep, she crept downstairs and slipped it under his door. She was afraid that if she did not do the thing at once her courage would fail. In the note she tried to be quite definite about what she wanted. "I want someone to love me and I want to love someone," she wrote. "If you are the one for me I want you to come into the orchard at night and make a noise under my window. It will be easy for me to crawl down over the shed and come to you. I am thinking about it all the time, so if you are to come at all you must come soon."

For a long time Louise did not know what would be the outcome of her bold attempt to secure for herself a lover. In a way she still did not know whether or not she wanted him to come. Sometimes it seemed to her that to be held tightly and kissed was the whole secret of life, and then a new impulse came and she was terribly afraid. The age-old woman's desire to be possessed had taken possession of her, but so vague was her notion of life that it seemed to her just the touch of John Hardy's hand upon her own hand would satisfy. She wondered if he would understand that. At the table next day while Albert Hardy talked and the two girls whispered and laughed, she did not look at John but at the table and as soon as possible escaped. In the evening she went out of the house until she was sure he had taken the wood to her room and gone away. When after several evenings of intense listening she heard no call from the darkness in the orchard, she was half beside herself with grief and decided that for her there was no way to break through the wall that had shut her off from the joy of life.

And then on a Monday evening two or three weeks after the writing of the note, John Hardy came for her. Louise had so entirely given up the thought of his coming that for a long time she did not hear the call that came up from the orchard. On the Friday evening before, as she was being driven back to the farm for the week-end by one of the hired men, she had on an impulse done a thing that had startled her, and as John Hardy stood in the darkness below and called her name softly and insistently, she walked about in her room and wondered what new impulse had led her to commit so ridiculous an act.

The farm hand, a young fellow with black curly hair, had come for her somewhat late on that Friday evening and they drove home in the darkness. Louise, whose mind was filled with thoughts of John Hardy, tried to make talk but the country boy was embarrassed and would say nothing. Her mind began to review the loneliness of her childhood and she remembered with a pang the sharp new loneliness that had just come to her. "I hate everyone," she cried suddenly, and then broke forth into a tirade that frightened her escort. "I hate father and old man Hardy, too," she declared vehemently. "I get my lessons there in the school in town but I hate that also."

Louise frightened the farm hand still more by turning and putting her cheek down upon his shoulder. Vaguely she hoped that he like that young man who had stood in the darkness with Mary would put his arms about her and kiss her, but the country boy was only alarmed. He struck the horse with the whip and began to whistle. "The road is rough, eh?" he said loudly. Louise was so angry that reaching up she snatched his hat from his head and threw it into the road. When he jumped out of the buggy and went to get it, she drove off and left him to walk the rest of the way back to the farm.

Louise Bentley took John Hardy to be her lover. That was not what she wanted but it was so the young man had interpreted her approach to him, and so anxious was she to achieve something else that she made no resistance. When after a few months they were both afraid that she was about to become a mother, they went one evening to the county seat and were married. For a few months they lived in the Hardy house and then took a house of their own. All during the first year Louise tried to make her husband understand the vague and intangible hunger that had led to the writing of the note and that was still unsatisfied. Again and again she crept into his arms and tried to talk of it, but always without success. Filled with his own notions of love between men and women, he did not listen but began to kiss her upon the lips. That confused her so that in the end she did not want to be kissed. She did not know what she wanted.

When the alarm that had tricked them into marriage proved to be groundless, she was angry and said bitter, hurtful things. Later when her son David was born, she could not nurse him and did not know whether she wanted him or not. Sometimes she stayed in the room with him all day, walking about and occasionally creeping close to touch him tenderly with her hands, and then other days came when she did not want to see or be near the tiny bit of humanity that had come into the house. When John Hardy reproached her for her cruelty, she laughed. "It is a man child and will get what it wants anyway," she said sharply. "Had it been a woman child there is nothing in the world I would not have done for it."

Part IV | TERROR

When David Hardy was a tall boy of fifteen, he, like his mother, had an adventure that changed the whole current of his life and sent him out of his quiet corner into the world.

The shell of the circumstances of his life was broken and he was compelled to start forth. He left Winesburg and no one there ever saw him again. After his disappearance, his mother and grandfather both died and his father became very rich. He spent much money in trying to locate his son, but that is no part of this story.

It was in the late fall of an unusual year on the Bentley farms. Everywhere the crops had been heavy. That spring, Jesse had bought part of a long strip of black swamp land that lay in the valley of Wine Creek. He got the land at a low price but had spent a large sum of money to improve it. Great ditches had to be dug and thousands of tile laid. Neighboring farmers shook their heads over the expense Some of them laughed and hoped that Jesse would lose heavily by the venture, but the old man went silently on with the work and said nothing.

When the land was drained he planted it to cabbages and onions, and again the neighbors laughed. The crop was, however, enormous and brought high prices. In the one year Jesse made enough money to pay for all the cost of preparing the land and had a surplus that enabled him to buy two more farms. He was exultant and could not conceal his delight. For the first time in all the history of his ownership of the farms, he went among his men with a smiling face.

Jesse bought a great many new machines for cutting down the cost of labor and of the remaining acres in the strip of black fertile swamp land. One day he went into Winesburg and bought a bicycle and a new suit of clothes for David and he gave his two sisters money with which to go to a religious convention at Cleveland, Ohio.

In the fall of that year when the frost came and the trees in the forests along Wine Creek were golden brown, David spent every moment when he did not have to attend school, out in the open. Alone or with other boys he went every afternoon into the woods to gather nuts. The other boys of the countryside, most of them sons of laborers on the Bentley farms, had guns with which they went hunting rabbits and squirrels, but David did not go with them. He made himself a sling with rubber bands and a forked stick and went off by himself to gather nuts. As he went about thoughts came to him. He realized that he was almost a man and wondered what he would do in life, but before they came to anything, the thoughts passed and he was a boy again. One day he killed a squirrel that sat on one of the lower branches of a tree and chattered at him. Home he ran with the squirrel in his hand. One of the Bentley sisters cooked the little animal and he ate it with great gusto. The skin he tacked on a board and suspended the board by a string from his bedroom window.

That gave his mind a new turn. After that he never went into the woods without carrying the sling in his pocket and he spent hours shooting at imaginary animals concealed among the brown leaves in the trees. Thoughts of his coming manhood passed and he was content to be a boy with a boy's impulses.

One Saturday morning when he was about to set off for the woods with the sling in his pocket and a bag for nuts on his shoulder, his grandfather stopped him. In the eyes of the old man was the strained serious look that always a little frightened David. At such times Jesse Bentley's eyes did not look straight ahead but wavered and seemed to be looking at nothing. Something like an invisible curtain appeared to have come between the man and all the rest of the world. "I want you to come with me," he said briefly, and his eyes looked over the boy's head into the sky. "We have something important to do today. You may bring the bag for nuts if you wish. It does not matter and anyway we will be going into the woods."

Jesse and David set out from the Bentley farmhouse in the old phaeton that was drawn by the white horse. When they had gone along in silence for a long way they stopped at the edge of a field where a flock of sheep were grazing. Among the sheep was a lamb that had been born out of season, and this David and his grandfather caught and tied so tightly that it looked like a little white ball. When they drove on again Jesse let David hold the lamb in his arms. "I saw it yesterday and it put me in mind of what I have long wanted to do," he said, and again he looked away over the head of the boy with the wavering, uncertain stare in his eyes.

After the feeling of exaltation that had come to the farmer as a result of his successful year, another mood had taken possession of him. For a long time he had been going about feeling very humble and prayerful. Again he walked alone at night thinking of God and as he walked he again connected his own figure with the figures of old days. Under the stars he knelt on the wet grass and raised up his voice in prayer. Now he had decided that like the men whose stories filled the pages of the Bible, he would make a sacrifice to God. "I have been given these abundant crops and God has also sent me a boy who is called David," he whispered to himself. "Perhaps I should have done this thing long ago." He was sorry the idea had not come into his mind in the days before his daughter Louise had been born and thought that surely now when he had erected a pile of burning sticks in some lonely place in the woods and had offered the body of a lamb as a burnt offering, God would appear to him and give him a message.

More and more as he thought of the matter, he thought also of David and his passionate self-love was partially forgotten. "It is time for the boy to begin thinking of going out into the world and the message will be one concerning him," he decided. "God will make a pathway for him. He will tell me what place David is to take in life and when he shall set out on his journey. It is right that the boy should be there. If I am fortunate and an angel of God should appear, David will see the beauty and glory of God made manifest to man. It will make a true man of God of him also."

In silence Jesse and David drove along the road until they came to that place where Jesse had once before appealed to God and had frightened his grandson. The morning had been bright and cheerful, but a cold wind now began to blow and clouds hid the sun. When David saw the place to which they had come he began to tremble with fright, and when they stopped by the bridge where the creek came down from among the trees, he wanted to spring out of the phaeton and run away.

A dozen plans for escape ran through David's head, but when Jesse stopped the horse and climbed over the fence into the wood, he followed. "It is foolish to be afraid. Nothing will happen," he told himself as he went along with the lamb in his arms. There was something in the helplessness of the little animal held so tightly in his arms that gave him courage. He could feel the rapid beating of the beast's heart and that made his own heart beat less rapidly. As he walked swiftly along behind his grandfather, he untied the string with which the four legs of the lamb were fastened together. "If anything happens we will run away together," he thought.

In the woods, after they had gone a long way from the road, Jesse stopped in an opening among the trees where a clearing, overgrown with small bushes, ran up from the creek. He was still silent but began at once to erect a heap of dry sticks which he presently set afire. The boy sat on the ground with the lamb in his arms. His imagination began to invest every movement of the old man with significance and he became every moment more afraid. "I must put the blood of the lamb on the head of the boy," Jesse muttered when the sticks had begun to blaze greedily, and taking a long knife from his pocket he turned and walked rapidly across the clearing toward David.

Terror seized upon the soul of the boy. He was sick with it. For a moment he sat perfectly still and then his body stiffened and he sprang to his feet. His face became as white as the fleece of the lamb that, now finding itself suddenly released, ran down the hill. David ran also. Fear made his feet fly. Over the low bushes and logs he leaped frantically. As he ran he put his hand into his pocket and took out the branched stick from which the sling for shooting squirrels was suspended. When he came to the creek that was shallow and splashed down over the stones, he dashed into the water and turned to look back, and when he saw his grandfather still running toward him with the long knife held tightly in his hand he did not hesitate, but reaching down, selected a stone and put it in the sling. With all his strength he drew back the heavy rubber bands and the stone whistled through the air. It hit Jesse, who had entirely forgotten the boy and was pursuing the lamb, squarely in the head. With a groan he pitched forward and fell almost at the boy's feet. When David saw that he lay still and that he was apparently dead, his fright increased immeasurably. It became an insane panic.

With a cry he turned and ran off through the woods weeping convulsively. "I don't care—I killed him, but I don't care," he sobbed. As he ran on and on he decided suddenly that he would never go back again to the Bentley farms or to the town of Winesburg. "I have killed the man of God and now I will myself be a man and go into the world," he said stoutly as he stopped running and walked rapidly down a road that followed the windings of Wine Creek as it ran through fields and forests into the west.

On the ground by the creek Jesse Bentley moved uneasily about. He groaned and opened his eyes. For a long time he lay perfectly still and looked at the sky. When at last he got to his feet, his mind was confused and he was not surprised by the boy's disappearance. By the roadside he sat down on a log and began to talk about God. That is all they ever got out of him. Whenever David's name was mentioned he looked vaguely at the sky and said that a messenger from God had taken the boy. "It happened because I was too greedy for glory," he declared, and would have no more to say in the matter.

A Man of Ideas

He lived with his mother, a grey, silent woman with a peculiar ashy complexion. The house in which they lived stood in a little grove of trees beyond where the main street of Winesburg crossed Wine Creek. His name was Joe Welling, and his father had been a man of some dignity in the community, a lawyer and a member of the state legislature at Columbus. Joe himself was small of body and in his character unlike anyone else in town. He was like a tiny little volcano that lies silent for days and then suddenly spouts fire. No, he wasn't like that—he was like a man who is subject to fits, one who walks among his fellow men inspiring fear because a fit may come upon him suddenly and blow him away into a strange uncanny physical state in which his eyes roll and his legs and arms jerk. He was like that, only that the visitation that descended upon Joe Welling was a mental and not a physical thing. He was beset by ideas and in the throes of one of his ideas was uncontrollable. Words rolled and tumbled from his mouth. A peculiar smile came upon his lips. The edges of his teeth that were tipped with gold glistened in the light. Pouncing upon a bystander he began to talk. For the bystander there was no escape. The excited man breathed into his face, peered into his eyes, pounded upon his chest with a shaking forefinger, demanded, compelled attention.

In those days the Standard Oil Company did not deliver oil to the consumer in big wagons and motor trucks as it does now, but delivered instead to retail grocers, hardware stores, and the like. Joe was the Standard Oil agent in Winesburg and in several towns up and down the railroad that went through Winesburg. He collected bills, booked orders, and did other things. His father, the legislator, had secured the job for him.

In and out of the stores of Winesburg went Joe Welling —silent, excessively polite, intent upon his business. Men watched him with eyes in which lurked amusement tempered by alarm. They were waiting for him to break forth, preparing to flee. Although the seizures that came upon him were harmless enough, they could not be laughed away. They were overwhelming. Astride an idea, Joe was overmastering. His personality became gigantic. It over-rode the man to whom he talked, swept him away, swept all away, all who stood within sound of his voice.

In Sylvester West's Drug Store stood four men who were talking of horse racing. Wesley Moyer's stallion, Tony Tip, was to race at the June meeting at Tiffin, Ohio, and there was a rumor that he would meet the stiffest competition of his career. It was said that Pop Geers, the great racing driver, would himself be there. A doubt of the success of Tony Tip hung heavy in the air of Winesburg.

Into the drug store came Joe Welling, brushing the screen door violently aside. With a strange absorbed light in his eyes he pounced upon Ed Thomas, he who knew Pop Geers and whose opinion of Tony Tip's chances was worth considering.

"The water is up in Wine Creek," cried Joe Welling with the air of Pheidippides bringing news of the victory of the Greeks in the struggle at Marathon. His finger beat a tattoo upon Ed Thomas's broad chest. "By Trunion bridge it is within eleven and a half inches of the flooring," he went on, the words coming quickly and with a little whistling noise from between his teeth. An expression of helpless annoyance crept over the faces of the four.

"I have my facts correct. Depend upon that. I went to Sinnings' Hardware Store and got a rule. Then I went back and measured. I could hardly believe my own eyes. It hasn't rained you see for ten days. At first I didn't know what to think. Thoughts rushed through my head. I thought of subterranean passages and springs. Down under the ground went my mind, delving about. I sat on the floor of the bridge and rubbed my head. There wasn't a cloud in the sky, not one. Come out into the street and you'll see. There wasn't a cloud. There isn't a cloud now. Yes, there was a cloud. I don't want to keep back any facts. There was a cloud in the west down near the horizon, a cloud no bigger than a man's hand.

"Not that I think that has anything to do with it. There it is, you see. You understand how puzzled I was.

"Then an idea came to me. I laughed. You'll laugh, too. Of course it rained over in Medina County. That's interesting, eh? If we had no trains, no mails, no telegraph, we would know that it rained over in Medina County. That's where Wine Creek comes from. Everyone knows that. Little old Wine Creek brought us the news. That's interesting. I laughed. I thought I'd tell you—it's interesting, eh?"

Joe Welling turned and went out at the door. Taking a book from his pocket, he stopped and ran a finger down one of the pages. Again he was absorbed in his duties as agent of the Standard Oil Company. "Hern's Grocery will be getting low on coal oil. I'll see them," he muttered, hurrying along the street, and bowing politely to the right and left at the people walking past.

When George Willard went to work for the *Winesburg Eagle* he was besieged by Joe Welling. Joe envied the boy. It seemed to him that he was meant by Nature to be a reporter on a newspaper. "It is what I should be doing, there is no doubt of that," he declared, stopping George Willard on the sidewalk before Daugherty's Feed Store. His eyes began to glisten and his forefinger to tremble. "Of course I make more money with the Standard Oil Company and I'm only telling you," he added. "I've got nothing against you but I should have your place. I could do the work at odd moments. Here and there I would run finding out things you'll never see."

Becoming more excited Joe Welling crowded the young reporter against the front of the feed store. He appeared to be lost in thought, rolling his eyes about and running a thin nervous hand through his hair. A smile spread over his face and his gold teeth glittered. "You get out your note book," he commanded. "You carry a little pad of paper in your pocket, don't you? I knew you did. Well, you set this down. I thought of it the other day. Let's take decay. Now what is decay? It's fire. It burns up wood and other things. You never thought of that? Of course not. This sidewalk here and this feed store, the trees down the street there—they're all on fire. They're burning up. Decay you see is always going on. It don't stop. Water and paint can't stop it. If a thing is iron, then what? It rusts, you see. That's fire, too. The world is on fire. Start your pieces in the paper that way. Just say in big letters *'The World Is On Fire.'* That will make 'em look up. They'll say you're a smart one. I don't care. I don't envy you. I just snatched that idea out of the air. I would make a newspaper hum. You got to admit that."

Turning quickly, Joe Welling walked rapidly away. When he had taken several steps he stopped and looked back. "I'm going to stick to you," he said. "I'm going to make you a regular hummer. I should start a newspaper myself, that's what I should do. I'd be a marvel. Everybody knows that."

When George Willard had been for a year on the *Winesburg Eagle*, four things happened to Joe Welling. His mother died, he came to live at the New Willard House, he became involved in a love affair, and he organized the Winesburg Baseball Club.

Joe organized the baseball club because he wanted to be a coach and in that position he began to win the respect of his townsmen. "He is a wonder," they declared after Joe's team had whipped the team from Medina County. "He gets everybody working together. You just watch him."

Upon the baseball field Joe Welling stood by first base, his whole body quivering with excitement. In spite of themselves all of the players watched him closely. The opposing pitcher became confused.

"Now! Now! Now! Now!" shouted the excited man. "Watch me! Watch me! Watch my fingers! Watch my hands! Watch my feet! Watch my eyes! Let's work together here! Watch me! In me you see all the movements of the game! Work with me! Work with me! Watch me! Watch me! Watch me!"

With runners of the Winesburg team on bases, Joe Welling became as one inspired. Before they knew what had come over them, the base runners were watching the man, edging off the bases, advancing, retreating, held as by an invisible cord. The players of the opposing team also watched Joe. They were fascinated. For a moment they watched and then, as though to break a spell that hung over them, they began hurling the ball wildly about, and amid a series of fierce animal-like cries from the coach, the runners of the Winesburg team scampered home.

Joe Welling's love affair set the town of Winesburg on edge. When it began everyone whispered and shook his head. When people tried to laugh, the laughter was forced and unnatural. Joe fell in love with Sarah King, a lean, sad-looking woman who lived with her father and brother in a brick house that stood opposite the gate leading to the Winesburg Cemetery.

The two Kings, Edward the father, and Tom the son, were not popular in Winesburg. They were called proud and dangerous. They had come to Winesburg from some place in the South and ran a cider mill on the Trunion Pike. Tom King was reported to have killed a man before he came to Winesburg. He was twenty-seven years old and rode about town on a grey pony. Also he had a long yellow mustache that dropped down over his teeth, and always carried a heavy, wicked-looking walking stick in his hand. Once he killed a dog with the stick. The dog belonged to Win Pawsey, the shoe merchant, and stood on the sidewalk wagging its tail. Tom King killed it with one blow. He was arrested and paid a fine of ten dollars.

Old Edward King was small of stature and when he passed people in the street laughed a queer unmirthful laugh. When he laughed he scratched his left elbow with his right hand. The sleeve of his coat was almost worn through from the habit. As he walked along the street, looking nervously about and laughing, he seemed more dangerous than his silent, fierce-looking son.

When Sarah King began walking out in the evening with Joe Welling, people shook their heads in alarm. She was tall and pale and had dark rings under her eyes. The couple looked ridiculous together. Under the trees they walked and Joe talked. His passionate eager protestations of love, heard coming out of the darkness by the cemetery wall, or from the deep shadows of the trees on the hill that ran up to the Fair Grounds from Waterworks Pond, were repeated in the stores. Men stood by the bar in the New Willard House laughing and talking of Joe's courtship. After the laughter came silence. The Winesburg baseball team, under his management, was winning game after game, and the town had begun to respect him. Sensing a tragedy, they waited, laughing nervously.

Late on a Saturday afternoon the meeting between Joe Welling and the two Kings, the anticipation of which had set the town on edge, took place in Joe Welling's room in the New Willard House. George Willard was a witness to the meeting. It came about in this way:

When the young reporter went to his room after the evening meal he saw Tom King and his father sitting in the half darkness in Joe's room. The son had the heavy walking stick in his hand and sat near the door. Old Edward King walked nervously about, scratching his left elbow with his right hand. The hallways were empty and silent.

George Willard went to his own room and sat down at his desk. He tried to write but his hand trembled so that he could not hold the pen. He also walked nervously up and down. Like the rest of the town of Winesburg he was perplexed and knew not what to do.

It was seven-thirty and fast growing dark when Joe Welling came along the station platform toward the New Willard House, In his arms he held a bundle of weeds and grasses. In spite of the terror that made his body shake, George Willard was amused at the sight of the small spry figure holding the grasses and half running along the platform.

Shaking with fright and anxiety, the young reporter lurked in the hallway outside the door of the room in which Joe Welling talked to the two Kings. There had been an oath, the nervous giggle of old Edward King, and then silence. Now the voice of Joe Welling, sharp and clear, broke forth. George Willard began to laugh. He understood. As he had swept all men before him, so now Joe Welling was carrying the two men in the room off their feet with a tidal wave of words. The listener in the hall walked up and down, lost in amazement.

Inside the room Joe Welling had paid no attention to the grumbled threat of Tom King. Absorbed in an idea he closed the door and, lighting a lamp, spread the handful of weeds and grasses upon the floor. "I've got something here," he announced solemnly. "I was going to tell George Willard about it, let him make a piece out of it for the paper. I'm glad you're here. I wish Sarah were here also. I've been going to come to your house and tell you of some of my ideas. They're interesting. Sarah wouldn't let me. She said we'd quarrel. That's foolish."

Running up and down before the two perplexed men, Joe Welling began to explain. "Don't you make a mistake now," he cried. "This is something big." His voice was shrill with excitement. "You just follow me, you'll be interested. I know you will. Suppose this—suppose all of the wheat, the corn, the oats, the peas, the potatoes, were all by some miracle swept away. Now here we are, you see, in this county. There is a high fence built all around us. We'll suppose that. No one can get over the fence and all the fruits of the earth are destroyed, nothing left but these wild things, these grasses. Would we be done for? I ask you that. Would we be done for?" Again Tom King growled and for a moment there was silence in the room. Then again Joe plunged into the exposition of his idea. "Things would go hard for a time. I admit that. I've got to admit that. No getting around it. We'd be hard put to it. More than one fat stomach would cave in. But they couldn't down us. I should say not."

Tom King laughed good naturedly and the shivery, nervous laugh of Edward King rang through the house. Joe Welling hurried on. "We'd begin, you see, to breed up new vegetables and fruits. Soon we'd regain all we had lost. Mind, I don't say the new things would be the same as the old. They wouldn't. Maybe they'd be better, maybe not so good. That's interesting, eh? You can think about that. It starts your mind working, now don't it?"

In the room there was silence and then again old Edward King laughed nervously. "Say, I wish Sarah was here," cried Joe Welling. "Let's go up to your house. I want to tell her of this."

There was a scraping of chairs in the room. It was then that George Willard retreated to his own room. Leaning out at the window he saw Joe Welling going along the street with the two Kings. Tom King was forced to take extraordinary long strides to keep pace with the little man. As he strode along, he leaned over, listening—absorbed, fascinated. Joe Welling again talked excitedly. "Take milkweed now," he cried. "A lot might be done with milkweed, eh? It's almost unbelievable. I want you to think about it. I want you two to think about it. There would be a new vegetable kingdom you see. It's interesting, eh? It's an idea. Wait till you see Sarah, she'll get the idea. She'll be interested. Sarah is always interested in ideas. You can't be too smart for Sarah, now can you? Of course you can't. You know that."

Adventure

Alice Hindman, a woman of twenty-seven when George Willard was a mere boy, had lived in Winesburg all her life. She clerked in Winney's Dry Goods Store and lived with her mother, who had married a second husband.

Alice's step-father was a carriage painter, and given to drink. His story is an odd one. It will be worth telling some day.

At twenty-seven Alice was tall and somewhat slight. Her head was large and overshadowed her body. Her shoulders were a little stooped and her hair and eyes brown. She was very quiet but beneath a placid exterior a continual ferment went on.

When she was a girl of sixteen and before she began to work in the store, Alice had an affair with a young man. The young man, named Ned Currie, was older than Alice. He, like George Willard, was employed on the *Winesburg Eagle* and for a long time he went to see Alice almost every evening. Together the two walked under the trees through the streets of the town and talked of what they would do with their lives. Alice was then a very pretty girl and Ned Currie took her into his arms and kissed her. He became excited and said things he did not intend to say and Alice, betrayed by her desire to have something beautiful come into her rather narrow life, also grew excited. She also talked. The outer crust of her life, all of her natural diffidence and reserve, was torn away and she gave herself over to the emotions of love. When, late in the fall of her sixteenth year, Ned Currie went away to Cleveland where he hoped to get a place on a city newspaper and rise in the world, she wanted to go with him. With a trembling voice she told him what was in her mind. "I will work and you can work," she said. "I do not want to harness you to a needless expense that will prevent your making progress. Don't marry me now. We will get along without that and we can be together. Even though we live in the same house no one will say anything. In the city we will be unknown and people will pay no attention to us."

Ned Currie was puzzled by the determination and abandon of his sweetheart and was also deeply touched. He had wanted the girl to become his mistress but changed his mind. He wanted to protect and care for her. "You don't know what you're talking about," he said sharply; "you may be sure I'll let you do no such thing. As soon as I get a good job I'll come back. For the present you'll have to stay here. It's the only thing we can do."

On the evening before he left Winesburg to take up his new life in the city, Ned Currie went to call on Alice. They walked about through the streets for an hour and then got a rig from Wesley Moyer's livery and went for a drive in the country. The moon came up and they found themselves unable to talk. In his sadness the young man forgot the resolutions he had made regarding his conduct with the girl.

They got out of the buggy at a place where a long meadow ran down to the bank of Wine Creek and there in the dim light became lovers. When at midnight they returned to town they were both glad. It did not seem to them that anything that could happen in the future could blot out the wonder and beauty of the thing that had happened. "Now we will have to stick to each other, whatever happens we will have to do that," Ned Currie said as he left the girl at her father's door.

The young newspaper man did not succeed in getting a place on a Cleveland paper and went west to Chicago. For a time he was lonely and wrote to Alice almost every day. Then he was caught up by the life of the city; he began to make friends and found new interests in life. In Chicago he boarded at a house where there were several women. One of them attracted his attention and he forgot Alice in Winesburg. At the end of a year he had stopped writing letters, and only once in a long time, when he was lonely or when he went into one of the city parks and saw the moon shining on the grass as it had shone that night on the meadow by Wine Creek, did he think of her at all.

In Winesburg the girl who had been loved grew to be a woman. When she was twenty-two years old her father, who owned a harness repair shop, died suddenly. The harness maker was an old soldier, and after a few months his wife received a widow's pension. She used the first money she got to buy a loom and became a weaver of carpets, and Alice got a place in Winney's store. For a number of years nothing could have induced her to believe that Ned Currie would not in the end return to her.

She was glad to be employed because the daily round of toil in the store made the time of waiting seem less long and uninteresting. She began to save money, thinking that when she had saved two or three hundred dollars she would follow her lover to the city and try if her presence would not win back his affections.

Alice did not blame Ned Currie for what had happened in the moonlight in the field, but felt that she could never marry another man. To her the thought of giving to another what she still felt could belong only to Ned seemed monstrous. When other young men tried to attract her attention she would have nothing to do with them. "I am his wife and shall remain his wife whether he comes back or not," she whispered to herself, and for all of her willingness to support herself could not have understood the growing modern idea of a woman's owning herself and giving and taking for her own ends in life.

Alice worked in the dry goods store from eight in the morning until six at night and on three evenings a week went back to the store to stay from seven until nine. As time passed and she became more and more lonely she began to practice the devices common to lonely people. When at night she went upstairs into her own room she knelt on the floor to pray and in her prayers whispered things she wanted to say to her lover. She became attached to inanimate objects, and because it was her own, could not bear to have anyone touch the furniture of her room. The trick of saving money, begun for a purpose, was carried on after the scheme of going to the city to find Ned Currie had been given up. It became a fixed habit, and when she needed new clothes she did not get them. Sometimes on rainy afternoons in the store she got out her bank book and, letting it lie open before her, spent hours dreaming impossible dreams of saving money enough so that the interest would support both herself and her future husband.

"Ned always liked to travel about," she thought. "I'll give him the chance. Some day when we are married and I can save both his money and my own, we will be rich. Then we can travel together all over the world."

In the dry goods store weeks ran into months and months into years as Alice waited and dreamed of her lover's return. Her employer, a grey old man with false teeth and a thin grey mustache that drooped down over his mouth, was not given to conversation, and sometimes, on rainy days and in the winter when a storm raged in Main Street, long hours passed when no customers came in. Alice arranged and rearranged the stock. She stood near the front window where she could look down the deserted street and thought of the evenings when she had walked with Ned Currie and of what he had said. "We will have to stick to each other now." The words echoed and re-echoed through the mind of the maturing woman. Tears came into her eyes. Sometimes when her employer had gone out and she was alone in the store she put her head on the counter and wept. "Oh, Ned, I am waiting," she whispered over and over, and all the time the creeping fear that he would never come back grew stronger within her.

In the spring when the rains have passed and before the long hot days of summer have come, the country about Winesburg is delightful. The town lies in the midst of open fields, but beyond the fields are pleasant patches of woodlands. In the wooded places are many little cloistered nooks, quiet places where lovers go to sit on Sunday afternoons. Through the trees they look out across the fields and see farmers at work about the barns or people driving up and down on the roads. In the town bells ring and occasionally a train passes, looking like a toy thing in the distance.

For several years after Ned Currie went away Alice did not go into the wood with other young people on Sunday, but one day after he had been gone for two or three years and when her loneliness seemed unbearable, she put on her best dress and set out. Finding a little sheltered place from which she could see the town and a long stretch of the fields, she sat down. Fear of age and ineffectuality took possession of her. She could not sit still, and arose. As she stood looking out over the land something, perhaps the thought of never ceasing life as it expresses itself in the flow of the seasons, fixed her mind on the passing years. With a shiver of dread, she realized that for her the beauty and freshness of youth had passed. For the first time she felt that she had been cheated. She did not blame Ned Currie and did not know what to blame. Sadness swept over her. Dropping to her knees, she tried to pray, but instead of prayers words of protest came to her lips. "It is not going to come to me. I will never find happiness. Why do I tell myself lies?" she cried, and an odd sense of relief came with this, her first bold attempt to face the fear that had become a part of her everyday life.

In the year when Alice Hindman became twenty-five two things happened to disturb the dull uneventfulness of her days. Her mother married Bush Milton, the carriage painter of Winesburg, and she herself became a member of the Winesburg Methodist Church. Alice joined the church because she had become frightened by the loneliness of her position in life. Her mother's second marriage had emphasized her isolation. "I am becoming old and queer. If Ned comes he will not want me. In the city where he is living men are perpetually young. There is so much going on that they do not have time to grow old," she told herself with a grim little smile, and went resolutely about the business of becoming acquainted with people. Every Thursday evening when the store had closed she went to a prayer meeting in the basement of the church and on Sunday evening attended a meeting of an organization called The Epworth League.

When Will Hurley, a middle-aged man who clerked in a drug store and who also belonged to the church, offered to walk home with her she did not protest. "Of course I will not let him make a practice of being with me, but if he comes to see me once in a long time there can be no harm in that," she told herself, still determined in her loyalty to Ned Currie.

Without realizing what was happening, Alice was trying feebly at first, but with growing determination, to get a new hold upon life. Beside the drug clerk she walked in silence, but sometimes in the darkness as they went stolidly along she put out her hand and touched softly the folds of his coat. When he left her at the gate before her mother's house she did not go indoors, but stood for a moment by the door. She wanted to call to the drug clerk, to ask him to sit with her in the darkness on the porch before the house, but was afraid he would not understand. "It is not him that I want," she told herself; "I want to avoid being so much alone. If I am not careful I will grow unaccustomed to being with people."

During the early fall of her twenty-seventh year a passionate restlessness took possession of Alice. She could not bear to be in the company of the drug clerk, and when, in the evening, he came to walk with her she sent him away. Her mind became intensely active and when, weary from the long hours of standing behind the counter in the store, she went home and crawled into bed, she could not sleep. With staring eyes she looked into the darkness. Her imagination, like a child awakened from long sleep, played about the room. Deep within her there was something that would not be cheated by phantasies and that demanded some definite answer from life.

Alice took a pillow into her arms and held it tightly against her breasts. Getting out of bed, she arranged a blanket so that in the darkness it looked like a form lying between the sheets and, kneeling beside the bed, she caressed it, whispering words over and over, like a refrain. "Why doesn't something happen? Why am I left here alone?" she muttered. Although she sometimes thought of Ned Currie, she no longer depended on him. Her desire had grown vague. She did not want Ned Currie or any other man. She wanted to be loved, to have something answer the call that was growing louder and louder within her.

And then one night when it rained Alice had an adventure. It frightened and confused her. She had come home from the store at nine and found the house empty. Bush Milton had gone off to town and her mother to the house of a neighbor. Alice went upstairs to her room and undressed in the darkness. For a moment she stood by the window hearing the rain beat against the glass and then a strange desire took possession of her. Without stopping to think of what she intended to do, she ran downstairs through the dark house and out into the rain. As she stood on the little grass plot before the house and felt the cold rain on her body a mad desire to run naked through the streets took possession of her.

She thought that the rain would have some creative and wonderful effect on her body. Not for years had she felt so full of youth and courage. She wanted to leap and run, to cry out, to find some other lonely human and embrace him. On the brick sidewalk before the house a man stumbled homeward. Alice started to run. A wild, desperate mood took possession of her. "What do I care who it is. He is alone, and I will go to him," she thought; and then without stopping to consider the possible result of her madness, called softly,

"Wait!" she cried. "Don't go away. Whoever you are, you must wait."

The man on the sidewalk stopped and stood listening. He was an old man and somewhat deaf. Putting his hand to his mouth, he shouted. "What? What say?" he called.

Alice dropped to the ground and lay trembling. She was so frightened at the thought of what she had done that when the man had gone on his way she did not dare get to her feet, but crawled on hands and knees through the grass to the house. When she got to her own room she bolted the door and drew her dressing table across the doorway. Her body shook as with a chill and her hands trembled so that she had difficulty getting into her nightdress. When she got into bed she buried her face in the pillow and wept brokenheartedly. "What is the matter with me? I will do something dreadful if I am not careful," she thought, and turning her face to the wall, began trying to force herself to face bravely the fact that many people must live and die alone, even in Winesburg.

Respectability

If you have lived in cities and have walked in the park on a summer afternoon, you have perhaps seen, blinking in a corner of his iron cage, a huge, grotesque kind of monkey, a creature with ugly, sagging, hairless skin below his eyes and a bright purple underbody. This monkey is a true monster. In the completeness of his ugliness he achieved a kind of perverted beauty. Children stopping before the cage are fascinated, men turn away with an air of disgust, and women linger for a moment, trying perhaps to remember which one of their male acquaintances the thing in some faint way resembles.

Had you been in the earlier years of your life a citizen of the village of Winesburg, Ohio, there would have been for you no mystery in regard to the beast in his cage. "It is like Wash Williams," you would have said. "As he sits in the corner there, the beast is exactly like old Wash sitting on the grass in the station yard on a summer evening after he has closed his office for the night."

Wash Williams, the telegraph operator of Winesburg, was the ugliest thing in town. His girth was immense, his neck thin, his legs feeble. He was dirty. Everything about him was unclean. Even the whites of his eyes looked soiled.

I go too fast. Not everything about Wash was unclean. He took care of his hands. His fingers were fat, but there was something sensitive and shapely in the hand that lay on the table by the instrument in the telegraph office. In his youth Wash Williams had been called the best telegraph operator in the state, and in spite of his degradement to the obscure office at Winesburg, he was still proud of his ability.

Wash Williams did not associate with the men of the town in which he lived. "I'll have nothing to do with them," he said, looking with bleary eyes at the men who walked along the station platform past the telegraph office. Up along Main Street he went in the evening to Ed Griffith's saloon, and after drinking unbelievable quantities of beer staggered off to his room in the New Willard House and to his bed for the night.

Wash Williams was a man of courage. A thing had happened to him that made him hate life, and he hated it wholeheartedly, with the abandon of a poet. First of all, he hated women. "Bitches," he called them. His feeling toward men was somewhat different. He pitied them. "Does not every man let his life be managed for him by some bitch or another?" he asked.

In Winesburg no attention was paid to Wash Williams and his hatred of his fellows. Once Mrs. White, the banker's wife, complained to the telegraph company, saying that the office in Winesburg was dirty and smelled abominably, but nothing came of her complaint. Here and there a man respected the operator. Instinctively the man felt in him a glowing resentment of something he had not the courage to resent. When Wash walked through the streets such a one had an instinct to pay him homage, to raise his hat or to bow before him. The superintendent who had supervision over the telegraph operators on the railroad that went through Winesburg felt that way. He had put Wash into the obscure office at Winesburg to avoid discharging him, and he meant to keep him there. When he received the letter of complaint from the banker's wife, he tore it up and laughed unpleasantly. For some reason he thought of his own wife as he tore up the letter.

Wash Williams once had a wife. When he was still a young man he married a woman at Dayton, Ohio. The woman was tall and slender and had blue eyes and yellow hair. Wash was himself a comely youth. He loved the woman with a love as absorbing as the hatred he later felt for all women.

In all of Winesburg there was but one person who knew the story of the thing that had made ugly the person and the character of Wash Williams. He once told the story to George Willard and the telling of the tale came about in this way:

George Willard went one evening to walk with Belle Carpenter, a trimmer of women's hats who worked in a millinery shop kept by Mrs. Kate McHugh. The young man was not in love with the woman, who, in fact, had a suitor who worked as bartender in Ed Griffith's saloon, but as they walked about under the trees they occasionally embraced. The night and their own thoughts had aroused something in them. As they were returning to Main Street they passed the little lawn beside the railroad station and saw Wash Williams apparently asleep on the grass beneath a tree. On the next evening the operator and George Willard walked out together. Down the railroad they went and sat on a pile of decaying railroad ties beside the tracks. It was then that the operator told the young reporter his story of hate.

Perhaps a dozen times George Willard and the strange, shapeless man who lived at his father's hotel had been on the point of talking. The young man looked at the hideous, leering face staring about the hotel dining room and was consumed with curiosity. Something he saw lurking in the staring eyes told him that the man who had nothing to say to others had nevertheless something to say to him. On the pile of railroad ties on the summer evening, he waited expectantly. When the operator remained silent and seemed to have changed his mind about talking, he tried to make conversation. "Were you ever married, Mr. Williams?" he began. "I suppose you were and your wife is dead, is that it?"

Wash Williams spat forth a succession of vile oaths. "Yes, she is dead," he agreed. "She is dead as all women are dead. She is a living-dead thing, walking in the sight of men and making the earth foul by her presence." Staring into the boy's eyes, the man became purple with rage. "My wife, she is dead; yes, surely. I tell you, all women are dead, my mother, your mother, that tall dark woman who works in the millinery store and with whom I saw you walking about yesterday— all of them, they are all dead. I tell you there is something rotten about them. I was married, sure. My wife was dead before she married me, she was a foul thing come out of a woman more foul. She was a thing sent to make life unbearable to me. I was a fool, do you see, as you are now, and so I married this woman. I would like to see men a little begin to understand women. They are sent to prevent men making the world worth while. It is a trick in Nature. Ugh! They are creeping, crawling, squirming things, they with their soft hands and their blue eyes. The sight of a woman sickens me. Why I don't kill every woman I see I don't know."

Half frightened and yet fascinated by the light burning in the eyes of the hideous old man, George Willard listened, afire with curiosity. Darkness came on and he leaned forward trying to see the face of the man who talked. When, in the gathering darkness, he could no longer see the purple, bloated face and the burning eyes, a curious fancy came to him. Wash Williams talked in low even tones that made his words seem the more terrible. In the darkness the young reporter found himself imagining that he sat on the railroad ties beside a comely young man with black hair and black shining eyes. There was something almost beautiful in the voice of Wash Williams, the hideous, telling his story of hate.

The telegraph operator of Winesburg, sitting in the darkness on the railroad ties, had become a poet. Hatred had raised him to that elevation. "It is because I saw you kissing the lips of that Belle Carpenter that I tell you my story," he said. "What happened to me may next happen to you. I want to put you on your guard. Already you may be having dreams in your head. I want to destroy them."

Wash Williams began telling the story of his married life with the tall blonde girl with blue eyes whom he had met when he was a young operator at Dayton, Ohio. Here and there his story was touched with moments of beauty intermingled with strings of vile curses. The operator had married the daughter of a dentist who was the youngest of three sisters. On his marriage day, because of his ability, he was promoted to a position as dispatcher at an increased salary and sent to an office at Columbus, Ohio. There he settled down with his young wife and began buying a house on the installment plan.

The young telegraph operator was madly in love. With a kind of religious fervor he had managed to go through the pitfalls of his youth and to remain virginal until after his marriage. He made for George Willard a picture of his life in the house at Columbus, Ohio, with the young wife. "In the garden back of our house we planted vegetables," he said, "you know, peas and corn and such things. We went to Columbus in early March and as soon as the day became warm I went to work in the garden. With a spade I turned up the black ground while she ran about laughing and pretending to be afraid of the worms I uncovered. Late in April came the planting. In the little paths among the seed beds she stood holding a paper bag in her hand. The bag was filled with seeds. A few at a time she handed me the seeds that I might thrust them into the warm, soft ground."

For a moment there was a catch in the voice of the man talking in the darkness. "I loved her," he said. "I don't claim not to be a fool. I love her yet. There in the dusk in the spring evening I crawled along the black ground to her feet and groveled before her. I kissed her shoes and the ankles above her shoes. When the hem of her garment touched my face I trembled. When after two years of that life I found she had managed to acquire three other lovers who came regularly to our house when I was away at work, I didn't want to touch them or her. I just sent her home to her mother and said nothing. There was nothing to say. I had four hundred dollars in the bank and I gave her that. I didn't ask her reasons. I didn't say anything. When she had gone I cried like a silly boy. Pretty soon I had a chance to sell the house and I sent that money to her."

Wash Williams and George Willard arose from the pile of

railroad ties and walked along the tracks toward town. The operator finished his tale quickly, breathlessly.

"Her mother sent for me," he said. "She wrote me a letter and asked me to come to their house at Dayton. When I got there it was evening about this time."

Wash Williams' voice rose to half scream. "I sat in the parlor of that house two hours. Her mother took me in there and left me. Their house was stylish. They were what is called respectable people. There were plush chairs and a couch in the room. I was trembling all over. I hated the men I thought had wronged her. I was sick of living alone and wanted her back. The longer I waited the more raw and tender I became. I thought that if she came in and just touched me with her hand I would perhaps faint away. I ached to forgive and forget."

Wash Williams stopped and stood staring at George Willard. The boy's body shook as from a chill. Again the man's voice became soft and low. "She came into the room naked," he went on. "Her mother did that. While I sat there she was taking the girl's clothes off, perhaps coaxing her to do it. First I heard voices at the door that led into a little hallway and then it opened softly. The girl was ashamed and stood perfectly still staring at the floor. The mother didn't come into the room. When she had pushed the girl in through the door she stood in the hallway waiting, hoping we would— well, you see—waiting."

George Willard and the telegraph operator came into the main street of Winesburg. The lights from the store windows lay bright and shining on the sidewalks. People moved about laughing and talking. The young reporter felt ill and weak. In imagination, he also became old and shapeless. "I didn't get the mother killed," said Wash Williams, staring up and down the street, "I struck her once with a chair and then the neighbors came in and took it away. She screamed so loud you see. I won't ever have a chance to kill her now. She died of a fever a month after that happened."

The Thinker

The house in which Seth Richmond of Winesburg lived with his mother had been at one time the show place of the town, but when young Seth lived there its glory had become somewhat dimmed. The huge brick house which Banker White had built on Buckeye Street had overshadowed it. The Richmond place was in a little valley far out at the end of Main Street. Farmers coming into town by a dusty road from the south passed by a grove of walnut trees, skirted the Fair Ground with its high board fence covered with advertisements, and trotted their horses down through the valley past the Richmond place into town. As much of the country north and south of Winesburg was devoted to fruit and berry raising. Seth saw wagon-loads of berry pickers—boys, girls, and women—going to the fields in the morning and returning covered with dust in the evening. The chattering crowd, with their rude jokes cried out from wagon to wagon, sometimes irritated him sharply. He regretted that he also could not laugh boisterously, shout meaningless jokes and make of himself a figure in the endless stream of moving, giggling activity that went up and down the road.

The Richmond house was built of limestone, and although it was said in the village to have become run down, had in reality grown more beautiful with every passing year. Already time had begun a little to color the stone, lending a golden richness to its surface and in the evening or on dark days touching the shaded places beneath the eaves with wavering patches of browns and blacks.

The house had been built by Seth's grandfather, a stone quarryman, and it, together with the stone quarries on Lake Erie eighteen miles to the north, had been left to his son, Clarence Richmond, Seth's father. Clarence Richmond, a quiet passionate man extraordinarily admired by his neighbors, had been killed in a street fight with the editor of a newspaper in Toledo, Ohio. The fight concerned the publication of Clarence Richmond's name coupled with that of a woman school teacher, and as the dead man had begun the row by firing upon the editor, the effort to punish the slayer was unsuccessful. After the quarryman's death it was found that much of the money left to him had been squandered in speculation and in insecure investments made through the influence of friends.

Left with but a small income, Virginia Richmond had settled down to a retired life in the village and to the raising of her son. Although she had been deeply moved by the death of the husband and father, she did not at all believe the stories concerning him that ran about after his death. To her mind, the sensitive, boyish man whom all had instinctively loved, was but an unfortunate, a being too fine for everyday life. "You'll be hearing all sorts of stories, but you are not to believe what you hear," she said to her son. "He was a good man, full of tenderness for everyone, and should not have tried to be a man of affairs. No matter how much I were to plan and dream of your future, I could not imagine anything better for you than that you turn out as good a man as your father."

Several years after the death of her husband, Virginia Richmond had become alarmed at the growing demands upon her income and had set herself to the task of increasing it. She had learned stenography and through the influence of her husband's friends got the position of court stenographer at the county seat. There she went by train each morning during the sessions of the court, and when no court sat, spent her days working among the rosebushes in her garden. She was a tall, straight figure of a woman with a plain face and a great mass of brown hair.

In the relationship between Seth Richmond and his mother, there was a quality that even at eighteen had begun to color all of his traffic with men. An almost unhealthy respect for the youth kept the mother for the most part silent in his presence. When she did speak sharply to him he had only to look steadily into her eyes to see dawning there the puzzled look he had already noticed in the eyes of others when he looked at them.

The truth was that the son thought with remarkable clearness and the mother did not. She expected from all people certain conventional reactions to life. A boy was your son, you scolded him and he trembled and looked at the floor. When you had scolded enough he wept and all was forgiven. After the weeping and when he had gone to bed, you crept into his room and kissed him.

Virginia Richmond could not understand why her son did not do these things. After the severest reprimand, he did not tremble and look at the floor but instead looked steadily at her, causing uneasy doubts to invade her mind. As for creeping into his room—after Seth had passed his fifteenth year, she would have been half afraid to do anything of the kind.

Once when he was a boy of sixteen, Seth in company with two other boys ran away from home. The three boys climbed into the open door of an empty freight car and rode some forty miles to a town where a fair was being held. One of the boys had a bottle filled with a combination of whiskey and blackberry wine, and the three sat with legs, dangling out of the car door drinking from the bottle. Seth's two companions sang and waved their hands to idlers about the stations of the towns through which the train passed. They planned raids upon the baskets of farmers who had come with their families to the fair. "We will live like kings and won't have to spend a penny to see the fair and horse races," they declared boastfully.

After the disappearance of Seth, Virginia Richmond walked up and down the floor of her home filled with vague alarms. Although on the next day she discovered, through an inquiry made by the town marshal, on what adventure the boys had gone, she could not quiet herself. All through the night she lay awake hearing the clock tick and telling herself that Seth, like his father, would come to a sudden and violent end. So determined was she that the boy should this time feel the weight of her wrath that, although she would not allow the marshal to interfere with his adventure, she got out pencil and paper and wrote down a series of sharp, stinging reproofs she intended to pour out upon him. The reproofs she committed to memory, going about the garden and saying them aloud like an actor memorizing his part.

And when, at the end of the week, Seth returned, a little weary and with coal soot in his ears and about his eyes, she again found herself unable to reprove him. Walking into the house he hung his cap on a nail by the kitchen door and stood looking easily at her. "I wanted to turn back within an hour after we had started," he explained. "I didn't know what to do. I knew you would be bothered, but I knew also that if I didn't go on I would be ashamed of myself. I went through with the thing for my own good. It was uncomfortable, sleeping on wet straw, and two drunken Negroes came and slept with us. When I stole a lunch basket out of a farmer's wagon I couldn't help thinking of his children going all day without food. I was sick of the whole affair, but I was determined to stick it out until the other boys were ready to come back."

"I'm glad you did stick it out," replied the mother, half resentfully, and kissing him upon the forehead pretended to busy herself with the work about the house.

On a summer evening Seth Richmond went to the New Willard House to visit his friend, George Willard. It had rained during the afternoon, but as he walked through Main Street, the sky had partially cleared and a golden glow lit up the west. Going around a corner, he turned in at the door of the hotel and began to climb the stairway leading up to his friend's room. In the hotel office the proprietor and two traveling men were engaged in a discussion of politics.

On the stairway Seth stopped and listened to the voices of the men below. They were excited and talked rapidly. Tom Willard was berating the traveling men. "I am a Democrat but your talk makes me sick," he said. "You don't understand McKinley. McKinley and Mark Hanna are friends. It is impossible perhaps for your mind to grasp that. If anyone tells you that a friendship can be deeper and bigger and more worth while than dollars and cents, or even more worth while than state politics, you snicker and laugh."

The landlord was interrupted by one of the guests, a tall, grey-mustached man who worked for a wholesale grocery house. "Do you think that I've lived in Cleveland all these years without knowing Mark Hanna?" he demanded. "Your talk is piffle. Hanna is after money and nothing else. This McKinley is his tool. He has McKinley bluffed and don't you forget it."

The young man on the stairs did not linger to hear the rest of the discussion, but went on up the stairway and into a little dark hall. Something in the voices of the men talking in the hotel office started a chain of thoughts in his mind. He was lonely and had begun to think that loneliness was a part of his character, something that would always stay with him. Stepping into a side hall he stood by a window that looked into an alleyway. At the back of his shop stood Abner Groff, the town baker. His tiny bloodshot eyes looked up and down the alleyway. In his shop someone called the baker, who pretended not to hear. The baker had an empty milk bottle in his hand and an angry sullen look in his eyes.

In Winesburg, Seth Richmond was called the "deep one." "He's like his father," men said as he went through the streets. "He'll break out some of these days. You wait and see."

The talk of the town and the respect with which men and boys instinctively greeted him, as all men greet silent people, had affected Seth Richmond's outlook on life and on himself. He, like most boys, was deeper than boys are given credit for being, but he was not what the men of the town, and even his mother, thought him to be. No great underlying purpose lay back of his habitual silence, and he had no definite plan for his life. When the boys with whom he associated were noisy and quarrelsome, he stood quietly at one side. With calm eyes he watched the gesticulating lively figures of his companions. He wasn't particularly interested in what was going on, and sometimes wondered if he would ever be particularly interested in anything. Now, as he stood in the half-darkness by the window watching the baker, he wished that he himself might become thoroughly stirred by something, even by the fits of sullen anger for which Baker Groff was noted. "It would be better for me if I could become excited and wrangle about politics like windy old Tom Willard," he thought, as he left the window and went again along the hallway to the room occupied by his friend, George Willard.

George Willard was older than Seth Richmond, but in the rather odd friendship between the two, it was he who was forever courting and the younger boy who was being courted. The paper on which George worked had one policy. It strove to mention by name in each issue, as many as possible of the inhabitants of the village. Like an excited dog, George Willard ran here and there, noting on his pad of paper who had gone on business to the county seat or had returned from a visit to a neighboring village. All day he wrote little facts upon the pad. "A. P. Wringlet had received a shipment of straw hats. Ed Byerbaum and Tom Marshall were in Cleveland Friday. Uncle Tom Sinnings is building a new barn on his place on the Valley Road."

The idea that George Willard would some day become a writer had given him a place of distinction in Winesburg, and to Seth Richmond he talked continually of the matter. "It's the easiest of all lives to live," he declared, becoming excited and boastful. "Here and there you go and there is no one to boss you. Though you are in India or in the South

Seas in a boat, you have but to write and there you are. Wait till I get my name up and then see what fun I shall have."

In George Willard's room, which had a window looking down into an alleyway and one that looked across railroad tracks to Biff Carter's Lunch Room facing the railroad station, Seth Richmond sat in a chair and looked at the floor. George Willard, who had been sitting for an hour idly playing with a lead pencil, greeted him effusively. "I've been trying to write a love story," he explained, laughing nervously. Lighting a pipe he began walking up and down the room. "I know what I'm going to do. I'm going to fall in love. I've been sitting here and thinking it over and I'm going to do it."

As though embarrassed by his declaration, George went to a window and turning his back to his friend leaned out. "I know who I'm going to fall in love with," he said sharply. "It's Helen White. She is the only girl in town with any 'get-up' to her."

Struck with a new idea, young Willard turned and walked toward his visitor. "Look here," he said "You know Helen White better than I do. I want you to tell her what I said. You just get to talking to her and say that I'm in love with her. See what she says to that. See how she takes it, and then you come and tell me."

Seth Richmond arose and went toward the door. The words of his comrade irritated him unbearably. 'Well, good-bye," he said briefly.

George was amazed. Running forward he stood in the darkness trying to look into Seth's face. "What's the matter? What are you going to do? You stay here and let's talk," he urged.

A wave of resentment directed against his friend the men of the town who were, he thought, perpetually talking of nothing, and most of all, against his own habit of silence, made Seth half desperate. "Aw, speak to her yourself," he burst forth and then, going quickly through the door, slammed it sharply in his friend's face. "I'm going to find Helen White and talk to her, but not about him," he muttered.

Seth went down the stairway and out at the front door

of the hotel muttering with wrath. Crossing a little dusty street and climbing a low iron railing, he went to sit upon the grass in the station yard. George Willard he thought a profound fool, and he wished that he had said so more vigorously. Although his acquaintanceship with Helen White, the banker's daughter, was outwardly but casual, she was often the subject of his thoughts and he felt that she was something private and personal to himself. "The busy fool with his love stories," he muttered staring back over his shoulder at George Willard's room, "why does he never tire of his eternal talking."

It was berry harvest time in Winesburg and upon the station platform men and boys loaded the boxes of red, fragrant berries into two express cars that stood upon the siding. A June moon was in the sky, although in the west a storm threatened, and no street lamps were lighted. In the dim light the figures of the men standing upon the express truck and pitching the boxes in at the doors of the cars were but dimly discernible. Upon the iron railing that protected the station lawn sat other men. Pipes were lighted. Village jokes went back and forth. Away in the distance a train whistled and the men loading the boxes into the cars worked with renewed activity.

Seth arose from his place on the grass and went silently past the men perched upon the railing and into Main Street. He had come to a resolution. "I'll get out of here," he told himself. "What good am I here? I'm going to some city and go to work. I'll tell mother about it tomorrow."

Seth Richmond went slowly along Main Street, past Wacker's Cigar Store and the Town Hall, and into Buckeye Street. He was depressed by the thought that he was not a part of the life in his own town, but the depression did not cut deeply as he did not think of himself as at fault. In the heavy shadows of a big tree before Doctor Welling's house, he stopped and stood watching half-witted Turk Smollet, who was pushing a wheelbarrow in the road. The old man with his absurdly boyish mind had a dozen long boards on the wheelbarrow, and, as he hurried along the road, balanced the load with extreme nicety. "Easy there, Turk! Steady now, old boy!" the old man shouted to himself, and laughed so that the load of boards rocked dangerously.

Seth knew Turk Smollet, the half dangerous old wood chopper whose peculiarities added so much of color to the life of the village. He knew that when Turk got into Main Street he would become the center of a whirlwind of cries and comments, that in truth the old man was going far out of his way in order to pass through Main Street and exhibit his skill in wheeling the boards. "If George Willard were here, he'd have something to say," thought Seth. "George belongs to this town. He'd shout at Turk and Turk would shout at him. They'd both be secretly pleased by what they had said. It's different with me. I don't belong. I'll not make a fuss about it, but I'm going to get out of here."

Seth stumbled forward through the half-darkness, feeling himself an outcast in his own town. He began to pity himself, but a sense of the absurdity of his thoughts made him smile. In the end he decided that he was simply old beyond his years and not at all a subject for self-pity. "I'm made to go to work. I may be able to make a place for myself by steady working, and I might as well be at it," he decided.

Seth went to the house of Banker White and stood in the darkness by the front door. On the door hung a heavy brass knocker, an innovation introduced into the village by Helen White's mother, who had also organized a women's club for the study of poetry. Seth raised the knocker and let it fall. Its heavy clatter sounded like a report from distant guns. "How awkard and foolish I am," he thought. "If Mrs. White comes to the door, I won't know what to say."

It was Helen White who came to the door and found Seth standing at the edge of the porch. Blushing with pleasure, she stepped forward, closing the door softly. "I'm going to get out of town. I don't know what I'll do, but I'm going to get out of here and go to work. I think I'll go to Columbus." he said. "Perhaps I'll get into the State University down there.

Anyway, I'm going. I'll tell mother tonight." He hesitated and looked doubtfully about. "Perhaps you wouldn't mind coming to walk with me?"

Seth and Helen walked through the streets beneath the trees. Heavy clouds had drifted across the face of the moon, and before them in the deep twilight went a man with a short ladder upon his shoulder. Hurrying forward, the man stopped at the street crossing and, putting the ladder against the wooden lamp-post, lighted the village lights so that their way was half lighted, half darkened, by the lamps and by the deepening shadows cast by the low branched trees. In the tops of the trees the wind began to play, disturbing the sleeping birds so that they flew about calling plaintively. In the lighted space before one of the lamps, two bats wheeled and circled, pursuing the gathering swarm of night flies.

Since Seth had been a boy in knee trousers there had been a half expressed intimacy between him and the maiden who now for the first time walked beside him. For a time she had been beset with a madness for writing notes which she addressed to Seth. He had found them concealed in his books at school and one had been given him by a child met in the street, while several had been delivered through the village post office.

The notes had been written in a round, boyish hand and had reflected a mind inflamed by novel reading. Seth had not answered them, although he had been moved and flattered by some of the sentences scrawled in pencil upon the stationery of the banker's wife. Putting them into the pocket of his coat, he went through the street or stood by the fence in the school yard with something burning at his side. He thought it fine that he should be thus selected as the favorite of the richest and most attractive girl in town.

Helen and Seth stopped by a fence near where a low dark building faced the street. The building had once been a factory for the making of barrel staves but was now vacant. Across the street upon the porch of a house a man and woman talked of their childhood, their voices coming clearly across to the half-embarrassed youth and maiden. There was the sound of scraping chairs and the man and woman came down the gravel path to a wooden gate. Standing outside the gate, the man leaned over and kissed the woman. "For old times' sake," he said and, turning, walked rapidly away along the sidewalk.

"That's Belle Turner," whispered Helen, and put her hand boldly into Seth's hand. "I didn't know she had a fellow. I thought she was too old for that." Seth laughed uneasily. The hand of the girl was warm and a strange, dizzy feeling crept over him. Into his mind came a desire to tell her something he had been determined not to tell. "George Willard's in love with you," he said, and in spite of his agitation his voice was low and quiet. "He's writing a story, and he wants to be in love. He wants to know how it feels. He wanted me to tell you and see what you said."

Again Helen and Seth walked in silence. They came to the garden surrounding the old Richmond place and going through a gap in the hedge sat on a wooden bench beneath a bush.

On the street as he walked beside the girl new and daring thoughts had come into Seth Richmond's mind. He began to regret his decision to get out of town. "It would be something new and altogether delightful to remain and walk often through the streets with Helen White." he thought. In imagination he saw himself putting his arm about her waist and feeling her arms clasped tightly about his neck. One of those odd combinations of events and places made him connect the idea of love-making with this girl and a spot he had visited some days before. He had gone on an errand to the house of a farmer who lived on a hillside beyond the Fair Ground and had returned by a path through a field. At the foot of the hill below the farmer's house Seth had stopped beneath a sycamore tree and looked about him. A soft humming noise had greeted his ears. For a moment he had thought the tree must be the home of a swarm of bees.

And then, looking down, Seth had seen the bees everywhere all about him in the long grass. He stood in a mass of weeds that grew waist-high in the field that ran away from the hillside. The weeds were abloom with tiny purple blossoms and gave forth an overpowering fragrance. Upon the weeds the bees were gathered in armies, singing as they worked.

Seth imagined himself lying on a summer evening, buried deep among the weeds beneath the tree. Beside him, in the scene built in his fancy, lay Helen White, her hand lying in his hand. A peculiar reluctance kept him from kissing her lips, but he felt he might have done that if he wished. Instead, he lay perfectly still, looking at her and listening to the army of bees that sang the sustained masterful song of labor above his head.

On the bench in the garden Seth stirred uneasily. Releasing the hand of the girl, he thrust his hands into his trouser pockets. A desire to impress the mind of his companion with the importance of the resolution he had made came over him and he nodded his head toward the house. "Mother'll make a fuss, I suppose," he whispered. "She hasn't thought at all about what I'm going to do in life. She thinks I'm going to stay on here forever just being a boy."

Seth's voice became charged with boyish earnestness. "You see, I've got to strike out. I've got to get to work. It's what I'm good for."

Helen White was impressed. She nodded her head and a feeling of admiration swept over her. "This is as it should be," she thought. "This boy is not a boy at all, but a strong, purposeful man." Certain vague desires that had been invading her body were swept away and she sat up very straight on the bench. The thunder continued to rumble and flashes of heat lightning lit up the eastern sky. The garden that had been so mysterious and vast, a place that with Seth beside her might have become the background for strange and wonderful adventures, now seemed no more than an ordinary Winesburg back yard, quite definite and limited in its outlines.

"What will you do up there?" she whispered.

Seth turned half around on the bench, striving to see her face in the darkness. He thought her infinitely more sensible and straightforward than George Willard, and was glad he had come away from his friend. A feeling of impatience with the town that had been in his mind returned, and he tried to tell her of it. "Everyone talks and talks," he began. I'm sick of it. I'll do something, get into some kind of work where talk don't count. Maybe I'll just be a mechanic in a shop. I don't know. I guess I don't care much. I just want to work and keep quiet. That's all I've got in my mind."

Seth arose from the bench and put out his hand. He did not want to bring the meeting to an end but could not think of anything more to say. "It's the last time we'll see each other," he whispered.

A wave of sentiment swept over Helen. Putting her hand upon Seth's shoulder, she started to draw his face down toward her own upturned face. The act was one of pure affection and cutting regret that some vague adventure that had been present in the spirit of the night would now never be realized. "I think I'd better be going along," she said, letting her hand fall heavily to her side. A thought came to her. "Don't you go with me; I want to be alone," she said. "You go and talk with your mother. You'd better do that now."

Seth hesitated and, as he stood waiting, the girl turned and ran away through the hedge. A desire to run after her came to him, but he only stood staring, perplexed and puzzled by her action as he had been perplexed and puzzled by all of the life of the town out of which she had come. Walking slowly toward the house, he stopped in the shadow of a large tree and looked at his mother sitting by a lighted window busily sewing. The feeling of loneliness that had visited him earlier in the evening returned and colored his thoughts of the adventure through which he had just passed. "Huh!" he exclaimed, turning and staring in the direction taken by Helen White. "That's how things'll turn out. She'll be like the rest. I suppose she'll begin now to look at me in a funny way." He looked at the ground and pondered this thought. "She'll be embarrassed and feel strange when I'm around," he whispered to himself. "That's how it'll be. That's how everything'll turn out. When it comes to loving someone, it won't never be me. It'll be someone else—some fool—someone who talks a lot—someone like that George Willard."

Tandy

Until she was seven years old she lived in an old unpainted house on an unused road that led off Trunion Pike. Her father gave her but little attention and her mother was dead. The father spent his time talking and thinking of religion. He proclaimed himself an agnostic and was so absorbed in destroying the ideas of God that had crept into the minds of his neighbors that he never saw God manifesting himself in the little child that, half forgotten, lived here and there on the bounty of her dead mother's relatives.

A stranger came to Winesburg and saw in the child what the father did not see. He was a tall, red-haired young man who was almost always drunk. Sometimes he sat in a chair before the New Willard House with Tom Hard, the father. As Tom talked, declaring there could be no God, the stranger smiled and winked at the bystanders. He and Tom became friends and were much together.

The stranger was the son of a rich merchant of Cleveland and had come to Winesburg on a mission. He wanted to cure himself of the habit of drink, and thought that by escaping from his city associates and living in a rural community he would have a better chance in the struggle with the appetite that was destroying him.

His sojourn in Winesburg was not a success. The dullness

of the passing hours led to his drinking harder than ever. But he did succeed in doing something. He gave a name rich with meaning to Tom Hard's daughter.

One evening when he was recovering from a long debauch the stranger came reeling along the main street of the town. Tom Hard sat in a chair before the New Willard House with his daughter, then a child of five, on his knees. Beside him on the board sidewalk sat young George Willard. The stranger dropped into a chair beside them. His body shook and when he tried to talk his voice trembled.

It was late evening and darkness lay over the town and over the railroad that ran along the foot of a little incline before the hotel. Somewhere in the distance, off to the west, there was a prolonged blast from the whistle of a passenger engine. A dog that had been sleeping in the roadway arose and barked. The stranger began to babble and made a prophecy concerning the child that lay in the arms of the agnostic.

"I came here to quit drinking," he said, and tears began to run down his checks. He did not look at Tom Hard, but leaned forward and stared into the darkness as though seeing a vision. "I ran away to the country to be cured, but I am not cured. There is a reason." He turned to look at the child who sat up very straight on her father's knee and returned the look.

The stranger touched Tom Hard on the arm. "Drink is not the only thing to which I am addicted," he said. "There is something else. I am a lover and have not found my thing to love. That is a big point if you know enough to realize what I mean. It makes my destruction inevitable, you see. There are few who understand that."

The stranger became silent and seemed overcome with sadness, but another blast from the whistle of the passenger engine aroused him. "I have not lost faith. I proclaim that. I have only been brought to the place where I know my faith will not be realized," he declared hoarsely. He looked hard at the child and began to address her, paying no more attention to the father. "There is a woman coming," he said, and his voice was now sharp and earnest. "I have missed her, you see. She did not come in my time. You may be the woman. It would be like fate to let me stand in her presence once, on such an evening as this, when I have destroyed myself with drink and she is as yet only a child."

The shoulders of the stranger shook violently, and when he tried to roll a cigarette the paper fell from his trembling fingers. He grew angry and scolded. "They think it's easy to be a woman, to be loved, but I know better," he declared. Again he turned to the child. "I understand," he cried. "Perhaps of all men I alone understand."

His glance again wandered away to the darkened street. "I know about her, although she has never crossed my path," he said softly. "I know about her struggles and her defeats. It is because of her defeats that she is to me the lovely one. Out of her defeats has been born a new quality in woman. I have a name for it. I call it Tandy. I made up the name when I was a true dreamer and before my body became vile. It is the quality of being strong to be loved. It is something men need from women and that they do not get."

The stranger arose and stood before Tom Hard. His body rocked back and forth and he seemed about to fall, but instead he dropped to his knees on the sidewalk and raised the hands of the little girl to his drunken lips. He kissed them ecstatically. "Be Tandy, little one," he pleaded. "Dare to be strong and courageous. That is the road. Venture anything. Be brave enough to dare to be loved. Be something more than man or woman. Be Tandy."

The stranger arose and staggered off down the street. A day or two later he got aboard a train and returned to his home in Cleveland. On the summer evening, after the talk before the hotel, Tom Hard took the girl child to the house of a relative where she had been invited to spend the night. As he went along in the darkness under the trees he forgot the babbling voice of the stranger and his mind returned to the making of arguments by which he might destroy men's faith in God. He spoke his daughter's name and she began to weep.

"I don't want to be called that," she declared. "I want to be called Tandy—Tandy Hard." The child wept so bitterly that Tom Hard was touched and tried to comfort her. He stopped beneath a tree and, taking her into his arms, began to caress her. "Be good, now," he said sharply; but she would not be quieted. With childish abandon she gave herself over to grief, her voice breaking the evening stillness of the street. "I want to be Tandy. I want to be Tandy. I want to be Tandy Hard," she cried, shaking her head and sobbing as though her young strength were not enough to bear the vision the words of the drunkard had brought to her.

The Strength of God

The Reverend Curtis Hartman was pastor of the Presbyterian Church of Winesburg, and had been in that position ten years. He was forty years old, and by his nature very silent and reticent. To preach, standing in the pulpit before the people, was always a hardship for him and from Wednesday morning until Saturday evening he thought of nothing but the two sermons that must be preached on Sunday. Early on Sunday morning he went into a little room called a study in the bell tower of the church and prayed. In his prayers there was one note that always predominated. "Give me strength and courage for Thy work, O Lord!" he pleaded, kneeling on the bare floor and bowing his head in the presence of the task that lay before him.

The Reverend Hartman was a tall man with a brown beard. His wife, a stout, nervous woman, was the daughter of a manufacturer of underwear at Cleveland, Ohio. The minister himself was rather a favourite in the town. The elders of the church liked him because he was quiet and unpretentious and Mrs. White, the banker's wife, thought him scholarly and refined.

The Presbyterian Church held itself somewhat aloof from the other churches of Winesburg. It was larger and more imposing and its minister was better paid. He even had a carriage of his own and on summer evenings sometimes drove about town with his wife. Through Main Street and up and down Buckeye Street he went, bowing gravely to the people, while his wife, afire with secret pride, looked at him out of the corners of her eyes and worried lest the horse become frightened and run away.

For a good many years after he came to Winesburg things went well with Curtis Hartman. He was not one to arouse keen enthusiasm among the worshippers in his church but on the other hand he made no enemies. In reality he was much in earnest and sometimes suffered prolonged periods of remorse because he could not go crying the word of God in the highways and byways of the town. He wondered if the flame of the spirit really burned in him and dreamed of a day when a strong sweet new current of power would come like a great wind into his voice and his soul and the people would tremble before the spirit of God made manifest in him. "I am a poor stick and that will never really happen to me," he mused dejectedly, and then a patient smile lit up his features. "Oh well, I suppose I'm doing well enough," he added philosophically.

The room in the bell tower of the church, where on Sunday mornings the minister prayed for an increase in him of the power of God, had but one window. It was long and narrow and swung outward on a hinge like a door. On the window, made of little leaded panes, was a design showing the Christ laying his hand upon the head of a child. One Sunday morning in the summer as he sat by his desk in the room with a large Bible opened before him, and the sheets of his sermon scattered about, the minister was shocked to see, in the upper room of the house next door, a woman lying in her bed and smoking a cigarette while she read a book. Curtis Hartman went on tiptoe to the window and closed it softly. He was horror stricken at the thought of a woman smoking and trembled also to think that his eyes, just raised from the pages of the book of God, had looked upon the bare shoulders and white throat of a woman. With his brain in a whirl he went down into the pulpit and preached a long sermon without once thinking of his gestures or his voice. The sermon attracted unusual attention because of its power and clearness. "I wonder if she is listening, if my voice is carrying a message into her soul," he thought and began to hope that on future Sunday mornings he might be able to say words that would touch and awaken the woman apparently far gone in secret sin.

The house next door to the Presbyterian Church, through the windows of which the minister had seen the sight that had so upset him, was occupied by two women. Aunt Elizabeth Swift, a grey competent-looking widow with money in the Winesburg National Bank, lived there with her daughter Kate Swift, a school teacher. The school teacher was thirty years old and had a neat trim-looking figure. She had few friends and bore a reputation of having a sharp tongue. When he began to think about her, Curtis Hartman remembered that she had been to Europe and had lived for two years in New York City. "Perhaps after all her smoking means nothing," he thought. He began to remember that when he was a student in college and occasionally read novels, good although somewhat worldly women, had smoked through the pages of a book that had once fallen into his hands. With a rush of new determination he worked on his sermons all through the week and forgot, in his zeal to reach the ears and the soul of this new listener, both his embarassment in the pulpit and the necessity of prayer in the study on Sunday mornings.

Reverend Hartman's experience with women had been somewhat limited. He was the son of a wagon maker from Muncie, Indiana, and had worked his way through college. The daughter of the underwear manufacturer had boarded in a house where he lived during his school days and he had married her after a formal and prolonged courtship, carried on for the most part by the girl herself. On his marriage day the underwear manufacturer had given his daughter five thousand dollars and he promised to leave her at least twice that amount in his will. The minister had thought himself fortunate in marriage and had never permitted himself to think of other women. He did not want to think of other women. What he wanted was to do the work of God quietly and earnestly.

In the soul of the minister a struggle awoke. From wanting to reach the ears of Kate Swift, and through his sermons to delve into her soul, he began to want also to look again at the figure lying white and quiet in the bed. On a Sunday morning when he could not sleep because of his thoughts he arose and went to walk in the streets. When he had gone along Main Street almost to the Old Richmond place he stopped and picking up a stone rushed off to the room in the bell tower. With the stone he broke out a corner of the window and then locked the door and sat down at the desk before the open Bible to wait. When the shade of the window to Kate Swift's room was raised he could see, through the hole, directly into her bed, but she was not there. She also had arisen and had gone for a walk and the hand that raised the shade was the hand of Aunt Elizabeth Swift.

The minister almost wept with joy at this deliverance from the carnal desire to "peep" and went back to his own house praising God. In an ill moment he forgot, however, to stop the hole in the window. The piece of glass broken out at the corner of the window just nipped off the bare heel of the boy standing motionless and looking with rapt eyes into the face of the Christ.

Curtis Hartman forgot his sermon on that Sunday morning. He talked to his congregation and in his talk said that it was a mistake for people to think of their minister as a man set aside and intended by nature to lead a blameless life. "Out of my own experience I know that we, who are the ministers of God's word, are beset by the same temptations that assail you," he declared. "I have been tempted and have surrendered to temptation. It is only the hand of God, placed beneath my head, that has raised me up. As he has raised me so also will he raise you. Do not despair. In your hour of sin raise your eyes to the skies and you will be again and again saved."

Resolutely the minister put the thoughts of the woman in

the bed out of his mind and began to be something like a lover in the presence of his wife. One evening when they drove out together he turned the horse out of Buckeye Street and in the darkness on Gospel Hill, above Waterworks Pond, put his arm about Sarah Hartman's waist. When he had eaten breakfast in the morning and was ready to retire to his study at the back of his house he went around the table and kissed his wife on the cheek. When thoughts of Kate Swift came into his head, he smiled and raised his eyes to the skies. "Intercede for me, Master," he muttered, "keep me in the narrow path intent on Thy work."

And now began the real struggle in the soul of the brown-bearded minister. By chance he discovered that Kate Swift was in the habit of lying in her bed in the evenings and reading a book. A lamp stood on a table by the side of the bed and the light streamed down upon her white shoulders and bare throat. On the evening when he made the discovery the minister sat at the desk in the study from nine until after eleven and when her light was put out stumbled out of the church to spend two more hours walking and praying in the streets. He did not want to kiss the shoulders and the throat of Kate Swift and had not allowed his mind to dwell on such thoughts. He did not know what he wanted. "I am God's child and he must save me from myself," he cried, in the darkness under the trees as he wandered in the streets. By a tree he stood and looked at the sky that was covered with hurrying clouds. He began to talk to God intimately and closely. "Please, Father, do not forget me. Give me power to go tomorrow and repair the hole in the window. Lift my eyes again to the skies. Stay with me, Thy servant, in his hour of need."

Up and down through the silent streets walked the minister and for days and weeks his soul was troubled. He could not understand the temptation that had come to him nor could he fathom the reason for its coming. In a way he began to blame God, saying to himself that he had tried to keep his feet in the true path and had not run about seeking sin. "Through my days as a young man and all through my life here I have gone quietly about my work," he declared. "Why now should I be tempted? What have I done that this burden should be laid on me?"

Three times during the early fall and winter of that year Curtis Hartman crept out of his house to the room in the bell tower to sit in the darkness looking at the figure of Kate Swift lying in her bed and later went to walk and pray in the streets. He could not understand himself. For weeks he would go along scarcely thinking of the school teacher and telling himself that he had conquered the carnal desire to look at her body. And then something would happen. As he sat in the study of his own house, hard at work on a sermon, he would become nervous and begin to walk up and down the room. "I will go out into the streets," he told himself and even as he let himself in at the church door he persistently denied to himself the cause of his being there "I will not repair the hole in the window and I will train myself to come here at night and sit in the presence of this woman without raising my eyes. I will not be defeated in this thing. The Lord has devised this temptation as a test of my soul and I will grope my way out of darkness into the light of righteousness."

One night in January when it was bitter cold and snow lay deep on the streets of Winesburg Curtis Hartman paid his last visit to the room in the bell tower of the church. It was past nine o'clock when he left his own house and he set out so hurriedly that he forgot to put on his overshoes. In Main Street no one was abroad but Hop Higgins the night watchman and in the whole town no one was awake but the watchman and young George Willard, who sat in the office of the *Winesburg Eagle* trying to write a story. Along the street to the church went the minister, plowing through the drifts and thinking that this time he would utterly give way to sin. "I want to look at the woman and to think of kissing her shoulders and I am going to let myself think what I choose," he declared bitterly and tears came into his eyes. He began to think that he would get out of the ministry and try some other way of life. "I shall go to some city and get into business," he declared. "If my nature is such that I cannot resist sin, I shall give myself over to sin. At least I shall not be a hypocrite, preaching the word of God with my mind thinking of the shoulders and neck of a woman who does not belong to me."

It was cold in the room of the bell tower of the church on that January night and almost as soon as he came into the room Curtis Hartman knew that if he stayed he would be ill. His feet were wet from tramping in the snow and there was no fire. In the room in the house next door Kate Swift had not yet appeared. With grim determination the man sat down to wait. Sitting in the chair and gripping the edge of the desk on which lay the Bible he stared into the darkness thinking the blackest thoughts of his life. He thought of his wife and for the moment almost hated her. "She has always been ashamed of passion and has cheated me," he thought. "Man has a right to expect living passion and beauty in a woman. He has no right to forget that he is an animal and in me there is something that is Greek. I will throw off the woman of my bosom and seek other women. I will besiege this school teacher. I will fly in the face of all men and if I am a creature of carnal lusts I will live then for my lusts."

The distracted man trembled from head to foot, partly from cold, partly from the struggle in which he was engaged. Hours passed and a fever assailed his body. His throat began to hurt and his teeth chattered. His feet on the study floor felt like two cakes of ice. Still he would not give up. "I will see this woman and will think the thoughts I have never dared to think," he told himself, gripping the edge of the desk and waiting.

Curtis Hartman came near dying from the effects of that night of waiting in the church, and also he found in the thing that happened what he took to be the way of life for him. On other evenings when he had waited he had not been able to see, through the little hole in the glass, any part of the school teacher's room except that occupied by her bed. In the darkness he had waited until the woman suddenly appeared sitting in the bed in her white night-robe. When the light was turned up she propped herself up among the pillows and read a book. Sometimes she smoked one of the cigarettes. Only her bare shoulders and throat were visible.

On the January night, after he had come near dying with cold and after his mind had two or three times actually slipped away into an odd land of fantasy so that he had by an exercise of will power to force himself back into consciousness, Kate Swift appeared. In the room next door a lamp was lighted and the waiting man stared into an empty bed. Then upon the bed before his eyes a naked woman threw herself. Lying face downward she wept and beat with her fists upon the pillow. With a final outburst of weeping she half arose, and in the presence of the man who had waited to look and to think thoughts the woman of sin began to pray. In the lamplight her figure, slim and strong, looked like the figure of the boy in the presence of the Christ on the leaded window.

Curtis Hartman never remembered how he got out of the church. With a cry he arose, dragging the heavy desk along the floor. The Bible fell, making a great clatter in the silence. When the light in the house next door went out he stumbled down the stairway and into the street. Along the street he went and ran in at the door of the *Winesburg Eagle*. To George Willard, who was tramping up and down in the office undergoing a struggle of his own, he began to talk half incoherently. "The ways of God are beyond human understanding," he cried, running in quickly and closing the door. He began to advance upon the young man, his eyes glowing and his voice ringing with fervor. "I have found the light," he cried. "After ten years in this town, God has manifested himself to me in the body of a woman." His voice dropped and he began to whisper. "I did not understand," he said. "What I took to be a trial of my soul was only a preparation for a new and more beautiful fervor of the spirit. God has appeared to me in the person of Kate Swift, the school teacher, kneeling naked on a bed. Do you know Kate Swift? Although she may not be aware of it, she is an instrument of God, bearing the message of truth."

Reverend Curtis Hartman turned and ran out of the office. At the door he stopped, and after looking up and down the deserted street, turned again to George Willard. "I am delivered. Have no fear." He held up a bleeding fist for the young man to see. "I smashed the glass of the window," he cried. "Now it will have to be wholly replaced. The strength of God was in me and I broke it with my fist."

The Teacher

Snow lay deep in the streets of Winesburg. It had begun to snow about ten o'clock in the morning and a wind sprang up and blew the snow in clouds along Main Street. The frozen mud roads that led into town were fairly smooth and in places ice covered the mud. "There will be good sleighing," said Will Henderson, standing by the bar in Ed Griffith's saloon. Out of the saloon he went and met Sylvester West the druggist stumbling along in the kind of heavy overshoes called arctics. "Snow will bring the people into town on Saturday," said the druggist. The two men stopped and discussed their affairs. Will Henderson, who had on a light overcoat and no overshoes, kicked the heel of his left foot with the toe of the right. "Snow will be good for the wheat," observed the druggist sagely.

Young George Willard, who had nothing to do, was glad because he did not feel like working that day. The weekly paper had been printed and taken to the post office Wednesday evening and the snow began to fall on Thursday. At eight o'clock, after the morning train had passed, he put a pair of skates in his pocket and went up to Waterworks Pond but did not go skating. Past the pond and along a path that followed Wine Creek he went until he came to a grove of beech trees. There he built a fire against the side of a log and sat down at the end of the log to think. When the snow began to fall and the wind to blow he hurried about getting fuel for the fire.

The young reporter was thinking of Kate Swift, who had once been his school teacher. On the evening before he had gone to her house to get a book she wanted him to read and had been alone with her for an hour. For the fourth or fifth time the woman had talked to him with great earnestness and he could not make out what she meant by her talk. He began to believe she might be in love with him and the thought was both pleasing and annoying.

Up from the log he sprang and began to pile sticks on the fire. Looking about to be sure he was alone he talked aloud pretending he was in the presence of the woman. "Oh, you're just letting on, you know you are," he declared. "I am going to find out about you. You wait and see."

The young man got up and went back along the path toward town leaving the fire blazing in the wood. As he went through the streets the skates clanked in his pocket. In his own room in the New Willard House he built a fire in the stove and lay down on top of the bed. He began to have lustful thoughts and pulling down the shade of the window closed his eyes and turned his face to the wall. He took a pillow into his arms and embraced it thinking first of the school teacher, who by her words had stirred something within him, and later of Helen White, the slim daughter of the town banker, with whom he had been for a long time half in love.

By nine o'clock of that evening snow lay deep in the streets and the weather had become bitter cold. It was difficult to walk about. The stores were dark and the people had crawled away to their houses. The evening train from Cleveland was very late but nobody was interested in its arrival. By ten o'clock all but four of the eighteen hundred citizens of the town were in bed.

Hop Higgins, the night watchman, was partially awake. He was lame and carried a heavy stick. On dark nights he carried a lantern. Between nine and ten o'clock he went his rounds. Up and down Main Street he stumbled through the drifts trying the doors of the stores. Then he went into alleyways and tried the back doors. Finding all tight he hurried around the corner to the New Willard House and beat on the door. Through the rest of the night he intended to stay by the stove. "You go to bed. I'll keep the stove going," he said to the boy who slept on a cot in the hotel office.

Hop Higgins sat down by the stove and took off his shoes. When the boy had gone to sleep he began to think of his own affairs. He intended to paint his house in the spring and sat by the stove calculating the cost of paint and labor. That led him into other calculations. The night watchman was sixty years old and wanted to retire. He had been a soldier in the Civil War and drew a small pension. He hoped to find some new method of making a living and aspired to become a professional breeder of ferrets. Already he had four of the strangely shaped savage little creatures, that are used by sportsmen in the pursuit of rabbits, in the cellar of his house. "Now I have one male and three females," he mused. "If I am lucky by spring I shall have twelve or fifteen. In another year I shall be able to begin advertising ferrets for sale in the sporting papers."

The night watchman settled into his chair and his mind became a blank. He did not sleep. By years of practice he had trained himself to sit for hours through the long nights neither asleep nor awake. In the morning he was almost as refreshed as though he had slept.

With Hop Higgins safely stowed away in the chair behind the stove only three people were awake in Winesburg. George Willard was in the office of the *Eagle* pretending to be at work on the writing of a story but in reality continuing the mood of the morning by the fire in the wood. In the bell tower of the Presbyterian Church the Reverend Curtis Hartman was sitting in the darkness preparing himself for a revelation from God, and Kate Swift, the school teacher, was leaving her house for a walk in the storm.

It was past ten o'clock when Kate Swift set out and the walk was unpremeditated. It was as though the man and the boy, by thinking of her, had driven her forth into the wintry streets. Aunt Elizabeth Swift had gone to the county seat concerning some business in connection with mortgages in which she had money invested and would not be back until the next day. By a huge stove, called a base burner, in the living room of the house sat the daughter reading a book. Suddenly she sprang to her feet and, snatching a cloak from a rack by the front door, ran out of the house.

At the age of thirty Kate Swift was not known in Winesburg as a pretty woman. Her complexion was not good and her face was covered with blotches that indicated ill health. Alone in the night in the winter streets she was lovely. Her back was straight, her shoulders square, and her features were as the features of a tiny goddess on a pedestal in a garden in the dim light of a summer evening.

During the afternoon the school teacher had been to see Doctor Welling concerning her health. The doctor had scolded her and had declared she was in danger of losing her hearing. It was foolish for Kate Swift to be abroad in the storm, foolish and perhaps dangerous.

The woman in the streets did not remember the words of the doctor and would not have turned back had she remembered. She was very cold but after walking for five minutes no longer minded the cold. First she went to the end of her own street and then across a pair of hay scales set in the ground before a feed barn and into Trunion Pike. Along Trunion Pike she went to Ned Winters' barn and turning east followed a street of low frame houses that led over Gospel Hill and into Sucker Road that ran down a shallow valley past Ike Smead's chicken farm to Waterworks Pond. As she went along, the bold, excited mood that had driven her out of doors passed and then returned again.

There was something biting and forbidding in the character of Kate Swift. Everyone felt it. In the schoolroom she was silent, cold, and stern, and yet in an odd way very close to her pupils. Once in a long while something seemed to have come over her and she was happy. All of the children in the schoolroom felt the effect of her happiness. For a time they did not work but sat back in their chairs and looked at her.

With hands clasped behind her back the school teacher

walked up and down in the schoolroom and talked very rapidly. It did not seem to matter what subject came into her mind. Once she talked to the children of Charles Lamb and made up strange, intimate little stories concerning the life of the dead writer. The stories were told with the air of one who had lived in a house with Charles Lamb and knew all the secrets of his private life. The children were somewhat confused, thinking Charles Lamb must be someone who had once lived in Winesburg.

On another occasion the teacher talked to the children of Benvenuto Cellini. That time they laughed. What a bragging, blustering, brave, lovable fellow she made of the old artist! Concerning him also she invented anecdotes. There was one of a German music teacher who had a room above Cellini's lodgings in the city of Milan that made the boys guffaw. Sugars McNutts, a fat boy with red cheeks, laughed so hard that he became dizzy and fell off his seat and Kate Swift laughed with him. Then suddenly she became again cold and stern.

On the winter night when she walked through the deserted snow-covered streets, a crisis had come into the life of the school teacher. Although no one in Winesburg would have suspected it, her life had been very adventurous. It was still adventurous. Day by day as she worked in the schoolroom or walked in the streets, grief, hope, and desire fought within her. Behind a cold exterior the most extraordinary events transpired in her mind. The people of the town thought of her as a confirmed old maid and because she spoke sharply and went her own way thought her lacking in all the human feeling that did so much to make and mar their own lives. In reality she was the most eagerly passionate soul among them, and more than once, in the five years since she had come back from her travels to settle in Winesburg and become a school teacher, had been compelled to go out of the house and walk half through the night fighting out some battle raging within. Once on a night when it rained she had stayed out six hours and when she came home had a quarrel with Aunt Elizabeth Swift. "I am glad you're not a man," said the mother sharply.

"More than once I've waited for your father to come home, not knowing what new mess he had got into. I've had my share of uncertainty and you cannot blame me if I do not want to see the worst of him reproduced in you."

Kate Swift's mind was ablaze with thoughts of George Willard. In something he had written as a school boy she thought she had recognized the spark of genius and wanted to blow on the spark. One day in the summer she had gone to the *Eagle* office and finding the boy unoccupied had taken him out Main Street to the Fair Ground, where the two sat on a grassy bank and talked. The school teacher tried to bring home to the mind of the boy some conception of the difficulties he would have to face as a writer. "You will have to know life," she declared, and her voice trembled with earnestness. She took hold of George Willard's shoulders and turned him about so that she could look into his eyes. A passer-by might have thought them about to embrace. "If you are to become a writer you'll have to stop fooling with words," she explained. "It would be better to give up the notion of writing until you are better prepared. Now it's time to be living. I don't want to frighten you, but I would like to make you understand the import of what you think of attempting. You must not become a mere peddler of words. The thing to learn is to know what people are thinking about, not what they say."

On the evening before that stormy Thursday night when the Reverend Curtis Hartman sat in the bell tower of the church waiting to look at her body, young Willard had gone to visit the teacher and to borrow a book. It was then the thing happened that confused and puzzled the boy. He had the book under his arm and was preparing to depart. Again Kate Swift talked with great earnestness. Night was coming on and the light in the room grew dim. As he turned to go she spoke his name softly and with an impulsive movement took hold of his hand. Because the reporter was rapidly becoming a man something of his man's appeal, combined with the winsomeness of the boy, stirred the heart of the lonely woman. A passionate desire to have him understand the import of life, to learn to interpret it truly and honestly, swept over her. Lean-

ing forward, her lips brushed his cheek. At the same moment
he for the first time became aware of the marked beauty of
her features. They were both embarrassed, and to relieve her
feeling she became harsh and domineering. "What's the use?
It will be ten years before you begin to understand what I
mean when I talk to you," she cried passionately.

On the night of the storm and while the minister sat in the
church waiting for her, Kate Swift went to the office of the
Winesburg Eagle, intending to have another talk with the boy.
After the long walk in the snow she was cold, lonely, and tired.
As she came through Main Street she saw the light from the
printshop window shining on the snow and on an impulse
opened the door and went in. For an hour she sat by the
stove in the office talking of life. She talked with passionate
earnestness. The impulse that had driven her out into the
snow poured itself out into talk. She became inspired as she
sometimes did in the presence of the children in school. A
great eagerness to open the door of life to the boy, who had
been her pupil and who she thought might possess a talent
for the understanding of life, had possession of her. So strong
was her passion that it became something physical. Again her
hands took hold of his shoulders and she turned him about.
In the dim light her eyes blazed. She arose and laughed, not
sharply as was customary with her, but in a queer, hesitating
way. "I must be going," she said. "In a moment, if I stay,
I'll be wanting to kiss you."

In the newspaper office a confusion arose. Kate Swift turned
and walked to the door. She was a teacher but she was also
a woman. As she looked at George Willard, the passionate
desire to be loved by a man, that had a thousand times before
swept like a storm over her body, took possession of her.
In the lamplight George Willard looked no longer a boy, but
a man ready to play the part of a man.

The school teacher let George Willard take her into his
arms. In the warm little office the air became suddenly heavy
and the strength went out of her body. Leaning against a low
counter by the door she waited. When he came and put a

hand on her shoulder she turned and let her body fall heavily against him. For George Willard the confusion was immediately increased. For a moment he held the body of the woman tightly against his body and then it stiffened. Two sharp little fists began to beat on his face. When the school teacher had run away and left him alone, he walked up and down in the office swearing furiously.

It was into this confusion that the Reverend Curtis Hartman protruded himself. When he came in George Willard thought the town had gone mad. Shaking a bleeding fist in the air, the minister proclaimed the woman George had only a moment before held in his arms an instrument of God bearing a message of truth.

George blew out the lamp by the window and locking the door of the printshop went home. Through the hotel office, past Hop Higgins lost in his dream of the raising of ferrets, he went and up into his own room. The fire in the stove had gone out and he undressed in the cold. When he got into bed the sheets were like blankets of dry snow.

George Willard rolled about in the bed on which he had lain in the afternoon hugging the pillow and thinking thoughts of Kate Swift. The words of the minister, who he thought had gone suddenly insane, rang in his ears. His eyes stared about the room. The resentment, natural to the baffled male, passed and he tried to understand what had happened. He could not make it out. Over and over he turned the matter in his mind. Hours passed and he began to think it must be time for another day to come. At four o'clock he pulled the covers up about his neck and tried to sleep. When he became drowsy and closed his eyes, he raised a hand and with it groped about in the darkness. "I have missed something. I have missed something Kate Swift was trying to tell me," he muttered sleepily. Then he slept and in all Winesburg he was the last soul on that winter night to go to sleep.

Loneliness

He was the son of Mrs. Al Robinson who once owned a farm on a side road leading off Trunion Pike, east of Winesburg and two miles beyond the town limits. The farmhouse was painted brown and the blinds to all of the windows facing the road were kept closed. In the road before the house a flock of chickens, accompanied by two guinea hens, lay in the deep dust. Enoch lived in the house with his mother in those days and when he was a young boy went to school at the Winesburg High School. Old citizens remembered him as a quiet, smiling youth inclined to silence. He walked in the middle of the road when he came into town and sometimes read a book. Drivers of teams had to shout and swear to make him realize where he was so that he would turn out of the beaten track and let them pass.

When he was twenty-one years old Enoch went to New York City and was a city man for fifteen years. He studied French and went to an art school, hoping to develop a faculty he had for drawing. In his own mind he planned to go to Paris and to finish his art education among the masters there, but that never turned out.

Nothing ever turned out for Enoch Robinson. He could draw well enough and he had many odd delicate thoughts hidden away in his brain that might have expressed themselves through the brush of a painter, but he was always a child and that was a handicap to his worldly development. He never grew up and of course he couldn't understand people and he couldn't make people understand him The child in him kept bumping against things, against actualities like money and sex and opinions. Once he was hit by a street car and thrown against an iron post. That made him lame. It was one of the many things that kept things from turning out for Enoch Robinson.

In New York City, when he first went there to live and before he became confused and disconcerted by the facts of life, Enoch went about a good deal with young men. He got into a group of other young artists, both men and women, and in the evenings they sometimes came to visit him in his room. Once he got drunk and was taken to a police station where a police magistrate frightened him horribly, and once he tried to have an affair with a woman of the town met on the sidewalk before his lodging house. The woman and Enoch walked together three blocks and then the young man grew afraid and ran away. The woman had been drinking and the incident amused her. She leaned against the wall of a building and laughed so heartily that another man stopped and laughed with her. The two went away together, still laughing, and Enoch crept off to his room trembling and vexed.

The room in which young Robinson lived in New York faced Washington Square and was long and narrow like a hallway. It is important to get that fixed in your mind. The story of Enoch is in fact the story of a room almost more than it is the story of a man.

And so into the room in the evening came young Enoch's friends. There was nothing particularly striking about them except that they were artists of the kind that talk. Everyone knows of the talking artists. Throughout all of the known history of the world they have gathered in rooms and talked. They talk of art and are passionately, almost feverishly, in earnest about it. They think it matters much more than it does.

And so these people gathered and smoked cigarettes and talked and Enoch Robinson, the boy from the farm near

Winesburg, was there. He stayed in a corner and for the most part said nothing. How his big blue childlike eyes stared about! On the walls were pictures he had made, crude things, half finished. His friends talked of these. Leaning back in their chairs, they talked and talked with their heads rocking from side to side. Words were said about line and values and composition, lots of words, such as are always being said.

Enoch wanted to talk too but he didn't know how. He was too excited to talk coherently. When he tried he sputtered and stammered and his voice sounded strange and squeaky to him. That made him stop talking. He knew what he wanted to say, but he knew also that he could never by any possibility say it. When a picture he had painted was under discussion, he wanted to burst out with something like this: "You don't get the point," he wanted to explain; "the picture you see doesn't consist of the things you see and say words about. There is something else, something you don't see at all, something you aren't intended to see. Look at this one over here, by the door here, where the light from the window falls on it. The dark spot by the road that you might not notice at all is, you see, the beginning of everything. There is a clump of elders there such as used to grow beside the road before our house back in Winesburg, Ohio, and in among the elders there is something hidden. It is a woman, that's what it is. She has been thrown from a horse and the horse has run away out of sight. Do you not see how the old man who drives a cart looks anxiously about? That is Thad Grayback who has a farm up the road. He is taking corn to Winesburg to be ground into meal at Comstock's mill. He knows there is something in the elders, something hidden away, and yet he doesn't quite know.

"It's a woman you see, that's what it is! It's a woman and, oh, she is lovely! She is hurt and is suffering but she makes no sound. Don't you see how it is? She lies quite still, white and still, and the beauty comes out from her and spreads over everything. It is in the sky back there and all around everywhere. I didn't try to paint the woman, of course. She is too beautiful to be painted. How dull to talk of composition and such things! Why do you not look at the sky and then run away as I used to do when I was a boy back there in Winesburg, Ohio?"

That is the kind of thing young Enoch Robinson trembled to say to the guests who came into his room when he was a young fellow in New York City, but he always ended by saying nothing. Then he began to doubt his own mind. He was afraid the things he felt were not getting expressed in the pictures he painted. In a half indignant mood he stopped inviting people into his room and presently got into the habit of locking the door. He began to think that enough people had visited him, that he did not need people any more. With quick imagination he began to invent his own people to whom he could really talk and to whom he explained the things he had been unable to explain to living people. His room began to be inhabited by the spirits of men and women among whom he went, in his turn saying words. It was as though everyone Enoch Robinson had ever seen had left with him some essence of himself, something he could mould and change to suit his own fancy, something that understood all about such things as the wounded woman behind the elders in the pictures.

The mild, blue-eyed young Ohio boy was a complete egotist, as all children are egotists. He did not want friends for the quite simple reason that no child wants friends. He wanted most of all the people of his own mind, people with whom he could really talk, people he could harangue and scold by the hour, servants, you see, to his fancy. Among these people he was always self-confident and bold. They might talk, to be sure, and even have opinions of their own, but always he talked last and best. He was like a writer busy among the figures of his brain, a kind of tiny blue-eyed king he was, in a six-dollar room facing Washington Square in the city of New York.

Then Enoch Robinson got married. He began to get lonely and to want to touch actual flesh-and-bone people with his hands. Days passed when his room seemed empty. Lust visited his body and desire grew in his mind. At night strange fevers, burning within, kept him awake. He married a girl who sat in a chair next to his own in the art school and went to live in an apartment house in Brooklyn. Two children were born to the woman he married, and Enoch got a job in a place where illustrations are made for advertisements.

That began another phase of Enoch's life. He began to play at a new game. For a while he was very proud of himself in the role of producing citizen of the world. He dismissed the essence of things and played with realities. In the fall he voted at an election and he had a newspaper thrown on his porch each morning. When in the evening he came home from work he got off a streetcar and walked sedately along behind some business man, striving to look very substantial and important. As a payer of taxes he thought he should post himself on how things are run. "I'm getting to be of some moment, a real part of things, of the state and the city and all that," he told himself with an amusing miniature air of dignity. Once, coming home from Philadelphia, he had a discussion with a man met on a train. Enoch talked about the advisability of the government's owning and operating the railroads and the man gave him a cigar. It was Enoch's notion that such a move on the part of the government would be a good thing, and he grew quite excited as he talked. Later he remembered his own words with pleasure. "I gave him something to think about, that fellow," he muttered to himself as he climbed the stairs to his Brooklyn apartment.

To be sure, Enoch's marriage did not turn out. He himself brought it to an end. He began to feel choked and walled in by the life in the apartment, and to feel toward his wife and even toward his children as he had felt concerning the friends who once came to visit him. He began to tell little lies about business engagements that would give him freedom to walk alone in the street at night and, the chance offering, he secretly re-rented the room facing Washington Square. Then Mrs. Al Robinson died on the farm near Winesburg, and he got eight thousand dollars from the bank that acted as trustee of her estate. That took Enoch out of the world of men altogether. He gave the money to his wife and told her he could not live in the apartment any more. She cried and was angry and threatened, but he only stared at her and went his own way. In reality the wife did not care much. She thought Enoch slightly insane and was a little afraid of him. When it was quite sure that he would never come back, she took the two children and went to a village in Connecticut where she had lived as a girl. In the end she married a man who bought and sold real estate and was contented enough.

And so Enoch Robinson stayed in the New York room among the people of his fancy, playing with them, talking to them, happy as a child is happy. They were an odd lot, Enoch's people. They were made, I suppose, out of real people he had seen and who had for some obscure reason made an appeal to him. There was a woman with a sword in her hand, an old man with a long white beard who went about followed by a dog, a young girl whose stockings were always coming down and hanging over her shoe tops. There must have been two dozen of the shadow people, invented by the child-mind of Enoch Robinson, who lived in the room with him.

And Enoch was happy. Into the room he went and locked the door. With an absurd air of importance he talked aloud, giving instructions, making comments on life. He was happy and satisfied to go on making his living in the advertising place until something happened. Of course something did happen. That is why he went back to live in Winesburg and why we know about him. The thing that happened was a woman. It would be that way. He was too happy. Something had to come into his world. Something had to drive him out of the New York room to live out of his life an obscure, jerky little figure, bobbing up and down on the streets of an Ohio town at evening when the sun was going down behind the roof of Wesley Moyer's livery barn.

About the thing that happened. Enoch told George Willard about it one night. He wanted to talk to someone, and he chose the young newspaper reporter because the two happened to be thrown together at a time when the younger man was in a mood to understand.

Youthful sadness, young man's sadness, the sadness of a growing boy in a village at the year's end, opened the lips of the old man. The sadness was in the heart of George Willard and was without meaning, but it appealed to Enoch Robinson.

It rained on the evening when the two met and talked, a drizzly wet October rain. The fruition of the year had come and the night should have been fine with a moon in the sky and the crisp sharp promise of frost in the air, but it wasn't that way. It rained and little puddles of water shone under the street lamps on Main Street. In the woods in the darkness beyond the Fair Ground water dripped from the black trees. Beneath the trees wet leaves were pasted against tree roots that protruded from the ground. In gardens back of houses in Winesburg dry shriveled potato vines lay sprawling on the ground. Men who had finished the evening meal and who had planned to go uptown to talk the evening away with other men at the back of some store changed their minds. George Willard tramped about in the rain and was glad that it rained. He felt that way. He was like Enoch Robinson on the evenings when the old man came down out of his room and wandered alone in the streets. He was like that only that George Willard had become a tall young man and did not think it manly to weep and carry on. For a month his mother had been very ill and that had something to do with his sadness, but not much. He thought about himself and to the young that always brings sadness.

Enoch Robinson and George Willard met beneath a wooden awning that extended out over the sidewalk before Voight's wagon shop on Maumee Street just off the main street of Winesburg. They went together from there through the rain-washed streets to the older man's room on the third floor of the Heffner Block. The young reporter went willingly enough. Enoch Robinson asked him to go after the two had talked for ten minutes. The boy was a little afraid but had never been more curious in his life. A hundred times he had heard the old man spoken of as a little off his head and he thought himself rather brave and manly to go at all. From the very beginning, in the street in the rain, the old man talked in a queer way, trying to tell the story of the room in Washington

Square and of his life in the room. "You'll understand if you try hard enough," he said conclusively. "I have looked at you when you went past me on the street and I think you can understand. It isn't hard. All you have to do is to believe what I say, just listen and believe, that's all there is to it."

It was past eleven o'clock that evening when old Enoch, talking to George Willard in the room in the Heffner Block, came to the vital thing, the story of the woman and of what drove him out of the city to live out his life alone and defeated in Winesburg. He sat on a cot by the window with his head in his hand and George Willard was in a chair by a table. A kerosene lamp sat on the table and the room, although almost bare of furniture, was scrupulously clean. As the man talked George Willard began to feel that he would like to get out of the chair and sit on the cot also. He wanted to put his arms about the little old man. In the half darkness the man talked and the boy listened, filled with sadness.

"She got to coming in there after there hadn't been anyone in the room for years," said Enoch Robinson. "She saw me in the hallway of the house and we got acquainted. I don't know just what she did in her own room. I never went there. I think she was a musician and played a violin. Every now and then she came and knocked at the door and I opened it. In she came and sat down beside me, just sat and looked about and said nothing. Anyway, she said nothing that mattered."

The old man arose from the cot and moved about the room. The overcoat he wore was wet from the rain and drops of water kept falling with a soft thump on the floor. When he again sat upon the cot George Willard got out of the chair and sat beside him.

"I had a feeling about her. She sat there in the room with me and She was too big for the room. I felt that she was driving everything else away. We just talked of little things, but I couldn't sit still. I wanted to touch her with my fingers and to kiss her. Her hands were so strong and her face was so good and she looked at me all the time."

The trembling voice of the old man became silent and his body shook as from a chill. "I was afraid," he whispered,

"I was terribly afraid. I didn't want to let her come in when she knocked at the door but I couldn't sit still. 'No, no,' I said to myself, but I got up and opened the door just the same. She was so grown up, you see. She was a woman. I thought she would be bigger than I was there in that room."

Enoch Robinson stared at George Willard, his childlike blue eyes shining in the lamplight. Again he shivered. "I wanted her and all the time I didn't want her," he explained. "Then I began to tell her about my people, about everything that meant anything to me. I tried to keep quiet, to keep myself to myself, but I couldn't. I felt just as I did about opening the door. Sometimes I ached to have her go away and never come back any more."

The old man sprang to his feet and his voice shook with excitement. "One night something happened. I became mad to make her understand me and to know what a big thing I was in that room. I wanted her to see how important I was. I told her over and over. When she tried to go away, I ran and locked the door. I followed her about. I talked and talked and then all of a sudden things went to smash. A look came into her eyes and I knew she did understand. Maybe she had understood all the time. I was furious. I couldn't stand it. I wanted her to understand but, don't you see, I couldn't let her understand. I felt that then she would know everything, that I would be submerged, drowned out, you see. That's how it is. I don't know why."

The old man dropped into a chair by the lamp and the boy listened, filled with awe. "Go away, boy," said the man. "Don't stay here with me any more. I thought it might be a good thing to tell you but it isn't. I don't want to talk any more. Go away."

George Willard shook his head and a note of command came into his voice. "Don't stop now. Tell me the rest of it," he commanded sharply. "What happened? Tell me the rest of the story."

Enoch Robinson sprang to his feet and ran to the window that looked down into the deserted main street of Winesburg. George Willard followed. By the window the two stood, the tall awkward boy-man and the little wrinkled man-boy. The childish, eager voice carried forward the tale. "I swore at her," he explained. "I said vile words. I ordered her to go away and not to come back. Oh, I said terrible things. At first she pretended not to understand but I kept at it. I screamed and stamped on the floor. I made the house ring with my curses. I didn't want ever to see her again and I knew, after some of the things I said, that I never would see her again."

The old man's voice broke and he shook his head. "Things went to smash," he said quietly and sadly. "Out she went through the door and all the life there had been in the room followed her out. She took all of my people away. They all went out through the door after her. That's the way it was."

George Willard turned and went out of Enoch Robinson's room. In the darkness by the window, as he went through the door, he could hear the thin old voice whimpering and complaining. "I'm alone, all alone here," said the voice. "It was warm and friendly in my room but now I'm all alone."

An Awakening

Belle Carpenter had a dark skin, grey eyes, and thick lips. She was tall and strong. When black thoughts visited her she grew angry and wished she were a man and could fight someone with her fists. She worked in the millinery shop kept by Mrs. Kate McHugh and during the day sat trimming hats by a window at the rear of the store. She was the daughter of Henry Carpenter, bookkeeper in the First National Bank of Winesburg, and lived with him in a gloomy old house far out at the end of Buck-eye Street. The house was surrounded by pine trees and there was no grass beneath the trees. A rusty tin eavestrough had slipped from its fastenings at the back of the house and when the wind blew it beat against the roof of a small shed, making a dismal drumming noise that sometimes persisted all through the night.

When she was a young girl Henry Carpenter made life almost unbearable for Belle, but as she emerged from girlhood into womanhood he lost his power over her. The bookkeeper's life was made up of innumerable little pettinesses. When he went to the bank in the morning he stepped into a closet and put on a black alpaca coat that had become shabby with age. At night when he returned to his home he donned another black alpaca coat. Every evening he pressed the clothes worn in the streets. He had invented an arrangement of boards for the purpose. The trousers to his street suit were placed between the boards and the boards were clamped together with heavy screws. In the morning he wiped the boards with a damp cloth and stood them upright behind the dining room door. If they were moved during the day he was speechless with anger and did not recover his equilibrium for a week.

The bank cashier was a little bully and was afraid of his daughter. She, he realized, knew the story of his brutal treatment of her mother and hated him for it. One day she went home at noon and carried a handful of soft mud, taken from the road, into the house. With the mud she smeared the face of the boards used for the pressing of trousers and then went back to her work feeling relieved and happy.

Belle Carpenter occasionally walked out in the evening with George Willard. Secretly she loved another man, but her love affair, about which no one knew, caused her much anxiety. She was in love with Ed Handby, bartender in Ed Griffith's Saloon, and went about with the young reporter as a kind of relief to her feelings. She did not think that her station in life would permit her to be seen in the company of the bartender and walked about under the trees with George Willard and let him kiss her to relieve a longing that was very insistent in her nature. She felt that she could keep the younger man within bounds. About Ed Handby she was somewhat uncertain.

Handby, the bartender, was a tall, broad-shouldered man of thirty who lived in a room upstairs above Griffith's saloon. His fists were large and his eyes unusually small, but his voice, as though striving to conceal the power back of his fists, was soft and quiet.

At twenty-five the bartender had inherited a large farm from an uncle in Indiana. When sold, the farm brought in eight thousand dollars, which Ed spent in six months. Going to Sandusky, on Lake Erie, he began an orgy of dissipation, the story of which afterward filled his home town with awe. Here and there he went throwing the money about, driving carriages through the streets, giving wine parties to crowds of men and women, playing cards for high stakes and keeping mistresses whose wardrobes cost him hundreds of dollars. One night at a resort called Cedar Point, he got into a fight and ran amuck like a wild thing. With his fist he broke a large mirror in the wash room of a hotel and later went about smashing windows and breaking chairs in dance halls for the joy of hearing the glass rattle on the floor and seeing the terror in the eyes of clerks who had come from Sandusky to spend the evening at the resort with their sweethearts.

The affair between Ed Handby and Belle Carpenter on the surface amounted to nothing. He had succeeded in spending but one evening in her company. On that evening he hired a horse and buggy at Wesley Moyer's livery barn and took her for a drive. The conviction that she was the woman his nature demanded and that he must get her settled upon him and he told her of his desires. The bartender was ready to marry and to begin trying to earn money for the support of his wife, but so simple was his nature that he found it difficult to explain his intentions. His body ached with physical longing and with his body he expressed himself. Taking the milliner into his arms and holding her tightly in spite of her struggles, he kissed her until she became helpless. Then he brought her back to town and let her out of the buggy. "When I get hold of you again I'll not let you go. You can't play with me," he declared as he turned to drive away. Then, jumping out of the buggy,, he gripped her shoulders with his strong hands. "I'll keep you for good the next time," he said. "You might as well make up your mind to that. It's you and me for it and I'm going to have you before I get through."

One night in January when there was a new moon George Willard, who was in Ed Handby's mind the only obstacle to his getting Belle Carpenter, went for a walk. Early that evening George went into Ransom Surbeck's pool room with Seth Richmond and Art Wilson, son of the town butcher. Seth Richmond stood with his back against the wall and remained silent, but George Willard talked. The pool room was filled with Winesburg boys and they talked of women. The young reporter got into that vein. He said that women should look out for themselves, that the fellow who went out with a girl was not responsible for what happened. As he talked he looked about, eager for attention. He held the floor for five minutes and then Art Wilson began to talk. Art was learning the barber's trade in Cal Prouse's shop and already began to consider himself an authority in such matters as baseball, horse racing, drinking, and going about with women. He began to tell of a night when he with two men from Winesburg went into a house of prostitution at the county seat. The butcher's son held a cigar in the side of his mouth and as he talked spat on the floor. "The women in the place couldn't embarrass me although they tried hard enough," he boasted. "One of the girls in the house tried to get fresh, but I fooled her. As soon as she began to talk I went and sat in her lap. Everyone in the room laughed when I kissed her. I taught her to let me alone."

George Willard went out of the pool room and into Main Street. For days the weather had been bitter cold with a high wind blowing down on the town from Lake Erie, eighteen miles to the north, but on that night the wind had died away and a new moon made the night unusually lovely. Without thinking where he was going or what he wanted to do, George went out of Main Street and began walking in dimly lighted streets filled with frame houses.

Out of doors under the black sky filled with stars he forgot his companions of the pool room. Because it was dark and he was alone he began to talk aloud. In a spirit of play he reeled along the street imitating a drunken man and then imagined himself a soldier clad in shining boots that reached to the knees and wearing a sword that jingled as he walked. As a soldier he pictured himself as an inspector, passing before a long line of men who stood at attention. He began to examine the accoutrements of the men. Before a tree he stopped and began to scold. "Your pack is not in order," he said sharply. "How many times will I have to speak of this matter? Everything must be in order here. We have a difficult task before us and no difficult task can be done without order."

Hypnotized by his own words, the young man stumbled along the board sidewalk saying more words. "There is a law for armies and for men too," he muttered, lost in reflection. "The law begins with little things and spreads out until it covers everything. In every little thing there must be order, in the place where men work, in their clothes, in their thoughts. I myself must be orderly. I must learn that law. I must get myself into touch with something orderly and big that swings through the night like a star. In my little way I must begin to learn something, to give and swing and work with life, with the law."

George Willard stopped by a picket fence near a street lamp and his body began to tremble. He had never before thought such thoughts as had just come into his head and he wondered where they had come from. For the moment it seemed to him that some voice outside of himself had been talking as he walked. He was amazed and delighted with his own mind and when he walked on again spoke of the matter with fervor. "To come out of Ransom Surbeck's pool room and think things like that," he whispered. "It is better to be alone. If I talked like Art Wilson the boys would understand me but they wouldn't understand what I've been thinking down here."

In Winesburg, as in all Ohio towns of twenty years ago, there was a section in which lived day laborers. As the time of factories had not yet come, the laborers worked in the fields or were section hands on the railroads. They worked twelve hours a day and received one dollar for the long day of toil. The houses in which they lived were small cheaply constructed wooden affairs with a garden at the back. The more comfortable among them kept cows and perhaps a pig, housed in a little shed at the rear of the garden.

With his head filled with resounding thoughts, George Willard walked into such a street on the clear January night. The street was dimly lighted and in places there was no sidewalk. In the scene that lay about him there was something that excited his already aroused fancy. For a year he had been devoting all of his odd moments to the reading of books and now some tale he had read concerning life in old world towns of the middle ages came sharply back to his mind so that he stumbled forward with the curious feeling of one revisiting a place that had been a part of some former existence. On an impulse he turned out of the street and went into a little dark alleyway behind the sheds in which lived the cows and pigs.

For a half hour he stayed in the alleyway, smelling the strong smell of animals too closely housed and letting his mind play with the strange new thoughts that came to him. The very rankness of the smell of manure in the clear sweet air awoke something heady in his brain. The poor little houses lighted by kerosene lamps, the smoke from the chimneys mounting straight up into the clear air, the grunting of pigs, the women clad in cheap calico dresses and washing dishes in the kitchens, the footsteps of men coming out of the houses and going off to the stores and saloons of Main Street, the dogs barking and the children crying—all of these things made him seem, as he lurked in the darkness, oddly detached and apart from all life.

The excited young man, unable to bear the weight of his own thoughts, began to move cautiously along the alleyway. A dog attacked him and had to be driven away with stones, and a man appeared at the door of one of the houses and swore at the dog. George went into a vacant lot and throwing back his head looked up at the sky. He felt unutterably big and remade by the simple experience through which he had been passing and in a kind of fervor of emotion put up his hands, thrusting them into the darkness above his head and muttering words. The desire to say words overcame him and he said words without meaning, rolling them over on his tongue and saying them because they were brave words, full of meaning. "Death," he muttered, "night, the sea, fear, loveliness."

George Willard came out of the vacant lot and stood again on the sidewalk facing the houses. He felt that all of the people in the little street must be brothers and sisters to him and he wished he had the courage to call them out of their houses and to shake their hands. "If there were only a woman here I would take hold of her hand and we would run until we were both tired out," he thought. "That would make me feel better." With the thought of a woman in his mind he walked out of the street and went toward the house where Belle Carpenter lived. He thought she would understand his mood and that he could achieve in her presence a position he had long been wanting to achieve. In the past when he had been with her and had kissed her lips he had come away filled with anger at himself. He had felt like one being used for some obscure purpose and had not enjoyed the feeling. Now he thought he had suddenly become too big to be used.

When George got to Belle Carpenter's house there had already been a visitor there before him. Ed Handby had come to the door and calling Belle out of the house had tried to talk to her. He had wanted to ask the woman to come away with him and to be his wife, but when she came and stood by the door he lost his self-assurance and became sullen. "You stay away from that kid," he growled, thinking of George Willard, and then, not knowing what else to say, turned to go away. "If I catch you together I will break your bones and his too," he added. The bartender had come to woo, not to threaten, and was angry with himself because of his failure.

When her lover had departed Belle went indoors and ran hurriedly upstairs. From a window at the upper part of the house she saw Ed Handby cross the street and sit down on a horse block before the house of a neighbor. In the dim light the man sat motionless holding his head in his hands. She was made happy by the sight, and when George Willard came to the door she greeted him effusively and hurriedly put on her hat. She thought that, as she walked through the streets with young Willard, Ed Handby would follow and she wanted to make him suffer.

For an hour Belle Carpenter and the young reporter walked about under the trees in the sweet night air. George Willard was full of big words. The sense of power that had come to him during the hour in the darkness in the alleyway remained with him and he talked boldly, swaggering along and swinging his arms about. He wanted to make Belle Carpenter realize that he was aware of his former weakness and that he had changed. "You'll find me different," he declared, thrusting his hands into his pockets and looking boldly into her eyes. "I don't know why but it is so. You've got to take me for a man or let me alone. That's how it is."

Up and down the quiet streets under the new moon went the woman and the boy. When George had finished talking they turned down a side street and went across a bridge into a path that ran up the side of a hill. The hill began at Waterworks Pond and climbed upward to the Winesburg Fair Grounds. On the hillside grew dense bushes and small trees and among the bushes were little open spaces carpeted with long grass, now stiff and frozen.

As he walked behind the woman up the hill George Willard's heart began to beat rapidly and his shoulders straightened. Suddenly he decided that Belle Carpenter was about to surrender herself to him. The new force that had manifested itself in him had, he felt, been at work upon her and had led to her conquest. The thought made him half drunk with the sense of masculine power. Although he had been annoyed that as they walked about she had not seemed to be listening to his words, the fact that she had accompanied him to this place took all his doubts away. "It is different. Everything has become different," he thought and taking hold of her shoulder turned her about and stood looking at her, his eyes shining with pride.

Belle Carpenter did not resist. When he kissed her upon the lips she leaned heavily against him and looked over his shoulder into the darkness. In her whole attitude there was a suggestion of waiting. Again, as in the alleyway, George Willard's mind ran off into words and, holding the woman tightly he whispered the words into the still night. "Lust," he whispered, "lust and night and women."

George Willard did not understand what happened to him that night on the hillside. Later, when he got to his own room, he wanted to weep and then grew half insane with anger and hate. He hated Belle Carpenter and was sure that all his life he would continue to hate her. On the hillside he had led the woman to one of the little open spaces among the bushes and had dropped to his knees beside her. As in the vacant lot, by the laborers' houses, he had put up his hands in gratitude for the new power in himself and was waiting for the woman to speak when Ed Handby appeared.

The bartender did not want to beat the boy, who he thought had tried to take his woman away. He knew that beating was unnecessary, that he had power within himself to accomplish his purpose without using his fists. Gripping George by the shoulder and pulling him to his feet, he held him with one hand while he looked at Belle Carpenter seated on the grass. Then with a quick wide movement of his arm he sent the younger man sprawling away into the bushes and began to bully the woman, who had risen to her feet. "You're no good," he said roughly. "I've half a mind not to bother with you. I'd let you alone if I didn't want you so much."

On his hands and knees in the bushes George Willard stared at the scene before him and tried hard to think. He prepared to spring at the man who had humiliated him. To be beaten seemed to be infinitely better than to be thus hurled ignominiously aside.

Three times the young reporter sprang at Ed Handby and each time the bartender, catching him by the shoulder, hurled him back into the bushes. The older man seemed prepared to keep the exercise going indefinitely but George Willard's head struck the root of a tree and he lay still. Then Ed Handby took Belle Carpenter by the arm and marched her away.

George heard the man and woman making their way through the bushes. As he crept down the hillside his heart was sick within him. He hated himself and he hated the fate that had brought about his humiliation. When his mind went back to the hour alone in the alleyway he was puzzled and stopping in the darkness listened, hoping to hear again the voice outside himself that had so short a time before put new courage into his heart. When his way homeward led him again into the street of frame houses he could not bear the sight and began to run, wanting to get quickly out of the neighborhood that now seemed to him utterly squalid and commonplace.

"Queer"

From his seat on a box in the rough board shed that stuck like a burr on the rear of Cowley & Son's store in Winesburg, Elmer Cowley, the junior member of the firm, could see through a dirty window into the printshop of the *Winesburg Eagle*. Elmer was putting new shoelaces in his shoes. They did not go in readily and he had to take the shoes off. With the shoes in his hand he sat looking at a large hole in the heel of one of his stockings. Then looking quickly up he saw George Willard, the only newspaper reporter in Winesburg, standing at the back door of the *Eagle* printshop and staring absent-mindedly about. "Well, well, what next!" exclaimed the young man with the shoes in his hand, jumping to his feet and creeping away from the window.

A flush crept into Elmer Cowley's face and his hands began to tremble. In Cowley & Son's store a Jewish traveling salesman stood by the counter talking to his father. He imagined the reporter could hear what was being said and the thought made him furious. With one of the shoes still held in his hand he stood in a corner of the shed and stamped with a stockinged foot upon the board floor.

Cowley & Son's store did not face the main street of Winesburg. The front was on Maumee Street and beyond it was Voight's wagon shop and a shed for the sheltering of farmers' horses. Beside the store an alleyway ran behind the main street stores and all day drays and delivery wagons, intent on bringing in and taking out goods, passed up and down. The store itself was indescribable. Will Henderson once said of it that it sold everything and nothing. In the window facing Maumee Street stood a chunk of coal as large as an apple barrel, to indicate that orders for coal were taken, and beside the black mass of the coal stood three combs of honey grown brown and dirty in their wooden frames.

The honey had stood in the store window for six months. It was for sale as were also the coat hangers, patent suspender buttons, cans of roof paint, bottles of rheumatism cure, and a substitute for coffee that companioned the honey in its patient willingness to serve the public.

Ebenezer Cowley, the man who stood in the store listening to the eager patter of words that fell from the lips of the traveling man, was tall and lean and looked unwashed. On his scrawny neck was a large wen partially covered by a grey beard. He wore a long Prince Albert coat. The coat had been purchased to serve as a wedding garment. Before he became a merchant Ebenezer was a farmer and after his marriage he wore the Prince Albert coat to church on Sundays and on Saturday afternoons when he came into town to trade. When he sold the farm to become a merchant he wore the coat constantly. It had become brown with age and was covered with grease spots, but in it Ebenezer always felt dressed up and ready for the day in town.

As a merchant Ebenezer was not happily placed in life and he had not been happily placed as a farmer. Still he existed. His family, consisting of a daughter named Mabel and the son, lived with him in rooms above the store and it did not cost them much to live. His troubles were not financial. His unhappiness as a merchant lay in the fact that when a traveling man with wares to be sold came in at the front door he was afraid. Behind the counter he stood shaking his head. He was afraid, first that he would stubbornly refuse to buy and thus lose the opportunity to sell again; second that he would not be stubborn enough and would in a moment of weakness buy what could not be sold.

In the store on the morning when Elmer Cowley saw George Willard standing and apparently listening at the back door of the *Eagle* printshop, a situation had arisen that always stirred the son's wrath. The traveling man talked and Ebenezer listened, his whole figure expressing uncertainty. "You see how quickly it is done," said the traveling man, who had for sale a small flat metal substitute for collar buttons. With one hand he quickly unfastened a collar from his shirt and then fastened it on again. He assumed a flattering wheedling tone. "I tell you what, men have come to the end of all this fooling with collar buttons and you are the man to make money out of the change that is coming. I am offering you the exclusive agency for this town. Take twenty dozen of these fasteners and I'll not visit any other store. I'll leave the field to you."

The traveling man leaned over the counter and tapped with his finger on Ebenezer's breast. "It's an opportunity and I want you to take it," he urged. "A friend of mine told me about you. 'See that man Cowley,' he said. 'He's a live one.'"

The traveling man paused and waited. Taking a book from his pocket he began writing out the order. Still holding the shoe in his hand Elmer Cowley went through the store, past the two absorbed men, to a glass showcase near the front door. He took a cheap revolver from the case and began to wave it about. "You get out of here!" he shrieked. "We don't want any collar fasteners here." An idea came to him. "Mind, I'm not making any threat," he added. "I don't say I'll shoot. Maybe I just took this gun out of the case to look at it. But you better get out. Yes sir, I'll say that. You better grab up your things and get out."

The young storekeeper's voice rose to a scream and going behind the counter he began to advance upon the two men. "We're through being fools here!" he cried. "We ain't going to buy any more stuff until we begin to sell. We ain't going to keep on being queer and have folks staring and listening. You get out of here!"

The traveling man left. Raking the samples of collar fasteners off the counter into a black leather bag, he ran. He was a small man and very bow-legged and he ran awkwardly. The black bag caught against the door and he stumbled and fell. "Crazy, that's what he is—crazy!" he sputtered as he arose from the sidewalk and hurried away.

In the store Elmer Cowley and his father stared at each other. Now that the immediate object of his wrath had fled, the younger man was embarrassed. "Well, I meant it. I think we've been queer long enough," he declared, going to the showcase and replacing the revolver. Sitting on a barrel he pulled on and fastened the shoe he had been holding in his hand. He was waiting for some word of understanding from his father but when Ebenezer spoke his words only served to reawaken the wrath in the son and the young man ran out of the store without replying. Scratching his grey beard with his long dirty fingers, the merchant looked at his son with the same wavering uncertain stare with which he had confronted the traveling man. "I'll be starched," he said softly. "Well, well, I'll be washed and ironed and starched!"

Elmer Cowley went out of Winesburg and along a country road that paralleled the railroad track. He did not know where he was going or what he was going to do. In the shelter of a deep cut where the road, after turning sharply to the right, dipped under the tracks he stopped and the passion that had been the cause of his outburst in the store began to again find expression. "I will not be queer—one to be looked at and listened to," he declared aloud. "I'll be like other people. I'll show that George Willard. He'll find out. I'll show him!"

The distraught young man stood in the middle of the road and glared back at the town. He did not know the reporter George Willard and had no special feeling concerning the tall boy who ran about town gathering the town news. The reporter had merely come, by his presence in the office and in the printshop of the *Winesburg Eagle,* to stand for something in the young merchant's mind. He thought the boy who passed and repassed Cowley & Son's store and who stopped to talk to people in the street must be thinking of him and perhaps laughing at him. George Willard, he felt, belonged to the town, typified the town, represented in his person the spirit of the town. Elmer Cowley could not have believed that George Willard had also his days of unhappiness, that vague hungers and secret unnamable desires visited also his mind. Did he not represent public opinion and had not the public opinion of Winesburg condemned the Cowleys to queerness? Did he not walk whistling and laughing through Main Street? Might not one by striking his person strike also the greater enemy—the thing that smiled and went its own way—the judgment of Winesburg?

Elmer Cowley was extraordinarily tall and his arms were long and powerful. His hair, his eyebrows, and the downy beard that had begun to grow upon his chin, were pale almost to whiteness. His teeth protruded from between his lips and his eyes were blue with the colorless blueness of the marbles called "aggies" that the boys of Winesburg carried in their pockets. Elmer had lived in Winesburg for a year and had made no friends. He was, he felt, one condemned to go through life without friends and he hated the thought.

Sullenly the tall young man tramped along the road with his hands stuffed into his trouser pockets. The day was cold with a raw wind, but presently the sun began to shine and the road became soft and muddy. The tops of the ridges of frozen mud that formed the road began to melt and the mud clung to Elmer's shoes. His feet became cold. When he had gone several miles he turned off the road, crossed a field and entered a wood. In the wood he gathered sticks to build a fire, by which he sat trying to warm himself, miserable in body and in mind.

For two hours he sat on the log by the fire and then, arising and creeping cautiously through a mass of underbrush, he went to a fence and looked across fields to a small farmhouse surrounded by low sheds. A smile came to his lips and he began making motions with his long arms to a man who was husking corn in one of the fields.

In his hour of misery the young merchant had returned to the farm where he had lived through boyhood and where there was another human being to whom he felt he could explain himself. The man on the farm was a half-witted old fellow named Mook. He had once been employed by Ebenezer Cowley and had stayed on the farm when it was sold. The old man lived in one of the unpainted sheds back of the farmhouse and puttered about all day in the fields.

Mook the half-wit lived happily. With childlike faith he believed in the intelligence of the animals that lived in the sheds with him, and when he was lonely held long conversations with the cows, the pigs, and even with the chickens that ran about the barnyard. He it was who had put the expression regarding being "laundered" into the mouth of his former employer. When excited or surprised by anything he smiled vaguely and muttered: "I'll be washed and ironed. Well, well, I'll be washed and ironed and starched."

When the half-witted old man left his husking of corn and came into the wood to meet Elmer Cowley, he was neither surprised nor especially interested in the sudden appearance of the young man. His feet also were cold and he sat on the log by the fire, grateful for the warmth and apparently indifferent to what Elmer had to say.

Elmer talked earnestly and with great freedom, walking up and down and waving his arms about. "You don't understand what's the matter with me so of course you don't care," he declared. "With me it's different. Look how it has always been with me. Father is queer and mother was queer, too. Even the clothes mother used to wear were not like other people's clothes, and look at that coat in which father goes about there in town, thinking he's dressed up, too. Why don't he get a new one? It wouldn't cost much. I'll tell you why. Father doesn't know and when mother was alive she didn't know either. Mabel is different. She knows but she won't say anything. I will, though. I'm not going to be stared at any longer. Why look here, Mook, father doesn't know that his store there in town is just a queer jumble, that he'll never sell the stuff he buys. He knows nothing about it. Sometimes he's a little worried that trade doesn't come and then he goes and buys something else. In the evenings he sits by the fire upstairs and says trade will come after a while. He isn't worried. He's queer. He doesn't know enough to be worried."

The excited young man became more excited. "He don't know but I know," he shouted, stopping to gaze down into the dumb, unresponsive face of the half-wit. "I know too well. I can't stand it. When we lived out here it was different. I worked and at night I went to bed and slept. I wasn't always seeing people and thinking as I am now. In the evening, there in town, I go to the post office or to the depot to see the train come in, and no one says anything to me. Everyone stands around and laughs and they talk but they say nothing to me. Then I feel so queer that I can't talk either. I go away. I don't say anything. I can't."

The fury of the young man became uncontrollable. "I won't stand it," he yelled, looking up at the bare branches of the trees. "I'm not made to stand it."

Maddened by the dull face of the man on the log by the fire, Elmer turned and glared at him as he had glared back along the road at the town of Winesburg. "Go on back to work," he screamed. "What good does it do me to talk to you?" A thought came to him and his voice dropped. "I'm a coward too, eh?" he muttered. "Do you know why I came clear out here afoot? I had to tell someone and you were the only one I could tell. I hunted out another queer one, you see. I ran away, that's what I did. I couldn't stand up to someone like that George Willard. I had to come to you. I ought to tell him and I will."

Again his voice arose to a shout and his arms flew about. "I will tell him. I won't be queer. I don't care what they think. I won't stand it."

Elmer Cowley ran out of the woods leaving the half-wit sitting on the log before the fire. Presently the old man arose and climbing over the fence went back to his work in the corn. "I'll be washed and ironed and starched," he declared.

"Well, well, I'll be washed and ironed." Mook was interested. He went along a lane to a field where two cows stood nibbling at a straw stack. "Elmer was here," he said to the cows. "Elmer is crazy. You better get behind the stack where he don't see you. He'll hurt someone yet, Elmer will."

At eight o'clock that evening Elmer Cowley put his head in at the front door of the office of the *Winesburg Eagle* where George Willard sat writing. His cap was pulled down over his eyes and a sullen determined look was on his face. "You come on outside with me," he said, stepping in and closing the door. He kept his hand on the knob as though prepared to resist anyone else coming in. "You just come along outside. I want to see you."

George Willard and Elmer Cowley walked through the main street of Winesburg. The night was cold and George Willard had on a new overcoat and looked very spruce and dressed up. He thrust his hands into the overcoat pockets and looked inquiringly at his companion. He had long been wanting to make friends with the young merchant and find out what was in his mind. Now he thought he saw a chance and was delighted. "I wonder what he's up to? Perhaps he thinks he has a piece of news for the paper. It can't be a fire because I haven't heard the fire bell and there isn't anyone running," he thought.

In the main street of Winesburg, on the cold November evening, but few citizens appeared and these hurried along bent on getting to the stove at the back of some store. The windows of the stores were frosted and the wind rattled the tin sign that hung over the entrance to the stairway leading to Doctor Wellings's office. Before Hern's Grocery a basket of apples and a rack filled with new brooms stood on the sidewalk. Elmer Cowley stopped and stood facing George Willard. He tried to talk and his arms began to pump up and down. His face worked spasmodically. He seemed about to shout. "Oh, you go on back," he cried. "Don't stay out here with me. I ain't got anything to tell you. I don't want to see you at all."

For three hours the distracted young merchant wandered

through the resident streets of Winesburg blind with anger, brought on by his failure to declare his determination not to be queer. Bitterly the sense of defeat settled upon him and he wanted to weep. After the hours of futile sputtering at nothingness that had occupied the afternoon and his failure in the presence of the young reporter, he thought he could see no hope of a future for himself.

And then a new idea dawned for him. In the darkness that surrounded him he began to see a light. Going to the now darkened store, where Cowley & Son had for over a year waited vainly for trade to come, he crept stealthily in and felt about in a barrel that stood by the stove at the rear. In the barrel beneath shavings lay a tin box containing Cowley & Son's cash. Every evening Ebenezer Cowley put the box in the barrel when he closed the store and went upstairs to bed. "They wouldn't never think of a careless place like that," he told himself, thinking of robbers.

Elmer took twenty dollars, two ten-dollar bills, from the little roll containing perhaps four hundred dollars, the cash left from the sale of the farm. Then replacing the box beneath the shavings he went quietly out at the front door and walked again in the streets.

The idea that he thought might put an end to all of his unhappiness was very simple. "I will get out of here, run away from home," he told himself. He knew that a local freight train passed through Winesburg at midnight and went on to Cleveland, where it arrived at dawn. He would steal a ride on the local and when he got to Cleveland would lose himself in the crowds there. He would get work in some shop and become friends with the other workmen and would be indistinguishable. Then he could talk and laugh. He would no longer be queer and would make friends. Life would begin to have warmth and meaning for him as it had for others.

The tall awkward young man, striding through the streets, laughed at himself because he had been angry and had been half afraid of George Willard. He decided he would have his talk with the young reporter before he left town, that he would tell him about things, perhaps challenge him, challenge all of Winesburg through him.

Aglow with new confidence Elmer went to the office of the New Willard House and pounded on the door. A sleep-eyed boy slept on a cot in the office. He received no salary but was fed at the hotel table and bore with pride the title of "night clerk." Before the boy Elmer was bold, insistent. "You wake him up," he commanded. "You tell him to come down by the depot. I got to see him and I'm going away on the local. Tell him to dress and come on down. I ain't got much time."

The midnight local had finished its work in Winesburg and the trainsmen were coupling cars, swinging lanterns and preparing to resume their flight east. George Willard, rubbing his eyes and again wearing the new overcoat, ran down to the station platform afire with curiosity. "Well, here I am. What do you want? You've got something to tell me, eh?" he said.

Elmer tried to explain. He wet his lips with his tongue and looked at the train that had begun to groan and get under way. "Well, you see," he began, and then lost control of his tongue. "I'll be washed and ironed. I'll be washed and ironed and starched," he muttered half incoherently.

Elmer Cowley danced with fury beside the groaning train in the darkness on the station platform. Lights leaped into the air and bobbed up and down before his eyes. Taking the two ten-dollar bills from his pocket he thrust them into George Willard's hand. "Take them," he cried. "I don't want them. Give them to father. I stole them." With a snarl of rage he turned and his long arms began to flay the air. Like one struggling for release from hands that held him he struck out, hitting George Willard blow after blow on the breast, the neck, the mouth. The young reporter rolled over on the platform half unconscious, stunned by the terrific force of the blows. Springing aboard the passing train and running over the tops of cars, Elmer sprang down to a flat car and lying on his face looked back, trying to see the fallen man in the darkness. Pride surged up in him. "I showed him," he cried. "I guess I showed him. I ain't so queer. I guess I showed him I ain't so queer."

The Untold Lie

Ray Pearson and Hal Winters were farm hands employed
on a farm three miles north of Winesburg. On Saturday
afternoons they came into town and wandered about through
the streets with other fellows from the country.

Ray was a quiet, rather nervous man of perhaps fifty with
a brown beard and shoulders rounded by too much and too
hard labor. In his nature he was as unlike Hal Winters as
two men can be unlike.

Ray was an altogether serious man and had a little sharp-
featured wife who had also a sharp voice. The two, with
half a dozen thin-legged children, lived in a tumbledown
frame house beside a creek at the back end of the Wills farm
where Ray was employed.

Hal Winters, his fellow employee, was a young fellow. He
was not of the Ned Winters family, who were very respectable
people in Winesburg, but was one of the three sons of the
old man called Windpeter Winters who had a sawmill near
Unionville, six miles away, and who was looked upon by
everyone in Winesburg as a confirmed old reprobate.

People from the part of Northern Ohio in which Winesburg
lies will remember old Windpeter by his unusual and tragic
death. He got drunk one evening in town and started to drive
home to Unionville along the railroad tracks. Henry Bratten-

burg, the butcher, who lived out that way, stopped him at the edge of the town and told him he was sure to meet the down train but Windpeter slashed at him with his whip and drove on. When the train struck and killed him and his two horses a farmer and his wife who were driving home along a nearby road saw the accident. They said that old Windpeter stood up on the seat of his wagon, raving and swearing at the onrushing locomotive, and that he fairly screamed with delight when the team, maddened by his incessant slashing at them, rushed straight ahead to certain death. Boys like young George Willard and Seth Richmond will remember the incident quite vividly because, although everyone in our town said that the old man would go straight to hell and that the community was better off without him, they had a secret conviction that he knew what he was doing and admired his foolish courage. Most boys have seasons of wishing they could die gloriously instead of just being grocery clerks and going on with their humdrum lives.

But this is not the story of Windpeter Winters nor yet of his son Hal who worked on the Wills farm with Ray Pearson. It is Ray's story. It will, however, be necessary to talk a little of young Hal so that you will get into the spirit of it.

Hal was a bad one. Everyone said that. There were three of the Winters boys in that family, John, Hal, and Edward, all broad-shouldered big fellows like old Windpeter himself and all fighters and woman-chasers and generally all-around bad ones.

Hal was the worst of the lot and always up to some devilment. He once stole a load of boards from his father's mill and sold them in Winesburg. With the money he bought himself a suit of cheap, flashy clothes. Then he got drunk and when his father came raving into town to find him, they met and fought with their fists on Main Street and were arrested and put into jail together.

Hal went to work on the Wills farm because there was a country school teacher out that way who had taken his fancy. He was only twenty-two then but had already been in two or three of what were spoken of in Winesburg as "women scrapes." Everyone who heard of his infatuation for the school teacher was sure it would turn out badly. "He'll only get her into trouble, you'll see," was the word that went around.

And so these two men, Ray and Hal, were at work in a field on a day in the late October. They were husking corn and occasionally something was said and they laughed. Then came silence. Ray, who was the more sensitive and always minded things more, had chapped hands and they hurt. He put them into his coat pockets and looked away across the fields. He was in a sad, distracted mood and was affected by the beauty of the country. If you knew the Winesburg country in the fall and how the low hills are all splashed with yellows and reds you would understand his feeling. He began to think of the time, long ago when he was a young fellow living with his father, then a baker in Winesburg, and how on such days he had wandered away to the woods to gather nuts, hunt rabbits, or just to loaf about and smoke his pipe. His marriage had come about through one of his days of wandering. He had induced a girl who waited on trade in his father's shop to go with him and something had happened. He was thinking of that afternoon and how it had affected his whole life when a spirit of protest awoke in him. He had forgotten about Hal and muttered words. "Tricked by Gad, that's what I was, tricked by life and made a fool of," he said in a low voice.

As though understanding his thoughts, Hal Winters spoke up. "Well, has it been worth while? What about it, eh? What about marriage and all that?" he asked and then laughed. Hal tried to keep on laughing but he too was in an earnest mood. He began to talk earnestly. "Has a fellow got to do it?" he asked. "Has he got to be harnessed up and driven through life like a horse?"

Hal didn't wait for an answer but sprang to his feet and began to walk back and forth between the corn shocks. He was getting more and more excited. Bending down suddenly he picked up an ear of the yellow corn and threw it at the fence. "I've got Nell Gunther in trouble," he said. "I'm telling you, but you keep your mouth shut."

Ray Pearson arose and stood staring. He was almost a foot shorter than Hal, and when the younger man came and put his two hands on the older man's shoulders they made a picture. There they stood in the big empty field with the quiet corn shocks standing in rows behind them and the red and yellow hills in the distance, and from being just two indifferent workmen they had become all alive to each other. Hal sensed it and because that was his way he laughed. "Well, old daddy," he said awkwardly, "come on, advise me. I've got Nell in trouble. Perhaps you've been in the same fix yourself. I know what everyone would say is the right thing to do, but what do you say? Shall I marry and settle down? Shall I put myself into the harness to be worn out like an old horse? You know me, Ray. There can't anyone break me but I can break myself. Shall I do it or shall I tell Nell to go to the devil? Come on, you tell me. Whatever you say, Ray, I'll do."

Ray couldn't answer. He shook Hal's hands loose and turning walked straight away toward the barn. He was a sensitive man and there were tears in his eyes. He knew there was only one thing to say to Hal Winters, son of old Windpeter Winters, only one thing that all his own training and all the beliefs of the people he knew would approve, but for his life he couldn't say what he knew he should say.

At half-past four that afternoon Ray was puttering about the barnyard when his wife came up the lane along the creek and called him. After the talk with Hal he hadn't returned to the cornfield but worked about the barn. He had already done the evening chores and had seen Hal, dressed and ready for a roistering night in town, come out of the farmhouse and go into the road. Along the path to his own house he trudged behind his wife, looking at the ground and thinking. He couldn't make out what was wrong. Every time he raised his eyes and saw the beauty of the country in the failing light he wanted to do something he had never done before, shout or scream or hit his wife with his fists or something equally unexpected and terrifying. Along the path he went scratching his head and trying to make it out. He looked hard at his wife's back but she seemed all right.

She only wanted him to go into town for groceries and as soon as she had told him what she wanted began to scold. "You're always puttering," she said. "Now I want you to hustle. There isn't anything in the house for supper and you've got to get to town and back in a hurry."

Ray went into his own house and took an overcoat from a hook back of the door. It was torn about the pockets and the collar was shiny. His wife went into the bedroom and presently came out with a soiled cloth in one hand and three silver dollars in the other. Somewhere in the house a child wept bitterly and a dog that had been sleeping by the stove arose and yawned. Again the wife scolded. "The children will cry and cry. Why are you always puttering?" she asked.

Ray went out of the house and climbed the fence into a field. It was just growing dark and the scene that lay before him was lovely. All the low hills were washed with color and even the little clusters of bushes in the corners by the fences were alive with beauty. The whole world seemed to Ray Pearson to have become alive with something just as he and Hal had suddenly become alive when they stood in the corn field staring into each other's eyes.

The beauty of the country about Winesburg was too much for Ray on that fall evening. That is all there was to it. He could not stand it. Of a sudden he forgot all about being a quiet old farm hand and throwing off the torn overcoat began to run across the field. As he ran he shouted a protest against his life, against all life, against everything that makes life ugly. "There was no promise made," he cried into the empty spaces that lay about him. "I didn't promise my Minnie anything and Hal hasn't made any promise to Nell. I know he hasn't. She went into the woods with him because she wanted to go. What he wanted she wanted. Why should I pay? Why should Hal pay? Why should anyone pay? I don't want Hal to become old and worn out. I'll tell him. I won't let it go on. I'll catch Hal before he gets to town and I'll tell him."

Ray ran clumsily and once he stumbled and fell down. "I must catch Hal and tell him," he kept thinking, and although his breath came in gasps he kept running harder and harder. As he ran he thought of things that hadn't come into his mind for years—how at the time he married he had planned to go west to his uncle in Portland, Oregon—how he hadn't wanted to be a farm hand, but had thought when he got out West he would go to sea and be a sailor or get a job on a ranch and ride a horse into Western towns, shouting and laughing and waking the people in the houses with his wild cries. Then as he ran he remembered his children and in fancy felt their hands clutching at him. All of his thoughts of himself were involved with the thoughts of Hal and he thought the children were clutching at the younger man also. "They are the accidents of life, Hal," he cried. "They are not mine or yours. I had nothing to do with them."

Darkness began to spread over the fields as Ray Pearson ran on and on. His breath came in little sobs. When he came to the fence at the edge of the road and confronted Hal Winters, all dressed up and smoking a pipe as he walked jauntily along, he could not have told what he thought or what he wanted.

Ray Pearson lost his nerve and this is really the end of the story of what happened to him. It was almost dark when he got to the fence and he put his hands on the top bar and stood staring. Hal Winters jumped a ditch and coming up close to Ray put his hands into his pockets and laughed. He seemed to have lost his own sense of what had happened in the corn field and when he put up a strong hand and took hold of the lapel of Ray's coat he shook the old man as he might have shaken a dog that had misbehaved.

"You came to tell me, eh?" he said. "Well, never mind telling me anything. I'm not a coward and I've already made up my mind." He laughed again and jumped back across the ditch. "Nell ain't no fool," he said. "She didn't ask me to marry her. I want to marry her. I want to settle down and have kids,"

Ray Pearson also laughed. He felt like laughing at himself and all the world.

As the form of Hal Winters disappeared in the dusk that lay over the road that led to Winesburg, he turned and walked slowly back across the fields to where he had left his torn overcoat. As he went some memory of pleasant evenings spent with the thin-legged children in the tumble-down house by the creek must have come into his mind, for he muttered words. "It's just as well. Whatever I told him would have been a lie," he said softly, and then his form also disappeared into the darkness of the fields.

Drink

Tom Foster came to Winesburg from Cincinnati when he was still young and could get many new impressions. His grandmother had been raised on a farm near the town and as a young girl had gone to school there when Winesburg was a village of twelve or fifteen houses clustered about a general store on the Trunion Pike.

What a life the old woman had led since she went away from the frontier settlement and what a strong, capable little old thing she was! She had been in Kansas, in Canada, and in New York City, traveling about with her husband, a mechanic, before he died. Later she went to stay with her daughter, who had also married a mechanic and lived in Covington, Kentucky, across the river from Cincinnati.

Then began the hard years for Tom Foster's grandmother. First her son-in-law was killed by a policeman during a strike and then Tom's mother became an invalid and died also. The grandmother had saved a little money, but it was swept away by the illness of the daughter and by the cost of the two funerals. She became a half wornout old woman worker and lived with the grandson above a junk shop on a side-street in Cincinnati. For five years she scrubbed the floors in an office building and then got a place as dish washer in a restaurant. Her hands were all twisted out of shape. When she took hold of a mop or a broom handle the hands looked like the dried stems of an old creeping vine clinging to a tree.

The old woman came back to Winesburg as soon as she got the chance. One evening as she was coming home from work she found a pocket-book containing thirty-seven dollars, and that opened the way. The trip was a great adventure for the boy. It was past seven o'clock at night when the grandmother came home with the pocket-book held tightly in her old hands and she was so excited she could scarcely speak. She insisted on leaving Cincinnati that night, saying that if they stayed until morning the owner of the money would be sure to find them out and make trouble. Tom, who was then sixteen years old, had to go trudging off to the station with the old woman, bearing all of their earthly belongings done up in a worn-out blanket and slung across his back. By his side walked the grandmother urging him forward. Her toothless old mouth twitched nervously, and when Tom grew weary and wanted to put the pack down at a street crossing, she snatched it up and if he had not prevented would have slung it across her own back. When they got into the train and it had run out of the city she was as delighted as a girl and talked as the boy had never heard her talk before.

All through the night as the train rattled along, the grand-mother told Tom tales of Winesburg and of how he would enjoy his life working in the fields and shooting wild things in the woods there. She could not believe that the tiny village of fifty years before had grown into a thriving town in her absence, and in the morning when the train came to Wines-burg did not want to get off. "It isn't what I thought. It may be hard for you here," she said, and then the train went on its way and the two stood confused, not knowing where to turn, in the presence of Albert Longworth, the Winesburg baggage master.

But Tom Foster did get along all right. He was one to get along anywhere. Mrs. White, the banker's wife, employed his grandmother to work in the kitchen and he got a place as stable boy in the banker's new brick barn.

In Winesburg servants were hard to get. The woman who wanted help in her housework employed a "hired girl" who insisted on sitting at the table with the family. Mrs. White was sick of hired girls and snatched at the chance to get hold of the old city woman. She furnished a room for the boy Tom upstairs in the barn. "He can mow the lawn and run errands when the horses do not need attention," she explained to her husband.

Tom Foster was rather small for his age and had a large head covered with stiff black hair that stood straight up. The hair emphasized the bigness of his head. His voice was the softest thing imaginable, and he was himself so gentle and quiet that he slipped into the life of the town without attracting the least bit of attention.

One could not help wondering where Tom Foster got his gentleness. In Cincinnati he had lived in a neighborhood where gangs of tough boys prowled through the streets, and all through his early formative years he ran about with tough boys. For a while he was messenger for a telegraph company and delivered messages in a neighborhood sprinkled with houses of prostitution. The women in the houses knew and loved Tom Foster and the tough boys in the gangs loved him also.

He never asserted himself. That was one thing that helped him escape. In an odd way he stood in the shadow of the wall of life, was meant to stand in the shadow. He saw the men and women in the houses of lust, sensed their casual and horrible love affairs, saw boys fighting and listened to their tales of thieving and drunkenness, unmoved and strangely unaffected.

Once Tom did steal. That was while he still lived in the city. The grandmother was ill at the time and he himself was out of work. There was nothing to eat in the house, and so he went into a harness shop on a side street and stole a dollar and seventy-five cents out of the cash drawer.

The harness shop was run by an old man with a long mustache. He saw the boy lurking about and thought nothing of it. When he went out into the street to talk to a teamster

Tom opened the cash drawer and taking the money walked away. Later he was caught and his grandmother settled the matter by offering to come twice a week for a month and scrub the shop. The boy was ashamed, but he was rather glad, too. "It is all right to be ashamed and makes me understand new things," he said to the grandmother, who didn't know what the boy was talking about but loved him so much that it didn't matter whether she understood or not.

For a year Tom Foster lived in the banker's stable and then lost his place there. He didn't take very good care of the horses and he was a constant source of irritation to the banker's wife. She told him to mow the lawn and he forgot. Then she sent him to the store or to the post office and he did not come back but joined a group of men and boys and spent the whole afternoon with them, standing about, listening and occasionally, when addressed, saying a few words. As in the city in the houses of prostitution and with the rowdy boys running through the streets at night, so in Winesburg among its citizens he had always the power to be a part of and yet distinctly apart from the life about him.

After Tom lost his place at Banker White's he did not live with his grandmother, although often in the evening she came to visit him. He rented a room at the rear of a little frame building belonging to old Rufus Whiting. The building was on Duane Street, just off Main Street, and had been used for years as a law office by the old man, who had become too feeble and forgetful for the practice of his profession but did not realize his inefficiency. He liked Tom and let him have the room for a dollar a month. In the late afternoon when the lawyer had gone home the boy had the place to himself and spent hours lying on the floor by the stove and thinking of things. In the evening the grandmother came and sat in the lawyer's chair to smoke a pipe while Tom remained silent, as he always did in the presence of everyone.

Often the old woman talked with great vigor. Sometimes she was angry about some happening at the banker's house and scolded away for hours. Out of her own earnings she bought a mop and regularly scrubbed the lawyer's office. Then when the place was spotlessly clean and smelled clean she lighted her clay pipe and she and Tom had a smoke together. "When you get ready to die then I will die also," she said to the boy lying on the floor beside her chair.

Tom Foster enjoyed life in Winesburg. He did odd jobs, such as cutting wood for kitchen stoves and mowing the grass before houses. In late May and early June he picked strawberries in the fields. He had time to loaf and he enjoyed loafing. Banker White had given him a cast-off coat which was too large for him, but his grandmother cut it down, and he had also an overcoat, got at the same place, that was lined with fur. The fur was worn away in spots, but the coat was warm and in the winter Tom slept in it. He thought his method of getting along good enough and was happy and satisfied with the way life in Winesburg had turned out for him.

The most absurd little things made Tom Foster happy. That, I suppose, was why people loved him. In Hern's Grocery they would be roasting coffee on Friday afternoon, preparatory to the Saturday rush of trade, and the rich odor invaded lower Main Street. Tom Foster appeared and sat on a box at the rear of the store. For an hour he did not move but sat perfectly still, filling his being with the spicy odor that made him half drunk with happiness. "I like it," he said gently. "It makes me think of things far away, places and things like that."

One night Tom Foster got drunk. That came about in a curious way. He never had been drunk before, and indeed in all his life had never taken a drink of anything intoxicating, but he felt he needed to be drunk that one time and so went and did it.

In Cincinnati, when he lived there, Tom had found out many things, things about ugliness and crime and lust. Indeed, he knew more of these things than anyone else in Winesburg. The matter of sex in particular had presented itself to him in a quite horrible way and had made a deep impression on his mind. He thought, after what he had seen of the women standing before the squalid houses on cold nights and the look he had seen in the eyes of the men who stopped to talk to them, that he would put sex altogether out of his own life. One of the women of the neighborhood tempted him once and he went into a room with her. He never forgot the smell of the room nor the greedy look that came into the eyes of the woman. It sickened him and in a very terrible way left a scar on his soul. He had always before thought of women as quite innocent things, much like his grandmother, but after that one experience in the room he dismissed women from his mind. So gentle was his nature that he could not hate anything and not being able to understand he decided to forget.

And Tom did forget until he came to Winesburg. After he had lived there for two years something began to stir in him. On all sides he saw youth making love and he was himself a youth. Before he knew what had happened he was in love also. He fell in love with Helen White, daughter of the man for whom he had worked, and found himself thinking of her at night.

That was a problem for Tom and he settled it in his own way. He let himself think of Helen White whenever her figure came into his mind and only concerned himself with the manner of his thoughts. He had a fight, a quiet determined little fight of his own, to keep his desires in the channel where he thought they belonged, but on the whole he was victorious.

And then came the spring night when he got drunk. Tom was wild on that night. He was like an innocent young buck of the forest that has eaten of some maddening weed. The thing began, ran its course, and was ended in one night, and you may be sure that no one in Winesburg was any the worse for Tom's outbreak.

In the first place, the night was one to make a sensitive nature drunk. The trees along the residence streets of the town were all newly clothed in soft green leaves, in the gardens behind the houses men were puttering about in vegetable gardens, and in the air there was a hush, a waiting kind of silence very stirring to the blood.

Tom left his room on Duane Street just as the young night

began to make itself felt. First he walked through the streets, going softly and quietly along, thinking thoughts that he tried to put into words. He said that Helen White was a flame dancing in the air and that he was a little tree without leaves standing out sharply against the sky. Then he said that she was a wind, a strong terrible wind, coming out of the darkness of a stormy sea and that he was a boat left on the shore of the sea by a fisherman.

That idea pleased the boy and he sauntered along playing with it. He went into Main Street and sat on the curbing before Wacker's tobacco store. For an hour he lingered about listening to the talk of men, but it did not interest him much and he slipped away. Then he decided to get drunk and went into Willy's saloon and bought a bottle of whiskey. Putting the bottle into his pocket, he walked out of town, wanting to be alone to think more thoughts and to drink the whiskey.

Tom got drunk sitting on a bank of new grass beside the road about a mile north of town. Before him was a white road and at his back an apple orchard in full bloom. He took a drink out of the bottle and then lay down on the grass. He thought of mornings in Winesburg and of how the stones in the graveled driveway by Banker White's house were wet with dew and glistened in the morning light. He thought of the night in the barn when it rained and he lay awake hearing the drumming of the raindrops and smelling the warm smell of horses and of hay. Then he thought of a storm that had gone roaring through Winesburg several days before and, his mind going back, he relived the night he had spent on the train with his grandmother when the two were coming from Cincinnati. Sharply he remembered how strange it had seemed to sit quietly in the coach and to feel the power of the engine hurling the train along through the night.

Tom got drunk in a very short time. He kept taking drinks from the bottle as the thoughts visited him and when his head began to reel got up and walked along the road going away from Winesburg. There was a bridge on the road that ran out of Winesburg north to Lake Erie and the drunken boy made his way along the road to the bridge. There he sat down.

He tried to drink again, but when he had taken the cork out of the bottle he became ill and put it quickly back. His head was rocking back and forth and so he sat on the stone approach to the bridge and sighed. His head seemed to be flying about like a pinwheel and then projecting itself off into space and his arms and legs flopped helplessly about.

At eleven o'clock Tom got back into town. George Willard found him wandering about and took him into the *Eagle* printshop. Then he became afraid that the drunken boy would make a mess on the floor and helped him into the alleyway.

The reporter was confused by Tom Foster. The drunken boy talked of Helen White and said he had been with her on the shore of a sea and had made love to her. George had seen Helen White walking in the street with her father during the evening and decided that Tom was out of his head. A sentiment concerning Helen White that lurked in his own heart flamed up and he became angry. "Now you quit that," he said. "I won't let Helen White's name be dragged into this. I won't let that happen." He began shaking Tom's shoulder, trying to make him understand. "You quit it," he said again.

For three hours the two young men, thus strangely thrown together, stayed in the printshop. When he had a little recovered George took Tom for a walk. They went into the country and sat on a log near the edge of a wood. Something in the still night drew them together and when the drunken boy's head began to clear they talked.

"It was good to be drunk." Tom Foster said. "It taught me something. I won't have to do it again. I will think more clearly after this. You see how it is."

George Willard did not see, but his anger concerning Helen White passed and he felt drawn toward the pale, shaken boy as he had never before been drawn toward anyone. With motherly solicitude, he insisted that Tom get to his feet and walk about. Again they went back to the printshop and sat in silence in the darkness.

The reporter could not get the purpose of Tom Foster's action straightened out in his mind. When Tom spoke again of Helen White he again grew angry and began to scold.

"You quit that," he said sharply. "You haven't been with her. What makes you say you have? What makes you keep saying such things? Now you quit it, do you hear?"

Tom was hurt. He couldn't quarrel with George Willard because he was incapable of quarreling, so he got up to go away. When George Willard was insistent he put out his hand, laying it on the older boy's arm, and tried to explain.

"Well," he said softly, "I don't know how it was. I was happy. You see how that was. Helen White made me happy and the night did too. I wanted to suffer, to be hurt somehow. I thought that was what I should do. I wanted to suffer, you see, because everyone suffers and does wrong. I thought of a lot of things to do, but they wouldn't work. They all hurt someone else."

Tom Foster's voice arose, and for once in his life he became almost excited. "It was like making love, that's what I mean," he explained. "Don't you see how it is? It hurt me to do what I did and made everything strange. That's why I did it. I'm glad, too. It taught me something, that's it, that's what I wanted. Don't you understand? I wanted to learn things, you see. That's why I did it."

Death

The stairway leading up to Doctor Reefy's office, in the Heffner Block above the Paris Dry Goods store, was but dimly lighted. At the head of the stairway hung a lamp with a dirty chimney that was fastened by a bracket to the wall. The lamp had a tin reflector, brown with rust and covered with dust. The people who went up the stairway followed with their feet the feet of many who had gone before. The soft boards of the stairs had yielded under the pressure of feet and deep hollows marked the way.

At the top of the stairway a turn to the right brought you to the doctor's door. To the left was a dark hallway filled with rubbish. Old chairs, carpenter's horses, step ladders and empty boxes lay in the darkness waiting for shins to be barked. The pile of rubbish belonged to the Paris Dry Goods Company. When a counter or a row of shelves in the store became useless, clerks carried it up the stairway and threw it on the pile.

Doctor Reefy's office was as large as a barn. A stove with a round paunch sat in the middle of the room. Around its base was piled sawdust, held in place by heavy planks nailed to the floor. By the door stood a huge table that had once been a part of the furniture of Herrick's Clothing Store and that had been used for displaying custom-made clothes. It was covered with books, bottles, and surgical instruments. Near the edge of the table lay three or four apples left by John Spaniard, a tree nurseryman who was Doctor Reefy's friend, and who had slipped the apples out of his pocket as he came in at the door.

At middle age Doctor Reefy was tall and awkward. The grey beard he later wore had not yet appeared, but on the upper lip grew a brown mustache. He was not a graceful man, as when he grew older, and was much occupied with the problem of disposing of his hands and feet.

On summer afternoons, when she had been married many years and when her son George was a boy of twelve or fourteen, Elizabeth Willard sometimes went up the worn steps to Doctor Reefy's office. Already the woman's naturally tall figure had begun to droop and to drag itself listlessly about. Ostensibly she went to see the doctor because of her health, but on the half dozen occasions when she had been to see him the outcome of the visits did not primarily concern her health. She and the doctor talked of that but they talked most of her life, of their two lives and of the ideas that had come to them as they lived their lives in Winesburg.

In the big empty office the man and the woman sat looking at each other and they were a good deal alike. Their bodies were different, as were also the color of their eyes, the length of their noses, and the circumstances of their existence, but something inside them meant the same thing, wanted the same release, would have left the same impression on the memory of an onlooker. Later, and when he grew older and married a young wife, the doctor often talked to her of the hours spent with the sick woman and expressed a good many things he had been unable to express to Elizabeth. He was almost a poet in his old age and his notion of what happened took a poetic turn. "I had come to the time in my life when prayer became necessary and so I invented gods and prayed to them," he said. "I did not say my prayers in words nor did I kneel down but sat perfectly still in my chair. In the late afternoon when it was hot and quiet on Main Street or in the winter when the days were gloomy, the gods came into the office and I thought no one knew about them. Then I found that this woman Elizabeth knew, that she worshipped also the same gods. I have a notion that she came to the office because she thought the gods would be there but she was happy to find herself not alone just the same. It was an experience that cannot be explained, although I suppose it is always happening to men and women in all sorts of places."

On the summer afternoons when Elizabeth and the doctor sat in the office and talked of their two lives they talked of other lives also. Sometimes the doctor made philosophic epigrams. Then he chuckled with amusement. Now and then after a period of silence, a word was said or a hint given that strangely illuminated the life of the speaker, a wish became a desire, or a dream, half dead, flared suddenly into life. For the most part the words came from the woman and she said them without looking at the man.

Each time she came to see the doctor the hotel keeper's wife talked a little more freely and after an hour or two in his presence went down the stairway into Main Street feeling renewed and strengthened against the dullness of her days. With something approaching a girlhood swing to her body she walked along, but when she had got back to her chair by the window of her room and when darkness had come on and a girl from the hotel dining room brought her dinner on a tray, she let it grow cold. Her thoughts ran away to her girlhood with its passionate longing for adventure and she remembered the arms of men that had held her when adventure was a possible thing for her. Particularly she remembered one who had for a time been her lover and who in the moment of his passion had cried out to her more than a hundred times, saying the same words madly over and over: "You dear! You dear! You lovely dear!" The words, she thought, expressed something she would have liked to have achieved in life.

In her room in the shabby old hotel the sick wife of the hotel keeper began to weep and, putting her hands to her face, rocked back and forth. The words of her one friend,

Doctor Reefy, rang in her ears. "Love is like a wind stirring the grass beneath trees on a black night," he had said. "You must not try to make love definite. It is the divine accident of life. If you try to be definite and sure about it and to live beneath the trees, where soft night winds blow, the long hot day of disappointment comes swiftly and the gritty dust from passing wagons gathers upon lips inflamed and made tender by kisses."

Elizabeth Willard could not remember her mother who had died when she was but five years old. Her girlhood had been lived in the most haphazard manner imaginable. Her father was a man who had wanted to be let alone and the affairs of the hotel would not let him alone. He also had lived and died a sick man. Every day he arose with a cheerful face, but by ten o'clock in the morning all the joy had gone out of his heart. When a guest complained of the fare in the hotel dining room or one of the girls who made up the beds got married and went away, he stamped on the floor and swore. At night when he went to bed he thought of his daughter growing up among the stream of people that drifted in and out of the hotel and was overcome with sadness. As the girl grew older and began to walk out in the evening with men he wanted to talk to her, but when he tried was not successful. He always forgot what he wanted to say and spent the time complaining of his own affairs.

In her girlhood and young womanhood Elizabeth had tried to be a real adventurer in life. At eighteen life had so gripped her that she was no longer a virgin but, although she had a half dozen lovers before she married Tom Willard, she had never entered upon an adventure prompted by desire alone. Like all the women in the world, she wanted a real lover. Always there was something she sought blindly, passionately, some hidden wonder in life. The tall beautiful girl with the swinging stride who had walked under the trees with men was forever putting out her hand into the darkness and trying to get hold of some other hand. In all the babble of words that fell from the lips of the men with whom she adventured she was trying to find what would be for her the true word.

Elizabeth had married Tom Willard, a clerk in her father's hotel, because he was at hand and wanted to marry at the time when the determination to marry came to her. For a while, like most young girls, she thought marriage would change the face of life. If there was in her mind a doubt of the outcome of the marriage with Tom she brushed it aside. Her father was ill and near death at the time and she was perplexed because of the meaningless outcome of an affair in which she had just been involved. Other girls of her age in Winesburg were marrying men she had always known, grocery clerks or young farmers. In the evening they walked in Main Street with their husbands and when she passed they smiled happily. She began to think that the fact of marriage might be full of some hidden significance. Young wives with whom she talked spoke softly and shyly. "It changes things to have a man of your own," they said.

On the evening before her marriage the perplexed girl had a talk with her father. Later she wondered if the hours alone with the sick man had not led to her decision to marry. The father talked of his life and advised the daughter to avoid being led into another such muddle. He abused Tom Willard, and that led Elizabeth to come to the clerk's defense. The sick man became excited and tried to get out of bed. When she would not let him walk about he began to complain. "I've never been let alone," he said. "Although I've worked hard I've not made the hotel pay. Even now I owe money at the bank. You'll find that out when I'm gone."

The voice of the sick man became tense with earnestness. Being unable to arise, he put out his hand and pulled the girl's head down beside his own. "There's a way out," he whispered. "Don't marry Tom Willard or anyone else here in Winesburg. There is eight hundred dollars in a tin box in my trunk. Take it and go away."

Again the sick man's voice became querulous. "You've got to promise," he declared. "If you won't promise not to marry, give me your word that you'll never tell Tom about the money. It is mine and if I give it to you I've the right to make that demand. Hide it away. It is to make up to you for my failure as a father. Some time it may prove to be a door, a great open door to you. Come now, I tell you I'm about to die, give me your promise."

In Doctor Reefy's office, Elizabeth, a tired gaunt old woman at forty-one, sat in a chair near the stove and looked at the floor. By a small desk near the window sat the doctor. His hands played with a lead pencil that lay on the desk. Elizabeth talked of her life as a married woman. She became impersonal and forgot her husband, only using him as a lay figure to give point to her tale. 'And then I was married and it did not turn out at all," she said bitterly. "As soon as I had gone into it I began to be afraid. Perhaps I knew too much before and then perhaps I found out too much during my first night with him. I don't remember.

"What a fool I was. When father gave me the money and tried to talk me out of the thought of marriage, I would not listen. I thought of what the girls who were married had said of it and I wanted marriage also. It wasn't Tom I wanted, it was marriage. When father went to sleep I leaned out of the windows and thought of the life I had led. I didn't want to be a bad woman. The town was full of stories about me. I even began to be afraid Tom would change his mind."

The woman's voice began to quiver with excitement. To Doctor Reefy, who without realizing what was happening had begun to love her, there came an odd illusion. He thought that as she talked the woman's body was changing, that she was becoming younger, straighter, stronger. When he could not shake off the illusion his mind gave it a professional twist. "It is good for both her body and her mind, this talking," he muttered.

The woman began telling of an incident that had happened one afternoon a few months after her marriage. Her voice became steadier. "In the late afternoon I went for a drive alone," she said. "I had a buggy and a little grey pony I kept in Moyer's Livery. Tom was painting and repapering rooms in the hotel. He wanted money and I was trying to make up my mind to tell him about the eight hundred dollars father had given to me. I couldn't decide to do it. I didn't like him well enough. There was always paint on his hands and face during those days and he smelled of paint. He was trying to fix up the old hotel, make it new and smart."

The excited woman sat up very straight in her chair and made a quick girlish movement with her hand as she told of the drive alone on the spring afternoon. "It was cloudy and a storm threatened," she said. "Black clouds made the green of the trees and the grass stand out so that the colors hurt my eyes. I went out Trunion Pike a mile or more and then turned into a side road. The little horse went quickly along up hill and down. I was impatient. Thoughts came and I wanted to get away from my thoughts. I began to beat the horse. The black clouds settled down and it began to rain. I wanted to go at a terrible speed, to drive on and on forever. I wanted to get out of town, out of my clothes, out of my marriage, out of my body, out of everything. I almost killed the horse, making him run, and when he could not run any more I got out of the buggy and ran afoot into the darkness until I fell and hurt my side. I wanted to run away from everything but I wanted to run towards something too. Don't you see, dear how it was?"

Elizabeth sprang out of the chair and began to walk about in the office. She walked as Doctor Reefy thought he had never seen anyone walk before. To her whole body there was a swing, a rhythm that intoxicated him. When she came and knelt on the floor beside his chair he took her into his arms and began to kiss her passionately. "I cried all the way home," she said, as she tried to continue the story of her wild ride, but he did not listen. "You dear! You lovely dear! Oh you lovely dear!" he muttered and thought he held in his arms not the tired-out woman of forty-one but a lovely and innocent girl who had been able by some miracle to project herself out of the husk of the body of the tired-out woman.

Doctor Reefy did not see the woman he had held in his arms again until after her death. On the summer afternoon in the office when he was on the point of becoming her lover a half grotesque little incident brought his love-making quickly to an end. As the man and woman held each other tightly heavy feet came tramping up the office stairs. The two sprang to their feet and stood listening and trembling. The noise on the stairs was made by a clerk from the Paris Dry Goods Company. With a loud bang he threw an empty box on the pile of rubbish in the hallway and then went heavily down the stairs. Elizabeth followed him almost immediately. The thing that had come to life in her as she talked to her one friend died suddenly. She was hysterical, as was also Doctor Reefy, and did not want to continue the talk. Along the streets she went with the blood still singing in her body, but when she turned out of Main Street and saw ahead the lights of the New Willard House, she began to tremble and her knees shook so that for a moment she thought she would fall in the street.

The sick woman spent the last few months of her life hungering for death. Along the road of death she went, seeking, hungering. She personified the figure of death and made him now a strong black-haired youth running over hills, now a stern quiet man marked and scarred by the business of living. In the darkness of her room she put out her hand, thrusting it from under the covers of her bed, and she thought that death like a living thing put out his hand to her. "Be patient, lover," she whispered. "Keep yourself young and beautiful and be patient."

On the evening when disease laid its heavy hand upon her and defeated her plans for telling her son George of the eight hundred dollars hidden away, she got out of bed and crept half across the room pleading with death for another hour of life. "Wait, dear! The boy! The boy! The boy!" she pleaded as she tried with all of her strength to fight off the arms of the lover she had wanted so earnestly.

Elizabeth died one day in March in the year when her son George became eighteen, and the young man had but little sense of the meaning of her death. Only time could give him that. For a month he had seen her lying white and still and speechless in her bed, and then one afternoon the doctor stopped him in the hallway and said a few words.

The young man went into his own room and closed the door. He had a queer empty feeling in the region of his stomach. For a moment he sat staring at the floor and then jumping up went for a walk. Along the station platform he went, and around through residence streets past the high-school building, thinking almost entirely of his own affairs. The notion of death could not get hold of him and he was in fact a little annoyed that his mother had died on that day. He had just received a note from Helen White, the daughter of the town banker, in answer to one from him. "Tonight I could have gone to see her and now it will have to be put off", he thought half angrily.

Elizabeth died on a Friday afternoon at three o'clock. It had been cold and rainy in the morning but in the afternoon the sun came out. Before she died she lay paralyzed for six days unable to speak or move and with only her mind and her eyes alive. For three of the six days she struggled, thinking of her boy, trying to say some few words in regard to his future, and in her eyes there was an appeal so touching that all who saw it kept the memory of the dying woman in their minds for years. Even Tom Willard, who had always half resented his wife, forgot his resentment and the tears ran out of his eyes and lodged in his mustache. The mustache had begun to turn grey and Tom colored it with dye. There was oil in the preparation he used for the purpose and the tears, catching in the mustache and being brushed away by his hand, formed a fine mist-like vapor. In his grief Tom Willard's face looked like the face of a little dog that has been out a long time in bitter weather.

George came home along Main Street at dark on the day of his mother's death and, after going to his own room to brush his hair and clothes, went along the hallway and into the room where the body lay. There was a candle on the dressing table by the door and Doctor Reefy sat in a chair by the bed. The doctor arose and started to go out. He put out his hand as though to greet the younger man and then awkwardly drew it back again. The air of the room was heavy with the presence of the two self-conscious human beings, and the man hurried away.

The dead woman's son sat down in a chair and looked at the floor. He again thought of his own affairs and definitely decided he would make a change in his life, that he would leave Winesburg. "I will go to some city. Perhaps I can get a job on some newspaper," he thought, and then his mind turned to the girl with whom he was to have spent this evening and again he was half angry at the turn of events that had prevented his going to her.

In the dimly lighted room with the dead woman the young man began to have thoughts. His mind played with thoughts of life as his mother's mind had played with the thought of death. He closed his eyes and imagined that the red young lips of Helen White touched his own lips. His body trembled and his hands shook. And then something happened. The boy sprang to his feet and stood stiffly. He looked at the figure of the dead woman under the sheets and shame for his thoughts swept over him so that he began to weep. A new notion came into his mind and he turned and looked guiltily about as though afraid he would be observed.

George Willard became possessed of a madness to lift the sheet from the body of his mother and look at her face. The thought that had come into his mind gripped him terribly. He became convinced that not his mother but someone else lay in the bed before him. The conviction was so real that it was almost unbearable. The body under the sheets was long and in death looked young and graceful. To the boy, held by some strange fancy, it was unspeakably lovely. The feeling that the body before him was alive, that in another moment a lovely woman would spring out of the bed and confront him, became so overpowering that he could not bear the suspense. Again and again he put out his hand. Once he touched and half lifted the white sheet that covered her, but his courage failed and he, like Doctor Reefy, turned and went out of the room. In the hallway outside the door he stopped and trembled so that he had to put a hand against the wall to support himself. "That's not my mother. That's not my mother in there," he whispered to himself and again his body shook with fright and uncertainty. When Aunt Elizabeth Swift, who had come to watch over the body, came out of an adjoining room he put his hand into hers and began to sob, shaking his head from side to side, half blind with grief. "My mother is dead," he said, and then forgetting the woman he turned and stared at the door through which he had just come. "The dear, the dear, oh the lovely dear," the boy, urged by some impulse outside himself, muttered aloud.

As for the eight hundred dollars the dead woman had kept hidden so long and that was to give George Willard his start in the city, it lay in the tin box behind the plaster by the foot of his mother's bed. Elizabeth had put it there a week after her marriage, breaking the plaster away with a stick. Then she got one of the workmen her husband was at that time employing about the hotel to mend the wall. "I jammed the corner of the bed against it," she had explained to her husband, unable at the moment to give up her dream of release, the release that after all came to her but twice in her life, in the moments when her lovers Death and Doctor Reefy held her in their arms.

Sophistication

It was early evening of a day in the late fall and the Winesburg County Fair had brought crowds of country people into town. The day had been clear and the night came on warm and pleasant. On the Trunion Pike, where the road after it left town stretched away between berry fields now covered with dry brown leaves, the dust from passing wagons arose in clouds. Children, curled into little balls, slept on the straw scattered on wagon beds. Their hair was full of dust and their fingers black and sticky. The dust rolled away over the fields and the departing sun set it ablaze with colors.

In the main street of Winesburg crowds filled the stores and the sidewalks. Night came on, horses whinnied, the clerks in the stores ran madly about, children became lost and cried lustily, an American town worked terribly at the task of amusing itself.

Pushing his way through the crowds in Main Street, young George Willard concealed himself in the stairway leading to Doctor Reefy's office and looked at the people. With feverish eyes he watched the faces drifting past under the store lights. Thoughts kept coming into his head and he did not want to think. He stamped impatiently on the wooden steps and looked sharply about. "Well, is she going to stay with him all day? Have I done all this waiting for nothing?" he muttered.

George Willard, the Ohio village boy, was fast growing into manhood and new thoughts had been coming into his mind. All that day, amid the jam of people at the Fair, he had gone about feeling lonely. He was about to leave Winesburg to go away to some city where he hoped to get work on a city newspaper and he felt grown up. The mood that had taken possession of him was a thing known to men and unknown to boys. He felt old and a little tired. Memories awoke in him. To his mind his new sense of maturity set him apart, made of him a half-tragic figure. He wanted someone to understand the feeling that had taken possession of him after his mother's death.

There is a time in the life of every boy when he for the first time takes the backward view of life. Perhaps that is the moment when he crosses the line into manhood. The boy is walking through the street of his town. He is thinking of the future and of the figure he will cut in the world. Ambitions and regrets awake within him. Suddenly something happens; he stops under a tree and waits as for a voice calling his name. Ghosts of old things creep into his consciousness; the voices outside of himself whisper a message concerning the limitations of life. From being quite sure of himself and his future he becomes not at all sure. If he be an imaginative boy a door is torn open and for the first time he looks out upon the world, seeing, as though they marched in procession before him, the countless figures of men who before his time have come out of nothingness into the world, lived their lives and again disappeared into nothingness. The sadness of sophistication has come to the boy. With a little gasp he sees himself as merely a leaf blown by the wind through the streets of his village. He knows that in spite of all the stout talk of his fellows he must live and die in uncertainty, a thing blown by the winds, a thing destined like corn to wilt in the sun. He shivers and looks eagerly about. The eighteen years he has lived seem but a moment, a breathing space in the long march of humanity. Already he hears death calling. With all his heart he wants to come close to some other human, touch someone with his hands, be touched by the hand of another.

If he prefers that the other be a woman, that is because he believes that a woman will be gentle, that she will understand. He wants, most of all, understanding.

When the moment of sophistication came to George Willard his mind turned to Helen White, the Winesburg banker's daughter. Always he had been conscious of the girl growing into womanhood as he grew into manhood. Once on a summer night when he was eighteen, he had walked with her on a country road and in her presence had given way to an impulse to boast, to make himself appear big and significant in her eyes. Now he wanted to see her for another purpose. He wanted to tell her of the new impulses that had come to him. He had tried to make her think of him as a man when he knew nothing of manhood and now he wanted to be with her and to try to make her feel the change he believed had taken place in his nature.

As for Helen White, she also had come to a period of change. What George felt, she in her young woman's way felt also. She was no longer a girl and hungered to reach into the grace and beauty of womanhood. She had come home from Cleveland, where she was attending college, to spend a day at the Fair. She also had begun to have memories. During the day she sat in the grand-stand with a young man, one of the instructors from the college, who was a guest of her mother's. The young man was of a pedantic turn of mind and she felt at once he would not do for her purpose. At the Fair she was glad to be seen in his company as he was well dressed and a stranger. She knew that the fact of his presence would create an impression. During the day she was happy, but when night came on she began to grow restless. She wanted to drive the instructor away, to get out of his presence. While they sat together in the grand-stand and while the eyes of former schoolmates were upon them, she paid so much attention to her escort that he grew interested. "A scholar needs money. I should marry a woman with money," he mused.

Helen White was thinking of George Willard even as he wandered gloomily through the crowds thinking of her. She remembered the summer evening when they had walked together and wanted to walk with him again. She thought that the months she had spent in the city, the going to theaters and the seeing of great crowds wandering in lighted thoroughfares, had changed her profoundly. She wanted him to feel and be conscious of the change in her nature.

The summer evening together that had left its mark on the memory of both the young man and woman had, when looked at quite sensibly, been rather stupidly spent. They had walked out of town along a country road. Then they had stopped by a fence near a field of young corn and George had taken off his coat and let it hang on his arm. "Well, I've stayed here in Winesburg—yes—I've not yet gone away but I'm growing up," he had said. "I've been reading books and I've been thinking. I'm going to try to amount to something in life.

"Well," he explained, "that isn't the point. Perhaps I'd better quit talking."

The confused boy put his hand on the girl's arm. His voice trembled. The two started to walk back along the road toward town. In his desperation George boasted, "I'm going to be a big man, the biggest that ever lived here in Winesburg," he declared. "I want you to do something, I don't know what. Perhaps it is none of my business. I want you to try to be different from other women. You see the point. It's none of my business I tell you. I want you to be a beautiful woman. You see what I want."

The boy's voice failed and in silence the two came back into town and went along the street to Helen White's house. At the gate he tried to say something impressive. Speeches he had thought out came into his head, but they seemed utterly pointless. "I thought—I used to think—I had it in my mind you would marry Seth Richmond. Now I know you won't," was all he could find to say as she went through the gate and toward the door of her house.

On the warm fall evening as he stood in the stairway and looked at the crowd drifting through Main Street, George thought of the talk beside the field of young corn and was ashamed of the figure he had made of himself. In the street the people surged up and down like cattle confined in a pen. Buggies and wagons almost filled the narrow thoroughfare. A band played and small boys raced along the sidewalk, diving between the legs of men. Young men with shining red faces walked awkwardly about with girls on their arms. In a room above one of the stores, where a dance was to be held, the fiddlers tuned their instruments. The broken sounds floated down through an open window and out across the murmur of voices and the loud blare of the horns of the band. The medley of sounds got on young Willard's nerves. Everywhere, on all sides, the sense of crowding, moving life closed in about him. He wanted to run away by himself and think. "If she wants to stay with that fellow she may. Why should I care? What difference does it make to me?" he growled and went along Main Street and through Hern's Grocery into a side street.

George felt so utterly lonely and dejected that he wanted to weep but pride made him walk rapidly along, swinging his arms. He came to Wesley Moyer's livery barn and stopped in the shadows to listen to a group of men who talked of a race Wesley's stallion, Tony Tip, had won at the Fair during the afternoon. A crowd had gathered in front of the barn and before the crowd walked Wesley, prancing up and down and boasting. He held a whip in his hand and kept tapping the ground. Little puffs of dust arose in the lamplight. "Hell, quit your talking," Wesley exclaimed. "I wasn't afraid, I knew I had 'em beat all the time. I wasn't afraid."

Ordinarily George Willard would have been intensely interested in the boasting of Moyer, the horseman. Now it made him angry. He turned and hurried away along the street. "Old windbag," he sputtered. "Why does he want to be bragging? Why don't he shut up?"

George went into a vacant lot and, as he hurried along, fell over a pile of rubbish. A nail protruding from an empty barrel tore his trousers. He sat down on the ground and swore. With a pin he mended the torn place and then arose and went on. "I'll go to Helen White's house, that's what I'll do. I'll walk right in. I'll say that I want to see her. I'll walk right in and sit down, that's what I'll do," he declared, climbing over a fence and beginning to run.

On the veranda of Banker White's house Helen was restless and distraught. The instructor sat between the mother and daughter. His talk wearied the girl. Although he had also been raised in an Ohio town, the instructor began to put on the airs of the city. He wanted to appear cosmopolitan. "I like the chance you have given me to study the background out of which most of our girls come," he declared. "It was good of you, Mrs. White, to have me down for the day." He turned to Helen and laughed. "Your life is still bound up with the life of this town?" he asked. "There are people here in whom you are interested?" To the girl his voice sounded pompous and heavy.

Helen arose and went into the house. At the door leading to a garden at the back she stopped and stood listening. Her mother began to talk. "There is no one here fit to associate with a girl of Helen's breeding," she said.

Helen ran down a flight of stairs at the back of the house and into the garden. In the darkness she stopped and stood trembling. It seemed to her that the world was full of meaningless people saying words. Afire with eagerness she ran through a garden gate and, turning a corner by the banker's barn, went into a little side street. "George! Where are you, George?" she cried, filled with nervous excitement. She stopped running, and leaned against a tree to laugh hysterically. Along the dark little street came George Willard, still saying words. "I'm going to walk right into her house. I'll go right in and sit down," he declared as he came up to her. He stopped and stared stupidly. "Come on," he said and took hold of her hand. With hanging heads they walked away along the street under the trees. Dry leaves rustled under foot. Now that he had found her George wondered what he had better do and say.

At the upper end of the Fair Ground, in Winesburg, there is a half decayed old grand-stand. It has never been painted and the boards are all warped out of shape. The Fair Ground stands on top of a low hill rising out of the valley of Wine Creek and from the grand-stand one can see at night, over a cornfield, the lights of the town reflected against the sky.

George and Helen climbed the hill to the Fair Ground, coming by the path past Waterworks Pond. The feeling of loneliness and isolation that had come to the young man in the crowded streets of his town was both broken and intensified by the presence of Helen. What he felt was reflected in her.

In youth there are always two forces fighting in people. The warm unthinking little animal struggles against the thing that reflects and remembers, and the older, the more sophisticated thing had possession of George Willard. Sensing his mood, Helen walked beside him filled with respect. When they got to the grand-stand they climbed up under the roof and sat down on one of the long bench-like seats.

There is something memorable in the experience to be had by going into a fair ground that stands at the edge of a Middle Western town on a night after the annual fair has been held. The sensation is one never to be forgotten. On all sides are ghosts, not of the dead, but of living people. Here, during the day just passed, have come the people pouring in from the town and the country around. Farmers with their wives and children and all the people from the hundreds of little frame houses have gathered within these board walls. Young girls have laughed and men with beards have talked of the affairs of their lives. The place has been filled to overflowing with life. It has itched and squirmed with life and now it is night and the life has all gone away. The silence is almost terrifying. One conceals oneself standing silently beside the trunk of a tree and what there is of a reflective tendency in his nature is intensified. One shudders at the thought of the meaninglessness of life while at the same instant, and if the people of the town are his people, one loves life so intensely that tears come into the eyes.

In the darkness under the roof of the grand-stand, George Willard sat beside Helen White and felt very keenly his own insignificance in the scheme of existence. Now that he had come out of town where the presence of the people stirring about, busy with a multitude of affairs, had been so irritating, the irritation was all gone. The presence of Helen renewed and refreshed him. It was as though her woman's hand was assisting him to make some minute readjustment of the machinery of his life. He began to think of the people in the town where he had always lived with something like reverence. He had reverence for Helen. He wanted to love and to be loved by her, but he did not want at the moment to be confused by her womanhood. In the darkness he took hold of her hand and when she crept close put a hand on her shoulder. A wind began to blow and he shivered. With all his strength he tried to hold and to understand the mood that had come upon him. In that high place in the darkness the two oddly sensitive human atoms held each other tightly and waited. In the mind of each was the same thought. "I have come to this lonely place and here is this other," was the substance of the thing felt.

In Winesburg the crowded day had run itself out into the long night of the late fall. Farm horses jogged away along lonely country roads pulling their portion of weary people. Clerks began to bring samples of goods in off the sidewalks and lock the doors of stores. In the Opera House a crowd had gathered to see a show and further down Main Street the fiddlers, their instruments tuned, sweated and worked to keep the feet of youth flying over a dance floor.

In the darkness in the grand-stand Helen White and George Willard remained silent. Now and then the spell that held them was broken and they turned and tried in the dim light to see into each other's eyes. They kissed but that impulse did not last. At the upper end of the Fair Ground a half dozen men worked over horses that had raced during the afternoon. The men had built a fire and were heating kettles of water. Only their legs could be seen as they passed back and forth in the light. When the wind blew the little flames of the fire danced crazily about.

George and Helen arose and walked away into the darkness. They went along a path past a field of corn that had not yet been cut. The wind whispered among the dry corn blades. For a moment during the walk back into town the spell that held them was broken. When they had come to the crest of Waterworks Hill they stopped by a tree and George again put his hands on the girl's shoulders. She embraced him eagerly and then again they drew quickly back from that impulse. They stopped kissing and stood a little apart. Mutual respect grew big in them. They were both embarrassed and to relieve their embarrassment dropped into the animalism of youth. They laughed and began to pull and haul at each other. In some way chastened and purified by the mood they had been in, they became, not man and woman, not boy and girl, but excited little animals.

It was so they went down the hill. In the darkness they played like two splendid young things in a young world. Once, running swiftly forward, Helen tripped George and he fell. He squirmed and shouted. Shaking with laughter, he rolled down the hill. Helen ran after him. For just a moment she stopped in the darkness. There is no way of knowing what woman's thoughts went through her mind but, when the bottom of the hill was reached and she came up to the boy, she took his arm and walked beside him in dignified silence. For some reason they could not have explained they had both got from their silent evening together the thing needed. Man or boy, woman or girl, they had for a moment taken hold of the thing that makes the mature life of men and women in the modern world possible.

Departure

Young George Willard got out of bed at four in the morning. It was April and the young tree leaves were just coming out of their buds. The trees along the residence streets in Winesburg are maple and the seeds are winged. When the wind blows they whirl crazily about, filling the air and making a carpet underfoot.

George came downstairs into the hotel office carrying a brown leather bag. His trunk was packed for departure. Since two o'clock he had been awake thinking of the journey he was about to take and wondering what he would find at the end of his journey. The boy who slept in the hotel office lay on a cot by the door. His mouth was open and he snored lustily. George crept past the cot and went out into the silent deserted main street. The east was pink with the dawn and long streaks of light climbed into the sky where a few stars still shone.

Beyond the last house on Trunion Pike in Winesburg there is a great stretch of open fields. The fields are owned by farmers who live in town and drive homeward at evening along Trunion Pike in light creaking wagons. In the fields are planted berries and small fruits. In the late afternoon in the hot summers when the road and the fields are covered with dust, a smoky haze lies over the great flat basin of land.

To look across it is like looking out across the sea. In the spring when the land is green the effect is somewhat different. The land becomes a wide green billiard table on which tiny human insects toil up and down.

All through his boyhood and young manhood George Willard had been in the habit of walking on Trunion Pike. He had been in the midst of the great open place on winter nights when it was covered with snow and only the moon looked down at him; he had been there in the fall when bleak winds blew and on summer evenings when the air vibrated with the song of insects. On the April morning he wanted to go there again, to walk again in the silence. He did walk to where the road dipped down by a little stream two miles from town and then turned and walked silently back again. When he got to Main Street clerks were sweeping the sidewalks before the stores. "Hey, you George. How does it feel to be going away?" they asked.

The westbound train leaves Winesburg at seven forty-five in the morning. Tom Little is conductor. His train runs from Cleveland to where it connects with a great trunk line railroad with terminals in Chicago and New York. Tom has what in railroad circles is called an "easy run." Every evening he returns to his family. In the fall and spring he spends his Sundays fishing in Lake Erie. He has a round red face and small blue eyes. He knows the people in the towns along his railroad better than a city man knows the people who live in his apartment building.

George came down the little incline from the New Willard House at seven o'clock. Tom Willard carried his bag. The son had become taller than the father.

On the station platform everyone shook the young man's hand. More than a dozen people waited about. Then they talked of their own affairs. Even Will Henderson, who was lazy and often slept until nine, had got out of bed. George was embarrassed. Gertrude Wilmot, a tall thin woman of fifty who worked in the Winesburg post office, came along the station platform. She had never before paid any attention to George. Now she stopped and put out her hand. In two words she voiced what everyone felt. "Good luck," she said sharply and then turning went on her way.

When the train came into the station George felt relieved. He scampered hurriedly aboard. Helen White came running along Main Street hoping to have a parting word with him, but he had found a seat and did not see her. When the train started Tom Little punched his ticket, grinned and, although he knew George well and knew on what adventure he was just setting out, made no comment. Tom had seen a thousand George Willards go out of their towns to the city. It was a commonplace enough incident with him. In the smoking car there was a man who had just invited Tom to go on a fishing trip to Sandusky Bay. He wanted to accept the invitation and talk over details.

George glanced up and down the car to be sure no one was looking, then took out his pocketbook and counted his money. His mind was occupied with a desire not to appear green. Almost the last words his father had said to him concerned the matter of his behavior when he got to the city. "Be a sharp one," Tom Willard had said. "Keep your eyes on your money. Be awake. That's the ticket. Don't let anyone think you're a greenhorn."

After George counted his money he looked out of the window and was surprised to see that the train was still in Winesburg.

The young man, going out of his town to meet the adventure of life, began to think but he did not think of anything very big or dramatic. Things like his mother's death, his departure from Winesburg, the uncertainty of his future life in the city, the serious and larger aspects of his life did not come into his mind.

He thought of little things—Turk Smollet wheeling boards through the main street of his town in the morning, a tall woman, beautifully gowned, who had once stayed overnight at his father's hotel, Butch Wheeler the lamp lighter of Winesburg hurrying through the streets on a summer evening and holding a torch in his hand, Helen White standing by a window in the Winesburg post office and putting a stamp on an envelope.

The young man's mind was carried away by his growing passion for dreams. One looking at him would not have thought him particularly sharp. With the recollection of little things occupying his mind he closed his eyes and leaned back in the car seat. He stayed that way for a long time and when he aroused himself and again looked out of the car window the town of Winesburg had disappeared and his life there had become but a background on which to paint the dreams of his manhood.

From

POOR WHITE

EDITOR'S NOTE

Poor White was first published in 1920. In his introduction to The Modern Library edition of the book (1925) Anderson wrote of how he conceived its characters while he was on the deck of a ship in the Gulf of Mexico; as he describes their arrival in his imagination, one is reminded of Edgar Lee Masters' description of how the people in his *Spoon River Anthology* came to life, interrupting the conduct of his affairs in his law office in Chicago. Both Masters and Anderson possessed strong historical imaginations, and each re-created in his own fashion the cultural life of the Middle West as it existed between the decade following the Civil War and 1900.

Of Anderson's seven novels, *Poor White* and *Dark Laughter* represent him writing at the height of his narrative style, but *Poor White* is richer in texture than *Dark Laughter,* and with its evocation of an American past already into the twentieth century has more to say to a present generation of readers. In that sense *Poor White* reintroduces the readers of the present mid-century to relatives of their ancestors, and readers will rediscover them, not as they are seen in faded photographs and formal portraits, but as active men and women whose emotions and ideas were shaped by the transition from agrarian to industrial civilization.

The following pages are excerpts from the novel, and the first tells of its hero's "poor white" origins.

Selections from "Poor White"

Hugh McVey was born in a little hole of a town stuck on a mud bank on the western shore of the Mississippi River in the State of Missouri. It was a miserable place in which to be born. With the exception of a narrow strip of black mud along the river, the land for ten miles back from the town—called in derision by river men "Mudcat Landing"—was almost entirely worthless and unproductive. The soil, yellow, shallow and stony, was tilled, in Hugh's time, by a race of long gaunt men who seemed as exhausted and no-account as the land on which they lived. They were chronically discouraged, and the merchants and artisans of the town were in the same state. The merchants, who ran their stores—poor tumble-down ramshackle affairs—on the credit system, could not get pay for the goods they handed out over their counters and the artisans, the shoemakers, carpenters and harnessmakers, could not get pay for the work they did. Only the town's two saloons prospered. The saloon keepers sold their wares for cash and, as the men of the town and the farmers who drove into town felt that without drink life was unbearable, cash always could be found for the purpose of getting drunk.

Hugh McVey's father, John McVey, had been a farm hand in his youth but before Hugh was born had moved into town to find employment in a tannery. The tannery ran for a year or two and then failed, but John McVey stayed in town. He also became a drunkard. It was the easy obvious thing for him to do. During the time of his employment in the tannery he had been married and his son had been born. Then his wife died and the idle workman took his child and went to live in a tiny fishing shack by the river. How the boy lived through the next few years no one ever knew. John McVey loitered in the streets and on the river bank and only awakened out of his habitual stupor when, driven by hunger or the craving for drink, he went for a day's work in some farmer's field at harvest time or joined a number of other idlers for an adventurous trip down river on a lumber raft. The baby was left shut up in the shack by the river or carried about wrapped in a soiled blanket. Soon after he was old enough to walk he was compelled to find work in order that he might eat. The boy of ten went listlessly about town at the heels of his father. The two found work, which the boy did while the man lay sleeping in the sun. They cleaned cisterns, swept out stores and saloons and at night went with a wheelbarrow and a box to remove and dump in the river the contents of outhouses. At fourteen Hugh was as tall as his father and almost without education. He could read a little and could write his own name, had picked up these accomplishments from other boys who came to fish with him in the river, but he had never been to school. For days sometimes he did nothing but lie half asleep in the shade of a bush on the river bank. The fish he caught on his more industrious days he sold for a few cents to some housewife, and thus got money to buy food for his big growing indolent body. Like an animal that has come to its maturity he turned away from his father, not because of resentment for his hard youth, but because he thought it time to begin to go his own way.

In his fourteenth year and when the boy was on the point of sinking into the sort of animal-like stupor in which his father had lived, something happened to him. A railroad pushed its way down along the river to his town and he got a job as man of all work for the station master. He swept out the station, put trunks on trains, mowed the grass in the station yard and helped in a hundred odd ways the man who held the combined jobs of ticket seller, baggage master and telegraph operator at the little out-of-the-way place.

Hugh began a little to awaken. He lived with his employer, Henry Shepard, and his wife, Sarah Shepard, and for the first time in his life sat down regularly at table. His life, lying on the river bank through long summer afternoons or sitting perfectly still for endless hours in a boat, had bred in him a dreamy detached outlook on life. He found it hard to be definite and to do definite things, but for all his stupidity the boy had a great store of patience, a heritage perhaps from his mother. In his new place the station master's wife, Sarah Shepard, a sharp-tongued, good-natured woman, who hated the town and the people among whom fate had thrown her, scolded at him all day long. She treated him like a child of six, told him how to sit at table, how to hold his fork when he ate, how to address people who came to the house or to the station. The mother in her was aroused by Hugh's helplessness and, having no children of her own, she began to take the tall awkward boy to her heart. She was a small woman and when she stood in the house scolding the great stupid boy who stared down at her with his small perplexed eyes, the two made a picture that afforded endless amusement to her husband, a short fat bald-headed man who went about clad in blue overalls and a blue cotton shirt. Coming to the back door of his house, that was within a stone's throw of the station, Henry Shepard stood with his hand on the doorjamb and watched the woman and the boy. Above the scolding voice of the woman his own voice arose. "Look out, Hugh," he called. "Be on the jump, lad! Perk yourself up. She'll be biting you if you don't go mighty careful in there."

Hugh got little money for his work at the railroad station but for the first time in his life he began to fare well. Henry Shepard bought the boy clothes, and his wife, Sarah, who was a master of the art of cooking, loaded the table with good things to eat. Hugh ate until both the man and woman declared he would burst if he did not stop. Then when they were not looking he went into the station yard and crawling under a bush went to sleep. The station master came to look for him. He cut a switch from the bush and began to beat the boy's bare feet. Hugh awoke and was overcome with confusion. He got to his feet and stood trembling, half afraid he was to be driven away from his new home. The man and the confused blushing boy confronted each other for a moment and then the man adopted the method of his wife and began to scold. He was annoyed at what he thought the boy's indolence and found a hundred little tasks for him to do. He devoted himself to finding tasks for Hugh, and when he could think of no new ones, invented them. "We will have to keep the big lazy fellow on the jump. That's the secret of things," he said to his wife.

The boy learned to keep his naturally indolent body moving and his clouded sleepy mind fixed on definite things. For hours he plodded straight ahead, doing over and over some appointed task. He forgot the purpose of the job he had been given to do and did it because it was a job and would keep him awake. One morning he was told to sweep the station platform and as his employer had gone away without giving him additional tasks and as he was afraid that if he sat down he would fall into the odd detached kind of stupor in which he had spent so large a part of his life, he continued to sweep for two or three hours. The station platform was built of rough boards and Hugh's arms were very powerful. The broom he was using began to go to pieces. Bits of it flew about and after an hour's work the platform looked more uncleanly than when he began. Sarah Shepard came to the door of her house and stood watching. She was about to call to him and to scold him again for his stupidity when a new impulse came to her. She saw the serious determined look on the boy's long gaunt face and a flash of understanding came to her. Tears came into her eyes and her arms ached to take the great boy and hold him tightly against her breast. With all her mother's soul she wanted to protect Hugh from a world she was sure would treat him always as a beast of burden and would take no account of what she thought of as the handicap of his birth. Her morning's work was done and without saying anything to Hugh, who continued to go up and down the platform laboriously sweeping, she went out at the front door of the house and to one of the town stores. There she bought a half dozen books, a geography, an arithmetic, a speller and two or three readers. She had made up her mind to become Hugh McVey's school teacher and with characteristic energy did not put the matter off, but went about it at once. When she got back to her house and saw the boy still going doggedly up and down the platform, she did not scold but spoke to him with a new gentleness in her manner. "Well, my boy, you may put the broom away now and come to the house," she suggested. "I've made up my mind to take you for my own boy and I don't want to be ashamed of you. If you're going to live with me I can't have you growing up to be a lazy good-for-nothing like your father and the other men in this hole of a place. You'll have to learn things and I suppose I'll have to be your teacher.

"Come on over to the house at once," she added sharply, making a quick motion with her hand to the boy who with the broom in his hands stood stupidly staring. "When a job is to be done there's no use putting it off. It's going to be hard work to make an educated man of you, but it has to be done. We might as well begin on your lessons at once."

Hugh McVey lived with Henry Shepard and his wife until he became a grown man. After Sarah Shepard became his school teacher things began to go better for him. The scolding of the New England woman, that had but accentuated his awkwardness and stupidity, came to an end and life in his adopted home became so quiet and peaceful that the boy thought of himself as one who had come into a kind of paradise. For a time the two older people talked of sending him to the town school, but the woman objected. She had begun to feel so close to Hugh that he seemed a part of her own flesh and blood and the thought of him, so huge and ungainly, sitting in a schoolroom with the children of the town, annoyed and irritated her. In imagination she saw him being laughed at by other boys and could not bear the thought. She did not like the people of the town and did not want Hugh to associate with them.

Sarah Shepard had come from a people and a country quite different in its aspect from that in which she now lived. Her own people, frugal New Englanders, had come west in the year after the Civil War to take up cut-over timber land in the southern end of the State of Michigan. The daughter was a grown girl when her father and mother took up the westward journey, and after they arrived at the new home, had worked with her father in the fields. The land was covered with huge stumps and was difficult to farm but the New Englanders were accustomed to difficulties and were not discouraged. The land was deep and rich and the people who had settled upon it were poor but hopeful. They felt that every day of hard work done in clearing the land was like laying up treasure against the future. In New England they had fought against a hard climate and had managed to find a living on stony unproductive soil. The milder climate and the rich deep soil of Michigan was, they felt, full of promise. Sarah's father like most of his neighbors had gone into debt for his land and for tools with which to clear and work it and every year spent most of his earnings in paying interest on a mortgage held by a banker in a nearby town, but that did not discourage him. He whistled as he went about his work and spoke often of a future of ease and plenty. "In a few years and when the land is cleared we'll make money hand over fist," he declared.

When Sarah grew into young womanhood and went about among the young people in the new country, she heard much talk of mortgages and of the difficulty of making ends meet, but everyone spoke of the hard conditions as temporary. In every mind the future was bright with promise. Throughout the whole Mid-American country, in Ohio, Northern Indiana and Illinois, Wisconsin and Iowa a hopeful spirit prevailed. In every breast hope fought a successful war with poverty and discouragement. Optimism got into the blood of the children and later led to the same kind of hopeful courageous development of the whole western country. The sons and daughters of these hardy people no doubt had their minds too steadily fixed on the problem of the paying off of mortgages and getting on in the world, but there was courage in them. If they, with the frugal and sometimes niggardly New Englanders from whom they were sprung, have given modern American life a too material flavor, they have at least created a land in which a less determinedly materialistic people may in their turn live in comfort.

In the midst of the little hopeless community of beaten men and yellow defeated women on the bank of the Mississippi River, the woman who had become Hugh McVey's second mother and in whose veins flowed the blood of the pioneers, felt herself undefeated and unbeatable. She and her husband would, she felt, stay in the Missouri town for a while and then move on to a larger town and a better position in life. They would move on and up until the little fat man was a railroad president or a millionaire. It was the way things were done. She had no doubt of the future. "Do everything well," she said to her husband, who was perfectly satisfied with his position in life and had no exalted notions as to his future. "Remember to make your reports out neatly and clearly. Show them you can do perfectly the task given you to do, and you will be given a chance at a larger task. Some day when you least expect it something will happen. You will be called up into a position of power. We won't be compelled to stay in this hole of a place very long."

The ambitious energetic little woman, who had taken the son of the indolent farm hand to her heart, constantly talked to him of her own people. Every afternoon when her housework was done she took the boy into the front room of the house and spent hours laboring with him over his lessons. She worked upon the problem of rooting the stupidity and dullness out of his mind as her father had worked at the problem of rooting the stumps out of the Michigan land. After the lesson for the day had been gone over and over until Hugh was in a stupor of mental weariness, she put the books aside and talked to him. With glowing fervor she made for him a picture of her own youth and the people and places where she had lived. In the picture she represented the New Englanders of the Michigan farming community as a strong godlike race, always honest, always frugal, and always pushing ahead. His own people she utterly condemned. She pitied him for the blood in his veins. The boy had then and all his life certain physical difficulties she could never understand. The blood did not flow freely through his long body. His feet and hands were always cold and there was for him an almost sensual satisfaction to be had from just lying perfectly still in the station yard and letting the hot sun beat down on him.

Sarah Shepard looked upon what she called Hugh's laziness as a thing of the spirit. "You have got to get over it," she declared. "Look at your own people—poor white trash—how lazy and shiftless they are. You can't be like them. It's a sin to be so dreamy and worthless."

Swept along by the energetic spirit of the woman, Hugh fought to overcome his inclination to give himself up to vaporous dreams. He became convinced that his own people were really of inferior stock, that they were to be kept away from and not to be taken into account. During the first year after he came to live with the Shepards, he sometimes gave way to a desire to return to his old lazy life with his father in the shack by the river. People got off steamboats at the town and took the train to other towns lying back from the river. He earned a little money by carrying trunks filled with clothes or traveling men's samples up an incline from the steamboat landing to the railroad station. Even at fourteen the strength in his long gaunt body was so great that he could outlift any man in town, and he put one of the trunks on his shoulder and walked slowly and stolidly away with it as a farm horse might have walked along a country road with a boy of six perched on his back.

The money earned in this way Hugh for a time gave to his father, and when the man had become stupid with drink he grew quarrelsome and demanded that the boy return to live with him. Hugh had not the spirit to refuse and sometimes did not want to refuse. When neither the station master nor his wife was about he slipped away and went with his father to sit for a half day with his back against the wall of the fishing shack, his soul at peace. In the sunlight he sat and stretched forth his long legs. His small sleepy eyes stared out over the river. A delicious feeling crept over him and for the moment he thought of himself as completely happy and made up his mind that he did not want to return again to the railroad station and to the woman who was so determined to arouse him and make of him a man of her own people.

Hugh looked at his father asleep and snoring in the long grass on the river bank. An odd feeling of disloyalty crept over him and he became uncomfortable. The man's mouth was open and he snored lustily. From his greasy and threadbare clothing arose the smell of fish. Flies gathered in swarms and alighted on his face. Disgust took possession of Hugh. A flickering but ever recurring light came into his eyes. With all the strength of his awakening soul he struggled against the desire to give way to the inclination to stretch himself out beside the man and sleep. The words of the New England woman, who was, he knew, striving to lift him out of slothfulness and ugliness into some brighter and better way of life, echoed dimly in his mind. When he arose and went back along the street to the station master's house and when the woman there looked at him reproachfully and muttered words about the poor white trash of the town, he was ashamed and looked at the floor.

Hugh began to hate his own father and his own people. He connected the man who had bred him with the dreaded inclination toward sloth in himself. When the farm hand came to the station and demanded the money he had earned by carrying trunks, he turned away and went across a dusty road to the Shepards' house. After a year or two he paid no more attention to the dissolute farm hand who came occasionally to the station to mutter and swear at him; and, when he had earned a little money, gave it to the woman to keep for him. "Well," he said, speaking slowly and with the hesitating drawl characteristic of his people, "if you give me time I'll learn. I want to be what you want me to be. If you stick to me I'll try to make a man of myself."

Hugh McVey lived in the Missouri town under the tutelage of Sarah Shepard until he was nineteen years old. Then the station master gave up railroading and went back to Michigan. Sarah Shepard's father had died after having cleared one hundred and twenty acres of the cut-over timber land and it had been left to her. The dream that had for years lurked in the back of the little woman's mind and in which she saw bald-headed, good-natured Henry Shepard become a power in the railroad world had begun to fade. In newspapers and magazines she read constantly of other men who, starting from a humble position in the railroad service, soon became rich and powerful, but nothing of the kind seemed likely to happen to her husband. Under her watchful eye he did his work well and carefully but nothing came of it. Officials of the railroad sometimes passed through the town riding in private cars hitched to the end of one of the through trains, but the trains did not stop and the officials did not alight and, calling Henry out of the station, reward his faithfulness by piling new responsibilities upon him, as railroad officials did in such cases in the stories she read. When her father died and she saw a chance to again turn her face eastward and to live again among her own people, she told her husband to resign his position with the air of one accepting an undeserved defeat. The station master managed to get Hugh appointed in his place, and the two people went away one gray morning in October, leaving the tall ungainly young man in charge of affairs. He had books to keep, freight waybills to make out, messages to receive, dozens of definite things to do. Early in the morning before the train that was to take her away came to the station, Sarah Shepard called the young man to her and repeated the instructions she had so often given her husband. "Do everything neatly and carefully," she said. "Show yourself worthy of the trust that has been given you."

The New England woman wanted to assure the boy, as she had so often assured her husband, that if he would but work hard and faithfully promotion would inevitably come; but in the face of the fact that Henry Shepard had for years done without criticism the work Hugh was to do and had received neither praise nor blame from those above him, she found it impossible to say the words that arose to her lips. The woman and the son of the people among whom she had lived for five years and had so often condemned, stood beside each other in embarrassed silence. Stripped of her assurance as to the purpose of life and unable to repeat her accustomed formula, Sarah Shepard had nothing to say. Hugh's tall figure, leaning against the post that supported the roof of the front porch of the little house where she had taught him his lessons day after day, seemed to her suddenly old and she thought his long solemn face suggested a wisdom older and more mature than her own. An odd revulsion of feeling swept over her. For the moment she began to doubt the advisability of trying to be smart and to get on in life. If Hugh had been somewhat smaller of frame so that her mind could have taken hold of the fact of his youth and immaturity, she would no doubt have taken him into her arms and said words regarding her doubts. Instead she also became silent and the minutes slipped away as the two people stood before each other and stared at the floor of the porch. When the train on which she was to leave blew a warning whistle, and Henry Shepard called to her from the station platform, she put a hand on the lapel of Hugh's coat and drawing his face down, for the first time kissed him on the cheek. Tears came into her eyes and into the eyes of the young man. When he stepped across the porch to get her bag Hugh stumbled awkwardly against a chair. "Well, you do the best you can here," Sarah Shepard said quickly and then out of long habit and half unconsciously did repeat her formula. "Do little things well and big opportunities are bound to come," she declared as she walked briskly along beside Hugh across the narrow road and to the station and the train that was to bear her away.

After the departure of Sarah and Henry Shepard Hugh

continued to struggle with his inclination to give way to dreams. It seemed to him a struggle it was necessary to win in order that he might show his respect and appreciation of the woman who had spent so many long hours laboring with him. Although, under her tutelage, he had received a better education than any other young man of the river town, he had lost none of his physical desire to sit in the sun and do nothing. When he worked, every task had to be consciously carried on from minute to minute. After the woman left, there were days when he sat in the chair in the telegraph office and fought a desperate battle with himself. A queer determined light shone in his small gray eyes. He arose from the chair and walked up and down the station platform. Each time as he lifted one of his long feet and set it slowly down a special little effort had to be made. To move about at all was a painful performance, something he did not want to do. All physical acts were to him dull but necessary parts of his training for a vague and glorious future that was to come to him some day in a brighter and more beautiful land that lay in the direction thought of rather indefinitely as the East. "If I do not move and keep moving I'll become like father, like all the people about here," Hugh said to himself. He thought of the man who had bred him and whom he occasionally saw drifting aimlessly along Main Street or sleeping away a drunken stupor on the river bank. He was disgusted with him and had come to share the opinion the station master's wife had always held concerning the people of the Missouri village. "They're a lot of miserable lazy louts," she had declared a thousand times, and Hugh agreed with her, but sometimes wondered if in the end he might not also become a lazy lout. That possibility he knew was in him and for the sake of the woman as well as for his own sake he was determined it should not be so.

[*The story of Hugh McVey's rise as an inventor in the town of Bidwell, Ohio.*]

As for Hugh McVey, he stayed in his home town and among

his own people for a year after the departure of the man and
woman who had been father and mother to him, and then
he also departed. All through the year he worked constantly
to cure himself of the curse of indolence. When he awoke in
the morning he did not dare lie in bed for a moment for fear
indolence would overcome him and he would not be able to
arise at all. Getting out of bed at once he dressed and went
to the station. During the day there was not much work to be
done and he walked for hours up and down the station platform. When he sat down he at once took up a book and put his
mind to work. When the pages of the book became indistinct
before his eyes and he felt within him the inclination to drift
off into dreams, he again arose and walked up and down the
platform. Having accepted the New England woman's opinion
of his own people and not wanting to associate with them his
life became utterly lonely and his loneliness also drove him
to labor.

Something happened to him. Although his body would not
and never did become active, his mind began suddenly to work
with feverish eagerness. The vague thoughts and feelings that
had always been a part of him but that had been indefinite,
ill-defined things, like clouds floating far away in a hazy sky,
began to grow definite. In the evening after his work was done
and he had locked the station for the night, he did not go to
the town hotel where he had taken a room and where he ate
his meals, but wandered about town and along the road that
ran south beside the great mysterious river. A hundred new
and definite desires and hungers awoke in him. He began to
want to talk with people, to know men and most of all to
know women, but the disgust for his fellows in the town,
engendered in him by Sarah Shephard's words and most of
all by the things in his nature that were like their natures,
made him draw back. When in the fall at the end of the year
after the Shepards had left and he began living alone, his
father was killed in a senseless quarrel with a drunken river
man over the ownership of a dog, a sudden, and what seemed
to him at the moment heroic, resolution came to him. He
went early one morning to one of the town's two saloon

keepers, a man who had been his father's nearest approach to a friend and companion, and gave him money to bury the dead man. Then he wired to the headquarters of the railroad company telling them to send a man to Mudcat Landing to take his place. On the afternoon of the day on which his father was buried, he bought himself a handbag and packed his few belongings. Then he sat down alone on the steps of the railroad station to wait for the evening train that would bring the man who was to replace him and that would at the same time take him away. He did not know where he intended to go, but knew that he wanted to push out into a new land and get among new people. He thought he would go east and north. He remembered the long summer evenings in the river town when the station master slept and his wife talked. The boy who listened had wanted to sleep also, but with the eyes of Sarah Shepard fixed on him, had not dared to do so. The woman had talked of a land dotted with towns where the houses were all painted in bright colors, where young girls dressed in white dresses went about in the evening, walking under trees beside streets paved with bricks. where there was no dust or mud, where stores were gay bright places filled with beautiful wares that the people had money to buy in abundance and where everyone was alive and doing things worth while and none was slothful and lazy. The boy who had now become a man wanted to go to such a place. His work in the railroad station had given him some idea of the geography of the country and, although he could not have told whether the woman who had talked so enticingly had in mind her childhood in New England or her girlhood in Michigan, he knew in a general way that to reach the land and the people who were to show him by their lives the better way to form his own life, he must go east. He decided that the further east he went the more beautiful life would become, and that he had better not try going too far in the beginning. "I'll go into the northern part of Indiana or Ohio," he told himself. "There must be beautiful towns in those places."

Hugh was boyishly eager to get on his way and to become at once a part of the life in a new place. The gradual awakening of his mind had given him courage, and he thought of himself as armed and ready for association with men. He wanted to become acquainted with and be the friend of people whose lives were beautifully lived and who were themselves beautiful and full of significance. As he sat on the steps of the railroad station in the poor little Missouri town with his bag beside him, and thought of all the things he wanted to do in life, his mind became so eager and restless that some of its restlessness was transmitted to his body. For perhaps the first time in his life he arose without conscious effort and walked up and down the station platform out of an excess of energy. He thought he could not bear to wait until the train came and brought the man who was to take his place. "Well, I'm going away, I'm going away to be a man among men," he said to himself over and over. The saying became a kind of refrain and he said it unconsciously. As he repeated the words his heart beat high in anticipation of the future he thought lay before him.

CHAPTER II

Hugh McVey left the town of Mudcat Landing in early September of the year eighteen eighty-six. He was then twenty years old and was six feet and four inches tall. The whole upper part of his body was immensely strong but his long legs were ungainly and lifeless. He secured a pass from the railroad company that had employed him, and rode north along the river in the night train until he came to a large town named Burlington in the State of Iowa. There a bridge went over the river, and the railroad tracks joined those of a trunk line and ran eastward toward Chicago; but Hugh did not continue his journey on that night. Getting off the train he went to a nearby hotel and took a room for the night.

It was a cool clear evening and Hugh was restless. The town of Burlington, a prosperous place in the midst of a rich farming country, overwhelmed him with its stir and bustle. For the first time he saw brick-paved streets and streets lighted with lamps. Although it was nearly ten o'clock at night when he arrived, people still walked about in the streets and many stores were open.

The hotel where he had taken a room faced the railroad tracks and stood at the corner of a brightly lighted street. When he had been shown to his room Hugh sat for a half hour by an open window, and then as he could not sleep, decided to go for a walk. For a time he walked in the streets where the people stood about before the doors of the stores but, as his tall figure attracted attention and he felt people staring at him, he went presently into a side street.

In a few minutes he became utterly lost. He went through what seemed to him miles of streets lined with frame and brick houses, and occasionally passed people, but was too timid and embarrassed to ask his way. The street climbed upward and after a time he got into open country and followed a road that ran along a cliff overlooking the Mississippi River. The night was clear and the sky brilliant with stars. In the open, away from the multitude of houses, he no longer felt awkward and afraid, and went cheerfully along. After a time he stopped and stood facing the river. Standing on a high cliff and with a grove of trees at his back, the stars seemed to have all gathered in the eastern sky. Below him the water of the river reflected the stars. They seemed to be making a pathway for him into the East.

The tall Missouri countryman sat down on a log near the edge of the cliff and tried to see the water in the river below. Nothing was visible but a bed of stars that danced and twinkled in the darkness. He had made his way to a place far above the railroad bridge, but presently a through passenger train from the West passed over it and the lights of the train looked also like stars, stars that moved and beckoned and that seemed to fly like flocks of birds out of the West into the East.

For several hours Hugh sat on the log in the darkness. He decided that it was hopeless for him to find his way back to the hotel, and was glad of the excuse for staying abroad. His body for the first time in his life felt light and strong and his mind was feverishly awake. A buggy in which sat a young man and woman went along the road at his back, and after the voices had died away silence came, broken only at long intervals during the hours when he sat thinking of his future by the barking of a dog in some distant house or the churning of the paddle wheels of a passing river boat.

All of the early formative years of Hugh McVey's life had been spent within sound of the lapping of the waters of the Mississippi River. He had seen it in the hot summer when the water receded and the mud lay baked and cracked along the edge of the water; in the spring when the floods raged and the water went whirling past, bearing tree logs and even parts of houses; in the winter when the water looked deathly cold and ice floated past; and in the fall when it was quiet and still and lovely, and seemed to have sucked an almost human quality of warmth out of the red trees that lined its shores. Hugh had spent hours and days sitting or lying in the grass beside the river. The fishing shack in which he had lived with his father until he was fourteen years old was within a half dozen long strides of the river's edge, and the boy had often been left there alone for a week at a time. When his father had gone for a trip on a lumber raft or to work for a few days on some farm in the country back from the river, the boy, left often without money and with but a few loaves of bread, went fishing when he was hungry and when he was not did nothing but idle the days away in the grass on the river bank. Boys from the town came sometimes to spend an hour with him, but in their presence he was embarrassed and a little annoyed. He wanted to be left alone with his dreams. One of the boys, a sickly, pale, undeveloped lad of ten, often stayed with him through an entire summer afternoon. He was the son of a merchant in the town and grew quickly tired when he tried to follow other boys about. On the river bank he lay beside Hugh in silence. The two got into Hugh's boat and went fishing and the merchant's son grew animated and talked. He taught Hugh to write his own name and to read a few words. The shyness that kept them apart had begun to break down, when the merchant's son caught some childhood disease and died.

In the darkness above the cliff that night in Burlington Hugh remembered things concerning his boyhood that had not come back to his mind in years. The very thoughts that had passed through his mind during those long days of idling on the river bank came streaming back.

After his fourteenth year when he went to work at the railroad station Hugh had stayed away from the river. With his work at the station, and in the garden back of Sarah Shepard's house, and the lessons in the afternoons, he had little idle time. On Sundays however things were different. Sarah Shepard did not go to church after she came to Mudcat Landing, but she would have no work done on Sundays. On Sunday afternoons in the summer she and her husband sat in chairs beneath a tree beside the house and went to sleep. Hugh got into the habit of going off by himself. He wanted to sleep also, but did not dare. He went along the river bank by the road that ran south from the town, and when he had followed it two or three miles, turned into a grove of trees and lay down in the shade.

The long summer Sunday afternoons had been delightful times for Hugh, so delightful that he finally gave them up, fearing they might lead him to take up again his old sleepy way of life. Now as he sat in the darkness above the same river he had gazed on through the long Sunday afternoons, a spasm of something like loneliness swept over him. For the first time he thought about leaving the river country and going into a new land with a keen feeling of regret.

On the Sunday afternoons in the woods south of Mudcat Landing Hugh had lain perfectly still in the grass for hours. The smell of dead fish that had always been present about the shack where he spent his boyhood, was gone and there were no swarms of flies. Above his head a breeze played through the branches of the trees, and insects sang in the grass. Everything about him was clean. A lovely stillness pervaded the river and the woods. He lay on his belly and gazed down over the river out of sleep-heavy eyes into hazy distances. Half-formed thoughts passed like visions through his mind. He dreamed, but his dreams were unformed and vaporous. For hours the half-dead, half-alive state into which he had got, persisted. He did not sleep but lay in a land between sleeping and waking. Pictures formed in his mind. The clouds that floated in the sky above the river took on strange, grotesque shapes. They began to move. One of the clouds separated itself from the others. It moved swiftly away into the dim distance and then returned. It became a half-human thing and seemed to be marshaling the other clouds. Under its influence they became agitated and moved restlessly about. Out of the body of the most active of the clouds long vaporous arms were extended. They pulled and hauled at the other clouds making them also restless and agitated.

Hugh's mind, as he sat in the darkness on the cliff above the river that night in Burlington, was deeply stirred. Again he was a boy lying in the woods above his river, and the visions that had come to him there returned with startling clearness. He got off the log and lying in the wet grass, closed his eyes. His body became warm.

Hugh thought his mind had gone out of his body and up into the sky to join the clouds and the stars, to play with them. From the sky he thought he looked down on the earth and saw rolling fields, hills and forests. He had no part in the lives of the men and women of the earth, but was torn away from them, left to stand by himself. From his place in the sky above the earth he saw the great river going majestically along. For a time it was quiet and contemplative as the sky had been when he was a boy down below lying on his belly in the wood. He saw men pass in boats and could hear their voices dimly. A great quiet prevailed and he looked abroad beyond the wide expanse of the river and saw fields and towns. They were all hushed and still. An air of waiting hung over them. And then the river was whipped into action by some strange unknown force, something that had come out of a distant place, out of the place to which the cloud had gone and from which it had returned to stir and agitate the other clouds.

The river now went tearing along. It overflowed its banks and swept over the land, uprooting trees and forests and towns. The white faces of drowned men and children, borne along by the flood, looked up into the mind's eye of the man Hugh, who, in the moment of his setting out into the definite world of struggle and defeat, had let himself slip back into the vaporous dreams of his boyhood.

As he lay in the wet grass in the darkness on the cliff Hugh tried to force his way back to consciousness, but for a long time was unsuccessful. He rolled and writhed about and his lips muttered words. It was useless. His mind also was swept away. The clouds of which he felt himself a part flew across the face of the sky. They blotted out the sun from the earth, and darkness descended on the land, on the troubled towns, on the hills that were torn open, on the forests that were destroyed, on the peace and quiet of all places. In the country stretching away from the river where all had been peace and quiet, all was now agitation and unrest. Houses were destroyed and instantly rebuilt. People gathered in whirling crowds.

The dreaming man felt himself a part of something significant and terrible that was happening to the earth and to the peoples of the earth. Again he struggled to awake, to force himself back out of the dream world into consciousness. When he did awake, day was breaking and he sat on the very edge of the cliff that looked down upon the Mississippi River, gray now in the dim morning light.

The towns in which Hugh lived during the first three years after he began his eastward journey were all small places containing a few hundred people, and were scattered through Illinois, Indiana and Western Ohio. All of the people among whom he worked and lived during that time were farmers and laborers. In the spring of the first year of his wandering he passed through the city of Chicago and spent two hours there, going in and out at the same railroad station.

He was not tempted to become a city man. The huge commercial city at the foot of Lake Michigan, because of its commanding position in the very center of a vast farming empire, had already become gigantic. He never forgot the two hours he spent standing in the station in the heart of the city and walking in the street adjoining the station. It was evening when he came into the roaring, clanging place. On the long wide plains west of the city he saw farmers at work with their spring plowing as the train went flying along. Presently the farms grew small and the whole prairie dotted with towns. In these the train did not stop but ran into a crowded network of streets filled with multitudes of people. When he got into the big dark station Hugh saw thousands of people rushing about like disturbed insects. Unnumbered thousands of people were going out of the city at the end of their day of work and trains waited to take them to towns on the prairies. They came in droves, hurrying along like distraught cattle, over a bridge and into the station. The inbound crowds that had alighted from through trains coming from cities of the East and West climbed up a stairway to the street, and those that were outbound tried to descend by the same stairway and at the same time. The result was a whirling churning mass of humanity. Everyone pushed and crowded his way along. Men swore, women grew angry, and children cried. Near the doorway that opened into the street a long line of cab drivers shouted and roared.

Hugh looked at the people who were whirled along past him, and shivered with the nameless fear of multitudes, common to country boys in the city. When the rush of people had a little subsided he went out of the station and, walking across a narrow street, stood by a brick store building. Presently the rush of people began again, and again men, women, and boys came hurrying across the bridge and ran wildly in at the doorway leading into the station. They came in waves as water washes along a beach during a storm. Hugh had a feeling that if he were by some chance to get caught in the crowd he would be swept away into some unknown and terrible place. Waiting until the rush had a little subsided, he went across the street and on to the bridge to look at the river that flowed past the station. It was narrow and filled with ships, and the water looked gray and dirty. A pall of black smoke covered the sky. From all sides of him and even in the air above his head a great clatter and roar of bells and whistles went on.

With the air of a child venturing into a dark forest Hugh went a little way into one of the streets that led westward from the station. Again he stopped and stood by a building. Near at hand a group of young city roughs stood smoking and talking before a saloon. Out of a nearby building came a young girl who approached and spoke to one of them. The man began to swear furiously. "You tell her I'll come in there in a minute and smash her face," he said, and, paying no more attention to the girl, turned to stare at Hugh. All of the young men lounging before the saloon turned to stare at the tall country man. They began to laugh and one of them walked quickly toward him.

Hugh ran along the street and into the station followed by the shouts of the young roughs. He did not venture out again, and when his train was ready, got aboard and went gladly out of the great complex dwelling-place of modern Americans.

Hugh went from town to town always working his way eastward, always seeking the place where happiness was to come to him and where he was to achieve companionship with men and women. He cut fence posts in a forest on a large farm in Indiana, worked in the fields, and in one place was a section hand on the railroad.

On a farm in Indiana, some forty miles east of Indianapolis, he was for the first time powerfully touched by the presence of a woman. She was the daughter of the farmer who was Hugh's employer, and was an alert, handsome woman of twenty-four who had been a school teacher but had given up the work because she was about to be married. Hugh thought the man who was to marry her the most fortunate being in the world. He lived in Indianapolis and came by train to spend the week ends at the farm. The woman prepared for his coming by putting on a white dress and fastening a rose in her hair. The two people walked about in an orchard beside the house or went for a ride along the country roads. The young man, who, Hugh had been told, worked in a bank, wore stiff white collars, a black suit and a black derby hat.

On the farm Hugh worked in the field with the farmer and ate at table with his family, but did not get acquainted with them. On Sunday when the young man came he took the day off and went into a nearby town. The courtship became a matter very close to him and he lived through the excitement of the weekly visits as though he had been one of the principals. The daughter of the house, sensing the fact that the silent farm hand was stirred by her presence, became interested in him. Sometimes in the evening as he sat on a little porch before the house, she came to join him, and sat looking at him with a peculiarly detached and interested air. She tried to make talk, but Hugh answered all her advances so briefly and with such a half-frightened manner that she gave up the attempt. One Saturday evening when her sweetheart had come she took him for a ride in the family carriage, and Hugh concealed himself in the hayloft of the barn to wait for their return.

Hugh had never seen or heard a man express in any way his affection for a woman. It seemed to him a terrifically heroic thing to do and he hoped by concealing himself in the barn to see it done. It was a bright moonlight night and he waited until nearly eleven o'clock before the lovers returned. In the hayloft there was an opening high up under the roof. Because of his great height he could reach and pull himself up, and when he had done so, found a footing on one of the beams that formed the framework of the barn. The lovers stood unhitching the horse in the barnyard below. When the city man had led the horse into the stable he hurried quickly out again and went with the farmer's daughter along a path toward the house. The two people laughed and pulled at each other like children. They grew silent and when they had come near the house, stopped by a tree to embrace.

Hugh saw the man take the woman into his arms and hold her tightly against his body. He was so excited that he nearly fell off the beam. His imagination was inflamed and he tried to picture himself in the position of the young city man. His fingers gripped the boards to which he clung and his body trembled. The two figures standing in the dim light by the tree became one. For a long time they clung tightly to each other and then drew apart. They went into the house and Hugh climbed down from his place on the beam and lay in the hay. His body shook as with a chill and he was half ill of jealousy, anger, and an overpowering sense of defeat. It did not seem to him at the moment that it was worth while for him to go further east or to try to find a place where he would be able to mingle freely with men and women, or where such a wonderful thing as had happened to the man in the barnyard below might happen to him.

Hugh spent the night in the hayloft and at daylight crept out and went into a nearby town. He returned to the farmhouse late on Monday when he was sure the city man had gone away. In spite of the protest of the farmer he packed his clothes at once and declared his intention of leaving. He did not wait for the evening meal but hurried out of the house. When he got into the road and had started to walk away, he looked back and saw the daughter of the house standing at an open door and looking at him. Shame for what he had done on the night before swept over him. For a moment he stared at the woman who, with an intense, interested air stared back at him, and then putting down his head he hurried away. The woman watched him out of sight and later when her father stormed about the house, blaming Hugh for leaving so suddenly and declaring the tall Missourian was no doubt a drunkard who wanted to go off on a drunk, she had nothing to say. In her own heart she knew what was the matter with her father's farm hand and was sorry he had gone before she had more completely exercised her power over him.

None of the towns Hugh visited during his three years of wandering approached realization of the sort of life Sarah Shepard had talked to him about. They were all very much alike. There was a main street with a dozen stores on each side, a blacksmith shop, and perhaps an elevator for the storage of grain. All day the town was deserted, but in the evening the citizens gathered on Main Street. On the sidewalks before the stores young farm hands and clerks sat on store boxes or on the curbing. They did not pay any attention to Hugh who, when he went to stand near them, remained silent and kept himself in the background. The farm hands talked of their work and boasted of the number of bushels of corn they could pick in a day, or of their skill in plowing. The clerks were intent upon playing practical jokes which pleased the farm hands immensely. While one of them talked loudly of his skill in his work a clerk crept out of the door of one of the stores and approached him. He held a pin in his hand and with it jabbed the talker in the back. The crowd yelled and shouted with delight. If the victim became angry a quarrel started, but this did not often happen. Other men came to join the party and the joke was told to them. "Well, you should have seen the look on his face. I thought I would die," one of the bystanders declared.

Hugh got a job with a carpenter who specialized in the building of barns and stayed with him all through one fall. Later he went to work as a section hand on a railroad. Nothing happened to him. He was like one compelled to walk through life with a bandage over his eyes. On all sides of him, in the towns and on the farms, an undercurrent of life went on that did not touch him. In even the smallest of the towns, inhabited only by farm laborers, a quaint interesting civilization was being developed. Men worked hard but were much in the open air and had time to think. Their minds reached out toward the solution of the mystery of existence. The schoolmaster and the country lawyer read Tom Paine's *Age of Reason* and Bellamy's *Looking Backward*. They discussed these books with their fellows. There was a feeling, ill-expressed, that America had something real and spiritual to offer to the rest of the world. Workmen talked to each other of the new tricks of their trades, and after hours of discussion of some new way to cultivate corn, shape a horseshoe or build a barn, spoke of God and his intent concerning man. Long-drawn-out discussions of religious beliefs and the political destiny of America were carried on.

And across the background of these discussions ran tales of action in a sphere outside the little world in which the inhabitants of the towns lived. Men who had been in the Civil War and who had climbed fighting over hills and in the terror of defeat had swum wide rivers, told the tale of their adventures.

In the evening, after his day of work in the field or on the railroad with the section hands, Hugh did not know what to do with himself. That he did not go to bed immediately after the evening meal was due to the fact that he looked upon his tendency to sleep and to dream as an enemy to his development; and a peculiarly persistent determination to make something alive and worth while out of himself—the result of the five years of constant talking on the subject by the New England woman—had taken possession of him. "I'll find the right place and the right people and then I'll begin," he continually said to himself.

And then, worn out with weariness and loneliness, he went to bed in one of the little hotels or boarding houses where he lived during those years and his dreams returned. The dream that had come that night as he lay on the cliff above the Mississippi River near the town of Burlington, came back time after time. He sat upright in bed in the darkness of his room and after he had driven the cloudy, vague sensation out of his brain, was afraid to go to sleep again. He did not want to disturb the people of the house and so got up and dressed and without putting on his shoes walked up and down in the room. Sometimes the room he occupied had a low ceiling and he was compelled to stoop. He crept out of the house carrying his shoes in his hand and sat down on the sidewalk to put them on. In all the towns he visited, people saw him walking alone through the streets late at night or in the early hours of the morning. Whispers concerning the matter ran about. The story of what was spoken of as his queerness came to the men with whom he worked, and they found themselves unable to talk freely and naturally in his presence. At the noon hour when the men ate the lunch they had carried to work, when the boss was gone and it was customary among the workers to talk of their own affairs, they went off by themselves. Hugh followed them about. They went to sit under a tree, and when Hugh came to stand nearby, they became silent or the more vulgar and shallow among them began to show off. While he worked with a half dozen other men as a section hand on the railroad, two men did all the talking. Whenever the boss went away an old man who had a reputation as a wit told stories concerning his relations with women. A young man with red hair took the cue from him. The two men talked loudly and kept looking at Hugh. The younger of the two wits turned to another workman who had a weak, timid face. "Well, you," he cried, "what about your old woman? What about her? Who is the father of your son? Do you dare tell?"

In the towns Hugh walked about in the evening and tried always to keep his mind fixed on definite things. He felt that humanity was for some unknown reason drawing itself away from him, and his mind turned back to the figure of Sarah Shepard. He remembered that she had never been without things to do. She scrubbed her kitchen floor and prepared food for cooking; she washed, ironed, kneaded dough for bread, and mended clothes. In the evening, when she made the boy read to her out of one of the school books or do sums on a slate, she kept her hands busy knitting socks for him or for her husband. Except when something had crossed her so that she scolded and her face grew red, she was always cheerful. When the boy had nothing to do at the station and had been sent by the station master to work about the house, to draw water from the cistern for a family washing, or pull weeds in the garden, he heard the woman singing as she went about the doing of her innumerable petty tasks. Hugh decided that he also must do small tasks, fix his mind upon definite things. In the town where he was employed as a section hand, the cloud dream in which the world became a whirling, agitated center of disaster came to him almost every night. Winter came on and he walked through the streets at night in the darkness and through the deep snow. He was almost frozen; but as the whole lower part of his body was habitually cold he did not much mind the added discomfort, and so great was the reserve of strength in his big frame that the loss of sleep did not affect his ability to labor all day without effort.

Hugh went into one of the residence streets of the town and counted the pickets in the fences before the houses. He returned to the hotel and made a calculation as to the number of pickets in all the fences in town. Then he got a rule at the hardware store and carefully measured the pickets. He tried to estimate the number of pickets that could be cut of certain sized trees and that gave his mind another opening. He counted the number of trees in every street in town. He learned to tell at a glance and with relative accuracy how much lumber could be cut out of a tree. He built imaginary houses with lumber cut from the trees that lined the streets. He even tried to figure out a way to utilize the small limbs cut from the tops of the trees, and one Sunday went into the wood back of the town and cut a great armful of twigs, which he carried to his room and later with great patience wove into the form of a basket.

Book II | CHAPTER III

Bidwell, Ohio, was an old town as the ages of towns go in the Central West, long before Hugh McVey, in his search for a place where he could penetrate the wall that shut him off from humanity, went there to live and to try to work out his problem. It is a busy manufacturing town now and has a population of nearly a hundred thousand people; but the time for the telling of the story of its sudden and surprising growth has not yet come.

From the beginning Bidwell has been a prosperous place. The town lies in the valley of a deep, rapid-flowing river that spreads out just above the town, becomes for the time wide and shallow, and goes singing swiftly along over stones. South of the town the river not only spreads out, but the hills recede. A wide flat valley stretches away to the north. In the days before the factories came the land immediately about town was cut up into small farms devoted to fruit and berry raising, and beyond the area of small farms lay larger tracts that were immensely productive and that raised huge crops of wheat, corn, and cabbage.

When Hugh was a boy sleeping away his days in the grass beside his father's fishing shack by the Mississippi River, Bidwell had already emerged out of the hardships of pioneer days. On the farms that lay in the wide valley to the north the timber had been cut away and the stumps had all been rooted out of the ground by a generation of men that had passed. The soil was easy to cultivate and had lost little of its virgin fertility. Two railroads, the Lake Shore and Michigan Central—later a part of the great New York Central System—and a less important coal-carrying road, called the Wheeling and Lake Erie, ran through the town. Twenty-five hundred people lived then in Bidwell. They were for the most part descendants of the pioneers who had come into the country by boat through the Great Lakes or by wagon roads over the mountains from the States of New York and Pennsylvania.

The town stood on a sloping incline running up from the river, and the Lake Shore and Michigan Central Railroad had its station on the river bank at the foot of Main Street. The Wheeling Station was a mile away to the north. It was to be reached by going over a bridge and along a piked road that even then had begun to take on the semblance of a street. A dozen houses had been built facing Turner's Pike and between these were berry fields and an occasional orchard planted to cherry, peach or apple trees. A hard path went down to the distant station beside the road, and in the evening this path, wandering along under the branches of the fruit trees that extended out over the farm fences, was a favorite walking place for lovers.

The small farms lying close about the town of Bidwell raised

berries that brought top prices in the two cities, Cleveland and
Pittsburgh, reached by its two railroads, and all of the people
of the town who were not engaged in one of the trades—in
shoemaking, carpentry, horseshoeing, house-painting or the
like—or who did not belong to the small merchant and
professional classes, worked in summer on the land. On
summer mornings, men, women and children went into the
fields. In the early spring when planting went on and all
through late May, June and early July when berries and
fruit began to ripen, everyone was rushed with work and the
streets of the town were deserted. Everyone went to the fields.
Great hay wagons loaded with children, laughing girls, and
sedate women set out from Main Street at dawn. Beside them
walked tall boys, who pelted the girls with green apples and
cherries from the trees along the road, and men who went
along behind smoking their morning pipes and talking of the
prevailing prices of the products of their fields. In the town
after they had gone a Sabbath quiet prevailed. The merchants
and clerks loitered in the shade of the awnings before the
doors of the stores, and only their wives and the wives of the
two or three rich men in town came to buy and to disturb
their discussions of horse racing, politics and religion.

In the evening when the wagons came home, Bidwell awoke.
The tired berry pickers walked home from the fields in the
dust of the roads swinging their dinner pails. The wagons
creaked at their heels, piled high with boxes of berries ready
for shipment. In the stores after the evening meal crowds
gathered. Old men lit their pipes and sat gossiping along the
curbing at the edge of the sidewalks on Main Street; women
with baskets on their arms did the marketing for the next
day's living; the young men put on stiff white collars and
their Sunday clothes, and girls, who all day had been crawling
over the fields between the rows of berries or pushing their
way among the tangled masses of raspberry bushes, put on
white dresses and walked up and down before the men.
Friendships begun between boys and girls in the fields ripened
into love. Couples walked along residence streets under the
trees and talked with sudbued voices. They became silent and

embarrassed. The bolder ones kissed. The end of the berry picking season brought each year a new outbreak of marriages to the town of Bidwell.

In all the towns of Midwestern America it was a time of waiting. The country having been cleared and the Indians driven away into a vast distant place spoken of vaguely as the West, the Civil War having been fought and won, and there being no great national problems that touched closely their lives, the minds of men were turned in upon themselves. The soul and its destiny was spoken of openly on the streets. Robert Ingersoll came to Bidwell to speak in Terry's Hall, and after he had gone the question of the divinity of Christ for months occupied the minds of the citizens. The ministers preached sermons on the subject and in the evening it was talked about in the stores. Everyone had something to say. Even Charley Mook, who dug ditches, who stuttered so that not a half dozen people in town could understand him, expressed his opinion.

In all the great Mississippi Valley each town came to have a character of its own, and the people who lived in the towns were to each other like members of a great family. The individual idiosyncrasies of each member of the great family stood forth. A kind of invisible roof beneath which everyone lived spread itself over each town. Beneath the roof boys and girls were born, grew up, quarreled, fought, and formed friendships with their fellows, were introduced into the mysteries of love, married, and became the fathers and mothers of children, grew old, sickened, and died.

Within the invisible circle and under the great roof everyone knew his neighbor and was known to him. Strangers did not come and go swiftly and mysteriously and there was no constant and confusing roar of machinery and of new projects afoot. For the moment mankind seemed about to take time to try to understand itself.

In Bidwell there was a man named Peter White who was a tailor and worked hard at his trade, but who once or twice a year got drunk and beat his wife. He was arrested each time and had to pay a fine, but there was a general understanding of the impulse that led to the beating. Most of the women knowing the wife sympathized with Peter. "She is a noisy thing and her jaw is never still," the wife of Henry Teeters, the grocer, said to her husband. "If he gets drunk it's only to forget he's married to her. Then he goes home to sleep it off and she begins jawing at him. He stands it as long as he can. It takes a fist to shut up that woman. If he strikes her it's the only thing he can do."

Allie Mulberry the half-wit was one of the highlights of life in the town. He lived with his mother in a tumbledown house at the edge of town on Medina Road. Besides being a half-wit he had something the matter with his legs. They were trembling and weak and he could only move them with great difficulty. On summer afternoons when the streets were deserted, he hobbled along Main Street with his lower jaw hanging down. Allie carried a large club, partly for the support of his weak legs and partly to scare off dogs and mischievous boys. He liked to sit in the shade with his back against a building and whittle, and he liked to be near people and have his talent as a whittler appreciated. He made fans out of pieces of pine, long chains of wooden beads, and he once achieved a singular mechanical triumph that won him wide renown. He made a ship that would float in a beer bottle half-filled with water and laid on its side. The ship had sails and three tiny wooden sailors who stood at attention with their hands to their caps in salute. After it was constructed and put into the bottle it was too large to be taken out through the neck. How Allie got it in no one ever knew. The clerks and merchants who crowded about to watch him at work discussed the matter for days. It became a never-ending wonder among them. In the evening they spoke of the matter to the berry pickers who came into the stores, and in the eyes of the people of Bidwell Allie Mulberry became a hero. The bottle, half-filled with water and securely corked, was laid on a cushion in the window of Hunter's Jewelry Store. As it floated about on its own little ocean crowds gathered to look at it. Over the bottle was a sign with the words—"Carved by Allie Mulberry of Bidwell"—prominently displayed. Below these words a query had been printed. "How Did He Get It Into The Bottle?" was the question asked. The bottle stayed in the window for months and merchants took the traveling men who visited them, to see it. Then they escorted their guests to where Allie, with his back against the wall of a building and his club beside him, was at work on some new creation of the whittler's art. The travelers were impressed and told the tale abroad. Allie's fame spread to other towns. "He has a good brain," the citizen of Bidwell said, shaking his head. "He don't appear to know very much, but look what he does. He must be carrying all sorts of notions around inside of his head."

Jane Orange, widow of a lawyer, and with the single exception of Thomas Butterworth, a farmer who owned over a thousand acres of land and lived with his daughter on a farm a mile south of town, the richest person in town, was known to everyone in Bidwell, but was not liked. She was called stingy and it was said that she and her husband had cheated everyone with whom they had dealings in order to get their start in life. The town ached for the privilege of doing what they called "bringing them down a peg." Jane's husband had once been the Bidwell town attorney and later had charge of the settlement of an estate belonging to Ed Lucas, a farmer who died leaving two hundred acres of land and two daughters. The farmer's daughters, everyone said, "came out at the small end of the horn," and John Orange began to grow rich. It was said he was worth fifty thousand dollars. All during the later part of his life the lawyer went to the city of Cleveland on business every week, and when he was at home and even in the hottest weather he went about dressed in a long black coat. When she went to the stores to buy supplies for her house, Jane Orange was watched closely by the merchants. She was suspected of carrying away small articles that could be slipped into the pockets of her dress. One afternoon in Toddmore's grocery, when she thought no one was looking, she took a half dozen eggs out of a basket and looking quickly around to be sure she was unobserved, put them into her dress pocket. Harry Toddmore, the grocer's son who had seen the theft, said nothing, but went unobserved out at the back door. He got three or four clerks from other stores and they waited for Jane Orange at a corner. When she came along they hurried out and Harry Toddmore fell against her. Throwing out his hand he struck the pocket containing the eggs a quick, sharp blow. Jane Orange turned and hurried away toward home, but as she half ran through Main Street clerks and merchants came out of the stores, and from the assembled crowd a voice called attention to the fact that the contents of the stolen eggs having run down the inside of her dress and over her stockings began to make a stream on the sidewalk. A pack of town dogs excited by the shouts of the crowd ran at her heels, barking and sniffing at the yellow stream that dripped from her shoes.

An old man with a long white beard came to Bidwell to live. He had been a carpetbag Governor of a Southern state in the reconstruction days after the Civil War and had made money. He bought a house on Turner's Pick close beside the river and spent his days puttering about in a small garden. In the evening he came across the bridge into Main Street and went to loaf in Birdie Spinks' drugstore. He talked with great frankness and candor of his life in the South during the terrible time when the country was trying to emerge from the black gloom of defeat, and brought to the Bidwell men a new point of view on their old enemies, the "Rebs."

The old man—the name by which he had introduced himself in Bidwell was that of Judge Horace Hanby—believed in the manliness and honesty of purpose of the men he had for a time governed and who had fought a long grim war with the North, with the New Englanders and sons of New Englanders from the West and Northwest. "They're all right," he said with a grin. "I cheated them and made some money, but I liked them. Once a crowd of them came to my house and threatened to kill me and I told them that I did not blame them very much, so they let me alone." The judge, an ex-politician from the city of New York who had been involved in some affair that made it uncomfortable for him to return to live in that city, grew prophetic and philo-

sophic after he came to live in Bidwell. In spite of the doubt
everyone felt concerning his past, he was something of a
scholar and a reader of books, and won respect by his
apparent wisdom. "Well, there's going to be a new war here,"
he said. "It won't be like the Civil War, just shooting off
guns and killing peoples' bodies. At first it's going to be a
war between individuals to see to what class a man must
belong; then it is going to be a long, silent war between classes,
between those who have and those who can't get. It'll be
the worst war of all."

The talk of Judge Hanby, carried along and elaborated
almost every evening before a silent, attentive group in the
drugstore, began to have an influence on the minds of Bidwell
young men. At his suggestion several of the town boys, Cliff
Bacon, Albert Small, Ed Prawl, and two or three others,
began to save money for the purpose of going east to college.
Also at his suggestion Tom Butterworth the rich farmer sent
his daughter away to school. The old man made many
prophecies concerning what would happen in America. "I tell
you, the country isn't going to stay as it is," he said earnestly.
"In eastern towns the change has already come. Factories
are being built and everyone is going to work in the factories.
It takes an old man like me to see how that changes their
lives. Some of the men stand at one bench and do one thing
not only for hours but for days and years. There are signs
hung up saying they mustn't talk. Some of them make more
money than they did before the factories came, but I tell you
it's like being in prison. What would you say if I told you
all America, all you fellows who talk so big about freedom,
are going to be put in a prison, eh?

"And there's something else. In New York there are
already a dozen men who are worth a million dollars. Yes,
sir, I tell you it's true, a million dollars. What do you think
of that, eh?"

Judge Hanby grew excited and, inspired by the absorbed
attention of his audience, talked of the sweep of events. In
England, he explained, the cities were constantly growing
larger, and already almost everyone either worked in a factory

or owned stock in a factory. "In New England it is getting the same way fast," he explained. "The same thing'll happen here. Farming'll be done with tools. Almost everything now done by hand'll be done by machinery. Some'll grow rich and some poor. The thing is to get educated, yes, sir, that's the thing, to get ready for what's coming. It's the only way. The younger generation has got to be sharper and shrewder."

The words of the old man, who had been in many places and had seen men and cities, were repeated in the streets of Bidwell. The blacksmith and the wheelwright repeated his words when they stopped to exchange news of their affairs before the post office. Ben Peeler, the carpenter, who had been saving money to buy a house and a small farm to which he could retire when he became too old to climb about on the framework of buildings, used the money instead to send his son to Cleveland to a new technical school. Steve Hunter, the son of Abraham Hunter the Bidwell jeweler, declared that he was going to get up with the times, and when he went into a factory, would go into the office, not into the shop. He went to Buffalo, New York, to attend a business college.

The air of Bidwell began to stir with talk of new times. The evil things said of the new life coming were soon forgotten. The youth and optimistic spirit of the country led it to take hold of the hand of the giant, industrialism, and lead him laughing into the land. The cry, "get on in the world," that ran all over America at that period and that still echoes in the pages of American newspapers and magazines, rang in the streets of Bidwell.

In the harness shop belonging to Joseph Wainsworth it one day struck a new note. The harness maker was a trades-man of the old school and was vastly independent. He had learned his trade after five years' service as apprentice, and had spent an additional five years in going from place to place as a journeyman workman, and felt that he knew his business. Also he owned his shop and his home and had twelve hundred dollars in the bank. At noon one day when he was alone in the shop, Tom Butterworth came in and told him he had ordered four sets of farm work harness from a factory in Philadelphia. "I came in to ask if you'll repair them if they get out of order," he said.

Joe Wainsworth began to fumble with the tools on his bench. Then he turned to look the farmer in the eye and to do what he later spoke of to his cronies as "laying down the law." "When the cheap things begin to go to pieces take them somewhere else to have them repaired," he said sharply. He grew furiously angry. "Take the damn things to Philadelphia where you got 'em," he shouted at the back of the farmer who had turned to go out of the shop.

Joe Wainsworth was upset and thought about the incident all the afternoon. When farmer-customers came in and stood about to talk of their affairs he had nothing to say. He was a talkative man and his apprentice, Will Sellinger, son of the Bidwell house painter, was puzzled by his silence.

When the boy and the man were alone in the shop it was Joe Wainsworth's custom to talk of his days as a journeyman workman when he had gone from place to place working at his trade. If a trace were being stitched or a bridle fashioned, he told how the thing was done at a shop where he had worked in the city of Boston and in another shop at Providence, Rhode Island. Getting a piece of paper he made drawings illustrating the cuts of leather that were made in the other places and the methods of stitching. He claimed to have worked out his own methods for doing things, and that his method was better than anything he had seen in all his travels. To the men who came into the shop to loaf during winter afternoons he presented a smiling front and talked of their affairs, of the price of cabbage in Cleveland or the effect of a cold snap on the winter wheat, but alone with the boy, he talked only of harness making. "I don't say anything about it. What's the good bragging? Just the same, I could learn something to all the harness makers I've ever seen, and I've seen the best of them," he declared emphatically.

During the afternoon, after he had heard of the four factory-made work harnesses brought into what he had always thought of as a trade that belonged to him by the rights of a first-class workman, Joe remained silent for two or three hours. He thought of the words of old Judge Hanby and the constant talk of the new times now coming. Turning suddenly to his apprentice, who was puzzled by his long silence and who knew nothing of the incident that had disturbed his employer, he broke forth into words. He was defiant and expressed his defiance. "Well, then, let 'em go to Philadelphia, let 'em go any damn place they please," he growled, and then, as though his own words had re-established his self-respect, he straightened his shoulders and glared at the puzzled and alarmed boy. "I know my trade and do not have to bow down to any man," he declared. He expressed the old trades-man's faith in his craft and the rights it gave the craftsman. "Learn your trade. Don't listen to talk," he said earnestly. "The man who knows his trade is a man. He can tell everyone to go to the devil."

CHAPTER IV

Hugh McVey was twenty-three years old when he went to live in Bidwell. The position of telegraph operator at the Wheeling station a mile north of town became vacant and, through an accidental encounter with a former resident of a neighboring town, he got the place.

The Missourian had been at work during the winter in a sawmill in the country near a Northern Indiana town. During the evenings he wandered on country roads and in the town streets, but he did not talk to anyone. As had happened to him in other places, he had the reputation of being queer. His clothes were worn threadbare and, although he had money in his pockets, he did not buy new ones. In the evening when he went through the town streets and saw the smartly dressed clerks standing before the stores, he looked at his own shabby person and was ashamed to enter. In his boyhood Sarah Shepard had always attended to the buying of his clothes, and he made up his mind that he would go to the place in Michigan to which she and her husband had retired, and pay her a visit. He wanted Sarah Shepard to buy him a new outfit of clothes, but wanted also to talk with her.

Out of the three years of going from place to place and working with other men as a laborer, Hugh had got no big impulse that he felt would mark the road his life should take; but the study of mathematical problems, taken up to relieve his loneliness and to cure his inclination to dreams, was beginning to have an effect on his character. He thought that if he saw Sarah Shepard again he could talk to her and through her get into the way of talking to others. In the sawmill where he worked he answered the occasional remarks made to him by his fellow workers in a slow, hesitating drawl, and his body was still awkward and his gait shambling, but he did his work more quickly and accurately. In the presence of his foster-mother and garbed in new clothes, he believed he could now talk to her in a way that had been impossible during his youth. She would see the change in his character and would be encouraged about him. They would get on to a new basis and he would feel respect for himself in another.

Hugh went to the railroad station to make inquiry regarding the fare to the Michigan town and there had the adventure that upset his plans. As he stood at the window of the ticket office, the ticket seller, who was also the telegraph operator, tried to engage him in conversation. When he had given the information asked, he followed Hugh out of the building and into the darkness of a country railroad station at night, and the two men stopped and stood together beside an empty baggage truck. The ticket agent spoke of the loneliness of life in the town and said he wished he could go back to his own place and be again with his own people. "It may not be any better in my own town, but I know everybody there," he said. He was curious concerning Hugh as were all the people of the Indiana town, and hoped to get him into talk in order that he might find out why he walked alone at night, why he sometimes worked all evening over books and figures in his room at the country hotel, and why he had so little to say to his fellows. Hoping to fathom Hugh's silence he abused the town in which they both lived. "Well," he began, "I guess I understand how you feel. You want to get out of this place." He explained his own predicament in life. "I got married," he said. "Already I have three children. Out here a man can make more money railroading than he can in my state, and living is pretty cheap. Just today I had an offer of a job in a good town near my own place in Ohio, but I can't take it. The job only pays forty a month. The town's all right, one of the best in the northern part of the State, but you see the job's no good. Lord, I wish I could go. I'd like to live again among people such as live in that part of the country."

The railroad man and Hugh walked along the street that ran from the station up into the main street of the town. Wanting to meet the advances that had been made by his companion and not knowing how to go about it, Hugh adopted the method he had heard his fellow laborers use with one another. "Well," he said slowly, "come have a drink."

The two men went into a saloon and stood by the bar. Hugh made a tremendous effort to overcome his embarrassment. As he and the railroad man drank foaming glasses of beer he explained that he also had once been a railroad man and knew telegraphy, but that for several years he had been doing other work. His companion looked at his shabby clothes and nodded his head. He made a motion with his head to indicate that he wanted Hugh to come with him outside into the darkness. "Well, well," he exclaimed, when they had again got outside and had started along the street toward the station. "I understand now. They've all been wondering about you and I've heard lots of talk. I won't say anything, but I'm going to do something for you."

Hugh went to the station with his new-found friend and sat down in the lighted office. The railroad man got out a sheet of paper and began to write a letter. "I'm going to get you that job," he said. "I'm writing the letter now and I'll get it off on the midnight train. You've got to get on your feet. I was a boozer myself, but I cut it all out. A glass of beer now and then, that's my limit."

He began to talk of the town in Ohio where he proposed to get Hugh the job that would set him up in the world and save him from the habit of drinking, and described it as an earthly paradise in which lived bright, clear-thinking men and beautiful women. Hugh was reminded sharply of the talk he had heard from the lips of Sarah Shepard, when in his youth she spent long evenings telling him of the wonder of her own Michigan and New England towns and people, and contrasted the life lived there with that lived by the people of his own place.

Hugh decided not to try to explain away the mistake made by his new acquaintance, and to accept the offer of assistance in getting the appointment as telegraph operator.

The two men walked out of the station and stood again in the darkness. The railroad man felt like one who has been given the privilege of plucking a human soul out of the darkness of despair. He was full of words that poured from his lips and he assumed a knowledge of Hugh and his character entirely unwarranted by the circumstances. "Well," he exclaimed heartily, "you see I've given you a send-off. I have told them you're a good man and a good operator, but that you will take the place with its small salary because you've been sick and just now can't work very hard." The excited man followed Hugh along the street. It was late and the store lights had been put out. From one of the town's two saloons that lay in their way arose a clatter of voices. The old boyhood dream of finding a place and a people among whom he could, by sitting still and inhaling the air breathed by others, come into a warm closeness with life, came back to Hugh. He stopped before the saloon to listen to the voices within, but the railroad man plucked at his coat sleeve and protested. "Now, now, you're going to cut it out, eh?" he asked anxiously and then hurriedly explained his anxiety. "Of course I know what's the matter with you. Didn't I tell you I've been there myself? You've been working around. I know why that is. You don't have to tell me. If there wasn't something the matter with him, no man who knows telegraphy would work in a sawmill.

"Well, there's no good talking about it," he added thought-fully. "I've given you a send-off. You're going to cut it out, eh?"

Hugh tried to protest and to explain that he was not addicted to the habit of drinking, but the Ohio man would not listen. "It's all right," he said again, and then they came to the hotel where Hugh lived and he turned to go back to the station and wait for the midnight train that would carry the letter away and that would, he felt, carry also his demand that a fellow-human, who had slipped from the modern path of work and progress should be given a new chance. He felt magnanimous and wonderfully gracious. "It's all right, my boy," he said heartily. "No use talking to me. Tonight when you came to the station to ask the fare to that hole of a place in Michigan I saw you were embarrassed. 'What's the matter with that fellow?' I said to myself. I got to thinking. Then I came uptown with you and right away you bought me a drink. I wouldn't have thought anything about that if I hadn't been there myself. You'll get on your feet. Bidwell, Ohio, is full of good men. You get in with them and they'll help you and stick by you. You'll like those people. They've got get-up to them. The place you'll work at there is far out of town. It's away out about a mile at a little kind of outside-like place called Pickleville. There used to be a saloon there and a fac-tory for putting up cucumber pickles, but they've both gone now. You won't be tempted to slip in that place. You'll have a chance to get on your feet. I'm glad I thought of sending you there."

The Wheeling and Lake Erie ran along a little wooded depression that cut across the wide expanse of open farm lands north of the town of Bidwell. It brought coal from the hill country of West Virginia and Southeastern Ohio to ports on Lake Erie, and did not pay much attention to the carrying of passengers. In the morning a train consisting of a combined express and baggage car and two passenger coaches went north and west toward the lake, and in the evening the same train returned, bound southeast into the hills. The Bidwell station of the road was, in an odd way, detached from the town's life. The invisible roof under which the life of the town and the surrounding country was lived did not cover it. As the Indiana railroad man had told Hugh, the station itself stood on a spot known locally as Pickleville. Back of the station there was a small building for the storage of freight and near at hand four or five houses facing Turner's Pike. The pickle factory, now deserted and with its windows gone, stood across the tracks from the station and beside a small stream that ran under a bridge and across country through a grove of trees to the river. On hot summer days a sour, pungent smell arose from the old factory, and at night its presence lent a ghostly flavor to the tiny corner of the world in which lived perhaps a dozen people.

All day and at night an intense persistent silence lay over Pickleville, while in Bidwell a mile away the stir of new life began. In the evenings and on rainy afternoons when men could not work in the fields, old Judge Hanby went along Turner's Pike and across the wagon bridge into Bidwell and sat in a chair at the back of Birdie Spink's drugstore. He talked. Men came in to listen to him and went out. New talk ran through the town. A new force that was being born into American life and into life everywhere all over the world was feeding on the old dying individualistic life. The new force stirred and aroused the people. It met a need that was universal. It was meant to seal men together, to wipe out national lines, to walk under seas and fly through the air, to change the entire face of the world in which men lived. Already the giant that was to be king in the place of old kings was calling his servants and his armies to serve him. He used the methods of old kings and promised his followers booty and gain. Everywhere he went unchallenged, surveying the land, raising a new class of men to positions of power. Railroads had already been pushed out across the plains; great coal fields from which was to be taken food to warm the blood in the body of the giant were being opened up; iron fields were being discovered; the roar and clatter of the breathing of the terrible new thing, half-hideous, half-beautiful in its possibilities, that was for so long to drown the voices and confuse the thinking of men, was heard not only in the towns but even in lonely farm houses, where its willing servants, the newspapers and magazines, had begun to circulate in ever increasing numbers. At the town of Gibsonville, near Bidwell, Ohio, and at Lima and Finley, Ohio, oil and gas fields were discovered. At Cleveland, Ohio, a precise, definite-minded man named Rockefeller bought and sold oil. From the first he served the new thing well and he soon found others to serve with him. The Morgans, Fricks, Goulds, Carnegies, Vanderbilts, servants of the new king, princes of the new faith, merchants all, a new kind of rulers of men, defied the world-old law of class that puts the merchant below the craftsman, and added to the confusion of men by taking on the air of creators. They were merchants glorified and dealt in giant things, in the lives of men and in mines, forests, oil and gas fields, factories, and railroads.

And all over the country, in the towns, the farm houses, and the growing cities of the new country, people stirred and awakened. Thought and poetry died or passed as a heritage to feeble fawning men who also became servants of the new order. Serious young men in Bidwell and in other American towns, whose fathers had walked together on moonlight nights along Turner's Pike to talk of God, went away to technical schools. Their fathers had walked and talked and thoughts had grown up in them. The impulse had reached back to their father's fathers on moonlit roads of England, Germany, Ireland, France, and Italy, and back of these to the moonlit hills of Judea where shepherds talked and serious young men, John and Matthew and Jesus, caught the drift of the talk and made poetry of it; but the serious-minded sons of these men in the new land were swept away from thinking and dreaming. From all sides the voice of the new age that was to do definite things shouted at them. Eagerly they took up the cry and ran with it. Millions of voices arose. The clamor became terrible, and confused the minds of all men. In making way for the newer, broader brotherhood into which men are some day to emerge, in extending the invisible roofs of the towns and cities to cover the world, men cut and crushed their way through the bodies of men.

And while the voices became louder and more excited and the new giant walked about making a preliminary survey of the land, Hugh spent his days at the quiet, sleepy railroad station at Pickleville and tried to adjust his mind to the realization of the fact that he was not to be accepted as fellow by the citizens of the new place to which he had come. During the day he sat in the tiny telegraph office or, pulling an express truck to the open window near his telegraph instrument, lay on his back with a sheet of paper propped on his bony knees and did sums. Farmers driving past on Turner's Pike saw him there and talked of him in the stores in town. "He's a queer silent fellow," they said. "What do you suppose he's up to?"

Hugh walked in the streets of Bidwell at night as he had walked in the streets of towns in Indiana and Illinois. He approached groups of men loafing on a street corner and then went hurriedly past them. On quiet streets as he went along under the trees, he saw women sitting in the lamplight in the houses and hungered to have a house and a woman of his own. One afternoon a woman school teacher came to the station to make inquiry regarding the fare to a town in West Virginia. As the station agent was not about Hugh gave her the information she sought and she lingered for a few moments to talk with him. He answered the questions she asked with monosyllables and she soon went away, but he was delighted and looked upon the incident as an adventure. At night he dreamed of the school teacher and when he awoke, pretended she was with him in his bedroom. He put out his hand and touched the pillow. It was soft and smooth as he imagined the cheek of a woman would be. He did not know the school teacher's name but invented one for her. "Be quiet, Elizabeth. Do not let me disturb your sleep," he murmured into the darkness. One evening he went to the house where the school teacher boarded and stood in the shadow of a tree until he saw her come out and go toward Main Street. Then he went by a roundabout way and walked past her on the sidewalk before the lighted stores. He did not look at her, but in passing her dress touched his arm and he was so excited later that he could not sleep and spent half the night walking about and thinking of the wonderful thing that had happened to him.

The ticket, express, and freight agent for the Wheeling and Lake Erie at Bidwell, a man named George Pike, lived in one of the houses near the station, and besides attending to his duties for the railroad company, owned and worked a small farm. He was a slender, alert, silent man with a long drooping mustache. Both he and his wife worked as Hugh had never seen a man and woman work before. Their arrangement of the division of labor was not based on sex but on convenience. Sometimes Mrs. Pike came to the station to sell tickets, load express boxes and trunks on the passenger trains and deliver heavy boxes of freight to draymen and farmers, while her husband worked in the fields back of his house or prepared the evening meal, and sometimes the matter was reversed and Hugh did not see Mrs. Pike for several days at a time.

During the day there was little for the station agent or his wife to do at the station and they disappeared. George Pike had made an arrangement of wires and pulleys connecting the station with a large bell hung on top of his house, and when someone came to the station to receive or deliver freight Hugh pulled at the wire and the bell began to ring. In a few minutes either George Pike or his wife came running from the house or fields, dispatched the business and went quickly away again.

Day after day Hugh sat in a chair by a desk in the station or went outside and walked up and down the station platform. Engines pulling long caravans of coal cars ground past. The brakemen waved their hands to him and then the train disappeared into the grove of trees that grew beside the creek along which the tracks of the road were laid. In Turner's Pike a creaking farm wagon appeared and then disappeared along the tree-lined road that led to Bidwell. The farmer turned on his wagon seat to stare at Hugh but unlike the railroad men did not wave his hand. Adventurous boys came out along the road from town and climbed, shouting and laughing, over the rafters in the deserted pickle factory across the tracks or went to fish in the creek in the shade of the factory walls. Their shrill voices added to the loneliness of the spot. It became almost unbearable to Hugh. In desperation he turned from the rather meaningless doing of sums and working out of problems regarding the number of fence pickets that could be cut from a tree or the number of steel rails or railroad ties consumed in building a mile of railroad, the innumerable petty problems with which he had been keeping his mind busy, and turned to more definite and practical problems. He remembered an autumn he had put in cutting corn on a farm in Illinois and, going into the station, waved his long arms about, imitating the movements of a man in the act of cutting corn. He wondered if a machine might not be made that would do the work, and tried to make drawings of the parts of such a machine. Feeling his inability to handle so difficult a problem he sent away for books and began the study of mechanics. He joined a correspondence school started by a man in Pennsylvania, and worked for days on the problems the man sent him to do. He asked questions and began a little to understand the mystery of the application of power. Like the other young men of Bidwell he began to put himself into touch with the spirit of the age, but unlike them he did not dream of suddenly acquired wealth. While they embraced new and futile dreams he worked to destroy the tendency to dreams in himself.

Hugh came to Bidwell in the early spring and during May, June and July the quiet station at Pickleville awoke for an hour or two each evening. A certain percentage of the sudden and almost overwhelming increase in express business that came with the ripening of the fruit and berry crop came to the Wheeling, and every evening a dozen express trucks, piled high with berry boxes, waited for the southbound train.

When the train came into the station a small crowd had assembled. George Pike and his stout wife worked madly, throwing the boxes in at the door of the express car. Idlers standing about became interested and lent a hand. The engineer climbed out of his locomotive, stretched his legs and crossing a narrow road got a drink from the pump in George Pike's yard.

Hugh walked to the door of his telegraph office and standing in the shadows watched the busy scene. He wanted to take part in it, to laugh and talk with the men standing about, to go to the engineer and ask questions regarding the locomotive and its construction, to help George Pike and his wife, and perhaps cut through their silence and his own enough to become acquainted with them. He thought of all these things but stayed in the shadow of the door that led to the telegraph office until, at a signal given by the train conductor, the engineer climbed into his engine and the train began to move away into the evening darkness. When Hugh came out of his office the station platform was deserted again. In the grass across the tracks and beside the ghostly looking old factory, crickets sang. Tom Wilder, the Bidwell hack driver, had got a traveling man off the train and the dust left by the heels of his team still hung in the air over Turner's Pike. From the darkness that brooded over the trees that grew along the creek beyond the factory came the hoarse croak of frogs. On Turner's Pike a half-dozen Bidwell young men accompanied by as many town girls walked along the path beside the road under the trees. They had come to the station to have somewhere to go, had made up a party to come, but now the half-unconscious purpose of their coming was apparent. The party split itself up into couples and each strove to get as far away as possible from the others. One of the couples came back along the path toward the station and went to the pump in George Pike's yard. They stood by the pump, laughing and pretending to drink out of a tin cup, and when they got again into the road the others had disappeared. They became silent. Hugh went to the end of the platform and watched as they walked slowly along. He became furiously jealous of the young man who put his arm about the waist of his companion and then, when he turned and saw Hugh staring at him, took it away again.

The telegraph operator went quickly along the platform until he was out of range of the young man's eyes, and, when he thought the gathering darkness would hide him, returned and crept along the path beside the road after him. Again a hungry desire to enter into the lives of the people about him took possession of the Missourian. To be a young man dressed in a stiff white collar, wearing neatly made clothes, and in the evening to walk about with young girls seemed like getting on the road to happiness. He wanted to run shouting along the path beside the road until he had overtaken the young man and woman, to beg them to take him with them, to accept him as one of themselves, but when the momentary impulse had passed and he returned to the telegraph office and lighted a lamp, he looked at his long awkward body and could not conceive of himself as ever by any chance becoming the thing he wanted to be. Sadness swept over him and his gaunt face, already cut and marked with deep lines, became longer and more gaunt. The old boyhood notion, put into his mind by the words of his foster-mother, Sarah Shepard, that a town and a people could remake him and erase from his body the marks of what he thought of as his inferior birth, began to fade. He tried to forget the people about him and turned with renewed energy to the study of the problems in the books that now lay in a pile upon his desk. His inclination to dreams, balked by the persistent holding of his mind to definite things, began to reassert itself in a new form, and his brain played no more with pictures of clouds and men in agitated movement but took hold of steel, wood, and iron. Dumb masses of materials taken out of the earth and the forests were molded by his mind into fantastic shapes. As he sat in the telegraph office during the day or walked alone through the streets of Bidwell at night, he saw in fancy a thousand new machines, formed by his hands and brain, doing the work that had been done by the hands of men. He had come to Bidwell, not only in the hope that there he would at last find companionship, but also because his mind was really aroused and he wanted leisure to begin trying to do tangible things. When the citizens of Bidwell would not take him into their town life but left him standing to one side, as the tiny dwelling place for men called Pickleville where he lived stood aside out from under the invisible roof of the town, he decided to try to forget men and to express himself wholly in work.

CHAPTER V

Hugh's first inventive effort stirred the town of Bidwell deeply. When word of it ran about, the men who had been listening to the talk of Judge Horace Hanby and whose minds had turned toward the arrival of the new forward-pushing impulse in American life thought they saw in Hugh the instrument of its coming to Bidwell. From the day of his coming to live among them, there had been much curiosity in the stores and houses regarding the tall, gaunt, slow-speaking stranger at Pickleville. George Pike had told Birdie Spinks the druggist how Hugh worked all day over books, and how he made drawings for parts of mysterious machines and left them on his desk in the telegraph office. Birdie Spinks told others and the tale grew. When Hugh walked alone in the streets during the evening and thought no one took account of his presence, hundreds of pairs of curious eyes followed him about.

A tradition in regard to the telegraph operator began to grow up. The tradition made Hugh a gigantic figure, one who walked always on a plane above that on which other men lived. In the imagination of his fellow citizens of the Ohio town, he went about always thinking great thoughts, solving mysterious and intricate problems that had to do with the new mechanical age Judge Hanby talked about to the eager listeners in the drugstore. An alert, talkative people saw among them one who could not talk and whose long face was habitually serious, and could not think of him as having daily to face the same kind of minor problems as themselves.

The Bidwell young man who had come down to the Wheeling station with a group of other young men, who had seen the evening train go away to the south, who had met at the station one of the town girls and had, in order to escape the others and be alone with her, taken her to the pump in George Pike's yard on the pretense of wanting a drink, walked away with her into the darkness of the summer evening with his mind fixed on Hugh. The young man's name was Ed Hall and he was apprentice to Ben Peeler, the carpenter who had sent his son to Cleveland to a technical school. He wanted to marry the girl he had met at the station and did not see how he could manage it on his salary as a carpenter's apprentice. When he looked back and saw Hugh standing on the station platform, he took the arm he had put around the girl's waist quickly away and began to talk. "I'll tell you what," he said earnestly, "if things don't pretty soon get on the stir around here I'm going to get out. I'll go over by Gibsonburg and get a job in the oil fields, that's what I'll do. I've got to have more money." He sighed heavily and looked over the girl's head into the darkness. "They say that telegraph fellow back there at the station is up to something," he ventured. "It's all the talk. Birdie Spinks says he is an inventor; says George Pike told him; says he is working all the time on new inventions to do things by machinery; that his passing off as a telegraph operator is only a bluff. Some think maybe he was sent here to see about starting a factory to make one of his inventions, sent by rich men maybe in Cleveland or some other place. Everybody says they'll bet there'll be factories here in Bidwell before very long now. I wish I knew. I don't want to go away if I don't have to, but I got to have more money. Ben Peeler won't never give me a raise so I can get married or nothing. I wish I knew that fellow back there so I could ask him what's up. They say he's smart. I suppose he wouldn't tell me nothing. I wish I was smart enough to invent something and maybe get rich. I wish I was the kind of fellow they say he is."

Ed Hall again put his arm about the girl's waist and walked away. He forgot Hugh and thought of himself and of how he wanted to marry the girl whose young body nestled close to his own—wanted her to be utterly his. For a few hours he passed out of Hugh's growing sphere of influence on the collective thought of the town, and lost himself in the immediate deliciousness of kisses.

And as he passed out of Hugh's influence others came in. On Main Street in the evening everyone speculated on the

Missourian's purpose in coming to Bidwell. The forty dollars a month paid him by the Wheeling railroad could not have tempted such a man. They were sure of that. Steve Hunter the jeweler's son had returned to town from a course in a business college at Buffalo, New York, and hearing the talk became interested. Steve had in him the making of a live man of affairs, and he decided to investigate. It was not, however, Steve's method to go at things directly, and he was impressed by the notion, then abroad in Bidwell, that Hugh had been sent to town by someone, perhaps by a group of capitalists who intended to start factories there.

Steve thought he would go easy. In Buffalo, where he had gone to the business college, he had met a girl whose father, E. P. Horn, owned a soap factory; had become acquainted with her at church and had been introduced to her father. The soap maker, an assertive positive man who manufactured a product called Horn's Household Friend Soap, had his own notion of what a young man should be and how he should make his way in the world, and had taken pleasure in talking to Steve. He told the Bidwell jeweler's son of how he had started his own factory with but little money and had succeeded and gave Steve many practical hints on the organization of companies. He talked a great deal of a thing called "control." "When you get ready to start for yourself keep that in mind," he said. "You can sell stock and borrow money at the bank, all you can get, but don't give up control. Hang on to that. That's the way I made my success. I always kept the control."

Steve wanted to marry Ernestine Horn, but felt that he should show what he could do as a business man before he attempted to thrust himself into so wealthy and prominent a family. When he returned to his own town and heard the talk regarding Hugh McVey and his inventive genius, he remembered the soap maker's words regarding control, and repeated them to himself. One evening he walked along Turner's Pike and stood in the darkness by the old pickle factory. He saw Hugh at work under a lamp in the telegraph office and was impressed. "I'll lay low and see what he's up to," he told himself. "If he's got an invention, I'll get up a company. I'll get money in and I'll start a factory. The people here'll tumble over each other to get into a thing like that. I don't believe anyone sent him here. I'll bet he's just an inventor. That kind always are queer. I'll keep my mouth shut and watch my chance. If there is anything starts, I'll start it and I'll get into control, that's what I'll do, I'll get into control."

In the country stretching away north beyond the fringe of small berry farms lying directly about town, were other and larger farms. The land that made up these larger farms was also rich and raised big crops. Great stretches of it were planted to cabbage for which a market had been built up in Cleveland, Pittsburgh, and Cincinnati. Bidwell was often in derision called Cabbageville by the citizens of nearby towns. One of the largest of the cabbage farms belonged to a man named Ezra French, and was situated on Turner's Pike, two miles from town and a mile beyond the Wheeling station.

On spring evenings when it was dark and silent about the station and when the air was heavy with the smell of new growth and of land fresh-turned by the plow, Hugh got out of his chair in the telegraph office and walked in the soft darkness. He went along Turner's Pike to town, saw groups of men standing on the sidewalks before the stores and young girls walking arm in arm along the street, and then came back to the silent station. Into his long and habitually cold body the warmth of desire began to creep. The spring rains came and soft winds blew down from the hill country to the south. One evening when the moon shone he went around the old pickle factory to where the creek went chattering under leaning willow trees, and as he stood in the heavy shadows by the factory wall, tried to imagine himself as one who had become suddenly clean-limbed, graceful, and agile. A bush grew beside the stream near the factory and he took hold of it with his powerful hands and tore it out by the roots. For a moment the strength in his shoulders and arms gave him an intense masculine satisfaction. He thought of how powerfully he could hold the body of a woman against his body and the spark of the fires of spring that had touched him became a flame. He felt new-made and tried to leap lightly and gracefully across the stream, but stumbled and fell in the water. Later he went soberly back to the station and tried again to lose himself in the study of the problems he had found in his books.

The Ezra French farm lay beside Turner's Pike a mile north of the Wheeling station and contained two hundred acres of land of which a large part was planted to cabbages. It was a profitable crop to raise and required no more care than corn, but the planting was a terrible task. Thousands of plants that had been raised from seeds planted in a seed-bed back of the barn had to be laboriously transplanted. The plants were tender and it was necessary to handle them carefully. The planter crawled slowly and painfully along, and from the road looked like a wounded beast striving to make his way to a hole in a distant wood. He crawled forward a little and then stopped and hunched himself up into a ball-like mass. Taking the plant, dropped on the ground by one of the plant droppers, he made a hole in the soft ground with a small three-cornered hoe, and with his hands packed the earth about the plant roots. Then he crawled on again.

Ezra the cabbage farmer had come west from one of the New England states and had grown comfortably wealthy, but he would not employ extra labor for the plant setting and the work was done by his sons and daughters. He was a short, bearded man whose leg had been broken in his youth by a fall from the loft of a barn. As it had not mended properly he could do little work and limped painfully about. To the men of Bidwell he was known as something of a wit, and in the winter he went to town every afternoon to stand in the stores and tell the Rabelaisian stories for which he was famous; but when spring came he became restlessly active, and in his own house and on the farm, became a tyrant. During the time of the cabbage setting he drove his sons and daughters like slaves. When in the evening the moon came up, he made them go back to the fields immediately after supper and work until midnight. They went in sullen silence, the girls to limp slowly along dropping the plants out of baskets carried on their arms, and the boys to crawl after them and set the plants. In the half darkness the little group of humans went slowly up and down the long fields. Ezra hitched a horse to a wagon and brought the plants from the seedbed behind the barn. He went here and there swearing and protesting against every delay in the work. When his wife, a tired little old woman, had finished the evening's work in the house, he made her come also to the fields. "Come, come," he said, sharply, "we need every pair of hands we can get." Although he had several thousand dollars in the Bidwell bank and owned mortgages on two or three neighboring farms, Ezra was afraid of poverty, and to keep his family at work pretended to be upon the point of losing all his possessions. "Now is our chance to save ourselves," he declared. "We must get in a big crop. If we do not work hard now we'll starve." When in the field his sons found themselves unable to crawl longer without resting, and stood up to stretch their tired bodies, he stood by the fence at the field's edge and swore. "Well, look at the mouths I have to feed, you lazies!" he shouted. "Keep at the work. Don't be idling around. In two weeks it'll be too late for planting and then you can rest. Now every plant we set will help to save us from ruin. Keep at the job. Don't be idling around."

In the spring of his second year in Bidwell, Hugh went often in the evening to watch the plant setters at work in the moonlight on the French farm. He did not make his presence known but hid himself in a fence corner behind bushes and watched the workers. As he saw the stooped misshapen figures crawling slowly along and heard the words of the old man driving them like cattle, his heart was deeply touched and he wanted to protest. In the dim light the slowly moving figures of women appeared, and after them came the crouched crawling men. They came down the long row toward him, wriggling into his line of sight like grotesquely misshapen animals driven by some god of the night to the performance of a terrible task. An arm went up. It came down again swiftly. The three-cornered hoe sank into the ground. The slow rhythm of the crawler was broken. He reached with his disengaged hand for the plant that lay on the ground before him and lowered it into the hole the hoe had made. With his fingers he packed the earth about the roots of the plant and then again began the slow crawl forward. There were four of the French boys and the two older ones worked in silence. The younger boys complained. The three girls and their mother, who were attending to the plant dropping, came to the end of the row and turning, went away into the darkness. "I'm going to quit this slavery," one of the younger boys said. "I'll get a job over in town. I hope it's true what they say, that factories are coming."

The four young men came to the end of the row and, as Ezra was not in sight, stood a moment by the fence near where Hugh was concealed. "I'd rather be a horse or a cow than what I am," the complaining voice went on. "What's the good being alive if you have to work like this?"

For a moment as he listened to the voices of the complaining workers, Hugh wanted to go to them and ask them to let him share in their labor. Then another thought came. The crawling figures came sharply into his line of vision. He no longer heard the voice of the youngest of the French boys that seemed to come out of the ground. The machine-like swing of the bodies of the plant setters suggested vaguely to his mind the possibility of building a machine that would do the work they were doing. His mind took eager hold of that thought and he was relieved. There had been something in the crawling figures and in the moonlight out of which the voices came that had begun to awaken in his mind the fluttering, dreamy state in which he had spent so much of his boyhood. To think of the possibility of building a plant-setting machine was safer. It fitted into what Sarah Shepard had so often told him was the safe way of life. As he went back through the darkness to the railroad station, he thought about the matter and decided that to become an inventor would be the sure way of placing his feet at last upon the path of progress he was trying to find.

Hugh became absorbed in the notion of inventing a machine

that would do the work he had seen the men doing in the field. All day he thought about it. The notion once fixed in his mind gave him something tangible to work upon. In the study of mechanics, taken up in a purely amateur spirit, he had not gone far enough to feel himself capable of undertaking the actual construction of such a machine, but thought the difficulty might be overcome by patience and by experimenting with combinations of wheels, gears and levers whittled out of pieces of wood. From Hunter's Jewelry Store he got a cheap clock and spent days taking it apart and putting it together again. He dropped the doing of mathematical problems and sent away for books describing the construction of machines. Already the flood of new inventions, that was so completely to change the methods of cultivating the soil in America, had begun to spread over the country, and many new and strange kinds of agricultural implements arrived at the Bidwell freight house of the Wheeling railroad. There Hugh saw a harvesting machine for cutting grain, a mowing machine for cutting hay and a long-nosed strange-looking implement that was intended to root potatoes out of the ground very much after the method pursued by energetic pigs. He studied these carefully. For a time his mind turned away from the hunger for human contact and he was content to remain an isolated figure, absorbed in the workings of his own awakening mind.

An absurd and amusing thing happened. After the impulse to try to invent a plant-setting machine came to him, he went every evening to conceal himself in the fence corner and watch the French family at their labors. Absorbed in watching the mechanical movements of the men who crawled across the fields in the moonlight, he forgot they were human. After he had watched them crawl into sight, turn at the end of the rows, and crawl away again into the hazy light that had reminded him of the dim distances of his own Mississipi River country, he was seized with a desire to crawl after them and to try to imitate their movements. Certain intricate mechanical problems, that had already come into his mind in connection with the proposed machine, he thought could be better understood if he could get the movements necessary to plant setting into his own body. His lips began to mutter words and getting out of the fence corner where he had been concealed he began to crawl across the field behind the French boys. "The down stroke will go so," he muttered, and bringing up his arm swung it above his head. His fist descended into the soft ground. He had forgotten the rows of new set plants and crawled directly over them, crushing them into the soft ground. He stopped crawling and waved his arm about. He tried to relate his arms to the mechanical arms of the machine that was being created in his mind. Holding one arm stiffly in front of him he moved it up and down. "The stroke will be shorter than that. The machine must be built close to the ground. The wheels and the horses will travel in paths between the rows. The wheels must be broad to provide traction. I will gear from the wheels to get power for the operation of the mechanism," he said aloud.

Hugh arose and stood in the moonlight in the cabbage field, his arms still going stiffly up and down. The great length of his figure and his arms was accentuated by the wavering uncertain light. The laborers, aware of some strange presence, sprang to their feet and stood listening and looking. Hugh advanced toward them, still muttering words and waving his arms. Terror took hold of the workers. One of the woman plant droppers screamed and ran away across the field, and the others ran crying at her heels. "Don't do it. Go away," the older of the French boys shouted, and then he with his brothers also ran.

Hearing the voices Hugh stopped and stared about. The field was empty. Again he lost himself in his mechanical calculations. He went back along the road to the Wheeling station and to the telegraph office where he worked half the night on a rude drawing he was trying to make of the parts of his plant setting machine, oblivious to the fact that he had created a myth that would run through the whole countryside. The French boys and their sisters stoutly declared that a ghost had come into the cabbage fields and had threatened them with death if they did not go away and quit working at night. In a trembling voice their mother backed up their assertion. Ezra French, who had not seen the apparition and did not believe the tale, scented a revolution. He swore. He threatened the entire family with starvation. He declared that a lie had been invented to deceive and betray him.

However, the work at night in the cabbage fields on the French farm was at an end. The story was told in the town of Bidwell, and as the entire French family except Ezra swore to its truth, was generally believed. Tom Foresby, an old citizen who was a spiritualist, claimed to have heard his father say that there had been in early days an Indian burying-ground on the Turner Pike.

The cabbage field on the French farm became locally famous. Within a year two other men declared they had seen the figure of a gigantic Indian dancing and singing a funeral dirge in the moonlight. Farmer boys, who had been for an evening in town and were returning late at night to lonely farmhouses, whipped their horses into a run when they came to the farm. When it was far behind them they breathed more freely. Although he continued to swear and threaten, Ezra never again succeeded in getting his family into the fields at night. In Bidwell he declared that the story of the ghost invented by his lazy sons and daughters had ruined his chance for making a decent living out of his farm.

CHAPTER VI

Steve Hunter decided that it was time something was done to wake up his native town. The call of the spring wind awoke something in him as in Hugh. It came up from the south bringing rain followed by warm fair days. Robins hopped about on the lawns before the houses on the residence streets of Bidwell, and the air was again sweet with the pregnant sweetness of new-plowed ground. Like Hugh, Steve walked about alone through the dark, dimly lighted residence streets during the spring evenings, but he did not try awkwardly to leap over creeks in the darkness or pull bushes out of the ground, nor did he waste his time dreaming of being physically young, clean-limbed and beautiful.

Before the coming of his great achievements in the industrial field, Steve had not been highly regarded in his home town. He had been a noisy boastful youth and had been spoiled by his father. When he was twelve years old what were called safety bicycles first came into use and for a long time he owned the only one in town. In the evening he rode it up and down Main Street, frightening the horses and arousing the envy of the town boys. He learned to ride without putting his hands on the handle-bars and the other boys began to call him Smarty Hunter and later, because he wore a stiff, white collar that folded down over his shoulders, they gave him a girl's name. "Hello, Susan," they shouted, "don't fall and muss your clothes."

In the spring that marked the beginning of his great industrial adventure, Steve was stirred by the soft spring winds into dreaming his own kind of dreams. As he walked about through the streets, avoiding the other young men and women, he remembered Ernestine, the daughter of the Buffalo soap maker, and thought a great deal about the magnificence of the big stone house in which she lived with her father. His body ached for her, but that was a matter he felt could be managed. How he could achieve a financial position that would make it possible for him to ask for her hand was a more difficult problem. Since he had come back from the business college to live in his home town, he had secretly, and at the cost of two new five dollar dresses, arranged a physical alliance with a girl named Louise Trucker whose father was a farm laborer, and that left his mind free for other things. He intended to become a manufacturer, the first one in Bidwell to make himself a leader in the new movement that was sweeping over the country. He had thought out what he wanted to do and it only remained to find something for him to manufacture to put his plans through. First of all he had selected with great care certain men he intended to ask to go in with him. There was John Clark the banker, his own

father, E. H. Hunter the town jeweler, Thomas Butterworth
the rich farmer, and young Gordon Hart, who had a job as
assistant cashier in the bank. For a month he had been
dropping hints to these men of something mysterious and
important about to happen. With the exception of his father
who had infinite faith in the shrewdness and ability of his
son, the men he wanted to impress were only amused. One
day Thomas Butterworth went into the bank and stood
talking the matter over with John Clark. "The young squirt
was always a smart aleck and a blowhard," he said. "What's
he up to now? What's he nudging and whispering about?"

As he walked in the main street of Bidwell, Steve began
to acquire that air of superiority that later made him so
respected and feared. He hurried along with a peculiarly
intense absorbed look in his eyes. He saw his fellow townsmen
as through a haze, and sometimes did not see them at all.
As he went along he took papers from his pocket, read them
hurriedly, and then quickly put them away again. When he
did speak—perhaps to a man who had known him from
boyhood—there was in his manner something gracious to the
edge of condescension. One morning in March he met Zebe
Wilson the town shoemaker on the sidewalk before the post-
office. Steve stopped and smiled. "Well, good morning,
Mr. Wilson," he said, "and how is the quality of leather you
are getting from the tanneries now?"

Word regarding this strange salutation ran about among
the merchants and artisans. "What's he up to now?" they
asked each other. "Mr. Wilson, indeed! Now what's wrong
between that young squirt and Zebe Wilson?"

In the afternoon, four clerks from the Main Street stores
and Ed Hall the carpenter's apprentice, who had a half day
off because of rain, decided to investigate. One by one they
went along Hamilton Street to Zebe Wilson's shop and
stepped inside to repeat Steve Hunter's salutation. "Well, good
afternoon, Mr. Wilson," they said, "and how is the quality
of leather you are getting from the tanneries now?" Ed Hall,
the last of the five who went into the shop to repeat the

formal and polite inquiry, barely escaped with his life. Zebe Wilson threw a shoemaker's hammer at him and it went through the glass in the upper part of the shop door.

Once when Tom Butterworth and John Clark the banker were talking of the new air of importance he was assuming, and half-indignantly speculated on what he meant by his whispered suggestion of something significant about to happen, Steve came along Main Street past the front door of the bank. John Clark called him in. The three men confronted each other and the jeweler's son sensed the fact that the banker and the rich farmer were amused by his pretensions. At once he proved himself to be what all Bidwell later acknowledged him to be, a man who could handle men and affairs. Having at that time nothing to support his pretensions he decided to put up a bluff. With a wave of his hand and an air of knowing just what he was about, he led the two men into the back room cf the bank and shut the door leading into the large room to which the general public was admitted. "You would have thought he owned the place," John Clark afterward said with a note of admiration in his voice to young Gordon Hart when he described what took place in the back room.

Steve plunged at once into what he had to say to the two solid moneyed citizens of his town. "Well, now, look here, you two," he began earnestly. "I'm going to tell you something, but you got to keep still." He went to the window that looked out upon an alleyway and glanced about as though fearful of being overheard, then sat down in the chair usually occupied by John Clark on the rare occasions when the directors of the Bidwell bank held a meeting. Steve looked over the heads of the two men who in spite of themselves were beginning to be impressed. "Well," he began, "there is a fellow out at Pickleville. You have maybe heard things said about him. He's telegraph operator out there. Perhaps you have heard how he is always making drawings of parts of machines. I guess everybody in town has been wondering what he's up to."

Steve looked at the two men and then got nervously out

of the chair and walked about the room. "That fellow is my man. I put him there," he declared. "I didn't want to tell anyone yet."

The two men nodded and Steve became lost in the notion created in his fancy. It did not occur to him that what he had just said was untrue. He began to scold the two men. "Well, I suppose I'm on the wrong track there," he said. "My man has made an invention that will bring millions in profits to those who get into it. In Cleveland and Buffalo I'm already in touch with big bankers. There's to be a big factory built, but you see yourself how it is, here I'm at home. I was raised as a boy here."

The excited young man plunged into an exposition of the spirit of the new times. He grew bold and scolded the older men. "You know yourself that factories are springing up everywhere, in towns all over the state," he said. "Will Bidwell wake up? Will we have factories here? You know well enough we won't, and I know why. It's because a man like me who was raised here has to go to a city to get money to back his plans. If I talked to you fellows you would laugh at me. In a few years I might make you more money than you have made in your whole lives, but what's the use talking? I'm Steve Hunter; you knew me when I was a kid. You'd laugh. What's the use my trying to tell you fellows my plans?"

Steve turned as though to go out of the room, but Tom Butterworth took hold of his arm and led him back to a chair. "Now, you tell us what you're up to," he demanded. In turn he grew indignant. "If you've got something to manufacture you can get backing here as well as anyplace," he said. He became convinced that the jeweler's son was telling the truth. It did not occur to him that a Bidwell young man would dare lie to such solid men as John Clark and himself. "You let them city bankers alone," he said emphatically. "You tell us your story. What you got to tell?"

In the silent little room the three men stared at each other. Tom Butterworth and John Clark in their turn began to have dreams. They remembered the tales they had heard of vast fortunes made quickly by men who owned new and valuable inventions. The land was at that time full of such tales. They were blown about on every wind. Quickly they realized that they had made a mistake in their attitude toward Steve, and were anxious to win his regard. They had called him into the bank to bully him and to laugh at him. Now they were sorry. As for Steve, he only wanted to get away— to get by himself and think. An injured look crept over his face. "Well," he said, "I thought I'd give Bidwell a chance. There are three or four men here. I have spoken to all of you and dropped a hint of something in the wind, but I'm not ready to be very definite yet."

Seeing the new look of respect in the eyes of the two men Steve became bold. "I was going to call a meeting when I was ready," he said pompously. " You two do what I've been doing. You keep your mouths shut. Don't go near that telegraph operator and don't talk to a soul. If you mean business I'll give you a chance to make barrels of money, more'n you ever dreamed of, but don't be in a hurry." He took a bundle of letters out of his inside coat pocket, and beat with them on the edge of the table that occupied the center of the room. Another bold thought came into his mind.

"I've got letters here offering me big money to take my factory either to Cleveland or Buffalo," he declared emphatically. "It isn't money that's hard to get. I can tell you men that. What a man wants in his home town is respect. He don't want to be looked on as a fool because he tries to do something to rise in the world."

Steve walked boldly out of the bank and into Main Street. When he had got out of the presence of the two men he was frightened. "Well, I've done it. I've made a fool of myself," he muttered aloud. In the bank he had said that Hugh McVey the telegraph operator was his man, that he had brought the fellow to Bidwell. What a fool he had been. In his anxiety to impress the two older men he had told a story, the falsehood of which could be discovered in a few minutes.

Why had he not kept his dignity and waited? There had been
no occasion for being so definite. He had gone too far, had
been carried away. To be sure he had told the two men not
to go near the telegraph operator, but that would no doubt
but serve to arouse their suspicions of the thinness of his
story. They would talk the matter over and start an investigation of their own. Then they would find out he had lied.
He imagined the two men as already engaged in a whispered
conversation regarding the probability of his tale. Like most
shrewd men he had an exalted notion regarding the shrewdness
of others. He walked a little away from the bank and then
turned to look back. A shiver ran over his body. Into his
mind came the sickening fear that the telegraph operator at
Pickleville was not an inventor at all. The town was full of
tales, and in the bank he had taken advantage of that fact
to make an impression; but what proof had he? No one had
seen one of the inventions supposed to have been worked
out by the mysterious stranger from Missouri. There had after
all been nothing but whispered suspicions, old wives' tales,
fables invented by men who had nothing to do but loaf in
the drugstore and make up stories.

The thought that Hugh McVey might not be an inventor
overpowered him and he put it quickly aside. He had something more immediate to think about. The story of the bluff
he had just made in the bank would be found out and the
whole town would rock with laughter at his expense. The
young men of the town did not like him. They would roll
the story over on their tongues. Ribald old fellows who had
nothing else to do would take up the story with joy and
would elaborate it. Fellows like the cabbage farmer Ezra
French, who had a talent for saying cutting things, would
exercise it. They would make up imaginary inventions,
grotesque, absurd inventions. Then they would get young
fellows to come to him and propose that he take them up,
promote them, and make everyone rich. Men would shout
jokes at him as he went along Main Street. His dignity would
be gone forever. He would be made a fool of by the very

school boys as he had been in his youth when he bought the bicycle and rode it about before the eyes of other boys in the evenings.

Steve hurried out of Main Street and went over the bridge that crossed the river into Turner's Pike. He did not know what he intended to do, but felt there was much at stake and that he would have to do something at once. It was a warm, cloudy day and the road that led to Pickleville was muddy. During the night before it had rained and more rain was promised. The path beside the road was slippery, and so absorbed was he that as he plunged along, his feet slipped out from under him and he sat down in a small pool of water. A farmer driving past along the road turned to laugh at him. "You go to hell," Steve shouted. "You just mind your own business and go to hell."

The distracted young man tried to walk sedately along the path. The long grass that grew beside the path wet his shoes, and his hands were wet and muddy. Farmers turned on their wagon seats to stare at him. For some obscure reason he could not himself understand, he was terribly afraid to face Hugh McVey. In the bank he had been in the presence of men who were trying to get the best of him, to make a fool of him, to have fun at his expense. He had felt that and had resented it. The knowledge had given him a certain kind of boldness; it had enabled his mind to make up the story of the inventor secretly employed at his own expense and the city bankers anxious to furnish him capital. Although he was terribly afraid of discovery, he felt a little glow of pride at the thought of the boldness with which he had taken the letters out of his pocket and had challenged the two men to call his bluff.

Steve, however, felt there was something different about the man in the telegraph office in Pickleville. He had been in town for nearly two years and no one knew anything about him. His silence might be indicative of anything. He was afraid the tall silent Missourian might decide to have nothing to do with him, and pictured himself as being brushed rudely aside, being told to mind his own business.

Steve knew instinctively how to handle business men. One simply created the notion of money to be made without effort. He had done that to the two men in the bank and it had worked. After all he had succeeded in making them respect him. He had handled the situation. He wasn't such a fool at that kind of a thing. The other thing he had to face might be very different. Perhaps after all Hugh McVey was a big inventor, a man with a powerful creative mind. It was possible he had been sent to Bidwell by a big business man of some city. Big business men did strange, mysterious things; they put wires out in all directions, controlled a thousand little avenues for the creation of wealth.

Just starting out on his own career as a man of affairs, Steve had an overpowering respect for what he thought of as the subtlety of men of affairs. With all the other American youths of his generation he had been swept off his feet by the propaganda that then went on and is still going on, and that is meant to create the illusion of greatness in connection with the ownership of money. He did not then know and, in spite of his own later success and his own later use of the machinery by which illusion is created, he never found out that in an industrial world reputations for greatness of mind are made as a Detroit manufacturer would make automobiles. He did not know that men are employed to bring up the name of a politician so that he may be called a statesman, as a new brand of breakfast food that it may be sold; that most modern great men are mere illusions sprung out of a national hunger for greatness. Some day a wise man, one who has not read too many books but who has gone about among men, will discover and set forth a very interesting thing about America. The land is vast and there is a national hunger for vastness in individuals. One wants an Illinois-sized man for Illinois, an Ohio-sized man for Ohio, and a Texas-sized man for Texas.

To be sure, Steve Hunter had no notion of all this. He never did get a notion of it. The men he had already begun to think of as great and to try to imitate were like the strange and gigantic protuberances that sometimes grow on the side of unhealthy trees, but he did not know it. He did not know that throughout the country, even in that early day, a system was being built up to create the myth of greatness. At the seat of the American government at Washington, hordes of somewhat clever and altogether unhealthy young men were already being employed for the purpose. In a sweeter age many of these young men might have become artists, but they had not been strong enough to stand against the growing strength of dollars. They had become instead newspaper correspondents and secretaries to politicians. All day and every day they used their minds and their talents as writers in the making of puffs and the creating of myths concerning the men by whom they were employed. They were like the trained sheep that are used at great slaughterhouses to lead other sheep into the killing pens. Having befouled their own minds for hire, they made their living by befouling the minds of others. Already they had found out that no great cleverness was required for the work they had to do. What was required was constant repetition. It was only necessary to say over and over that the man by whom they were employed was a great man. No proof had to be brought forward to substantiate the claims they made; no great deeds had to be done by the men who were thus made great, as brands of crackers or breakfast food are made salable. Stupid and prolonged and insistent repetition was what was necessary.

As the politicians of the industrial age have created a myth about themselves, so also have the owners of dollars, the big bankers, the railroad manipulators, the promoters of industrial enterprise. The impulse to do so is partly sprung from shrewdness but for the most part it is due to a hunger within to be of some real moment in the world. Knowing that the talent that had made them rich is but a secondary talent, and being a little worried about the matter, they employ men to glorify it. Having employed a man for the purpose, they are themselves children enough to believe the myth they have paid money to have created. Every rich man in the country unconsciously hates his press agent.

Although he had never read a book, Steve was a constant

reader of the newspapers and had been deeply impressed by the stories he had read regarding the shrewdness and ability of the American captains of industry. To him they were supermen and he would have crawled on his knees before a Gould or a Cal Price—the commanding figures among moneyed men of that day. As he went down along Turner's Pike that day when industry was born in Bidwell, he thought of these men and of lesser rich men of Cleveland and Buffalo, and was afraid that in approaching Hugh he might be coming into competition with one of these men. As he hurried along under the gray sky, he however realized that the time for action had come and that he must at once put the plans that he had formed in his mind to the test of practicability; that he must at once see Hugh McVey, find out if he really did have an invention that could be manufactured, and if he did try to secure some kind of rights of ownership over it. "If I do not act at once, either Tom Butterworth or John Clark will get in ahead of me," he thought. He knew they were both shrewd capable men. Had they not become well-to-do? Even during the talk in the bank, when they had seemed to be impressed by his words, they might well have been making plans to get the better of him. They would act, but he must act first.

Steve hadn't the courage of the lie he had told. He did not have imagination enough to understand how powerful a thing is a lie. He walked quickly along until he came to the Wheeling Station at Pickleville, and then, not having the courage to confront Hugh at once, went past the station and crept in behind the deserted pickle factory and stood across the tracks. Through a broken window at the back he climbed, and crept like a thief across the earth floor until he came to a window that looked out upon the station. A freight train rumbled slowly past and a farmer came to the station to get a load of goods that had arrived by freight. George Pike came running from his house to attend to the wants of the farmer. He went back to his house and Steve was left alone in the presence of the man on whom he felt all of his future depended. He was as excited as a village girl in the presence of a lover. Through the windows of the telegraph office he could see Hugh seated at a desk with a book before him. The presence of the book frightened him. He decided that the mysterious Missourian must be some strange sort of intellectual giant. He was sure that one who could sit quietly reading hour after hour in such a lonely isolated place could be of no ordinary clay. As he stood in the deep shadows inside the old building and stared at the man he was trying to find courage to approach, a citizen of Bidwell named Dick Spearsman came to the station and going inside, talked to the telegraph operator. Steve trembled with anxiety. The man who had come to the station was an insurance agent who also owned a small berry farm at the edge of town. He had a son who had gone west to take up land in the State of Kansas, and the father thought of visiting him. He came to the station to make inquiry regarding the railroad fare, but when Steve saw him talking to Hugh, the thought came into his mind that John Clark or Thomas Butterworth might have sent him to the station to make an investigation of the truth of the statements he had made in the bank. "It would be like them to do it that way," he muttered to himself. "They wouldn't come themselves. They would send someone they thought I wouldn't suspect. They would play safe, damn 'em."

Trembling with fear, Steve walked up and down in the empty factory. Cobwebs hanging down brushed against his face and he jumped aside as though a hand had reached out of the darkness to touch him. In the corners of the old building shadows lurked and distorted thoughts began to come into his head. He rolled and lighted a cigarette and then remembered that the flare of the match could probably be seen from the station. He cursed himself for his carelessness. Throwing the cigarette on the earth floor he ground it under his heel. When at last Dick Spearsman had disappeared up the road that led to Bidwell and he came out of the old factory and got again into Turner's Pike, he felt that he was in no shape to talk of business but nevertheless must act at once. In front of the factory he stopped in the road and tried to wipe the mud off the seat of his trousers with a handkerchief. Then he went to the creek and washed his soiled hands. With wet hands he arranged his tie and straightened the collar of his coat. He had an air of one about to ask a woman to become his wife. Striving to look as important and dignified as possible, he went along the station platform and into the telegraph office to confront Hugh and to find out at once and finally what fate the gods had in store for him.

It no doubt contributed to Steve's happiness in after life, in the days when he was growing rich, and later when he reached out for public honors, contributed to campaign funds, and even in secret dreamed of getting into the United States Senate or being Governor of his state, that he never knew how badly he overreached himself that day in his youth when he made his first business deal with Hugh at the Wheeling Station at Pickleville. Later Hugh's interest in the Steven Hunter industrial enterprises was taken care of by a man who was as shrewd as Steve himself. Tom Butterworth, who had made money and knew how to make and handle money, managed such things for the inventor, and Steve's chance was gone forever.

That is, however, a part of the story of the development of the town of Bidwell and a story that Steve never understood. When he overreached himself that day he did not know what he had done. He made a deal with Hugh and was happy to escape the predicament he thought he had got himself into when he talked too much of the two men in the bank.

Although Steve's father had always a great faith in his son's shrewdness and when he talked to other men represented him as a peculiarly capable and unappreciated man, the two did not in private get on well. In the Hunter household they quarreled and snarled at each other. Steve's mother had died when he was a small boy and his one sister, two years older than himself, kept herself always in the house and seldom appeared on the streets. She was a semi-invalid. Some obscure nervous disease had twisted her body out of shape, and her face twitched incessantly. One morning in the barn back of the Hunter house Steve, then a lad of fourteen, was oiling his bicycle when his sister appeared and stood watching him. A small wrench lay on the ground and she picked it up. Suddenly and without warning she began to beat him on the head. He was compelled to knock her down in order to tear the wrench out of her hand. After the incident she was ill in bed for a month.

Elsie Hunter was always a source of unhappiness to her brother. As he began to get up in life Steve had a growing passion for being respected by his fellows. It got to be something of an obsession with him and among other things he wanted very much to be thought of as one who had good blood in his veins. A man whom he hired searched out his ancestry, and with the exception of his immediate family it seemed very satisfactory. The sister, with her twisted body and her face that twitched so persistently, seemed to be everlastingly sneering at him. He grew half-afraid to come into her presence. After he began to grow rich he married Ernestine, the daughter of the soap maker at Buffalo, and when her father died she also had a great deal of money. His own father died and he set up a household of his own. That was in the time when big houses began to appear at the edge of the berry lands and on the hills south of Bidwell. On his father's death Steve became guardian for his sister. The jeweler had left a small estate and it was entirely in the son's hands. Elsie lived with one servant in a small house in town and was put in the position of being entirely dependent on her brother's bounty. In a sense it might be said that she lived by her hatred of him. When on rare occasions he came to her house she would not see him. A servant came to the door and reported her asleep. Almost every month she wrote a letter demanding that her share of her father's money be handed over to her, but it did no good. Steve occasionally spoke to an acquaintance of his difficulty with her. "I am more sorry for the woman than I can say," he declared. "It's the dream of my life to make the poor afflicted soul happy. You see yourself that I provide her with every comfort of life. Ours is an old family. I have it from an expert in such matters that we are descendants of one Hunter, a courtier in the court of Edward the Second of England. Our blood has perhaps become a little thin. All the vitality of the family was centered in me. My sister does not understand me and that has been the cause of much unhappiness and heart burning, but I shall always do my duty by her."

In the late afternoon of the spring day that was also the most eventful day of his life, Steve went quickly along the Wheeling Station platform to the door of the telegraph office. It was a public place, but before going in he stopped, again straightened his tie and brushed his clothes, and then knocked at the door. As there was no response he opened the door softly and looked in. Hugh was at his desk but did not look up. Steve went in and closed the door. By chance the moment of his entrance was also a big moment in the life of the man he had come to see. The mind of the young inventor, that had for so long been dreamy and uncertain, had suddenly become extraordinarily clear and free. One of the inspired moments that come to intense natures, working intensely, had come to him. The mechanical problem he was trying so hard to work out became clear. It was one of the moments that Hugh afterwards thought of as justifying his existence, and in later life he came to live for such moments. With a nod of his head to Steve he arose and hurried out to the building that was used by the Wheeling as a freight warehouse. The jeweler's son ran at his heels. On an elevated platform before the freight warehouse sat an odd-looking agricultural implement, a machine for rooting potatoes out of the ground that had been received on the day before and was now awaiting delivery to some farmer. Hugh dropped to his knees beside the machine and examined it closely. Muttered exclamations broke from his lips. For the first time in his life he was not embarrassed in the presence of another person. The two men, the one almost grotesquely tall, the other short of stature and already inclined toward corpulency, stared at each other. "What is it you're inventing? I came to see you about that," Steve said timidly.

Hugh did not answer the question directly. He stepped across the narrow platform to the freight warehouse and began to make a rude drawing on the side of the building. Then he tried to explain his plantsetting machine. He spoke of it as a thing already achieved. At the moment he thought of it in that way. "I had not thought of the use of a large wheel with the arms attached at regular intervals," he said absentmindedly. "I will have to find money now. That'll be the next step. It will be necessary to make a working model of the machine now. I must find out what changes I'll have to make in my calculations."

The two men returned to the telegraph office and while Hugh listened Steve made his proposal. Even then he did not understand what the machine that was to be made was to do. It was enough for him that a machine was to be made and he wanted to share in its ownership at once. As the two men walked back from the freight warehouse, his mind took hold of Hugh's remark about getting money. Again he was afraid. "There's someone in the background," he thought. "Now I must make a proposal he can't refuse. I mustn't leave until I've made a deal with him."

Fairly carried away by his anxiety, Steve proposed to provide money out of his own pocket to make the model of the machine. "We'll rent the old pickle factory across the track," he said, opening the door and pointing with a trembling finger. "I can get it cheap. I'll have windows and a floor put in. Then I'll get you a man to whittle out a model of the machine. Allie Mulberry can do it. I'll get him for you. He can whittle anything if you only show him what you want. He's halfcrazy and won't get on to our secret. When the model is made, leave it to me, you just leave it to me."

Rubbing his hands together Steve walked boldly to the telegrapher's desk and picking up a sheet of paper began to write out a contract. It provided that Hugh was to get a royalty of ten per cent of the selling price on the machine he had invented and that was to be manufactured by a company to be organized by Steven Hunter. The contract also stated that a promoting company was to be organized at once and money provided for the experimental work Hugh had yet to do. The

Missourian was to begin getting a salary at once. He was to risk nothing, as Steve elaborately explained. When he was ready for them mechanics were to be employed and their salaries paid. When the contract had been written and read aloud, a copy was made and Hugh, who was again embarrassed beyond words, signed his name.

With a flourish of his hand Steve laid a little pile of money on the desk. "That's for a starter," he said and turned to frown at George Pike who at that moment came to the door. The freight agent went quickly away and the two men were left alone together. Steve shook hands with his new partner. He went out and then came in again. "You understand," he said mysteriously. "The fifty dollars is your first month's salary. I was ready for you. I brought it along. You just leave everything to me, just you leave it to me." Again he went out and Hugh was left alone. He saw the young man go across the tracks to the old factory and walk up and down before it. When a farmer came along and shouted at him, he did not reply, but stepping back into the road swept the deserted old building with his eyes as a general might have looked over a battlefield. Then he went briskly down the road toward town and the farmer turned on his wagon seat to stare after him.

Hugh McVey also stared. When Steve had gone away, he walked to the end of the station platform and looked along the road toward town. It seemed to him wonderful that he had at last held conversation with a citizen of Bidwell. A little of the import of the contract he had signed came to him, and he went into the station and got his copy of it and put it in his pocket. Then he came out again. When he read it over and realized anew that he was to be paid a living wage and have time and help to work out the problem that had now become vastly important to his happiness, it seemed to him that he had been in the presence of a kind of god. He remembered the words of Sarah Shepard concerning the bright alert citizens of eastern towns and realized that he had been in the presence of such a being, that he had in some way become connected in his new work with such a one. The realization overcame him completely. Forgetting entirely his duties as a telegrapher, he closed the office and went for a walk across the meadows and in the little patches of woodlands that still remained standing in the open plain north of Pickleville. He did not return until late at night, and when he did, had not solved the puzzle as to what had happened. All he got out of it was the fact that the machine he had been trying to make was of great and mysterious importance to the civilization into which he had come to live and of which he wanted so keenly to be a part. There seemed to him something almost sacred in that fact. A new determination to complete and perfect his plant-setting machine had taken possession of him.

Weaving through the fabric of the novel is the story of Clara Butterworth, daughter of the township's wealthiest farmer. She has been educated at Ohio's university in Columbus and is among the "emancipated" young women of her day, with a mind and will of her own. On her return to Bidwell from college, she fixes her eyes on McVey, and it is she who does more than half the wooing, its progress quickened by rumors of her adventures with other men. She marries him.

One day in the month of October, four years after the time of his first motor ride with Clara and Tom, Hugh went on a business trip to the city of Pittsburgh. He left Bidwell in the morning and got to the steel city at noon. At three o'clock his business was finished and he was ready to return.

Although he had not yet realized it, Hugh's career as a successful inventor had received a sharp check. The trick of driving directly at the point, of becoming utterly absorbed in the thing before him, had been lost. He went to Pittsburgh to see about the casting of new parts for the hay-loading machine, but what he did in Pittsburgh was of no importance to the men who would manufacture and sell that worthy, labor-saving tool. Although he did not know it, a young man from Cleveland, in the employ of Tom and Steve, had already done what Hugh was striving half-heartedly to do. The machine had been finished and ready to market in October three years before, and after repeated tests a lawyer had made formal application for patent. Then it was discovered that an Iowa man had already made application for and been granted a patent on a similar apparatus.

When Tom came to the shop and told him what had happened Hugh had been ready to drop the whole matter, but that was not Tom's notion. "The devil!" he said. "Do you think we're going to waste all this money and labor?"

Drawings of the Iowa man's machine were secured. and Tom set Hugh at the task of doing what he called "getting round" the other fellow's patents. "Do the best you can and we'll go ahead," he said. "You see we've got the money and that means power. Make what changes you can and then we'll go on with our manufacturing plans. We'll whipsaw this other fellow through the courts. We'll fight him till he's sick of fight and then we'll buy him out cheap. I've had the fellow looked up and he hasn't any money and is a boozer besides. You go ahead. We'll get that fellow all right."

Hugh had tried valiantly to go along the road marked out for him by his father-in-law and had put aside other plans to rebuild the machine he had thought of as completed and out of the way. He made new parts, changed other parts, studied the drawings of the Iowa man's machine, did what he could to accomplish his task.

Nothing happened. A conscientious determination not to infringe on the work of the Iowa man stood in his way.

Then something did happen. At night as he sat alone in his shop after a long study of the drawings of the other man's machine, he put them aside and sat staring into the darkness beyond the circle of light cast by his lamp. He forgot the machine and thought of the unknown inventor, the man far away over forests, lakes and rivers, who for months had worked on the same problem that had occupied his mind. Tom had said the man had no money and was a boozer. He could be defeated, bought cheap. He was himself at work on the instrument of the man's defeat.

Hugh left his shop and went for a walk, and the problem connected with the twisting of the iron and steel parts of the hay-loading apparatus into new forms was again left unsolved. The Iowa man had become a distinct, almost understandable personality to Hugh. Tom had said he drank, got drunk. His own father had been a drunkard. Once a man, the very man who had been the instrument of his own coming to Bidwell, had taken it for granted he was a drunkard. He wondered if some twist of life might not have made him one.

Thinking of the Iowa man, Hugh began to think of other men. He thought of his father and of himself. When he was striving to come out of the filth, the flies, the poverty, the fishy smells, the shadowy dreams of his life by the river, his father had often tried to draw him back into that life. In imagination he saw before him the dissolute man who had bred him. On afternoons of summer days in the river town, when Henry Shepard was not about, his father sometimes came to the station where he was employed. He had begun to earn a little money and his father wanted it to buy drinks. Why?

There was a problem for Hugh's mind, a problem that could not be solved in wood and steel. He walked and thought about it when he should have been making new parts for the hay-loading apparatus. He had lived but little in the life of the imagination, had been afraid to live that life, had been warned and rewarned against living it. The shadowy figure of the unknown inventor in the State of Iowa, who had been brother to himself, who had worked on the same problems and had come to the same conclusions, slipped away, followed by the almost equally shadowy figure of his father. Hugh tried to think of himself and his own life.

For a time that seemed a simple and easy way out of the new and intricate task he had set for his mind. His own life was a matter of history. He knew about himself. Having walked far out of town, he turned and went back toward his shop. His way led through the new city that had grown up since his coming to Bidwell. Turner's Pike that had been a country road along which on summer evenings lovers strolled to the Wheeling Station and Pickleville was now a street. All that section of the new city was given over to workers' homes and here and there a store had been built. The Widow

McCoy's place was gone and in its place was a warehouse, black and silent under the night sky. How grim the street in the late night! The berry pickers who once went along the road at evening were now gone forever. Like Ezra French's sons they had perhaps become factory hands. Apple and cherry trees once grew along the road. They had dropped their blossoms on the heads of strolling lovers. They also were gone. Hugh had once crept along the road at the heels of Ed Hall, who walked with his arm about a girl's waist. He had heard Ed complaining of his lot in life and crying out for new times. It was Ed Hall who had introduced the piece-work plan in the factories of Bidwell and brought about the strike, during which three men had been killed and ill-feeling engendered in hundreds of silent workers. That strike had been won by Tom and Steve and they had since that time been victorious in a larger and more serious strike. Ed Hall was now at the head of a new factory being built along the Wheeling tracks. He was growing fat and was prosperous.

When Hugh got to his shop he lighted his lamp and again got out the drawings he had come from home to study. They lay unnoticed on the desk. He looked at his watch. It was two o'clock. "Clara may be awake. I must go home," he thought vaguely. He now owned his own motor car and it stood in the road before the shop. Getting in he drove away into the darkness over the bridge, out of Turner's Pike and along a street lined with factories and railroad sidings. Some of the factories were working and were ablaze with lights. Through lighted windows he could see men stationed along benches and bending over huge, iron machines. He had come from home that evening to study the work of an unknown man from the faraway State of Iowa, to try to circumvent that man. Then he had gone to walk and to think of himself and his own life. "The evening has been wasted. I have done nothing," he thought gloomily as his car climbed up a long street lined with the homes of the wealthier citizens of his town and turned into the short stretch of Medina Road still left between the town and the Butterworth farmhouse.

On the day when he went to Pittsburgh, Hugh got to the station where he was to take the homeward train at three, and the train did not leave until four. He went into a big waiting-room and sat on a bench in a corner. After a time he arose and going to a stand bought a newspaper, but did not read it. It lay unopened on the bench beside him. The station was filled with men, women, and children who moved restlessly about. A train came in and a swarm of people departed, were carried into faraway parts of the country, while new people came into the station from a nearby street. He looked at those who were going out into the train shed. "It may be that some of them are going to that town in Iowa where that fellow lives," he thought. It was odd how thoughts of the unknown Iowa man clung to him. . . .

On that day when he went to Sandusky, Hugh had several hours to wait for his homebound train and went to walk by the shores of a bay. Some brightly colored stones attracted his attention and he picked several of them up and put them in his pockets. In the station at Pittsburgh he took them out and held them in his hand. A light came in at a window, a long slanting light that played over the stones. His roving, disturbed mind was caught and held. He rolled the stones back and forth. The colors blended and then separated again. When he raised his eyes, a woman and a child on a nearby bench, also attracted by the flashing bit of color held like a flame in his hand, were looking at him intently.

He was confused and walked out of the station into the street. "What a silly fellow I have become, playing with colored stones like a child," he thought, but at the same time put the stones carefully into his pockets. . . .

Hugh got into his homebound train at four o'clock and went into the smoking car. The somewhat distorted and twisted fragment of thoughts that had all day been playing through his mind stayed with him. "What difference does it make if the new parts I have ordered for the machine have to be thrown away?" he thought. "If I never complete the machine, it's all right. The one the Iowa man had made does the work."

For a long time he struggled with that thought. Tom, Steve, all the Bidwell men with whom he had been associated, had a philosophy into which the thought did not fit. "When you put your hand to the plow do not turn back," they said. Their language was full of such sayings. To attempt to do a thing and fail was the great crime, the sin against the Holy Ghost. There was unconscious defiance of a whole civilization in Hugh's attitude toward the completion of the parts that would help Tom and his business associates "get around" the Iowa man's patent.

The train from Pittsburgh went through northern Ohio to a junction where Hugh would get another train for Bidwell. Great booming towns, Youngstown, Akron, Canton, Massilon —manufacturing towns all—lay along the way. In the smoker Hugh sat, again playing with the colored stones held in his hand. There was relief for his mind in the stones. The light continually played about them, and their color shifted and changed. One could look at the stones and get relief from thoughts. Raising his eyes he looked out of the car window. The train was passing through Youngstown. His eyes looked along grimy streets of workers' houses clustered closely about huge mills. The same light that had played over the stones in his hand began to play over his mind, and for a moment he became not an inventor but a poet. The revolution within had really begun. A new declaration of independence wrote itself within him. "The gods have thrown the towns like stones over the flat country, but the stones have no color. They do not burn and change in the light," he thought.

Two men who sat in a seat in the westward-bound train began to talk, and Hugh listened. One of them had a son in college. "I want him to be a mechanical engineer," he said. "If he doesn't do that I'll get him started in business. It's a mechanical age and a business age. I want to see him succeed. I want him to keep in the spirit of the times."

Hugh's train was due in Bidwell at ten, but did not arrive until half after eleven. He walked from the station through the town toward the Butterworth farm.

At the end of their first year of marriage a daughter had been born to Clara, and some time before his trip to Pittsburgh she had told him she was again pregnant. "She may be sitting up. I must get home," he thought, but when he got to the bridge near the farmhouse, the bridge on which he had stood beside Clara that first time they were together, he got out of the road and went to sit on a fallen log at the edge of a grove of trees.

"How quiet and peaceful the night!" he thought and leaning forward held his long, troubled face in his hands. He wondered why peace and quiet would not come to him, why life would not let him alone. "After all, I've lived a simple life and have done good work," he thought. "Some of the things they've said about me are true enough. I've invented machines that save useless labor, I've lightened men's labor."

Butterworth, Clara's father, attempts to drive McVey into rivalry with another inventor, and McVey's response to his father-in-law's demands brings the book to a close.

Now his eyes looked at the towns, at Bidwell, Akron, Youngstown, and all the great, new towns scattered up and down Midwestern America as on the train and in the station at Pittsburgh he had looked at the colored stones held in his hand. He looked at the towns and wanted light and color to play over them as they played over the stones, and when that did not happen, his mind, filled with strange new hungers engendered by the disease of thinking, made up words over which lights played. "The gods have scattered towns over the flat lands," his mind had said, as he sat in the smoking car of the train, and the phrase came back to him later, as he sat in the darkness on the log with his head held in his hands. It was a good phrase and lights could play over it as they played over the colored stones, but it would in no way answer the problem of how to "get around" the Iowa man's patent on the hay-loading device.

Hugh did not get to the Butterworth farmhouse until two o'clock in the morning, but when he got there his wife was awake and waiting for him. She heard his heavy, dragging footsteps in the road as he turned in at the farm gate, and getting quickly out of bed, threw a cloak over her shoulders and came out to the porch facing the barns. A late moon had come up and the barnyard was washed with moonlight. From the barns came the low, sweet sound of contented animals nibbling at the hay in the mangers before them, from a row of sheds back of one of the barns came the soft bleating of sheep and in a faraway field a calf bellowed loudly and was answered by its mother.

When Hugh stepped into the moonlight around the corner of the house, Clara ran down the steps to meet him, and taking his arm, led him past the barns and over the bridge where as a child she had seen the figures of her fancy advancing towards her. Sensing his troubled state her mother spirit was aroused. He was unfilled by the life he led. She understood that. It was so with her. By a lane they went to a fence where nothing but open fields lay between the farm and the town far below. Although she sensed his troubled state, Clara was not thinking of Hugh's trip to Pittsburgh nor of the problems connected with the completion of the hay-loading machine. It may be that like her father she had dismissed from her mind all thoughts of him as one who would continue to help solve the mechanical problems of his age. Thoughts of his continued success had never meant much to her, but during the evening something had happened to Clara and she wanted to tell him about it, to take him into the joy of it. Their first child had been a girl and she was sure the next would be a man child. "I felt him tonight," she said, when they had got to the place by the fence and saw below the lights of the town. "I felt him tonight," she said again, "and oh, he was strong! He kicked like anything. I am sure this time it's a boy."

For perhaps ten minutes Clara and Hugh stood by the fence. The disease of thinking that was making Hugh useless for the work of his age had swept away many old things within him and he was not self-conscious in the presence of his woman. When she told him of the struggle of the man of another generation, striving to be born he put his arm about her and held her close against his long body. For a time they stood in silence, and then started to return to the house and sleep. As they went past the barns and the bunkhouse where several men now slept they heard, as though coming out of the past, the loud snoring of the rapidly aging farm hand, Jim Priest, and then above that sound and above the sound of the animals stirring in the barns arose another sound, a sound shrill and intense, greetings perhaps to an unborn Hugh McVey. For some reason, perhaps to announce a shift in crews, the factories of Bidwell that were engaged in night work set up a great whistling and screaming. The sound ran up the hillside and rang in the ears of Hugh as, with his arm about Clara's shoulders, he went up the steps and in at the farm-house door.

SELECTED
STORIES

_____

The Contract

EDITOR'S NOTE

"The Contract," an early story which appeared first in 1921, has been selected to counterbalance "The Man Who Became a Woman." The pastoral quality of the final love scene in it, and the scene witnessed at a distance by two boys, are among the best examples of Anderson's descriptive powers. Here, as in "A Meeting South", the action of the story is not spectacular; there is little outward show of emotion, yet the feeling of being betrayed and of being trapped by love is clearly conveyed by the speeches of the man and woman. The same feeling (which in Anderson's writings is a theme) enters his novels *Many Marriages* (1923) and *Beyond Desire* (1932). The story plays on the theme with greater poignancy than the longer pieces, and one is not likely to forget the sensations of a man who "felt like a beast who in playing about at night in a forest has suddenly put his foot in a trap."

One evening he kissed her, and she got abruptly up from the bench in the garden back of her father's house and went to stand by a tree. How soft and still and lovely the night seemed to him! He felt absurdly set up, a little, perhaps, he thought, smiling indulgently at himself, as a warrior might feel after securing a position of advantage for a coming great battle. For the moment he had forgotten her and continued to sit alone on the bench smiling at himself. Had the stillness of the garden been broken by the blast of a trumpet and himself proclaimed some kind of a conquering male hero, he would not have been too surprised. The notion of being a conqueror clung to him, and although he laughed at himself, he went on playing with the idea. There was Napoleon following his star of destiny and Alexander sighing for more worlds to conquer! Had he not suddenly kissed her without asking permission? Had he not stormed the fortress? It was the way things were done among the bolder males. He laughed softly.

In a way she had been expecting the kiss, although she had been telling herself she did not want it. Still she was prepared for it as he was not. It was the third time they had been together.

For her the first time she had seen him had been the most stirring of all. He had come into town unheralded and then word had gone around that he was a figure of consequence in the intellectual world. He was invited to speak before an organization called the Thursday Club and she went with her father, the editor of the town's one newspaper.

His figure had swept like a flame across the field of her fancy that first evening. In what a daring way he had talked! His subject was the effect of Christianity on civilization and he spoke of Jesus, the man of Nazareth, in a way that disturbed and irritated the Thursday Club. With what fire and eloquence he talked. There was the sacred young man, a carpenter in an obscure village. He had thought his own thoughts, ignored the teachings of older men. When he was not at work at his trade, he went alone to talk in the hills. His own intense nature and the long hours and days of silent contemplation of life had made him a profound mystic. Had anyone thought, had anyone dared think, of the man Jesus as just an ordinary human being who had, in the face of the commonplace standards of life, had the courage to use his life as an adventurous experiment for the benefit of society!

The speaker before the Thursday Club, organized by her father and several other men for the purpose of studying literature, had quite startled his audience. After the meeting several of the members protested, saying the club had been organized for another purpose and that it was too bad to start a religious discussion.

They had, she felt, missed the whole point of his talk. It was not a religious discussion. As she sat beside her father and looked about at the other club members and their wives and at the few unmarried men scattered among them, a great gladness that such a man had come to live in her town swept over her. As he continued talking of the man of Galilee and how he walked up and down through many towns in a far-away country casting out devils by the power of his bold and lovely presence, she was so overcome with emotion that tears came to her eyes. The speaker was himself a man of thirty, and Jesus, the Christ of whom he talked so eloquently, had been a man of thirty when he set out on his mission to civilization. After the meeting and as the speaker walked home with herself and her father, she remained silent while the two men talked. Even then he was a little too conscious of her. She had wanted to worship from afar. She had wanted to repeat aloud the words of the officers of the Pharisees, sent to seize Jesus in the temple, the men who had returned from their mission empty-handed. "Never man spake like this man," they had said, filled with wonder.

As the three people walked under the trees, he continued to speak on the subject that had been the foundation of his talk before the club. "They evidently misunderstood," he said, laughing. "I did not intend my talk to be concerned with religion. I was thinking only of the barbaric background of the life of Jesus Christ and its dramatic possibilities. You understand what I mean, the soft smiling land of Galilee, the lake with the white cities on the shore, ruled over by the cruel Herod Antipas, the fishermen leaving their nets to follow the man who taught the strange new doctrine of peace, for-giveness and love. And then the strange crowds in the streets of the towns and in the city of Jerusalem, the paralytic at Bethesda, the pool by the Sheep-gate, the prostitute who wiped his feet with her hair as he sat at the feast, the scene in the garden on the night before the crucifixion, the crucifixion itself—why should all this not be taken as profound and beautiful literature? This is how, I am sure, it has had its greatest effect upon mankind."

As he had talked to her father during the walk homeward on that first evening, the speaker had occasionally turned to her and once he had made a feeble apology for the seriousness of the talk. "Does all this bore you?" he asked, and a chill ran over her body. She made a gesture with her hand and looked away, and as soon as they had arrived at her father's house, she excused herself and went upstairs.

The two men continued talking for a long time and she undressed and lay in bed with her door open so she could hear the voices. What an evening that had been for her! Her father, usually a rather prosaic man, was excited and talked well, and she thought the newcomer the most wonderful being that had ever come into her consciousness. His strong boyish voice ran up the stairs and through the halls of the house and she sat up in bed and listened, her whole being strangely alive. The voice had carried her out of herself and into the land of Galilee he had described so vividly, and she stood in a vast crowd of people listening to another stranger of thirty who had suddenly come out of another place and was talking. A phrase remembered from her Bible-reading ran through her mind and she repeated it aloud. She became, not herself, but a strange woman in a strange land. "Blessed be the womb that bare Thee and the breasts that Thou hast sucked," she imagined herself shouting, quite carried away.

She saw him for the second time two weeks after that first meeting, and it was strange and also sad to think that during that second meeting he came off his pedestal with a thump.

He wrote her a note and asked her to go with him to a concert and she was stirred at the thought of sitting close beside him all evening and hearing music. Before the evening came, she went about her father's house, attending to the household affairs, with her mind floating away out of her body into a land of spiritual adventure. When her father spoke to her at the table, she was confused and her cheeks grew red. "What's the matter with you?" he asked, laughing. "You've begun acting like a schoolgirl. What's happened to you?"

After all, she was not very young and the new man was not the first who had been attracted to her. Already two men of the town had asked her to marry them—but she had never before got into such a strange exalted state. "Between him and myself it will be different. We will go along a new road into a strange beautiful place," she whispered to herself. She had no plan. It was enough, she thought, that the new man had come to town, that she could occasionally sit in silence beside him, that she could hear his voice, that she could come into the presence of his mind at work making beautiful images.

"It is quite true. There is a religion of the beautiful," she thought. Her mother, who had died when she was fifteen, had been a devout church member, and as a young girl she had also given herself, for a time, to religious enthusiasm. Later she had given up churchgoing and had thought of herself as an intellectual woman.

Now she laughed at herself. "I am a child beside him," she thought, remembering how glowingly he had talked before the Thursday Club. Contentment settled down upon her. "In every life there should be a deeply spiritual love," she told herself. "I am like that woman in the Bible who on a scorching day came down alone, out of a village, to the well in the dusty plain and found lying there on a stone bench the sacred man, he who knew the true way of life."

At the concert he did several things to disturb her.

In the first place he was not at all absorbed or carried away by the music and all evening he kept looking at her with hungry eyes. As they walked homeward he did not talk, giving himself with abandon to ideas, but was silent and self-conscious.

And then he kissed her and her exalted mood went quickly away and something shrewd and determined took entire possession of her.

It was ten o'clock when they got to the house and her

father was at the newspaper office. The moon shone and they went into the garden and sat together on a bench. After he had kissed her, she went to stand by the three because it was necessary for her to make a new adjustment. She had been allowing herself to be a child and her child's hands had been building a temple. Now all the bricks and stone of the temple had fallen down and there was a great dust and racket.

To relieve the tenseness of the situation she led him out of the garden into the street. After all, she had not finished with him. There was something she wanted. They walked down a silent street under trees and a group of young men went past them singing some foolish love-song.

Presently they came to the end of the street and into a field, and it was then she understood the depth of his stupidity. Some elders grew in a little gully beside the field and he wanted her to go in among them. When she drew back, a little startled, he was angry. "The kiss you let me take back there was a lie, then?" he asked sharply. "It didn't mean anything? You are like all the other women who give kisses having no meaning?"

It was during the third time they were together that everything between them was settled. A war had broken out between the forces sleeping in each of them, but after that third meeting peace came. One Saturday afternoon they went together to spend a day in the country. She wore a heavy sweater and stout boots and on his shoulder he carried a small bag filled with the luncheon she had prepared. She was in a smiling, confident mood and he was disturbed and unhappy. When he looked at her he felt like one condemned to beat with bare hands against a cold stone wall. The wall was as hard as adamant, but was surfaced with some warm soft growth.

For a time after they set out, things went well and then the final struggle between them began. Several times during the afternoon, as they walked in a little strip of woodland among dry leaves and under the fragrant trees just in the fullness of the new spring life, she seemed about to yield to the hunger gnawing at him, but, as evening came on and when they had eaten the luncheon and sat on the grassy bank of a small stream, she became very business-like and determined. "We must get back toward town before darkness comes," she said, leading the way across a field and into a dusty road.

The battle came to a crisis quickly. When they had got almost to town, her energetic mood left her and they got out of the road and into an orchard. He built a little fire of twigs beside a rail fence and they leaned against the fence and watched it burn in silence. The thin column of smoke went up through the branches of the trees. "It's like incense," she said, creeping close to him. Their bodies pressed against each other. As the moon was full, darkness did not come and the day passed imperceptibly into night.

Two boys from a nearby farmhouse, who had been driving cows homeward along a lane, saw them standing thus, their arms about each other. They crawled over a fence and crept along in the shadows to wait and watch.

Overcome by a sudden fear she pushed herself out of his arms and moved slowly away along the fence. He followed, pressing her close. A wavering uncertainty had taken possession of her and the battle seemed lost. She wanted to escape and at the same time did not want to escape. She was tired.

With an effort she turned and walked in a very determined way across the orchard and he stood by the fence and let her go. One of the farm boys called to the other. "Nothing's going to happen. She's going away," he called. The boys climbed a fence and ran off along a lane toward a distant barn and again silence settled over the orchard. She returned to him, her eyes shining and her hands trembling.

"You see what you have brought me to, what has happened?" she asked sharply. For a moment she felt mean, beaten, and then quickly she became quite sure of herself. The whole fact of organized life stood back of her trembling figure.

He did not understand. "There will be a scandal," she said. "I don't blame you. I blame myself. Why did I let myself make a show of myself with you?"

She tried to explain. "Of course those boys know me," she said, turning her face away. "They have seen us, in this place, holding each other in that way and kissing. It's light enough to see everything. It's horrible. You are a man, but I'm a woman. There'll be a scandal and my name will be dragged in the mud."

He watched her, perplexed and puzzled. The fact that they had been seen at the love-making had rather amused him and he had been on the point of breaking into laughter. Now he felt ashamed and penitent.

She went and put her face down on the top rail of the fence and her body shook with sobs. He stood awkwardly watching.

A thought came to him. "Well," he said hesitatingly, "we could marry, we could get married."

He looked away over her head and out into an open country washed with moonlight. A wind came up and clouds raced across the sky making fugitive shadows that played madly over the face of the fields. Some shadowy, lovely thing seemed fleeing out of him and out of her. He felt like a beast who in playing about at night in a forest has suddenly put his foot into a trap. A madness to run away from her, to flit half-crazily away over the field like one of the cloud shadows and then to disappear forever into an unknown, mysterious distance, had possession of him, but his feet had become heavy. He was held fast, bound down to the earth, not by desire now, but by a strange hesitating sympathy with the thing that bound her to earth.

When she looked up, he took her into his arms and held her tightly while he continued looking over her head and into the distance. Her body that had been quivering with excitement became quiet. "We had better be married at once," he said. "There are things I have never understood before. Let's go back to town and be married at once, tonight. That will solve all our difficulties, you see."

The Egg

EDITOR'S NOTE

The Triumph of the Egg (1921), from which "the Egg" is taken, is a book which represents Anderson's writings in their widest range of experimentation, in transit from the pages of *The Little Review* to the more formal atmosphere of *The Dial*, which in 1920 had been "revived" for the third time since its founding in 1840 by Margaret Fuller (with the advice and friendship of Emerson) and was being published as a non-political monthly of "arts and letters" in New York. As Anderson's memoirs and autobiographies reveal, he shared the enthusiasms and fortunes of those who edited and wrote for "little magazines." His advice as well as his writings was welcomed and sought for; although he had "found himself," he enjoyed the freedom of doing short pieces in a variety of forms: further verses in the manner of his *Mid-American Chants*, descriptive pieces, and brief critical essays. In *The Little Review* he shared the company of the early Ben Hecht, W. B. Yeats, James Joyce, Ezra Pound, and H. D., and in *The Dial* the company of Vachel Lindsay, George Moore, Thomas Mann, and T. S. Eliot. He shared the fortunes of "advance-guard" writers outside as well as within Chicago— and he entered the 1920's as one who held affinities with the international reaches of the "little magazines" as well as a regional kinship with Dreiser, Sinclair Lewis, Edgar Lee

Masters, Sandburg, and Ernest Hemingway. In this broad milieu "The Egg" established Anderson's individuality, his gift of humor, or what his critics called his understanding of a "tragi-comic" situation. This story, not unlike the stories which follow it in *Horses and Men*, is told with a wandering, reminiscent air. He offers his readers the luxury of relaxing with him, and throughout "The Egg" he makes it seem as though the "real plot" of the story is being withheld.

How far *The Triumph of the Egg* had taken Anderson into an "international" company of artists and writers is shown in Virginia Woolf's essay on American fiction (1925): "In *The Triumph of the Egg* there is some rearrangement of the old elements of art which makes us rub our eyes. The feeling recalls that with which we read Chekhov for the first time. . . . Mr. Anderson has bored into that deeper and warmer layer of human nature which it would be frivolous to ticket new or old, American or European."

My Father was, I am sure, intended by nature to be a cheerful, kindly man. Until he was thirty-four years old he worked as a farm hand for a man named Thomas Butterworth whose place lay near the town of Bidwell. Ohio. He had then a horse of his own and on Saturday evenings drove into town to spend a few hours in social intercourse with other farm hands. In town he drank several glasses of beer and stood about in Ben Head's saloon—crowded on Saturday evenings with visiting farm hands. Songs were sung and glasses thumped on the bar. At ten o'clock father drove home along a lonely country road, made his horse comfortable for the night and himself went to bed, quite happy in his position in life. He had at that time no notion of trying to rise in the world.

It was in the spring of his thirty-fifth year that father married my mother, then a country school teacher, and in the following spring I came wriggling and crying into the world. Something happened to the two people. They became ambitious. The American passion for getting up in the world took possession of them.

It may have been that mother was responsible. Being a school teacher she had no doubt read books and magazines. She had, I presume, read of how Garfield, Lincoln, and other Americans rose from poverty to fame and greatness and as I lay beside her—in the days of her lying-in—she may have dreamed that I would some day rule men and cities. At any rate she induced father to give up his place as a farm hand, sell his horse and embark on an independent enterprise of his own. She was a tall silent woman with a long nose and troubled gray eyes. For herself she wanted nothing. For father and myself she was incurably ambitious.

The first venture into which the two people went turned out badly. They rented ten acres of poor stony land on Griggs's Road, eight miles from Bidwell, and launched into chicken raising. I grew into boyhood on the place and got my first impressions of life there. From the beginning they were impressions of disaster and if, in my turn, I am a gloomy man inclined to see the darker side of life, I attribute it to the fact that what should have been for me the happy joyous days of childhood were spent on a chicken farm.

One unversed in such matters can have no notion of the many and tragic things that can happen to a chicken. It is born out of an egg, lives for a few weeks as a tiny fluffy thing such as you will see pictured on Easter cards, then becomes hideously naked, eats quantities of corn and meal bought by the sweat of your father's brow, gets diseases called pip, cholera, and other names, stands looking with stupid eyes at the sun, becomes sick and dies. A few hens and now and then a rooster, intended to serve God's mysterious ends, struggle through to maturity. The hens lay eggs out of which come other chickens and the dreadful cycle is thus made complete. It is all unbelievably complex. Most philosophers must have been raised on chicken farms. One hopes for so much from a chicken and is so dreadfully disillusioned. Small chickens, just setting out on the journey of life, look so bright and alert and they are in fact so dreadfully stupid. They are so much like people they mix one up in one's judgments of life. If disease does not kill them they wait until your expectations are thoroughly aroused and then walk under the wheels of a wagon—to go squashed and dead back to their maker. Vermin infest their youth, and fortunes must be spent for curative powders. In later life I have seen how a literature has been built up on the subject of fortunes to be made out of the raising of chickens. It is intended to be read by the gods who have just eaten of the tree of the knowledge of good and evil. It is a hopeful literature and declares that much may be done by simple ambitious people who own a few hens. Do not be led astray by it. It was not written for you. Go hunt for gold on the frozen hills of Alaska, put your faith in the honesty of a politician, believe if you will that the world is daily growing better and that good will triumph over evil, but do not read and believe the literature that is written concerning the hen. It was not written for you.

I, however, digress. My tale does not primarily concern itself with the hen. If correctly told it will center on the egg. For ten years my father and mother struggled to make our chicken farm pay and then they gave up that struggle and began another. They moved into the town of Bidwell, Ohio, and embarked in the restaurant business. After ten years of worry with incubators that did not hatch, and with tiny—and in their own way lovely—balls of fluff that passed on into semi-naked pullethood and from that into dead henhood, we threw all aside and packing our belongings on a wagon drove down Grigg's Road toward Bidwell, a tiny caravan of hope looking for a new place from which to start on our upward journey through life.

We must have been a sad looking lot, not, I fancy, unlike refugees fleeing from a battlefield. Mother and I walked in the road. The wagon that contained our goods had been borrowed for the day from Mr. Albert Griggs, a neighbor. Out of its sides stuck the legs of cheap chairs and at the back of the pile of beds, tables, and boxes filled with kitchen utensils was a crate of live chickens, and on top of that the baby carriage in which I had been wheeled about in my infancy. Why we stuck to the baby carriage I don't know. It was unlikely other children would be born and the wheels were broken. People who have few possessions cling tightly to those they have. That is one of the facts that make life so discouraging.

Father rode on top of the wagon. He was then a bald-headed man of forty-five, a little fat and from long association with mother and the chickens he had become habitually silent and discouraged. All during our ten years on the chicken farm he had worked as a laborer on neighboring farms and most of the money he had earned had been spent for remedies to cure chicken diseases, on Wilmer's White Wonder Cholera Cure or Professor Bidlow's Egg Producer or some other preparations that mother found advertised in the poultry papers. There were two little patches of hair on father's head just above his ears. I remember that as a child I used to sit looking at him when he had gone to sleep in a chair before the stove on Sunday afternoons in the winter. I had at that time already begun to read books and have notions of my own and the bald path that led over the top of his head was, I fancied, something like a broad road, such a road as Caesar might have made on which to lead his legions out of Rome and into the wonders of an unknown world. The tufts of hair that grew above father's ears were, I thought, like forests. I fell into a half-sleeping, half-waking state and dreamed I was a tiny thing going along the road into a far beautiful place where there were no chicken farms and where life was a happy eggless affair.

One might write a book concerning our flight from the chicken farm into town. Mother and I walked the entire eight miles—she to be sure that nothing fell from the wagon and I to see the wonders of the world. On the seat of the wagon beside father was his greatest treasure. I will tell you of that.

On a chicken farm where hundreds and even thousands of chickens come out of eggs surprising things sometimes happen. Grotesques are born out of eggs as out of people. The accident does not often occur—perhaps once in a thousand births. A chicken is, you see, born that has four legs, two pairs of wings, two heads or what not. The things do not live. They go quickly back to the hand of their maker that has for a moment trembled. The fact that the poor little things could not live was one of the tragedies of life to father. He had some sort of notion that if he could but bring into henhood or roosterhood a five-legged hen or a two-headed rooster his fortune would be made. He dreamed of taking the wonder about to county fairs and of growing rich by exhibiting it to other farm hands.

At any rate he saved all the little monstrous things that had been born on our chicken farm. They were preserved in alcohol and put each in its own glass bottle. These he had carefully put into a box and on our journey into town it was carried on the wagon seat beside him. He drove the horses with one hand and with the other clung to the box. When we got to our destination the box was taken down at once and the bottles removed. All during our days as keepers of a restaurant in the town of Bidwell, Ohio, the grotesques in their little glass bottles sat on a shelf back of the counter. Mother sometimes protested but father was a rock on the subject of his treasure. The grotesques were, he declared, valuable. People, he said, liked to look at strange and wonderful things.

Did I say that we embarked in the restaurant business in the town of Bidwell, Ohio? I exaggerated a little. The town itself lay at the foot of a low hill and on the shore of a small river. The railroad did not run through the town and the station was a mile away to the north at a place called Pickleville. There had been a cider mill and pickle factory at the station, but before the time of our coming they had both gone out of business. In the morning and in the evening busses came down to the station along a road called Turner's Pike from the hotel on the main street of Bidwell. Our going to the out-of-the-way place to embark in the restaurant business was mother's idea. She talked of it for a year and then one day went off and rented an empty store building opposite the railroad station. It was her idea that the restaurant would be profitable. Traveling men, she said, would be always waiting around to take trains out of town and town people would come to the station to await incoming trains. They would come to the restaurant to buy pieces of pie and drink coffee. Now that I am older I know that she had another motive in going. She was ambitious for me. She wanted me to rise in the world, to get into a town school and become a man of the towns.

At Pickleville father and mother worked hard as they always had done. At first there was the necessity of putting our place into shape to be a restaurant. That took a month. Father built a shelf on which he put tins of vegetables. He painted a sign on which he put his name in large red letters. Below his name was the sharp command—"EAT HERE"—that was so seldom obeyed. A showcase was bought and filled with cigars and tobacco. Mother scrubbed the floor and the walls of the room. I went to school in the town and was glad to be away from the farm and from the presence of the discouraged, sad-looking chickens. Still I was not very joyous. In the evening I walked home from school along Turner's Pike and remembered the children I had seen playing in the town school yard. A troop of little girls had gone hopping about and singing. I tried that. Down along the frozen road I went hopping solemnly on one leg. "Hippity Hop To The Barber Shop," I sang shrilly. Then I stopped and looked doubtfully about. I was afraid of being seen in my gay mood. It must have seemed to me that I was doing a thing that should not be done by one who, like myself, had been raised on a chicken farm where death was a daily visitor.

Mother decided that our restaurant should remain open at night. At ten in the evening a passenger train went north past our door followed by a local freight. The freight crew had switching to do in Pickleville and when the work was done they came to our restaurant for hot coffee and food. Sometimes one of them ordered a fried egg. In the morning at four they returned northbound and again visited us. A little trade began to grow up. Mother slept at night and during the day tended the restaurant and fed our boarders while father slept. He slept in the same bed mother had occupied during the night and I went off to the town of

Bidwell and to school. During the long nights, while mother and I slept, father cooked meats that were to go into sandwiches for the lunch baskets of our boarders. Then an idea in regard to getting up in the world came into his head. The American spirit took hold of him. He also became ambitious.

In the long nights when there was little to do father had time to think. That was his undoing. He decided that he had in the past been an unsuccessful man because he had not been cheerful enough and that in the future he would adopt a cheerful outlook on life. In the early morning he came upstairs and got into bed with mother. She woke and the two talked. From my bed in the corner I listened.

It was father's idea that both he and mother should try to entertain the people who came to eat at our restaurant. I cannot now remember his words, but he gave the impression of one about to become in some obscure way a kind of public entertainer. When people, particularly young people from the town of Bidwell, came into our place, as on very rare occasions they did, bright entertaining conversation was to be made. From father's words I gathered that something of the jolly innkeeper effect was to be sought. Mother must have been doubtful from the first, but she said nothing discouraging. It was father's notion that a passion for the company of himself and mother would spring up in the breasts of the younger people of the town of Bidwell. In the evening bright happy groups would come singing down Turner's Pike. They would troop shouting with joy and laughter into our place. There would be song and festivity. I do not mean to give the impression that father spoke so elaborately of the matter. He was as I have said an uncommunicative man. "They want some place to go. I tell you they want some place to go," he said over and over. That was as far as he got. My own imagination has filled in the blanks.

For two or three weeks this notion of father's invaded our house. We did not talk much, but in our daily lives tried earnestly to make smiles take the place of glum looks. Mother smiled at the boarders and I, catching the infection, smiled at our cat. Father became a little feverish in his anxiety to please. There was no doubt, lurking somewhere in him, a touch of the spirit of the showman. He did not waste much of his ammunition on the railroad men he served at night but seemed to be waiting for a young man or woman from Bidwell to come in to show what he could do. On the counter in the restaurant there was a wire basket kept always filled with eggs, and it must have been before his eyes when the idea of being entertaining was born in his brain. There was something pre-natal about the way eggs kept themselves connected with the development of his idea. At any rate an egg ruined his new impulse in life. Late one night I was awakened by a roar of anger coming from father's throat. Both mother and I sat upright in our beds. With trembling hands she lighted a lamp that stood on a table by her head. Downstairs the front door of our restaurant went shut with a bang and in a few minutes father tramped up the stairs. He held an egg in his hand and his hand trembled as though he were having a chill. There was a half-insane light in his eyes. As he stood glaring at us I was sure he intended throwing the egg at either mother or me. Then he laid it gently on the table beside the lamp and dropped on his knees beside mother's bed. He began to cry like a boy and I, carried away by his grief, cried with him. The two of us filled the little upstairs room with our wailing voices. It is ridiculous, but of the picture we made I can remember only the fact that mother's hand continually stroked the bald path that ran across the top of his head. I have forgotton what mother said to him and how she induced him to tell her of what had happened downstairs. His explanation also has gone out of my mind. I remember only my own grief and fright and the shiny path over father's head glowing in the lamp light as he knelt by the bed.

As to what happened downstairs. For some unexplainable reason I know the story as well as though I had been a witness to my father's discomfiture. One in time gets to know many unexplainable things. On that evening young Joe Kane, son of a merchant of Bidwell, came to Pickleville to meet his father, who was expected on the ten o'clock evening train from the South. The train was three hours late and Joe came into our place to loaf about and to wait for its arrival. The local freight train came in and the freight crew were fed. Joe was left alone in the restaurant with father.

From the moment he came into our place the Bidwell young man must have been puzzled by my father's actions. It was his notion that father was angry at him for hanging around. He noticed that the restaurant keeper was apparently disturbed by his presence and he thought of going out. However, it began to rain and he did not fancy the long walk to town and back. He bought a five-cent cigar and ordered a cup of coffee. He had a newspaper in his pocket and took it out and began to read. "I'm waiting for the evening train. It's late," he said apologetically.

For a long time father, whom Joe Kane had never seen before, remained silently gazing at his visitor. He was no doubt suffering from an attack of stage fright. As so often happens in life he had thought so much and so often of the situation that now confronted him that he was somewhat nervous in its presence.

For one thing, he did not know what to do with his hands. He thrust one of them nervously over the counter and shook hands with Joe Kane. "How-de-do," he said. Joe Kane put his newspaper down and stared at him. Father's eye lighted on the basket of eggs that sat on the counter and he began to talk. "Well," he began hesitatingly, "well, you have heard of Christopher Columbus, eh?" He seemed to be angry. "That Christopher Columbus was a cheat," he declared emphatically. "He talked of making an egg stand on its end. He talked, he did, and then he went and broke the end of the egg."

My father seemed to his visitor to be beside himself at the duplicity of Christopher Columbus. He muttered and swore. He declared it was wrong to teach children that Christopher Columbus was a great man when, after all, he cheated at the critical moment. He had declared he would make an egg stand on end and then when his bluff had been called he had done a trick. Still grumbling at Columbus, father took an egg from the basket on the counter and began to walk up and down. He rolled the egg between the palms of his hands. He smiled genially. He began to mumble words regarding the effect to be produced on an egg by the electricity that comes out of the human body. He declared that without breaking its shell and by virtue of rolling it back and forth in his hands he could stand the egg on its end. He explained that the warmth of his hands and the gentle rolling movement he gave the egg created a new center of gravity, and Joe Kane was mildly interested. "I have handled thousands of eggs," father said. "No one knows more about eggs than I do."

He stood the egg on the counter and it fell on its side. He tried the trick again and again, each time rolling the egg between the palms of his hands and saying the words regarding the wonders of electricity and the laws of gravity. When after a half hour's effort he did succeed in making the egg stand for a moment he looked up to find that his visitor was no longer watching. By the time he had succeeded in calling Joe Kane's attention to the success of his effort the egg had again rolled over and lay on its side.

Afire with the showman's passion and at the same time a good deal disconcerted by the failure of his first effort, father now took the bottles containing the poultry monstrosities down from their place on the shelf and began to show them to his visitor. "How would you like to have seven legs and two heads like this fellow?" he asked, exhibiting the most remarkable of his treasures. A cheerful smile played over his face. He reached over the counter and tried to slap Joe Kane on the shoulder as he had seen men do in Ben Head's saloon when he was a young farm hand and drove to town on Saturday evenings. His visitor was made a little ill by the sight of the body of the terribly deformed bird floating in the alcohol in the bottle and got up to go. Coming from behind the counter father took hold of the young man's arm and led him back to his seat. He grew a little angry and for a moment had to turn his face away and force himself to smile. Then he put the bottles back on the shelf. In an outburst of generosity he fairly compelled Joe Kane to have a fresh cup of coffee and another cigar at his expense. Then he took a pan and filling it with vinegar, taken from a jug that sat beneath the counter, he declared himself about to do a new trick. "I will heat this egg in this pan of vinegar," he said. "Then I will put it through the neck of a bottle without breaking the shell. When the egg is inside the bottle it will resume its normal shape and the shell will become hard again. Then I will give the bottle with the egg in it to you. You can take it about with you wherever you go. People will want to know how you got the egg in the bottle. Don't tell them. Keep them guessing. That is the way to have fun with this trick."

Father grinned and winked at his visitor. Joe Kane decided that the man who confronted him was mildly insane but harmless. He drank the cup of coffee that had been given him and began to read his paper again. When the egg had been heated in vinegar father carried it on a spoon to the counter and going into a back room got an empty bottle. He was angry because his visitor did not watch him as he began to do his trick, but nevertheless went cheerfully to work. For a long time he struggled, trying to get the egg to go through the neck of the bottle. He put the pan of vinegar back on the stove, intending to reheat the egg, then picked it up and burned his fingers. After a second bath in the hot vinegar the shell of the egg had been softened a little but not enough for his purpose. He worked and worked and a spirit of desperate determination took possession of him. When he thought that at last the trick was about to be consummated the delayed train came in at the station and Joe Kane started to go nonchalantly out at the door. Father made a last desperate effort to conquer the egg and make it do the thing that would establish his reputation as one who knew how to entertain guests who came into his restaurant. He worried the egg. He attempted to be somewhat rough with it. He swore and the sweat stood out on his forehead. The egg broke under his hand. When the contents spurted over his clothes, Joe Kane, who had stopped at the door, turned and laughed.

A roar of anger rose from my father's throat. He danced

and shouted a string of inarticulate words. Grabbing another egg from the basket on the counter, he threw it, just missing the head of the young man as he dodged through the door and escaped.

Father came upstairs to mother and me with an egg in his hand. I do not know what he intended to do. I imagine he had some idea of destroying it, of destroying all eggs, and that he intended to let mother and me see him begin. When, however, he got into the presence of mother something happened to him. He laid the egg gently on the table and dropped on his knees by the bed as I have already explained. He later decided to close the restaurant for the night and to come upstairs and get into bed. When he did so he blew out the light and after much muttered conversation both he and mother went to sleep. I suppose I went to sleep also, but my sleep was troubled. I awoke at dawn and for a long time looked at the egg that lay on the table. I wondered why eggs had to be and why from the egg came the hen who again laid the egg. The question got into my blood. It has stayed there, I imagine, because I am the son of my father. At any rate, the problem remains unsolved in my mind. And that, I conclude, is but another evidence of the complete and final triumph of the egg—at least as far as my family is concerned.

I'm a Fool

EDITOR'S NOTE

"I'm a Fool" and "The Man Who Became a Woman"
(p. 364) are reprinted from *Horses and Men* (1923). Scenes
from the race track provide the general setting for the book,
and the title of one of its stories, "An Ohio Pagan," became
a phrase, a name for Anderson himself; as in *The Triumph
of the Egg* Anderson's "tragi-comic" spirit prevails throughout the volume. The stories "I'm a Fool" and "The Man
Who Became a Woman" are told in a reminiscent, yet high-
spirited fashion—their seriousness is more than half concealed.
"I'm a Fool" is one of Anderson's masterpieces in the art
of making a dramatic monologue turn into a story; it is the
best of his very short short stories. Even its touches of rural
slang have an air of permanence because they display the
character of the boy who tells the story, his eagerness to
be glib, quick-witted, up-to-date, and to hide his innocence
behind a guise of being tough and worldly.

Of Anderson's world of the race track, Virginia Woolf
has written: "It is a world in which the senses flourish; it is
dominated by instincts rather than by ideas; race-horses make
the hearts of little boys beat high; cornfields flow around the
cheap towns like golden seas, illimitable and profound. . . .
Anderson will leave what he has found exposed, defenseless,
naked to scorn and laughter."

In describing the reminiscent air with which Anderson tells the story of "The Man Who Became a Woman". Mrs. Woolf also spoke of the "shell-less" quality of his stories, as though they were "wrapped about in a soft caressing envelope, which always seems a little bit too loose to fit the shape." It is the "shell-less" quality that makes the bar-room scene in this story so effective, the scene in which the boy looks in the mirror across the bar and fears that his own face has become that of a woman; it is here that the boy has found himself "exposed, defenseless, naked to scorn and laughter."

It was a hard jolt for me, one of the most bitterest I ever had to face. And it all came about through my own foolishness, too. Even yet sometimes, when I think of it, I want to cry or swear or kick myself. Perhaps, even now, after all this time, there will be a kind of satisfaction in making myself look cheap by telling of it.

It began at three o'clock one October afternoon as I sat in the grandstand at the fall trotting and pacing meet at Sandusky, Ohio.

To tell the truth, I felt a little foolish that I should be sitting in the grandstand at all. During the summer before I had left my home town with Harry Whitehead and, with a nigger named Burt, had taken a job as swipe with one of the two horses Harry was campaigning through the fall race meets that year. Mother cried and my sister Mildred, who wanted to get a job as a school teacher in our town that fall, stormed and scolded about the house all during the week before I left. They both thought it something disgraceful that one of our family should take a place as a swipe with race horses. I've an idea Mildred thought my taking the place would stand in the way of her getting the job she'd been working so long for.

But after all I had to work, and there was no other work to be got. A big lumbering fellow of nineteen couldn't just hang around the house and I had got too big to mow people's lawns and sell newspapers. Little chaps who could get next to people's sympathies by their sizes were always getting jobs away from me. There was one fellow who kept saying to everyone who wanted a lawn mowed or a cistern cleaned, that he was saving money to work his way through college, and I used to lay awake nights thinking up ways to injure him without being found out. I kept thinking of wagons running over him and bricks falling on his head as he walked along the street. But never mind him.

I got the place with Harry and I liked Burt fine. We got along splendid together. He was a big nigger with a lazy sprawling body and soft, kind eyes, and when it came to a fight he could hit like Jack Johnson. He had Bucephalus, a big black pacing stallion that could do 2.09 or 2.10, if he had to, and I had a little gelding named Doctor Fritz that never lost a race all fall when Harry wanted him to win.

We set out from home late in July in a box car with the two horses and after that, until late November, we kept moving along to the race meets and the fairs. It was a peachy time for me, I'll say that. Sometimes now I think that boys who are raised regular in houses, and never have a fine nigger like Burt for best friend, and go to high schools and college, and never steal anything, or get drunk a little, or learn to swear from fellows who know how, or come walking up in front of a grandstand in their shirt sleeves and with dirty horsey pants on when the races are going on and the grandstand is full of people all dressed up—What's the use of talking about it? Such fellows don't know nothing at all. They've never had no opportunity.

But I did. Burt taught me how to rub down a horse and put the bandages on after a race and steam a horse out and a lot of valuable things for any man to know. He could wrap a bandage on a horse's leg so smooth that if it had been the same color you would think it was his skin, and I guess he'd have been a big driver, too, and got to the top like Murphy and Walter Cox and the others if he hadn't been black.

Gee whiz, it was fun. You got to a county seat town, maybe say on a Saturday or Sunday, and the fair began the next Tuesday and lasted until Friday afternoon. Doctor Fritz would be, say in the 2.25 trot on Tuesday afternoon and on Thursday afternoon Bucephalus would knock 'em cold in the "free-for-all" pace. It left you a lot of time to hang around and listen to horse talk, and see Burt knock some yap cold that got too gay, and you'd find out about horses and men and pick up a lot of stuff you could use all the rest of your life, if you had some sense and salted down what you heard and felt and saw.

And then at the end of the week when the race meet was over, and Harry had run home to tend up to his livery stable business, you and Burt hitched the two horses to carts and drove slow and steady across country, to the place for the next meeting, so as to not overheat the horses, etc., etc., you know.

Gee whizz, Gosh amighty, the nice hickorynut and beechnut and oaks and other kinds of trees along the roads, all brown and red, and the good smells, and Burt singing a song that was called Deep River, and the country girls at the windows of houses and everything. You can stick your colleges up your nose for all me. I guess I know where I got my education.

Why, one of those little burgs of towns you come to on the way, say now on a Saturday afternoon, and Burt says, "let's lay up here." And you did.

And you took the horses to a livery stable and fed them, and you got your good clothes out of a box and put them on.

And the town was full of farmers gaping, because they could see you were race-horse people, and the kids maybe never see a nigger before and was afraid and run away when the two of us walked down their main street.

And that was before prohibition and all that foolishness, and so you went into a saloon, the two of you, and all the yaps come and stood around, and there was always someone pretended he was horsey and knew things and spoke up and began asking questions, and all you did was to lie and lie all you could about what horses you had, and I said I owned them, and then some fellow said, "will you have a drink of whisky" and Burt knocked his eye out the way he could say, offhandlike, "Oh well, all right, I'm agreeable to a little nip. I'll split a quart with you." Gee whizz.

But that isn't what I want to tell my story about. We got home late in November and I promised mother I'd quit the race horses for good. There's a lot of things you've got to promise a mother because she don't know any better.

And so, there not being any work in our town any more than when I left there to go to the races, I went off to Sandusky and got a pretty good place taking care of horses for a man who owned a teaming and delivery and storage and coal and real estate business there. It was a pretty good place with good eats, and a day off each week, and sleeping on a cot in a big barn, and mostly just shoveling in hay and oats to a lot of big good-enough skates of horses, that couldn't have trotted a race with a toad. I wasn't dissatisfied and I could send money home.

And then, as I started to tell you, the fall races come to Sandusky and I got the day off and I went. I left the job at noon and had on my good clothes and my new brown derby hat, I'd just bought the Saturday before, and a stand-up collar.

First of all I went downtown and walked about with the dudes. I've always thought to myself, "put up a good front" and so I did it. I had forty dollars in my pocket and so I went into the West House, a big hotel, and walked up to the cigar stand. "Give me three twenty-five cent cigars," I said. There was a lot of horsemen and strangers and dressed-up people from other towns standing around in the lobby and in the bar, and I mingled amongst them. In the bar there was a fellow with a cane and a Windsor tie on, that it made me sick to look at him. I like a man to be a man and dress up, but not to go put on that kind of airs. So I pushed him aside, kind of rough, and had me a drink of whisky. And then he looked at me, as though he thought maybe he'd get gay, but he changed his mind and didn't say anything. And then I had another drink of whisky, just to show him something, and went out and had a hack out to the races, all to myself, and when I got there I bought myself the best seat I could get up in the grandstand, but didn't go in for any of these boxes. That's putting on too many airs.

And so there I was, sitting up in the grandstand as gay as you please and looking down on the swipes coming out with their horses, and with their dirty horsey pants on and the horse blankets swung over their shoulders, same as I had been doing all the year before I liked one thing about the same as the other, sitting up there and feeling grand and being down there and looking up at the yaps and feeling grander and more important, too. One thing's about as good as another, if you take it just right. I've often said that.

Well, right in front of me, in the grandstand that day, there was a fellow with a couple of girls and they was about my age. The young fellow was a nice guy all right. He was the kind maybe that goes to college and then comes to be a lawyer or maybe a newspaper editor or something like that, but he wasn't stuck on himself. There are some of that kind are all right and he was one of the ones.

He had his sister with him and another girl and the sister looked around over his shoulder, accidental at first, not intending to start anything—she wasn't that kind—and her eyes and mine happened to meet.

You know how it is. Gee, she was a peach! She had on a soft dress, kind of a blue stuff and it looked carelessly made, but was well sewed and made and everything. I knew that much. I blushed when she looked right at me and so did she. She was the nicest girl I've ever seen in my life. She wasn't stuck on herself and she could talk proper grammar without being like a school teacher or something like that. What I mean is, she was O. K. I think maybe her father was well-to-do, but not rich to make her chesty because she was his daughter, as some are. Maybe he owned a drugstore or a drygoods store in their home town, or something like that. She never told me and I never asked.

My own people are all O. K. too, when you come to that. My grandfather was Welsh and over in the old country, in Wales he was—But never mind that.

The first heat of the first race come off and the young fellow setting there with the two girls left them and went down to make a bet. I knew what he was up to, but he didn't talk big and noisy and let everyone around know he was a sport, as some do. He wasn't that kind. Well, he come back and I heard him tell the two girls what horse he'd bet on, and when the heat was trotted they all half got to their feet and acted in the excited, sweaty way people do when they've got money down on a race, and the horse they bet on is up there pretty close at the end, and they think maybe he'll come on with a rush, but he never does because he hasn't got the old juice in him, come right down to it.

And then, pretty soon, the horses came out for the 2.18 pace and there was a horse in it I knew. He was a horse Bob French had in his string but Bob didn't own him. He was a horse owned by a Mr. Mathers down at Marietta, Ohio. This Mr. Mathers had a lot of money and owned some coal mines or something, and he had a swell place out in the country, and he was stuck on race horses, but was a Presbyterian or something, and I think more than likely his wife was one, too, maybe a stiffer one than himself. So he never raced his horses hisself, and the story round the Ohio race tracks was that when one of his horses got ready to go to the races he turned him over to Bob French and pretended to his wife he was sold.

So Bob had the horses and he did pretty much as he pleased and you can't blame Bob, at least, I never did. Sometimes he was out to win and sometimes he wasn't. I never cared much about that when I was swiping a horse. What I did want to know was that my horse had the speed and could go out in front, if you wanted him to.

And, as I'm telling you, there was Bob in this race with one of Mr. Mather's horses, was named "About Ben Ahem" or something like that, and was fast as a streak. He was a gelding and had a mark of 2.21, but could step in .08 or .09.

Because when Burt and I were out, as I've told you, the

year before, there was a nigger, Burt knew, worked for Mr. Mathers and we went out there one day when we didn't have no race on at the Marietta Fair and our boss Harry was gone home.

And so everyone was gone to the fair but just this one nigger and he took us all through Mr. Mather's swell house and he and Burt tapped a bottle of wine Mr. Mathers had hid in his bedroom, back in a closet, without his wife knowing, and he showed us this Ahem horse. Burt was always stuck on being a driver but didn't have much chance to get to the top, being a nigger, and he and the other nigger gulped that whole bottle of wine and Burt got a little lit up.

So the nigger let Burt take this About Ben Ahem and step him a mile in a track Mr. Mathers had all to himself, right there on the farm. And Mr. Mathers had one child, a daughter, kinda sick and not very good-looking, and she came home and we had to hustle and get About Ben Ahem stuck back in the barn.

I'm only telling you to get everything straight. At Sandusky, that afternoon I was at the fair, this young fellow with the two girls was fussed, being with the girls and losing his bet. You know how a fellow is that way. One of them was his girl and the other his sister. I had figured that out.

"Gee whizz," I says to myself, "I'm going to give him the dope."

He was mighty nice when I touched him on the shoulder. He and the girls were nice to me right from the start and clear to the end. I'm not blaming them.

And so he leaned back and I give him the dope on About Ben Ahem. "Don't bet a cent on this first heat because he'll go like an oxen hitched to a plow, but when the first heat is over go right down and lay on your pile." That's what I told him.

Well, I never saw a fellow treat anyone sweller. There was a fat man sitting beside the little girl, that had looked at me twice by this time, and I at her, and both blushing, and what did he do but have the nerve to turn and ask the fat man to get up and change places with me so I could set with his crowd.

Gee whizz, craps amighty. There I was. What a chump I was to go and get gay up there in the West House bar, and just because that dude was standing there with a cane and that kind of a necktie on, to go and get all balled up and drink that whisky, just to show off.

Of course she would know, me setting right beside her and letting her smell of my breath. I could have kicked myself right down out of that grandstand and all around that race track and made a faster record than most of the skates of horses they had there that year.

Because that girl wasn't any mutt of a girl. What wouldn't I have give right then for a stick of chewing gum to chew, or a lozenger, or some liquorice, or most anything. I was glad I had those twenty-five cent cigars in my pocket and right away I give that fellow one and lit one myself. Then that fat man got up and we changed places and there I was, plunked right down beside her.

They introduced themselves and the fellow's best girl, he had with him, was named Miss Elinor Woodbury, and her father was a manufacturer of barrels from a place called Tiffin, Ohio. And the fellow himself was named Wilbur Wessen and his sister was Miss Lucy Wessen.

I suppose it was their having such swell names got me off my trolley. A fellow, just because he has been a swipe with a race horse, and works taking care of horses for a man in the teaming, delivery, and storage business, isn't any better or worse than anyone else. I've often thought that, and said it too.

But you know how a fellow is. There's something in that kind of nice clothes, and the kind of nice eyes she had, and the way she had looked at me, awhile before, over her brother's shoulder, and me looking back at her, and both of us blushing.

I couldn't show her up for a boob, could I?

I made a fool of myself, that's what I did. I said my name

was Walter Mathers from Marietta, Ohio, and then I told all three of them the smashingest lie you ever heard. What I said was that my father owned the horse About Ben Ahem and that he had let him out to this Bob French for racing purposes, because our family was proud and had never gone into racing that way, in our own name, I mean. Then I had got started and they were all leaning over and listening, and Miss Lucy Wessen's eyes were shining, and I went the whole hog.

I told about our place down a Marietta, and about the big stables and the grand brick house we had on a hill, up above the Ohio River, but I knew enough not to do it in no bragging way. What I did was to start things and then let them drag the rest out of me. I acted just as reluctant to tell as I could. Our famiy hasn't got any barrel factory, and, since I've known us, we've always been pretty poor, but not asking anything of anyone at that, and my grandfather, over in Wales—But never mind that.

We set there talking like we had known each other for years and years, and I went and told them that my father had been expecting maybe this Bob French wasn't on the square, and had sent me up to Sandusky on the sly to find out what I could.

And I bluffed it through I had found out all about the 2.18 pace, in which About Ben Ahem was to start.

I said he would lose the first heat by pacing like a lame cow and then he would come back and skin 'em alive after that. And to back up what I said I took thirty dollars out of my pocket and handed it to Mr. Wilbur Wessen and asked him, would he mind, after the first heat, to go down and place it on About Ben Ahem for whatever odds he could get. What I said was that I didn't want Bob French to see me and none of the swipes.

Sure enough the first heat come off and About Ben Ahem went off his stride, up the back stretch, and looked like a wooden horse or a sick one, and come in to be last. Then this Wilbur Wessen went down to the betting place under the grandstand and there I was with the two girls, and when that

Miss Woodbury was looking the other way once, Lucy Wessen kinda, with her shoulder you know, kinda touched me. Not just tucking down, I don't mean. You know how a woman can do. They get close, but not getting gay either. You know what they do. Gee whizz.

And then they give me a jolt. What they had done, when I didn't know, was to get together, and they had decided Wilbur Wessen would bet fifty dollars, and the two girls had gone and put in ten dollars each, of their own money, too. I was sick then, but I was sicker later.

About the gelding, About Ben Ahem, and their winning their money, I wasn't worried a lot about that. It come out O K. Ahem stepped the next three heats like a bushel of spoiled eggs going to market before they could be found out, and Wilbur Wessen had got nine to two for the money. There was something else eating at me.

Because Wilbur come back, after he had bet the money, and after that he spent most of his time talking to that Miss Woodbury, and Lucy Wessen and I was left alone together like on a desert island. Gee, if I'd only been on the square or if there had been any way of getting myself on the square. There ain't any Walter Mathers, like I said to her and them, and there hasn't ever been one, but if there was, I bet I'd go to Marietta, Ohio, and shoot him tomorrow.

There I was, big boob that I am. Pretty soon the race over, and Wilbur had gone down and collected our money, and we had a hack downtown, and he stood us a swell supper at the West House, and a bottle of champagne beside.

And I was with that girl and she wasn't saying much, and I wasn't saying much either. One thing I know. She wasn't stuck on me because of the lie about my father being rich and all that. There's a way you know. . . . Craps amighty. There's a kind of girl, you see just once in your life, and if you don't get busy and make hay, then you're gone for good and all, and might as well go jump off a bridge. They give you a look from inside of them somewhere, and it ain't no vamping, and what it means is—you want that girl to be your wife, and you want nice things around her like flowers and

swell clothes, and you want her to have the kids you're going
to have, and you want good music played and no rag-time.
Gee whizz.

There's a place over near Sandusky, across a kind of bay,
and it's called Cedar Point. And after we had supper we went
over to it in a launch, all by ourselves. Wilbur and Miss Lucy
and that Miss Woodbury had to catch a ten o'clock train
back to Tiffin, Ohio, because, when you're out with girls like
that you can't get careless with some kinds of Janes.

And Wilbur blowed himself to the launch and it cost him
fifteen cold plunks, but I wouldn't never have knew if I hadn't
listened. He wasn't no tin horn kind of a sport.

Over at the Cedar Point place, we didn't stay around where
there was a gang of common kind of cattle at all.

There was big dance halls and dining places for yaps, and
there was a beach you could walk along and get where it was
dark, and we went there.

She didn't talk hardly at all and neither did I, and I was
thinking how glad I was my mother was all right, and always
made us kids learn to eat with a fork at table, and not swill
soup, and not be noisy and rough like a gang you see around
a race track that way.

Then Wilbur and his girl went away up the beach and
Lucy and I sat down in a dark place, where there was some
roots of old trees, the water had washed up, and after that
the time, till we had to go back in the launch and they had
to catch their trains, wasn't nothing at all. It went like winking
your eye.

Here's how it was. The place we were setting in was dark,
like I said, and there was the roots from that old stump
sticking up like arms, and there was a watery smell, and the
night was like—as if you could put your hand out and feel
it—so warm and soft and dark and sweet like an orange.

I most cried and I most swore and I most jumped up and
danced, I was so mad and happy and sad.

When Wilbur come back from being alone with his girl,
and she saw him coming, Lucy she says, "we got to go to
the train now", and she was most crying too, but she never

knew nothing I knew, and she couldn't be so all busted up. And then, before Wilbur and Miss Woodbury got up to where we was, she put her face up and kissed me quick and put her head up against me and she was all quivering and— Gee whizz.

Sometimes I hope I have cancer and die. I guess you know what I mean. We went in the launch across the bay to the train like that, and it was dark, too. She whispered and said it was like she and I could get out of the boat and walk on the water, and it sounded foolish, but I knew what she meant.

And then quick we were right at the depot, and there was a big gang of yaps, the kind that goes to the fairs, and crowded and milling around like cattle, and how could I tell her? "It won't be long because you'll write and I'll write to you." That's all she said.

I got a chance like a hay barn afire. A swell chance I got.

And maybe she would write me, down at Marietta that way, and the letter would come back, and stamped on the front of it by the U.S.A. "there ain't any such guy," or something like that, whatever they stamp on a letter that way.

And me trying to pass myself off for a bigbug and a swell— to her, as decent a little body as God ever made. Craps amighty—a swell chance I got!

And then the train come in, and she got on it, and Wilbur Wessen he come and shook hands with me, and that Miss Woodbury was nice too and bowed to me, and I at her, and the train went and I busted out and cried like a kid.

Gee, I could have run after that train and made Dan Patch look like a freight train after a wreck but, socks amighty, what was the use? Did you ever see such a fool?

I'll bet you what—if I had an arm broke right now or a train had run over my foot—I wouldn't go to no doctor at all. I'd go set down and let her hurt and hurt—that's what I'd do.

I'll bet you what—if I hadn't a drunk that booze I'd a never been such a boob as to go tell such a lie—that couldn't never be made straight to a lady like her.

I wish I had that fellow right here that had on a Windsor

tie and carried a cane. I'd smash him for fair. Gosh darn his eyes. He's a big fool—that's what he is.

And if I'm not another you just go find me one and I'll quit working and be a bum and give him my job. I don't care nothing for working, and earning money, and saving it for no such boob as myself.

The Man Who Became a Woman[1]

My father was a retail druggist in our town, out in Nebraska, which was so much like a thousand other towns I've been in since that there's no use fooling around and taking up your time and mine trying to describe it.

Anyway I became a drug clerk and after father's death the store was sold and mother took the money and went west, to her sister in California, giving me four hundred dollars with which to make my start in the world. I was only nineteen years old then.

I came to Chicago, where I worked as a drug clerk for a time, and then, as my health suddenly went back on me, perhaps because I was so sick of my lonely life in the city and of the sight and smell of the drugstore, I decided to set out on what seemed to me then the great adventure and became for a time a tramp, working now and then, when I had no money, but spending all the time I could loafing around out of doors or riding up and down the land on freight trains and trying to see the world. I even did some stealing in lonely towns at night—once a pretty good suit of clothes that someone had left hanging out on a clothesline, and once some shoes out of a box in a freight car—but I was in constant

[1]For Editor's Note see p. 350.

terror of being caught and put into jail so realized that success as a thief was not for me.

The most delightful experience of that period of my life was when I once worked as a groom, or swipe, with race horses and it was during that time I met a young fellow of about my own age who has since become a writer of some prominence.

The young man of whom I now speak had gone into race track work as a groom, to bring a kind of flourish, a high spot he used to say, into his life.

He was then unmarried and had not been successful as a writer. What I mean is he was free and I guess, with him as with me, there was something he liked about the people who hang about a race track, the touts, swipes, drivers, niggers and gamblers. You know what a gaudy undependable lot they are—if you've ever been around the tracks much—about the best liars I've seen, and not saving money or thinking about morals, like most druggists, drygoods merchants and the others who used to be my father's friends in our Nebraska town—and not bending the knee much either, or kowtowing to people, they thought must be grander or richer or more powerful than themselves.

What I mean is, they were an independent, go-to-the-devil, come-have-a-drink-of-whisky, kind of a crew and when one of them won a bet, "knocked 'em off," we called it, his money was just dirt to him while it lasted. No king or president or soap manufacturer—gone on a trip with his family to Europe —could throw on more dog than one of them, with his big diamond rings and the diamond horseshoe stuck in his necktie and all.

I liked the whole blamed lot pretty well and he did too.

He was groom temporarily for a pacing gelding named Lumpy Joe owned by a tall black-mustached man named Alfred Kreymborg and trying the best he could to make the bluff to himself he was a real one. It happened that we were on the same circuit, doing the West Pennsylvania county fairs all that fall, and on fine evenings we spent a good deal of time walking and talking together.

Let us suppose it to be a Monday or Tuesday evening and our horses had been put away for the night. The racing didn't start until later in the week, maybe, Wednesday, usually. There was always a little place called a dining-hall, run mostly by the Woman's Christian Temperance Associations of the towns, and we would go there to eat where we could get a pretty good meal for twenty-five cents. At least then we thought it pretty good.

I would manage it so that I sat beside this fellow, whose name was Tom Means and when we had got through eating we would go look at our two horses again and when we got there Lumpy Joe would be eating his hay in his box stall and Alfred Kreymborg would be standing there, pulling his mustache and looking as sad as a sick crane.

But he wasn't really sad. "You two boys want to go downtown to see the girls. I'm an old duffer and way past that myself. You go along. I'll be setting here anyway, and I'll keep an eye on both the horses for you," he would say.

So we would set off, going, not into the town to try to get in with some of the town girls, who might have taken up with us because we were strangers and race track fellows, but out into the country. Sometimes we got into a hilly country and there was a moon. The leaves were falling off the trees and lay in the road so that we kicked them up with the dust as we went along.

To tell the truth I suppose I got to love Tom Means, who was five years older than me, although I wouldn't have dared say so, then. Americans are shy and timid about saying things like that and a man here don't dare own up he loves another man, I've found out, and they are afraid to admit such feelings to themselves even. I guess they're afraid it may be taken to mean something it don't need to at all.

Anyway we walked along and some of the trees were already bare and looked like people standing solemnly beside the road and listening to what we had to say. Only I didn't say much. Tom Means did most of the talking.

Sometimes we came back to the race track and it was late and the moon had gone down and it was dark. Then we often walked round and round the track, sometimes a dozen times, before we crawled into the hay to go to bed.

Tom talked always on two subjects, writing and race horses, but mostly about race horses. The quiet sounds about the race tracks and the smells of horses, and the things that go with horses, seemed to get him all excited. "Oh, hell, Herman Dudley," he would burst out suddenly, "don't go talking to me. I know what I think. I've been around more than you have and I've seen a world of people. There isn't any man or woman, not even a fellow's own mother, as fine as a horse, that is to say a thoroughbred horse."

Sometimes he would go on like that a long time, speaking of people he had seen and their characteristics. He wanted to be a writer later and what he said was that when he came to be one he wanted to write the way a well bred horse runs or trots or paces. Whether he ever did it or not I can't say. He has written a lot, but I'm not too good a judge of such things. Anyway I don't think he has.

But when he got on the subject of horses he certainly was a darby. I would never have felt the way I finally got to feel about horses or enjoyed my stay among them half so much if it hadn't been for him. Often he would go on talking for an hour maybe, speaking of horses' bodies and of their minds and wills as though they were human beings. "Lord help us, Herman," he would say, grabbing hold of my arm, "don't it get you up in the throat? I say now, when a good one, like that Lumpy Joe I'm swiping, flattens himself at the head of the stretch and he's coming, and you know he's coming, and you know his heart's sound, and he's game, and you know he isn't going to let himself get licked—don't it get you Herman, don't it get you like the old Harry?"

That's the way he would talk, and then later, sometimes, he'd talk about writing and get himself all het up about that too. He had some notions about writing I've never got myself around to thinking much about but just the same maybe his talk, working in me, has led me to want to begin to write this story myself.

There was one experience of that time on the tracks that I am forced, by some feeling inside myself, to tell.

Well, I don't know why but I've just got to. It will be kind of like confession is, I suppose, to a good Catholic, or maybe, better yet, like cleaning up the room you live in, if you are a bachelor, like I was for so long. The room gets pretty mussy and the bed not made some days and clothes and things thrown on the closet floor and maybe under the bed. And then you clean all up and put on new sheets, and then you take off all your clothes and get down on your hands and knees, and scrub the floor so clean you could eat bread off it, and then take a walk and come home after a while and your room smells sweet and you feel sweetened-up and better inside yourself too.

What I mean is, this story has been on my chest, and I've often dreamed about the happenings in it, even after I married Jessie and was happy. Sometimes I even screamed out at night and so I said to myself, "I'll write the dang story," and here goes.

Fall had come on and in the mornings now when we crept out of our blankets, spread out on the hay in the tiny lofts above the horse stalls, and put our heads out to look around, there was a white rime of frost on the ground. When we woke the horses woke too. You know how it is at the tracks—the little barnlike stalls with the tiny lofts above are all set along in a row and there are two doors to each stall, one coming up to a horse's breast and then a top one, that is only closed at night and in bad weather.

In the mornings the upper door is swung open and fastened back and the horses put their heads out. There is the white rime on the grass over inside the gray oval the track makes. Usually there is some outfit that has six, ten or even twelve horses, and perhaps they have a Negro cook who does his cooking at an open fire in the clear space before the row of stalls and he is at work now and the horses with their big fine eyes are looking about and whinnying, and a stallion looks out at the door of one of the stalls and sees a sweet-eyed mare looking at him and sends up his trumpet-call, and a man's voice laughs, and there are no women anywhere in sight or no sign of one anywhere, and everyone feels like laughing and usually does.

It's pretty fine but I didn't know how fine it was until I got to know Tom Means and heard him talk about it all.

At the time the thing happened of which I am trying to tell now Tom was no longer with me. A week before his owner, Alfred Kreymborg, had taken his horse Lumpy Joe over into the Ohio Fair Circuit and I saw no more of Tom at the tracks.

There was a story going about the stalls that Lumpy Joe, a big rangy brown gelding, wasn't really named Lumpy Joe at all, that he was a ringer who had made a fast record out in Iowa and up through the northwest country the year before, and that Kreymborg had picked him up and had kept him under wraps all winter and had brought him over into the Pennsylvania country under this new name and made a clean-up in the books.

I know nothing about that and never talked to Tom about it but anyway he, Lumpy Joe and Kreymborg were all gone now.

I suppose I'll always remember those days, and Tom's talk at night, and before that in the early September evenings how we sat around in front of the stalls and Kreymborg sitting on an upturned feed box and pulling at his long black mustache and sometimes humming a little ditty one couldn't catch the words of. It was something about a deep well and a little gray squirrel crawling up the sides of it, and he never laughed or smiled much but there was something in his solemn gray eyes, not quite a twinkle, something more delicate than that.

The others talked in low tones and Tom and I sat in silence. He never did his best talking except when he and I were alone.

For his sake—if he ever sees my story—I should mention that at the only big track we ever visited, at Readville, Pennsylvania, we saw old Pop Geers, the great racing driver, himself. His horses were at a place far away across the tracks from where we were stabled. I suppose a man like him was likely to get the choice of all the good places for his horses.

We went over there one evening and stood about and there was Geers himself, sitting before one of the stalls on a box tapping the ground with a riding whip. They called him, around the tracks, "The silent man from Tennessee" and he was silent—that night anyway. All we did was to stand and look at him for maybe a half hour and then we went away and that night Tom talked better than I had ever heard him. He said that the ambition of his life was to wait until Pop Geers died and then write a book about him, and to show in the book that there was at least one American who never went nutty about getting rich or owning a big factory or being any other kind of a hell of fellow. "He's satisfied I think to sit around like that and wait until the big moments of his life come, when he heads a fast one into the stretch and then, darn his soul, he can give all of himself to the thing right in front of him," Tom said, and then he was so worked up he began to blubber. We were walking along the fence on the inside of the tracks and it was dusk and, in some trees nearby, some birds, just sparrows maybe, were making a chirping sound, and you could hear insects singing and, where there was a little light, off to the west between some trees, motes were dancing in the air. Tom said that about Pop Geers, although I think he was thinking most about something he wanted to be himself and wasn't, and then he went and stood by the fence and sort of blubbered and I began to blubber too, although I didn't know what about.

But perhaps I did know, after all. I suppose Tom wanted to feel, when he became a writer, like he thought old Pop must feel when his horse swung around the upper turn, and there lay the stretch before him, and if he was going to get his horse home in front he had to do it right then. What Tom said was that any man had something in him that understands about a thing like that but that no woman ever did except up in her brain. He often got off things like that about women but I notice he later married one of them just the same.

But to get back to my knitting. After Tom had left, the stable I was with kept drifting along through nice little Pennsylvania county seat towns. My owner, a strange excitable kind of a man from over in Ohio, who had lost a lot of money on horses but was always thinking he would maybe get it all back in some big killing, had been playing in pretty good luck that year. The horse I had, a tough little gelding, a five-year-old, had been getting home in front pretty regular and so he took some of his winnings and bought a three-year-old black pacing stallion named "O My Man." My gelding was called "Pick-it-boy" because when he was in a race and had gone into the stretch my owner always got half wild with excitement and shouted so you could hear him a mile and a half. "Go, pick it boy, pick it boy, pick it boy," he kept shouting and so when he had got hold of this good little gelding he had named him that.

The gelding was a fast one, all right. As the boys at the tracks used to say, he "picked 'em up sharp and set 'em down clean," and he was what we called a natural race horse, right up to all the speed he had, and didn't require much training. "All you got to do is to drop him down on the track and he'll go," was what my owner was always saying to other men, when he was bragging about his horse.

And so you see, after Tom left, I hadn't much to do evenings and then the new stallion, the three-year-old, came on with a Negro swipe named Burt.

I liked him fine and he liked me but not the same as Tom and me. We got to be friends all right and I suppose Burt would have done things for me, and maybe me for him, that Tom and me wouldn't have done for each other.

But with a Negro you couldn't be close friends like you can with another white man. There's some reason you can't understand but it's true. There's been too much talk about the difference between whites and blacks and you're both shy, and anyway no use trying and I suppose Burt and I both knew it and so I was pretty lonesome.

Something happened to me that happened several times, when I was a young fellow, that I have never exactly understood. Sometimes now I think it was all because I had got to be almost a man and had never been with a woman. I don't know what's the matter with me. I can't ask a woman. I've tried it a good many times in my life but every time I've tried the same thing happened.

Of course, with Jessie now, it's different, but at the time of which I'm speaking Jessie was a long ways off and a good many things were to happen to me before I got to her.

Around a race track, as you may suppose, the fellows who are swipes and drivers and strangers in the towns do not go without women. They don't have to. In any town there are always some fly girls will come around a place like that. I suppose they think they are fooling with men who lead romantic lives. Such girls will come along by the front of the stalls where the race horses are and, if you look all right to them, they will stop and make a fuss over your horse. They rub their little hands over the horse's nose and then is the time for you—if you aren't a fellow like me who can't get up the nerve—then is the time for you to smile and say, "Hello, kid," and make a date with one of them for that evening uptown after supper. I couldn't do that, although the Lord knows I tried hard enough, often enough. A girl would come along alone, and she would be a little thing and give me the eye, and I would try and try but couldn't say anything. Both Tom, and Burt afterwards, used to laugh at me about it sometimes but what I think is that, had I been able to speak up to one of them and had managed to make a date with her, nothing would have come of it. We would probably have walked around the town and got off together in the dark somewhere, where the town came to an end, and then she would have had to knock me over with a club before it got any further.

And so there I was, having got used to Tom and our talks together, and Burt of course had his own friends among the black men. I got lazy and mopey and had a hard time doing my work.

It was like this. Sometimes I would be sitting, perhaps under a tree in the late afternoon when the races were over for the day and the crowds had gone away. There were always a lot of other men and boys who hadn't any horses in the races that day and they would be standing or sitting about in front of the stalls and talking.

I would listen for a time to their talk and then their voices would seem to go far away. The things I was looking at would go far away too. Perhaps there would be a tree, not more than a hundred yards away, and it would just come out of the ground and float away like a thistle. It would get smaller and smaller, away off there in the sky, and then suddenly— bang, it would be back where it belonged, in the ground, and I would begin hearing the voices of the men talking again.

When Tom was with me that summer the nights were splendid. We usually walked about and talked until pretty late and then I crawled up into my hole and went to sleep. Always out of Tom's talk I got something that stayed in my mind, after I was off by myself, curled up in my blanket. I suppose he had a way of making pictures as he talked and the pictures stayed by me as Burt was always saying pork chops did by him. "Give me the old pork chops, they stick to the ribs," Burt was always saying and with the imagination it was always that way about Tom's talks. He started something inside you that went on and on, and your mind played with it like walking about in a strange town and seeing the sights, and you slipped off to sleep and had splendid dreams and woke up in the morning feeling fine.

And then he was gone and it wasn't that way any more and I got into the fix I have described. At night I kept seeing women's bodies and women's lips and things in my dreams, and woke up in the morning feeling like the old Harry.

Burt was pretty good to me. He always helped me cool Pick-it-boy out after a race and he did the things himself that take the most skill and quickness, like getting the bandages on a horse's leg smooth, and seeing that every strap is setting just right, and every buckle drawn up to just the right hole, before your horse goes out on the track for a heat.

Burt knew there was something wrong with me and put himself out not to let the boss know. When the boss was around he was always bragging about me. "The brightest kid

I've ever worked with around the tracks," he would say and grin, and that at a time when I wasn't worth my salt.

When you go out with the horses there is one job that always takes a lot of time. In the late afternoon, after your horse has been in a race and after you have washed him and rubbed him out, he has to be walked slowly, sometimes for hours and hours, so he'll cool out slowly and won't get musclebound. I got so I did that job for both our horses and Burt did the more important things. It left him free to go talk or shoot dice with the other niggers and I didn't mind. I rather liked it and after a hard race even the stallion, O My Man, was tame enough, even when there were mares about.

You walk and walk and walk, around a little circle, and your horse's head is right by your shoulder, and all around you the life of the place you are in is going on, and in a queer way you get so you aren't really a part of it at all. Perhaps no one ever gets as I was then, except boys that aren't quite men yet and who like me have never been with girls or women— to really be with them, up to the hilt, I mean. I used to wonder if young girls got that way too before they married or did what we used to call "go on the town."

If I remember it right though, I didn't do much thinking then. Often I would have forgotten supper if Burt hadn't shouted at me and reminded me, and sometimes he forgot and went off to town with one of the other niggers and I did forget.

There I was with the horse, going slow slow slow, around a circle that way. The people were leaving the fair grounds now, some afoot, some driving away to the farms in wagons and Fords. Clouds of dust floated in the air and over to the west, where the town was, maybe the sun was going down, a red ball of fire through the dust. Only a few hours before the crowd had been all filled with excitement and everyone shouting. Let us suppose my horse had been in a race that afternoon and I had stood in front of the grandstand with my horse blanket over my shoulder, alongside of Burt perhaps, and when they came into the stretch my owner began to call, in that queer high voice of his that seemed to float over the top of all the shouting up in the grandstand. And his voice was saying over and over, "Go, pick it boy, pick it boy, pick it boy," the way he always did, and my heart was thumping so I could hardly breathe, and Burt was leaning over and snapping his fingers and muttering. "Come, little sweet. Come on home. Your Mama wants you. Come get your 'lasses and bread, little Pick-it-boy."

Well, all that was over now and the voices of the people left around were all low. And Pick-it-boy—I was leading him slowly around the little ring, to cool him out slowly, as I've said—he was different too. Maybe he had pretty nearly broken his heart trying to get down to the wire in front, or getting down there in front, and now everything inside him was quiet and tired, as it was nearly all the time those days in me, except in me tired but not quiet.

You remember I've told you we always walked in a circle, round and round and round. I guess something inside me got to going round and round and round too. The sun did sometimes and the trees and the clouds of dust. I had to think sometimes about putting down my feet so they went down in the right place and I didn't get to staggering like a drunken man.

And a funny feeling came that it is going to be hard to describe. It had something to do with the life in the horse and in me. Sometimes, these late years, I've thought maybe Negroes would understand what I'm trying to talk about now better than any white man ever will. I mean something about men and animals, something between them, something that can perhaps only happen to a white man when he has slipped off his base a little, as I suppose I had then. I think maybe a lot of horsey people feel it sometimes though. It's something like this, maybe—do you suppose it could be that something we whites have got, and think such a lot of, and are so proud about, isn't much of any good after all?

It's something in us that wants to be big and grand and important maybe and won't let us just be, like a horse or a dog or a bird can. Let's say Pick-it-boy had won his race that day. He did that pretty often that summer. Well, he was neither proud, like I would have been in his place, or mean in one part of the inside of him either. He was just himself, doing something with a kind of simplicity. That's what Pick-it-boy was like and I got to feeling it in him as I walked with him slowly in the gathering darkness. I got inside him in some way I can't explain and he got inside me. Often we would stop walking for no cause and he would put his nose up against my face.

I wished he was a girl sometimes or that I was a girl and he was a man. It's an odd thing to say but it's a fact. Being with him that way, so long, and in such a quiet way, cured something in me a little. Often after an evening like that I slept all right and did not have the kind of dreams I've spoken about.

But I wasn't cured for very long and couldn't get cured. My body seemed all right and just as good as ever but there wasn't no pep in me.

Then the fall got later and later and we came to the last town we were going to make before my owner laid his horses up for the winter, in his home town over across the state line in Ohio, and the track was up a hill, or rather in a kind of high plain above the town.

It wasn't much of a place and the sheds were rather rickety and the track bad, especially at the turns. As soon as we got to the place and got stabled it began to rain and kept it up all week so the fair had to be put off.

As the purses weren't very large a lot of the owners shipped right out but our owner stayed. The fair owners guaranteed expenses, whether the races were held the next week or not.

And all week there wasn't much of anything for Burt and me to do but clean manure out of the stalls in the morning, watch for a chance when the rain let up a little to jog the horses around the track in the mud and then clean them off, blanket them and stick them back in their stalls.

It was the hardest time of all for me. Burt wasn't so bad off as there were a dozen or two blacks around and in the evening they went off to town, got liquored up a little and came home late, singing and talking, even in the cold rain.

And then one night I got mixed up in the thing I'm trying to tell you about.

It was a Saturday evening and when I look back at it now it seems to me everyone had left the tracks but just me. In early evening swipe after swipe came over to my stall and asked me if I was going to stick around. When I said I was he would ask me to keep an eye out for him, that nothing happened to his horse. "Just take a stroll down that way now and then, eh, kid," one of them would say, "I just want to run up to town for an hour or two."

I would say "yes" to be sure, and so pretty soon it was dark as pitch up there in that little ruined fair-ground and nothing living anywhere around but the horses and me.

I stood it as long as I could, walking here and there in the mud and rain, and thinking all the time I wished I was someone else and not myself. "If I were someone else," I thought, "I wouldn't be here but down there in town with the others." I saw myself going into saloons and having drinks and later going off to a house maybe and getting myself a woman.

I got to thinking so much that, as I went stumbling around up there in the darkness, it was as though what was in my mind was actually happening.

Only I wasn't with some cheap woman, such as I would have found had I had the nerve to do what I wanted but with such a woman as I thought then I should never find in this world. She was slender and like a flower and with something in her like a race horse too, something in her like Pick-it-boy in the stretch, I guess.

And I thought about her and thought about her until I couldn't stand thinking any more. "I'll do something anyway," I said to myself.

So, although I had told all the swipes I would stay and watch their horses, I went out of the fair grounds and down the hill a ways. I went down until I came to a little low saloon, not in the main part of the town itself but halfway up the hillside. The saloon had once been a residence, a farmhouse perhaps, but if it was ever a farmhouse I'm sure the farmer who lived there and worked the land on that hillside hadn't made out very well. The country didn't look like a farming country, such as one sees all about the other county-seat towns we had been visiting all through the late summer and fall. Everywhere you looked there were stones sticking out of the ground and the trees mostly of the stubby, stunted kind. It looked wild and untidy and ragged, that's what I mean. On the flat plain, up above, where the fair ground was, there were a few fields and pastures, and there were some sheep raised and in the field right next to the tracks, on the furtherest side from town, on the back stretch side, there had once been a slaughterhouse, the ruins of which were still standing. It hadn't been used for quite some time but there were bones of animals lying all about in the field, and there was a smell coming out of the old building that would curl your hair.

The horses hated the place, just as we swipes did, and in the morning when we were jogging them around the track in the mud, to keep them in racing condition, Pick-it-boy and O My Man both raised old Ned every time we headed them up the back stretch and got near to where the old slaughterhouse stood. They would rear and fight at the bit, and go off their stride and run until they got clear of the rotten smells, and neither Burt nor I could make them stop it. "It's a hell of a town down there and this is a hell of a track for racing," Burt kept saying. "If they ever have their danged old fair someone's going to get spilled and maybe killed back here." Whether they did or not I don't know as I didn't stay for the fair, for reasons I'll tell you pretty soon, but Burt was speaking sense all right. A race horse isn't like a human being. He won't stand for it to have to do his work in any rotten ugly kind of a dump the way a man will, and he won't stand for the smells a man will either.

But to get back to my story again. There I was, going down the hillside in the darkness and the cold soaking rain and breaking my word to all the others about staying up above and watching the horses. When I got to the little saloon I decided to stop and have a drink or two. I'd found out long before that about two drinks upset me so I was two-thirds piped and couldn't walk straight, but on that night I didn't care a tinker's dam.

So I went up a kind of path, out of the road, toward the front door of the saloon. It was in what must have been the parlor of the place when it was a farmhouse and there was a little front porch.

I stopped before I opened the door and looked about a little. From where I stood I could look right down into the main street of the town, like being in a big city, like New York or Chicago, and looking down out of the fifteenth floor of an office building into the street.

The hillside was mighty steep and the road up had to wind and wind or no one could ever have come up out of the town to their plagued old fair at all.

It wasn't much of a town I saw—a main street with a lot of saloons and a few stores, one or two dinky moving-picture places, a few fords, hardly any women or girls in sight and a raft of men. I tried to think of the girl I had been dreaming about, as I walked around in the mud and darkness up at the fair ground, living in the place but I couldn't make it. It was like trying to think of Pick-it-boy getting himself worked up to the state I was in then, and going into the ugly dump I was going into. It couldn't be done.

All the same I knew the town wasn't all right there in sight. There must have been a good many of the kinds of houses Pennsylvania miners live in back in the hills, or around a turn in the valley in which the main street stood.

What I suppose is that, it being Saturday night and raining, the women and kids had all stayed at home and only the men were out, intending to get themselves liquored up. I've been in some other mining towns since and if I was a miner and had to live in one of them, or in one of the houses they live in with their women and kids, I'd get out and liquor myself up too.

So there I stood looking, and as sick as a dog inside myself, and as wet and cold as a rat in a sewer pipe. I could see the mass of dark figures moving about down below, and beyond the main street there was a river that made a sound you could

hear distinctly, even up where I was, and over beyond the
river were some railroad tracks with switch engines going up
and down. I suppose they had something to do with the mines
in which the men of the town worked. Anyway, as I stood
watching and listening there was, now and then, a sound like
thunder rolling down the sky, and I suppose that was a lot
of coal, maybe a whole carload, being let down plunk into a
coal car.

And then besides there was, on the side of a hill far away,
a long row of coke ovens. They had little doors, through which
the light from the fire within leaked out and as they were
set closely, side by side, they looked like the teeth of some
big man-eating giant lying and waiting over there in the hills.

The sight of it all, even the sight of the kind of hell-holes
men are satisfied to go on living in, gave me the fantods and
the shivers right down in my liver, and on that night I guess
I had in me a kind of contempt for all men, including myself,
that I've never had so thoroughly since. Come right down to
it, I suppose women aren't so much to blame as men. They
aren't running the show.

Then I pushed open the door and went into the saloon.
There were about a dozen men, miners I suppose, playing
cards at tables in a little long dirty room, with a bar at one
side of it, and with a big red-faced man with a mustache
standing back of the bar.

The place smelled, as such places do where men hang
around who have worked and sweated in their clothes and
perhaps slept in them too, and have never had them washed
but have just kept on wearing them. I guess you know what
I mean if you've ever been in a city. You smell that smell
in a city, in streetcars on rainy nights when a lot of factory
hands get on. I got pretty used to that smell when I was
a tramp and pretty sick of it too.

And so I was in the place now, with a glass of whisky in
my hand, and I thought all the miners were staring at me,
which they weren't at all, but I thought they were and so I felt

just the same as though they had been. And then I looked up and saw my own face in the old cracked looking-glass back of the bar. If the miners had been staring, or laughing at me, I wouldn't have wondered when I saw what I looked like.

It—I mean my own face—was white and pasty-looking, and for some reason, I can't tell exactly why, it wasn't my own face at all. It's a funny business I'm trying to tell you about and I know what you may be thinking of me as well as you do, so you needn't suppose I'm innocent or ashamed. I'm only wondering. I've thought about it a lot since and I can't make it out. I know I was never that way before that night and I know I've never been that way since. Maybe it was lonesomeness, just lonesomeness, gone on in me too long. I've often wondered if women generally are lonesomer than men.

The point is that the face I saw in the looking-glass back of that bar, when I looked up from my glass of whisky that evening, wasn't my own face at all but the face of a woman. It was a girl's face, that's what I mean. That's what it was. It was a girl's face, and a lonesome and scared girl too. She was just a kid at that.

When I saw that the glass of whisky came pretty near falling out of my hand but I gulped it down, put a dollar on the bar, and called for another. "I've got to be careful here— I'm up against something new," I said to myself. "If any of these men in here get on to me there's going to be trouble." When I had got the second drink in me I called for a third and I thought, "When I get this third drink down I'll get out of here and back up the hill to the fair ground before I make a fool of myself and begin to get drunk."

And then, while I was thinking and drinking my third glass of whisky, the men in the room began to laugh and of course I thought they were laughing at me. But they weren't. No one in the place had really paid any attention to me.

What they were laughing at was a man who had just come in at the door. I'd never seen such a fellow. He was a huge big man, with red hair, that stuck straight up like bristles out of his head, and he had a red-haired kid in his arms. The kid was just like himself, big, I mean, for his age, and with the same kind of stiff red hair.

He came and set the kid up on the bar, close beside me, and called for a glass of whisky for himself and all the men in the room began to shout and laugh at him and his kid. Only they didn't shout and laugh when he was looking, so he could tell which ones did it, but did all their shouting and laughing when his head was turned the other way. They kept calling him "cracked." "The crack is getting wider in the old tin pan," someone sang and then they all laughed.

I'm puzzled you see, just how to make you feel as I felt that night. I suppose, having undertaken to write this story, that's what I'm up against, trying to do that. I'm not claiming to be able to inform you or to do you any good. I'm just trying to make you understand some things about me, as I would like to understand some things about you, or anyone, if I had the chance. Anyway the whole blamed thing, the thing that went on I mean in that little saloon on that rainy Saturday night, wasn't like anything quite real. I've already told you how I had looked into the glass back of the bar and had seen there, not my own face but the face of a scared young girl. Well, the men, the miners, sitting at the tables in the half-dark room, the red-faced bartender, the unholy looking big man who had come in and his queer-looking kid, now sitting on the bar—all of them were like characters in some play, not like real people at all.

There was myself, that wasn't myself—and I'm not any fairy. Anyone who has ever known me knows better than that.

And then there was the man who had come in. There was a feeling came out of him that wasn't like the feeling you get from a man at all. It was more like the feeling you get maybe from a horse, only his eyes weren't like a horse's eyes. Horses' eyes have a kind of calm something in them and his hadn't. If you've ever carried a lantern through a wood at night, going along a path, and then suddenly you felt something funny in the air and stopped, and there ahead of you somewhere were the eyes of some little animal, gleaming out at you from a dead wall of darkness—The eyes shine big and quiet but there is a point right in the center of each, where there is something dancing and wavering. You aren't afraid the little animal will jump at you, you are afraid the little eyes will jump at you—that's what's the matter with you.

Only of course a horse, when you go into his stall at night, or a little animal you had disturbed in a wood that way, wouldn't be talking and the big man who had come in there with his kid was talking. He kept talking all the time, saying something under his breath, as they say, and I could only understand now and then a few words. It was his talking made him kind of terrible. His eyes said one thing and his lips another. They didn't seem to get together, as though they belonged to the same person.

For one thing the man was too big. There was about him an unnatural bigness. It was in his hands, his arms, his shoulders, his body, his head, a bigness like you might see in trees and bushes in a tropical country perhaps. I've never been in a tropical country but I've seen pictures. Only his eyes were small. In his big head they looked like the eyes of a bird. And I remember that his lips were thick, like Negroes' lips.

He paid no attention to me or to the others in the room but kept on muttering to himself, or to the kid sitting on the bar—I couldn't tell to which.

First he had one drink and then, quick, another. I stood staring at him and thinking—a jumble of thoughts, I suppose.

What I must have been thinking was something like this. "Well he's one of the kind you are always seeing about towns," I thought. I meant he was one of the cracked kind. In almost any small town you go to you will find one, and sometimes two or three cracked people, walking around. They go through the street, muttering to themselves and people generally are cruel to them. Their own folks make a bluff at being kind, but they aren't really, and the others in the town, men and boys, like to tease them. They send such a fellow, the mild silly kind, on some fool errand after a round square or a dozen post-holes or tie cards on his back saying "Kick me," or something like that, and then carry on and laugh as though they had done something funny.

And so there was this cracked one in that saloon and I could see the men in there wanted to have some fun putting up some kind of horseplay on him, but they didn't quite dare. He wasn't one of the mild kind, that was a cinch. I kept looking at the man and at his kid, and then up at that strange unreal reflection of myself in the cracked looking-glass back of the bar. "Rats, rats, digging in the ground—miners are rats, little jackrabbit," I heard him say to his solemn-faced kid. I guess, after all, maybe he wasn't so cracked.

The kid sitting on the bar kept blinking at his father, like an owl caught out in the daylight, and now the father was having another glass of whisky. He drank six glasses, one right after the other, and it was cheap tencent stuff. He must have had cast-iron insides all right.

Of the men in the room there were two or three (maybe they were really more scared than the others so had to put up a bluff of bravery by showing off) who kept laughing and making funny cracks about the big man and his kid and there was one fellow was the worst of the bunch. I'll never forget that fellow because of his looks and what happened to him afterwards.

He was one of the showing-off kind all right, and he was the one that had started the song about the crack getting bigger in the old tin pan. He sang it two or three times, and then the room singing it over and over. He was a showy kind of he grew bolder and got up and began walking up and down man with a fancy vest, on which there were brown tobacco spots, and he wore glasses. Every time he made some crack he thought was funny, he winked at the others as though to say, "You see me. I'm not afraid of this big fellow," and then the others laughed.

The proprietor of the place must have known what was going on, and the danger in it, because he kept leaning over the bar and saying, "Shush, now quit it," to the showy-off man, but it didn't do any good. The fellow kept prancing like a turkey-cock and he put his hat on one side of his head and stopped right back of the big man and sang that song about the crack in the old tin pan. He was one of the kind you can't shush until they get their blocks knocked off, and it didn't take him long to come to it that time anyhow.

Because the big fellow just kept on muttering to his kid and drinking his whisky, as though he hadn't heard anything, and then suddenly he turned and his big hand flashed out and he grabbed, not the fellow who had been showing off, but me. With just a sweep of his arm he brought me up against his big body. Then he shoved me over with my breast jammed against the bar and looking right into his kid's face and he said, "Now you watch him, and if you let him fall I'll kill you," in just quite ordinary tones as though he was saying "good morning" to some neighbor.

Then the kid leaned over and threw his arms around my head, and in spite of that I did manage to screw my head around enough to see what happened.

It was a sight I'll never forget. The big fellow had whirled around, and he had the showy-off man by the shoulder now, and the fellow's face was a sight. The big man must have had some reputation as a bad man in the town, even though he was cracked for the man with the fancy vest had his mouth open now, and his hat had fallen off his head, and he was silent and scared. Once, when I was a tramp, I saw a kid killed by a train. The kid was walking on the rail and showing off before some other kids, by letting them see how close he could let an engine come to him before he got out of the way. And the engine was whistling and a woman, over on the porch of a house nearby, was jumping up and down and screaming, and the kid let the engine get nearer and nearer, wanting more and more to show off, and then he stumbled and fell. God, I'll never forget the look on his face, in just the second before he got hit and killed, and now, there in the saloon, was the same terrible look on another face.

I closed my eyes for a moment and was sick all through me and then, when I opened my eyes, the big man's fist was just coming down in the other man's face. The one blow knocked him cold and he fell down like a beast hit with an axe.

And then the most terrible thing of all happened. The big man had on heavy boots, and he raised one of them and brought it down on the other man's shoulder, as he lay white and groaning on the floor. I could hear the bones crunch and it made me so sick I could hardly stand up, but I had to stand up and hold on to that kid or I knew it would be my turn next.

Because the big fellow didn't seem excited or anything, but kept on muttering to himself as he had been doing when he was standing peacefully by the bar drinking his whisky, and now he had raised his foot again, and maybe this time he would bring it down in the other man's face and, "just eliminate his map for keeps," as sports and prize-fighters sometimes say. I trembled, like I was having a chill, but thank God at that moment the kid, who had his arms around me and one hand clinging to my nose, so that there were the marks of his fingernails on it the next morning, at that moment the kid, thank God, began to howl, and his father didn't bother any more with the man on the floor but turned around, knocked me aside, and taking the kid in his arms tramped out of that place, muttering to himself as he had been doing ever since he came in.

I went out too but I didn't prance out with any dignity, I'll tell you that. I slunk out like a thief or a coward, which perhaps I am, partly anyhow.

And so there I was, outside there in the darkness, and it was as cold and wet and black and Godforsaken a night as any man ever saw. I was so sick at the thought of human beings that night I could have vomited to think of them at all. For a while I just stumbled along in the mind of the road, going up the hill, back to the fair ground, and then, almost before I knew where I was, I found myself in the stall with Pick-it-boy.

That was one of the best and sweetest feelings I've ever had in my whole life, being in that warm stall alone with that horse that night. I had told the other swipes that I would go up and down the row of stalls now and then and have an eye on the other horses, but I had altogether forgotten my promise now. I went and stood with my back against the side of the stall, thinking how mean and low and all balled-up and twisted-up human beings can become, and how the best of them are likely to get that way any time, just because they are human beings and not simple and clear in their minds, and inside themselves, as animals are, maybe.

Perhaps you know how a person feels at such a moment. There are things you think of, odd little things you had thought you had forgotten. Once, when you were a kid, you were with your father, and he was all dressed up, as for a funeral or Fourth of July, and was walking along a street holding your hand. And you were going past a railroad station, and there was a woman standing. She was a stranger in your town and was dressed as you had never seen a woman dressed before, and never thought you would see one, looking so nice. Long afterwards you knew that was because she had lovely taste in clothes, such as so few women have really, but then you thought she must be a queen. You had read about queens in fairy stories and the thoughts of them thrilled you. What lovely eyes the strange lady had and what beautiful rings she wore on her fingers.

Then your father came out, from being in the railroad station, maybe to set his watch by the station clock, and took you by the hand and he and the woman smiled at each other, in an embarrassed kind of way, and you kept looking longingly back at her, and when you were out of her hearing you asked your father if she really were a queen. And it may be that your father was one who wasn't so very hot on democracy and a free country and talked-up bunk about a free citizenry, and he said he hoped she was a queen, and maybe, for all he knew, she was.

Or maybe, when you get jammed up as I was that night, and can't get things clear about yourself or other people and why you are alive, or for that matter why anyone you can think about is alive, you think, not of people at all but of other things you have seen and felt—like walking along a road in the snow in the winter, perhaps out in Iowa, and hearing soft warm sounds in a barn close to the road, or of another time when you were on a hill and the sun was going down and the sky suddenly became a great soft-colored bowl, all glowing like a jewel-handled bowl, a great queen in some faraway mighty kingdom might have put on a vast table out under the tree, once a year, when she invited all her loyal and loving subjects to come and dine with her.

I can't, of course, figure out what you try to think about when you are as desolate as I was that night. Maybe you are like me and inclined to think of women, and maybe you are like a man I met once, on the road, who told me that when he was up against it he never thought of anything but grub and a big nice clean warm bed to sleep in. "I don't care about anything else and I don't ever let myself think of anything else," he said. "If I was like you and went to thinking about women sometime I'd find myself hooked up to some skirt, and she'd have the old double cross on me, and the rest of my life maybe I'd be working in some factory for her and her kids."

As I say, there I was anyway, up there alone with that horse in that warm stall in that dark lonesome fair ground and I had that feeling about being sick at the thought of human beings and what they could be like.

Well, suddenly I got again the queer feeling I'd had about him once or twice before, I mean the feeling about our understanding each other in some way I can't explain.

So having it again I went over to where he stood and began running my hands all over his body, just because I loved the feel of him and as sometimes, to tell the plain truth, I've felt about touching with my hands the body of a woman I've seen and who I thought was lovely too. I ran my hands over his head and neck and then down over his hard firm round body and then over his flanks and down his legs. His flanks quivered a little I remember and once he turned his head and stuck his cold nose down along my neck and nipped my shoulder a little, in a soft playful way. It hurt a little but I didn't care.

So then I crawled up through a hole into the loft above thinking that night was over anyway and glad of it, but it wasn't, not by a long sight.

As my clothes were all soaking wet and as we race track swipes didn't own any such things as nightgowns or pajamas I had to go to bed naked, of course.

But we had plenty of horse blankets and so I tucked myself in between a pile of them and tried not to think any more that night. The being with Pick-it-boy and having him close right under me that way made me feel a little better.

Then I was sound asleep and dreaming and—bang like being hit with a club by someone who has sneaked up behind you—I got another wallop.

What I suppose is that, being upset the way I was, I had forgotten to bolt the door to Pick-it-boy's stall down below and two Negro men had come in there, thinking they were in their own place, and had climbed up through the hole where I was. They were half lit-up but not what you might call dead drunk, and I suppose they were up against something a couple of white swipes, who had some money in their pockets, wouldn't have been up against.

What I mean is that a couple of white swipes, having liquored themselves up and being down there in the town on a bat, if they wanted a woman or a couple of women would have been able to find them. There is always a few women of that kind can be found around any town I've ever seen or heard of, and of course a bartender would have given them the tip where to go.

But a Negro, up there in that country, where there aren't any, or anyway mighty few Negro women, wouldn't know what to do when he felt that way and would be up against it.

It's so always. Burt and several other Negroes I've known pretty well have talked to me about it, lots of times. You take now a young Negro man—not a race track swipe or a tramp or any other low-down kind of a fellow—but, let us say, one who has been to college, and has behaved himself and tried to be a good man, the best he could, and be clean, as they say. He isn't any better off, is he? If he has made himself some money and wants to go sit in a swell restaurant, or go to hear some good music, or see a good play at the theater, he gets what we used to call on the tracks, "the messy end of the dung fork," doesn't he?

And even in such a lowdown place as what people call a "bad house" it's the same way. The white swipes and others can go into a place where they have Negro women fast enough, and they do it too, but you let a Negro swipe try it the other way around and see how he comes out.

You see, I can think this whole thing out fairly now, sitting here in my own house and writing, and with my wife Jessie in the kitchen making a pie or something, and I can show just how the two Negro men who came into that loft, where I was asleep, were justified in what they did, and I can preach about how the Negroes are up against it in this country, like a daisy, but I tell you what, I didn't think things out that way that night.

For, you understand, what they thought, they being half liquored-up, and when one of them had jerked the blankets off me, was that I was a woman. One of them carried a lantern but it was smoky and dirty and didn't give out much light. So they must have figured it out—my body being pretty white and slender then, like a young girl's body I suppose—that some white swipe had brought me up there. The kind of girls around a town that will come with a swipe to a race track on a rainy night aren't very fancy females but you'll find that kind in the towns all right. I've seen many a one in my day.

And so, I figure, these two big buck niggers, being piped that way, just made up their minds they would snatch me away from the white swipe who had brought me out there, and who had left me lying carelessly around.

"Jes' you lie still honey. We ain't gwine hurt you none," one of them said, with a little chuckling laugh that had something in it besides a laugh, too. It was the kind of laugh that gives you the shivers.

The devil of it was I couldn't say anything, not even a word. Why I couldn't yell out and say "What the hell," and just kid them a little and shoo them out of there I don't know, but I couldn't. I tried and tried so that my throat hurt but I didn't say a word. I just lay there staring at them.

It was a mixed-up night. I've never gone through another night like it.

Was I scared? Lord Almighty, I'll tell you what, I was scared.

Because the two black faces were leaning right over me now, and I could feel their liquored-up breaths on my cheeks, and their eyes were shining in the dim light from that smoky lantern, and right in the center of their eyes was that dancing flickering light I've told you about your seeing in the eyes of wild animals, when you were carrying a lantern through the woods at night.

It was a puzzler! All my life, you see—me never having had any sisters, and at that time never having had a sweetheart either—I had been dreaming and thinking about women, and I suppose I'd always been dreaming about a pure innocent one, for myself, made for me by God, maybe. Men are that way. No matter how big they talk about "let the women go hang," they've always got that notion tucked away inside themselves, somewhere. It's a kind of chesty man's notion, I suppose, but they've got it and the kind of up-and-coming women we have nowadays who are always saying, "I'm as good as a man and will do what the men do," are on the wrong trail if they really ever want to, what you might say "hog-tie" a fellow of their own.

So I had invented a kind of princess, with black hair and a slender willowy body to dream about. And I thought of her as being shy and afraid to ever tell anything she really felt to anyone but just me. I suppose I fancied that if I ever found such a woman in the flesh I would be the strong sure one and she the timid shrinking one.

And now I was that woman, or something like her, myself.

I gave a kind of wriggle, like a fish you have just taken off the hook. What I did next wasn't a thought-out thing. I was caught and I squirmed, that's all.

The two niggers both jumped at me but somehow—the

lantern having been kicked over and having gone out the first move they made—well in some way, when they both lunged at me they missed.

As good luck would have it my feet found the hole, where you put hay down to the horse in the stall below, and through which we crawled up when it was time to go to bed in our blankets up in the hay, and down I slid, not bothering to try to find the ladder with my feet but just letting myself go.

In less than a second I was out of doors in the dark and the rain and the two blacks were down the hole and out the door of the stall after me.

How long or how far they really followed me I suppose I'll never know. It was black dark and raining hard now and a roaring wind had begun to blow. Of course, my body being white, it must have made some kind of a faint streak in the darkness as I ran, and anyway I thought they could see me and I knew I couldn't see them and that made my terror ten times worse. Every minute I thought they would grab me.

You know how it is when a person is all upset and full of terror as I was. I suppose maybe the two niggers followed me for a while, running across the muddy race track and into the grove of trees that grew in the oval inside the track, but likely enough, after just a few minutes, they gave up the chase and went back, found their own place and went to sleep. They were liquored-up, as I've said, and maybe partly funning too.

But I didn't know that, if they were. As I ran I kept hearing sounds, sounds made by the rain coming down through the dead old leaves left on the trees and by the wind blowing, and it may be that the sound that scared me most of all was my own bare feet stepping on a dead branch and breaking it or something like that.

There was something strange and scary, a steady sound, like a heavy man running and breathing hard, right at my shoulder. It may have been my own breath, coming quick and fast. And I thought I heard that chuckling laugh I'd heard up in the loft, the laugh that sent the shivers right down through me. Of course every tree I came close to looked like a man standing there, ready to grab me, and I kept dodging and going—bang—into other trees. My shoulders kept knocking against trees in that way and the skin was all knocked off, and every time it happened I thought a big black hand had come down and clutched at me and was tearing my flesh.

How long it went on I don't know, maybe an hour, maybe five minutes. But anyway the darkness didn't let up, and the terror didn't let up, and I couldn't, to save my life, scream or make any sound.

Just why I couldn't I don't know. Could it be because at the time I was a woman, while at the same time I wasn't a woman? It may be that I was too ashamed of having turned into a girl and being afraid of a man to make any sound. I don't know about that. It's over my head.

But anyway I couldn't make a sound. I tried and tried and my throat hurt from trying and no sound came.

And then, after a long time, or what seemed like a long time, I got out from among the trees inside the track and was on the track itself again. I thought the two black men were still after me, you understand, and I ran like a madman.

Of course, running along the track that way, it must have been up the back stretch, I came after a time to where the old slaughterhouse stood, in that field, beside the track. I knew it by its ungodly smell, scared as I was. Then, in some way, I managed to get over the high old fair ground fence and was in the field, where the slaughterhouse was.

All the time I was trying to yell or scream, or be sensible and tell those two black men that I was a man and not a woman, but I couldn't make it. And then I heard a sound like a board cracking or breaking in the fence and thought they were still after me.

So I kept on running like a crazy man, in the field, and just then I stumbled and fell over something. I've told you how the old slaughterhouse field was filled with bones, that had been lying there a long time and had all been washed white. There were heads of sheep and cows and all kinds of things.

And when I fell and pitched forward I fell right into the midst of something, still and cold and white.

It was probably the skeleton of a horse lying there. In small towns like that, they take an old worn-out horse, that has died, and haul him off to some field outside of town and skin him for the hide, that they can sell for a dollar or two. It doesn't make any difference what the horse has been, that's the way he usually ends up. Maybe even Pick-it-boy, or O My Man, or a lot of other good fast ones I've seen and known have ended that way by this time.

And so I think it was the bones of a horse lying there and he must have been lying on his back. The birds and wild animals had picked all his flesh away and the rain had washed his bones clean.

Anyway I fell and pitched forward and my side got cut pretty deep and my hands clutched at something. I had fallen right in between the ribs of the horse and they seemed to wrap themselves around me close. And my hands, clutching upwards, had got hold of the cheeks of that dead horse and the bones of his cheeks were cold as ice with the rain washing over them. White bones wrapped around me and white bones in my hands.

There was a new terror now that seemed to go down to the very bottom of me, to the bottom of the inside of me, I mean. It shook me like I have seen a rat in a barn shaken by a dog. It was a terror like a big wave that hits you when you are walking on a seashore, maybe. You see it coming and you try to run and get away but when you start to run inshore there is a stone cliff you can't climb. So the wave comes high as a mountain, and there it is, right in front of you and nothing in all this world can stop it. And now it had knocked you down and rolled and tumbled you over and over and washed you clean, clean, but dead maybe.

And that's the way I felt—I seemed to myself dead with blind terror. It was a feeling like the finger of God running down your back and burning you clean, I mean.

It burned all that silly nonsense about being a girl right out of me.

I screamed at last and the spell that was on me was broken. I'll bet the scream I let out of me could have been heard a mile and a half.

Right away I felt better and crawled out from among the pile of bones, and then I stood on my own feet again and I wasn't a woman, or a young girl any more but a man and my own self, and as far as I know I've been that way ever since. Even the black night seemed warm and alive now, like a mother might be to a kid in the dark.

Only I couldn't go back to the race track because I was blubbering and crying and was ashamed of myself and of what a fool I had made of myself. Someone might see me and I couldn't stand that, not at that moment.

So I went across the field, walking now, not running like a crazy man, and pretty soon I came to a fence and crawled over and got into another field, in which there was a straw stack, I just happened to find in the pitch darkness.

The straw stack had been there a long time and some sheep had nibbled away at it until they had made a pretty deep hole, like a cave, in the side of it. I found the hole and crawled in and there were some sheep in there, about a dozen of them.

When I came in, creeping on my hands and knees, they didn't make much fuss, just stirred around a little and then settled down.

So I settled down amongst them too. They were warm and gentle and kind, like Pick-it-boy, and being in there with them made me feel better than I would have felt being with any human person I knew at that time.

So I settled down and slept after a while, and when I woke up it was daylight and not very cold and the rain was over. The clouds were breaking away from the sky now and maybe there would be a fair the next week but if there was I knew I wouldn't be there to see it.

Because what I expected to happen did happen. I had to go back across the fields and the fair ground to the place where my clothes were, right in the broad daylight, and me stark naked, and of course I knew someone would be up and would raise a shout, and every swipe and every driver would stick his head out and would whoop with laughter.

And there would be a thousand questions asked, and I would be too mad and too ashamed to answer, and would perhaps begin to blubber, and that would make me more ashamed than ever.

It all turned out just as I expected, except that when the noise and the shouts of laughter were going it the loudest, Burt came out of the stall where O My Man was kept, and when he saw me he didn't know what was the matter but he knew something was up that wasn't on the square and for which I wasn't to blame.

So he got so all-fired mad he couldn't speak for a minute, and then he grabbed a pitchfork and began prancing up and down before the other stalls, giving that gang of swipes and drivers such a royal old dressing-down as you never heard. You should have heard him sling language. It was grand to hear.

And while he was doing it I sneaked up into the loft, blubbering because I was so pleased and happy to hear him swear that way, and I got my wet clothes on quick and got down, and gave Pick-it-boy a good-bye kiss on the cheek and lit out.

The last I saw of all that part of my life was Burt, still going it, and yelling out for the man who had put up a trick on me to come out and get what was coming to him. He had the pitchfork in his hand and was swinging it around, and every now and then he would make a kind of lunge at a tree or something, he was so mad through, and there was no one else in sight at all. And Burt didn't even see me cutting out along the fence through a gate and down the hill and out of the race-horse and the tramp life for the rest of my days.

A Meeting South

EDITOR'S NOTE

"A Meeting South" first appeared between the covers of a book among "articles written during the author's life as a story-teller" in *Sherwood Anderson's Notebook* (1926). And in 1933 it was reprinted in Anderson's last book of stories, *Death in the Woods and Other Stories*. It was written in 1924, during the period in which Anderson employed his widest variations on the short story form, and the following year it was published in *The Dial*. Was the piece an essay, a fragment of autobiography, or a story? It had the character of being all three in one—but Anderson's final decision to call the piece a story was correct. It is, properly speaking, a story about a young post-World War I southern writer and a woman, and it is one of the finest examples of Anderson's art in lightly sketching characters. The woman has been transplanted from the Middle West to New Orleans, and she shared with Anderson a spirit of agelessness and an almost maternal concern for the young half-crippled ex-aviator, who drinks heavily and has come home to die.

In "A Meeting South" Anderson re-creates the romantic atmosphere of the South and makes it seem inevitable that the lives of Aunt Sally, who once kept a disreputable "hotel," and the young writer should cross. Anderson's references to the Shelley-like spirit of the young writer bring to mind

Shelley's lines on "the sensitive plant," and through this association the lyrical lightness of the story is sustained. Since Anderson knew and encouraged William Faulkner to write long before Faulkner became a famous novelist, there is little doubt that the younger man (who then thought of himself as a poet) served as a model for David, the young poet, in the story.

He told me the story of his ill-fortune—a crack-up in an airplane—with a very gentlemanly little smile on his very sensitive, rather thin, lips. Such things happened. He might well have been speaking of another. I liked his tone and I liked him.

This happened in New Orleans, where I had gone to live. When he came, my friend, Fred, for whom he was looking, had gone away, but immediately I felt a strong desire to know him better and so suggested we spend the evening together. When we went down the stairs from my apartment I noticed that he was a cripple. The slight limp, the look of pain that occasionally drifted across his face, the little laugh that was intended to be jolly, but did not quite achieve its purpose, all these things began at once to tell me the story I have now set myself to write.

"I shall take him to see Aunt Sally," I thought. One does not take every caller to Aunt Sally. However, when she is in fine feather, when she has taken a fancy to her visitor, there is no one like her. Although she has lived in New Orleans for thirty years, Aunt Sally is Middle Western, born and bred.

However I am plunging a bit too abruptly into my story.

First of all I must speak more of my guest, and for convenience's sake I shall call him David. I felt at once that he would be wanting a drink and, in New Orleans—dear city of Latins and hot nights—even in Prohibition times such things can be managed. We achieved several and my own head became somewhat shaky but I could see that what we had taken had not affected him. Evening was coming, the abrupt waning of the day and the quick smoky soft-footed coming of night, characteristic of the semitropic city, when he produced a bottle from his hip pocket. It was so large that I was amazed. How had it happened that the carrying of so large a bottle had not made him look deformed? His body was very small and delicately built. "Perhaps, like the kangaroo, his body has developed some kind of a natural pouch for taking care of supplies," I thought. Really he walked as one might fancy a kangaroo would walk when out for a quiet evening stroll. I went along thinking of Darwin and the marvels of Prohibition. "We are a wonderful people, we Americans," I thought. We were both in fine humor and had begun to like each other immensely.

He explained the bottle. The stuff, he said, was made by a Negro man on his father's plantation somewhere over in Alabama. We sat on the steps of a vacant house deep down in the old French Quarter of New Orleans—the Vieux Carré—while he explained that his father had no intention of breaking the law—that is to say, in so far as the law remained reasonable. "Our nigger just makes whisky for us," he said. "We keep him for that purpose. He doesn't have anything else to do, just makes the family whisky, that's all. If he went selling any, we'd raise hell with him. I dare say Dad would shoot him if he caught him up to any such unlawful trick, and you bet, Jim, our nigger, I'm telling you of, knows it too.

"He's a good whisky-maker, though, don't you think?" David added. He talked of Jim in a warm friendly way. "Lord, he's been with us always, was born with us. His wife cooks for us and Jim makes our whisky. It's a race to see which is best at his job, but I think Jim will win. He's getting a little better all the time and all of our family—well, I reckon we just like and need our whisky more than we do our food."

Do you know New Orleans? Have you lived there in the summer when it is hot, in the winter when it rains, and through the glorious late fall days? Some of its own, more progressive, people scorn it now. In New Orleans there is a sense of shame because the city is not more like Chicago or Pittsburgh.

It, however, suited David and me. We walked slowly, on account of his bad leg, through many streets of the Old Town, Negro women laughing all around us in the dusk, shadows playing over old buildings, children with their shrill cries dodging in and out of old hallways. The old city was once almost altogether French, but now it is becoming more and more Italian. It however remains Latin. People live out of doors. Families were sitting down to dinner within full sight of the street—all doors and windows open. A man and his wife quarreled in Italian. In a patio back of an old building a Negress sang a French song.

We came out of the narrow little streets and had a drink in front of the dark cathedral and another in a little square in front. There is a statue of General Jackson, always taking off his hat to Northern tourists who in winter come down to see the city. At his horse's feet an inscription—"The Union must and will be preserved." We drank solemnly to that declaration and the general seemed to bow a bit lower. "He was sure a proud man," David said, as we went over toward the docks to sit in the darkness and look at the Mississippi. All good New Orleanians go to look at the Mississippi at least once a day. At night it is like creeping into a dark bedroom to look at a sleeping child—something of that sort—gives you the same warm nice feeling, I mean. David is a poet and so in the darkness by the river we spoke of Keats and Shelley, the two English poets all good Southern men love.

All of this, you are to understand, was before I took him to see Aunt Sally.

Both Aunt Sally and myself are Middle Westerners. We are but guests down here, but perhaps we both in some queer way belong to this city. Something of the sort is in the wind. I don't quite know how it has happened.

A great many Northern men and women come down our way and, when they go back North, write things about the South. The trick is to write nigger stories. The North likes them. They are so amusing. One of the best-known writers of nigger stories was down here recently and a man I know, a Southern man, went to call on him. The writer seemed a bit nervous. "I don't know much about the South or Southerners," he said. "But you have your reputation," my friend said. "You are so widely known as a writer about the South and about Negro life." The writer had a notion he was being made sport of. "Now look here," he said, "I don't claim to be a highbrow. I'm a business man myself. At home, up North, I associate mostly with business men and when I am not at work I go out to the country club. I want you to understand I am not setting myself up as a highbrow.

"I give them what they want," he said. My friend said he appeared angry. "About what now, do you fancy?" he asked innocently.

However, I am not thinking of the Northern writer of Negro stories. I am thinking of the Southern poet, with the bottle clasped firmly in his hands, sitting in the darkness beside me on the docks facing the Mississippi.

He spoke at some length of his gift for drinking. "I didn't always have it. It is a thing built up," he said. The story of how he chanced to be a cripple came out slowly. You are to remember that my own head was a bit unsteady. In the darkness the river, very deep and very powerful off New Orleans, was creeping away to the gulf. The whole river seemed to move away from us and then to slip noiselessly into the darkness like a vast moving sidewalk.

When he had first come to me, in the late afternoon, and when we had started for our walk together I had noticed that one of his legs dragged as we went along and that he kept putting a thin hand to an equally thin cheek.

Sitting over by the river he explained, as a boy would explain when he has stubbed his toe running down a hill.

When the World War broke out he went over to England and managed to get himself enrolled as an aviator, very much, I gathered, in the spirit in which a countryman, in a city for a night, might take in a show.

The English had been glad enough to take him on. He was one more man. They were glad enough to take anyone on just then. He was small and delicately built but after he got in he turned out to be a first-rate flyer, serving all through the War with a British flying squadron, but at the last got into a crash and fell.

Both legs were broken, one of them in three places, the scalp was badly torn and some of the bones of the face had been splintered.

They had put him into a field hospital and had patched him up. "It was my fault if the job was rather bungled," he said. "You see it was a field hospital, a hell of a place. Men were torn all to pieces, groaning and dying. Then they moved me back to a base hospital and it wasn't much better. The fellow who had the bed next to mine had shot himself in the foot to avoid going into a battle. A lot of them did that, but why they picked on their own feet that way is beyond me. It's a nasty place, full of small bones. If you're ever going to shoot yourself don't pick on a spot like that. Don't pick on your feet. I tell you it's a bad idea.

"Anyway, the man in the hospital was always making a fuss and I got sick of him and the place too. When I got better I faked, said the nerves of my leg didn't hurt. It was a lie, of course. The nerves of my leg and of my face have never quit hurting. I reckon maybe, if I had told the truth, they might have fixed me up all right."

I got it. No wonder he carried his drinks so well. When I understood, I wanted to keep on drinking with him, wanted to stay with him until he got tired of me as he had of the man who lay beside him in the base hospital over there somewhere in France.

The point was that he never slept, could not sleep, except when he was a little drunk. "I'm a nut," he said smiling.

It was after we got over to Aunt Sally's that he talked most. Aunt Sally had gone to bed when we got there, but she got up when we rang the bell and we all went to sit together in the little patio back of her house. She is a large woman with great arms and rather a paunch, and she had put on nothing but a light flowered dressing-gown over a thin, ridiculously girlish, nightgown. By this time the moon had come up and, outside, in the narrow street of the Vieux Carré, three drunken sailors from a ship in the river were sitting on a curb and singing a song,

> "I've got to get it,
> You've got to get it,
> We've all got to get it
> In our own good time."

They had rather nice boyish voices and every time they sang a verse and had done the chorus they all laughed together heartily.

In Aunt Sally's patio there are many broad-leafed banana plants and a Chinaberry tree throwing its soft purple shadows on a brick floor.

As for Aunt Sally, she is as strange to me as he was. When we came and when we were all seated at a little table in the patio, she ran into her house and presently came back with a bottle of whisky. She, it seemed, had understood him at once, had understood without unnecessary words that the little Southern man lived always in the black house of pain, that whisky was good to him, that it quieted his throbbing nerves, temporarily at least. "Everything is temporary, when you come to that," I can fancy Aunt Sally saying.

We sat for a time in silence, David having shifted his allegiance and taken two drinks out of Aunt Sally's bottle. Presently he rose and walked up and down the patio floor, crossing and recrossing the network of delicately outlined shadows on the bricks. "It's really all right, the leg," he said, "something just presses on the nerves, that's all." In me there was a self-satisfied feeling. I had done the right thing. I had brought him to Aunt Sally. "I have brought him to a mother." She has always made me feel that way since I have known her.

And now I shall have to explain her a little. It will not be so easy. That whole neighborhood in New Orleans is alive with tales concerning her.

Aunt Sally came to New Orleans in the old days, when

the town was wild, in the wide-open days. What she had been before she came no one knew, but anyway she opened a place. That was very, very long ago when I was myself but a lad, up in Ohio. As I have already said Aunt Sally came from somewhere up in the Middle-Western country. In some obscure subtle way it would flatter me to think she came from my state.

The house she had opened was one of the older places in the French Quarter down here, and when she had got her hands on it, Aunt Sally had a hunch. Instead of making the place modern, cutting it up into small rooms, all that sort of thing, she left it just as it was and spent her money rebuilding falling old walls, mending winding broad old stairways, repairing dim high-ceilinged old rooms, soft-colored old marble mantels. After all, we do seem attached to sin and there are so many people busy making sin unattractive. It is good to find someone who takes the other road. It would have been so very much to Aunt Sally's advantage to have made the place modern, that is to say, in the business she was in at that time. If a few old rooms, wide old stairways, old cooking ovens built into the walls, if all these things did not facilitate the stealing in of couples on dark nights, they at least did something else. She had opened a gambling and drinking house, but one can have no doubt about the ladies stealing in. "I was on the make all right," Aunt Sally told me once.

She ran the place and took in money, and the money she spent on the place itself . A falling wall was made to stand up straight and fine again, the banana plants were made to grow in the patio, the Chinaberry tree got started and was helped through the years of adolescence. On the wall the lovely Rose of Montana bloomed madly. The fragrant Lantana grew in a dense mass at a corner of the wall.

When the Chinaberry tree, planted at the very center of the patio, began to get up into the light it filled the whole neighborhood with fragrance in the spring.

Fifteen, twenty years of that, with Mississippi River

gamblers and race-horse men sitting at tables by windows in the huge rooms upstairs in the house that had once, no doubt, been the town house of some rich planter's family—in the boom days of the Forties. Women stealing in, too, in the dusk of evenings. Drinks being sold. Aunt Sally raking down the kitty from the game, raking in her share, quite ruthlessly.

At night, getting a good price too from the lovers. No questions asked, a good price for drinks. Moll Flanders might have lived with Aunt Sally. What a pair they would have made! The Chinaberry tree beginning to be lusty. The Lantana blossoming—in the fall the Rose of Montana.

Aunt Sally getting hers. Using the money to keep the old house in fine shape. Salting some away all the time.

A motherly soul, good, sensible Middle-Western woman, eh? Once a race-horse man left twenty-four thousand dollars with her and disappeared. No one knew she had it. There was a report the man was dead. He had killed a gambler in a place down by the French Market and while they were looking for him he managed to slip in to Aunt Sally's and leave his swag. Some time later a body was found floating in the river and it was identified as the horseman but in reality he had been picked up in a wire-tapping haul in New York City and did not get out of his Northern prison for six years.

When he did get out, naturally, he skipped for New Orleans. No doubt he was somewhat shaky. She had him. If he squealed there was a murder charge to be brought up and held over his head. It was night when he arrived and Aunt Sally went at once to an old brick oven built into the wall of the kitchen and took out a bag. "There it is," she said. The whole affair was part of the day's work for her in those days.

Gamblers at the tables in some of the rooms upstairs, lurking couples, from the old patio below the fragrance of growing things.

When she was fifty, Aunt Sally had got enough and had put them all out. She did not stay in the way of sin too long and she never went in too deep, like that Moll Flanders, and so she was all right and sitting pretty. "They wanted to gamble and drink and play with the ladies. The ladies liked it all right. I never saw none of them come in protesting too much. The worst was in the morning when they went away. They looked so sheepish and guilty. If they felt that way, what made them come? If I took a man, you bet I'd want him and no monkey-business or nothing doing.

"I got a little tired of all of them, that's the truth." Aunt Sally laughed. "But that wasn't until I had got what I went after. Oh, pshaw, they took up too much of my time, after I got enough to be safe."

Aunt Sally is now sixty-five. If you like her and she likes you she will let you sit with her in her patio gossiping of the old times, of the old river days. Perhaps—well, you see there is still something of the French influence at work in New Orleans, a sort of matter-of-factness about life—what I started to say is that if you know Aunt Sally and she likes you, and if, by chance, your lady likes the smell of flowers growing in a patio at night—really, I am going a bit too far, I only meant to suggest that Aunt Sally at sixty-five is not harsh. She is a motherly soul.

We sat in the garden talking, the little Southern poet, Aunt Sally and myself—or rather they talked and I listened. The Southerner's great-grandfather was English, a younger son, and he came over here to make his fortune as a planter, and did it. Once he and his sons owned several great plantations with slaves, but now his father had but a few hundred acres left, about one of the old houses—somewhere over in Alabama. The land is heavily mortgaged and most of it has not been under cultivation for years. Negro labor is growing more and more expensive and unsatisfactory since so many Negroes have run off to Chicago, and the poet's father and the one brother at home are not much good at working the land. "We aren't strong enough and we don't know how," the poet said.

The Southerner had come to New Orleans to see Fred, to talk with Fred about poetry, but Fred was out of town. I could only walk about with him, help him drink his home-made whisky. Already I had taken nearly a dozen drinks. In the morning I would have a headache.

I drew within myself, listening while David and Aunt Sally talked. The Chinaberry tree had been so and so many years growing—she spoke of it as she might have spoken of a daughter. "It had a lot of different sickness when it was young, but it pulled through." Someone had built a high wall on one side of her patio so that the climbing plants did not get as much sunlight as they needed. The banana plants, however, did very well and now the Chinaberry tree was big and strong enough to take care of itself. She kept giving David drinks of whisky and he talked.

He told her of the place in his leg where something, a bone perhaps, pressed on the nerve, and of the place on his left cheek. A silver plate had been set under the skin. She touched the spot with her fat old fingers. The moonlight fell softly down on the patio floor. "I can't sleep except somewhere out of doors," David said.

He explained how that, at home on his father's plantation, he had to be thinking all day whether or not he would be able to sleep at night.

"I go to bed and then I get up. There is always a bottle of whisky on the table downstairs and I take three or four drinks. Then I go out doors." Often very nice things happened.

"In the fall it's best," he said. "You see the niggers are making molasses." Every Negro cabin on the place had a little clump of ground back of it where cane grew and in the fall the Negroes were making their 'lasses. "I take the bottle in my hand and go into the fields, unseen by the niggers. Having the bottle with me, that way, I drink a good deal and then lie down on the ground. The mosquitoes bite me some, but I don't mind much. I reckon I get drunk enough not to mind. The little pain makes a kind of rhythm for the great pain—like poetry.

"In a kind of shed the niggers are making the 'lasses, that is to say, pressing the juice out of the cane and boiling it down. They keep singing as they work. In a few years now

I reckon our family won't have any land. The banks could take it now if they wanted it. They don't want it. It would be too much trouble for them to manage, I reckon.

"In the fall, at night, the niggers are pressing the cane. Our niggers live pretty much on 'lasses and grits.

"They like working at night and I'm glad they do. There is an old mule going round and round in a circle and beside the press a pile of the dry cane. Niggers come, men and women, old and young. They build a fire outside the shed. The old mule goes round and round.

"The niggers sing. They laugh and shout. Sometimes the young niggers with their gals make love on the dry cane pile. I can hear it rattle.

"I have come out of the big house, me and my bottle, and I creep along, low on the ground, 'til I get up close. There I lie. I'm a little drunk. It all makes me happy. I can sleep some, on the ground like that, when the niggers are singing, when no one knows I'm there.

"I could sleep here, on these bricks here," David said, pointing to where the shadows cast by the broad leaves of the banana plants were broadest and deepest.

He got up from his chair and went limping, dragging one foot after the other, across the patio and lay down on the bricks.

For a long time Aunt Sally and I sat looking at each other, saying nothing, and presently she made a sign with her fat finger and we crept away into the house. I'll let you out at the front door. You let him sleep, right where he is," she said. In spite of her huge bulk and her age she walked across the patio floor as soft as a kitten. Beside her I felt awkward and uncertain. When we had got inside she whispered to me. She had some champagne left from the old days, hidden away somewhere in the old house. "I'm going to send a magnum up to his dad when he goes home," she explained.

She, it seemed, was very happy, having him there, drunk and asleep on the brick floor of the patio. "We used to have some good men come here in the old days too," she said. As we went into the house through the kitchen door I had looked back at David, asleep now in the heavy shadows at a

corner of the wall. There was no doubt he also was happy,
had been happy ever since I had brought him into the
presence of Aunt Sally. What a small huddled figure of a man
he looked, lying thus on the brick, under the night sky, in the
deep shadows of the banana plants.

I went into the house and out at the front door and into
a dark narrow street, thinking. Well, I was, after all, a
Northern man. It was possible Aunt Sally had become completely Southern, being down here so long.

I remembered that it was the chief boast of her life that
once she had shaken hands with John L. Sullivan and that
she had known P. T. Barnum.

"I knew Dave Gears. You mean to tell me you don't know
who Dave Gears was? Why, he was one of the biggest
gamblers we ever had in this city."

As for David and his poetry—it is in the manner of Shelley.
"If I could write like Shelley I would be happy. I wouldn't
care what happened to me," he had said during our walk of
the early part of the evening.

I went along enjoying my thoughts. The street was dark and
occasionally I laughed. A notion had come to me. It kept
dancing in my head and I thought it very delicious. It had
something to do with aristocrats, with such people as Aunt
Sally and David. "Lordy," I thought, "maybe I do understand
them a little. I'm from the Middle West myself and it seems
we can produce our aristocrats too." I kept thinking of Aunt
Sally and of my native state, Ohio. "Lordy, I hope she comes
from up there, but I don't think I had better inquire too
closely into her past," I said to myself, as I went smiling away
into the soft smoky night.

Death in the Woods

EDITOR'S NOTE

Anderson rewrote the story "Death in the Woods" several times until he was at last content with the version which gave the title to his last book of selected stories (1933). As Paul Rosenfeld observed in his introduction to *The Sherwood Anderson Reader* (1947), among Anderson's favorite books was Turgenev's *Memoirs of a Sportsman*, and he quoted Anderson's remark that Turgenev's writings were "like low fine music." It is more than likely that among other examples Anderson held in mind as he rewrote "Death in the Woods," the example of Turgenev's long short story, "A Lear of the Steppes," was not forgotten. Turgenev's "low fine music" sounds throughout it, and the view of the peasant in Turgenev's "Lear" has the same clarity that Anderson achieved in his description of the old woman who met her death in the woods. Turgenev's story was also a story-teller's story, and its overtones are not unlike those over which Anderson had masterly control. Those who read Anderson for his "universal" qualities, qualities which make him seem European as well as American have their proof of what they have discovered in "Death in the Woods."

She was an old woman and lived on a farm near the town

in which I lived. All country and small-town people have seen such old women, but no one knows much about them. Such an old woman comes into town driving an old worn-out horse or she comes afoot carrying a basket. She may own a few hens and have eggs to sell. She brings them in a basket and takes them to a grocer. There she trades them in. She gets some salt pork and some beans. Then she gets a pound or two of sugar and some flour.

Afterwards she goes to the butcher's and asks for some dog-meat. She may spend ten or fifteen cents, but when she does she asks for something. Formerly the butchers gave liver to anyone who wanted to carry it away. In our family we were always having it. Once one of my brothers got a whole cow's liver at the slaughterhouse near the fair grounds in our town. We had it until we were sick of it. It never cost a cent. I have hated the thought of it ever since.

The old farm woman got some liver and a soup-bone. She never visited with anyone, and as soon as she got what she wanted she lit out for home. It made quite a load for such an old body. No one gave her a lift. People drive right down a road and never notice an old woman like that.

There was such an old woman who used to come into town past our house one summer and fall when I was a young boy and was sick with what was called inflammatory rheumatism. She went home later carrying a heavy pack on her back. Two or three large gaunt-looking dogs followed at her heels.

The old woman was nothing special. She was one of the nameless ones that hardly anyone knows, but she got into my thoughts. I have just suddenly now, after all these years, remembered her and what happened. It is a story. Her name was Grimes, and she lived with her husband and son in a small unpainted house on the bank of a small creek four miles from town.

The husband and son were a tough lot. Although the son was but twenty-one, he had already served a term jail. It was whispered about that the woman's husband stole horses and ran them off to some other county. Now and then, when a horse turned up missing, the man had also disappeared. No one ever caught him. Once, when I was loafing at Tom Whitehead's livery-barn, the man came there and sat on the bench in front. Two or three other men were there, but no one spoke to him. He sat for a few minutes and then got up and went away. When he was leaving he turned around and stared at the men. There was a look of defiance in his eyes. "Well, I have tried to be friendly. You don't want to talk to me. It has been so wherever I have gone in this town. If, some day, one of your fine horses turns up missing, well, then what?" He did not say anything actually. "I'd like to bust one of you on the jaw," was about what his eyes said. I remember how the look in his eyes made me shiver.

The old man belonged to a family that had had money once. His name was Jake Grimes. It all comes back clearly now. His father, John Grimes, had owned a sawmill when the country was new, and had made money. Then he got to drinking and running after women. When he died there wasn't much left.

Jake blew in the rest. Pretty soon there wasn't any more lumber to cut and his land was nearly all gone.

He got his wife off a German farmer, for whom he went to work one June day in the wheat harvest. She was a young thing then and scared to death. You see, the farmer was up to something with the girl—she was, I think, a bound girl and his wife had her suspicions. She took it out on the girl when the man wasn't around. Then, when the wife had to go off to town for supplies, the farmer got after her. She told young Jake that nothing really ever happened, but he didn't know whether to believe it or not.

He got her pretty easy himself, the first time he was out with her. He wouldn't have married her if the German farmer hadn't tried to tell him where to get off. He got her to go riding with him in his buggy one night when he was threshing on the place, and then he came for her the next Sunday night.

She managed to get out of the house without her employer's seeing, but when she was getting into the buggy he showed up. It was almost dark, and he just popped up suddenly at the horse's head. He grabbed the horse by the bridle and Jake got out his buggy-whip.

They had it out all right! The German was a tough one. Maybe he didn't care whether his wife knew or not. Jake hit him over the face and shoulders with the buggy-whip, but the horse got to acting up and he had to get out.

Then the two men went for it. The girl didn't see it. The horse started to run away and went nearly a mile down the road before the girl got him stopped. Then she managed to tie him to a tree beside the road. (I wonder how I know all this. It must have stuck in my mind from small-town tales when I was a boy.) Jake found her there after he got through with the German. She was huddled up in the buggy seat, crying, scared to death. She told Jake a lot of stuff, how the German had tried to get her, how he chased her once into the barn, how another time, when they happened to be alone in the house together, he tore her dress open clear down the front. The German, she said, might have got her that time if he hadn't heard his old woman drive in at the gate. She had been off to town for supplies. Well, she would be putting the horse in the barn. The German managed to sneak off to the fields without his wife seeing. He told the girl he would kill her if she told. What could she do? She told a lie about ripping her dress in the barn when she was feeding the stock. I remember now that she was a bound girl and did not know where her father and mother were. Maybe she did not have any father. You know what I mean.

Such bound children were often enough cruelly treated. They were children who had no parents, slaves really. There were very few orphan homes then. They were legally bound into some home. It was a matter of pure luck how it came out.

II

She married Jake and had a son and daughter, but the daughter died.

Then she settled down to feed stock. That was her job. At the German's place she had cooked the food for the German and his wife. The wife was a strong woman with big hips and worked most of the time in the fields with her husband. She fed them and fed the cows in the barn, fed the pigs, the horses and the chickens. Every moment of every day, as a young girl, was spent feeding something.

Then she married Jake Grimes and he had to be fed. She was a slight thing, and when she had been married for three or four years, and after the two children were born, her slender shoulders became stooped.

Jake always had a lot of big dogs around the house, that stood near the unused sawmill near the creek. He was always trading horses when he wasn't stealing something and had a lot of poor bony ones about. Also he kept three or four pigs and a cow. They were all pastured in the few acres left of the Grimes place and Jake did little enough work.

He went into debt for a threshing outfit and ran it for several years, but it did not pay. People did not trust him. They were afraid he would steal the grain at night. He had to go a long way off to get work and it cost too much to get there. In the winter he hunted and cut a little firewood, to be sold in some nearby town. When the son grew up he was just like the father. They got drunk together. If there wasn't anything to eat in the house when they came home the old man gave his old woman a cut over the head. She had a few chickens of her own and had to kill one of them in a hurry. When they were all killed she wouldn't have any eggs to sell when she went to town, and then what would she do?

She had to scheme all her life about getting things fed, getting the pigs fed so they would grow fat and could be butchered in the fall. When they were butchered her husband took most of the meat off to town and sold it. If he did not do it first the boy did. They fought sometimes and when they fought the old woman stood aside trembling.

She had got the habit of silence anyway—that was fixed. Sometimes, when she began to look old—she wasn't forty yet—and when the husband and son were both off, trading horses or drinking or hunting or stealing, she went around the house and the barnyard muttering to herself.

How was she going to get everything fed?—that was her problem. The dogs had to be fed. There wasn't enough hay in the barn for the horses and the cow. If she didn't feed the chickens how could they lay eggs? Without eggs to sell how could she get things in town, things she had to have to keep the life of the farm going? Thank heaven, she did not have to feed her husband—in a certain way. That hadn't lasted long after their marriage and after the babies came. Where he went on his long trips she did not know. Sometimes he was gone from home for weeks, and after the boy grew up they went off together.

They left everything at home for her to manage and she had no money. She knew no one. No one ever talked to her in town. When it was winter she had to gather sticks of wood for her fire, had to try to keep the stock fed with very little grain.

The stock in the barn cried to her hungrily, the dogs followed her about. In the winter the hens laid few enough eggs. They huddled in the corners of the barn and she kept watching them. If a hen lays an egg in the barn in the winter and you do not find it, it freezes and breaks.

One day in winter the old woman went off to town with a few eggs and the dogs followed her. She did not get started until nearly three o'clock and the snow was heavy. She hadn't been feeling very well for several days and so she went muttering along, scantily clad, her shoulders stooped. She had an old grain bag in which she carried her eggs, tucked away down in the bottom. There weren't many of them, but in winter the price of eggs is up. She would get a little meat in exchange for the eggs, some salt pork, a little sugar, and some coffee perhaps. It might be the butcher would give her a piece of liver.

When she had got to town and was trading in her eggs the dogs lay by the door outside. She did pretty well, got the things she needed, more than she had hoped. Then she went to the butcher and he gave her some liver and some dog-meat.

It was the first time anyone had spoken to her in a friendly way for a long time. The butcher was alone in his shop when she came in and was annoyed by the thought of such a sick-looking old woman out on such a day. It was bitter cold and the snow, that had let up during the afternoon, was falling again. The butcher said something about her husband and her son, swore at them, and the old woman stared at him, a look of mild surprise in her eyes as he talked. He said that if either the husband or the son were going to get any of the liver or the heavy bones with scraps of meat hanging to them that he had put into the grain bag, he'd see him starve first.

Starve, eh? Well, things had to be fed. Men had to be fed, and the horses that weren't any good but maybe could be traded off, and the poor thin cow that hadn't given any milk for three months.

Horses, cows, pigs, dogs, men.

III

The old woman had to get back before darkness came if she could. The dogs followed at her heels, sniffing at the heavy grain bag she had fastened on her back. When she got to the edge of town she stopped by a fence and tied the bag on her back with a piece of rope she had carried in her dress-pocket for just that purpose. That was an easier way to carry it. Her arms ached. It was hard when she had to crawl over fences and once she fell over and landed in the snow. The dogs went frisking about. She had to struggle to get to her feet again, but she made it. The point of climbing over the fences was that there was a short cut over a hill and through a woods. She might have gone around by the road, but it was a mile farther that way. She was afraid she couldn't make it. And then, besides, the stock had to be fed. There was a little hay left and a little corn. Perhaps her husband and son would bring some home when they came. They had driven off in the only buggy the Grimes family had, a rickety thing, a rickety horse hitched to the buggy, two other rickety horses led by halters. They were going to trade horses, get a little money if they could. They might come home drunk. It would be well to have something in the house when they came back.

The son had an affair on with a woman at the county seat, fifteen miles away. She was a rough enough woman, a tough one. Once, in the summer, the son had brought her to the house. Both she and the son had been drinking. Jake Grimes was away and the son and his woman ordered the old woman about like a servant. She didn't mind much; she was used to it. Whatever happened she never said anything. That was her way of getting along. She had managed that way when she was a young girl at the German's and ever since she had married Jake. That time her son brought his woman to the house they stayed all night, sleeping together just as though they were married. It hadn't shocked the old woman, not much. She had got past being shocked early in life.

With the pack on her back she went painfully along across an open field, wading in the deep snow, and got into the woods.

There was a path, but it was hard to follow. Just beyond the top of the hill, where the woods was thickest, there was a small clearing. Had someone once thought of building a house there? The clearing was as large as a building lot in town, large enough for a house and a garden. The path ran along the side of the clearing, and when she got there the old woman sat down to rest at the foot of a tree.

It was a foolish thing to do. When she got herself placed, the pack against the tree's trunk, it was nice, but what about getting up again? She worried about that for a moment and then quietly closed her eyes.

She must have slept for a time. When you are about

so cold you can't get any colder. The afternoon grew a little warmer and the snow came thicker than ever. Then after a time the weather cleared. The moon even came out.

There were four Grimes dogs that had followed Mrs. Grimes into town, all tall gaunt fellows. Such men as Jake Grimes and his son always keep just such dogs. They kick and abuse them, but they stay. The Grimes dogs, in order to keep from starving, had to do a lot of foraging for themselves, and they had been at it while the old woman slept with her back to the tree at the side of the clearing. They had been chasing rabbits in the woods and in adjoining fields and in their ranging had picked up three other farm dogs.

After a time all the dogs came back to the clearing. They were excited about something. Such nights, cold and clear and with a moon, do things to dogs. It may be that some old instinct, come down from the time when they were wolves and ranged the woods in packs on winter nights, comes back into them.

The dogs in the clearing, before the old woman, had caught two or three rabbits and their immediate hunger had been satisfied. They began to play, running in circles in the clearing. Round and round they ran, each dog's nose at the tail of the next dog. In the clearing, under the snow-laden trees and under the wintry moon they made a strange picture, running thus silently, in a circle their running had beaten in the soft snow. The dogs made no sound. They ran around and around in the circle.

It may have been that the old woman saw them doing that before she died. She may have awakened once or twice and looked at the strange sight with dim old eyes.

She wouldn't be very cold now, just drowsy. Life hangs on a long time. Perhaps the old woman was out of her head. She may have dreamed of her girlhood, at the German's, and before that, when she was a child and before her mother lit out and left her.

Her dreams couldn't have been very pleasant. Not many pleasant things had happened to her. Now and then one of the Grimes dogs left the running circle and came to stand before her. The dog thrust his face close to her face. His red tongue was hanging out.

The running of the dogs may have been a kind of death ceremony. It may have been that the primitive instinct of the wolf, having been aroused in the dogs by the night and the running, made them somehow afraid.

"Now we are no longer wolves. We are dogs, the servants of men. Keep alive, man! When man dies we become wolves again."

When one of the dogs came to where the old woman sat with her back against the tree and thrust his nose close to her face he seemed satisfied and went back to run with the pack. All the Grimes dogs did it at some time during the evening, before she died. I knew all about it afterward, when I grew to be a man, because once in a woods in Illinois, on another winter night, I saw a pack of dogs act just like that. The dogs were waiting for me to die as they had waited for the old woman that night when I was a child, but when it happened to me I was a young man and had no intention whatever of dying.

The old woman died softly and quietly. When she was dead and when one of the Grimes dogs had come to her and had found her dead all the dogs stopped running.

They gathered about her.

Well, she was dead now. She had fed the Grimes dogs when she was alive, what about now?

There was the pack on her back, the grain bag containing the piece of salt pork, the liver the butcher had given her, the dog-meat, the soup bones. The butcher in town, having been suddenly overcome with a feeling of pity, had loaded her grain bag heavily. It had been a big haul for the old woman.

It was a big haul for the dogs now.

IV

One of the Grimes dogs sprang suddenly out from among the others and began worrying the pack on the old woman's back. Had the dogs really been wolves that one would have been the leader of the pack. What he did, all the others did.

All of them sank their teeth into the grain bag the old woman had fastened with ropes to her back.

They dragged the old woman's body out into the open clearing. The worn-out dress was quickly torn from her shoulders. When she was found, a day or two later, the dress had been torn from her body clear to the hips, but the dogs had not touched her body. They had got the meat out of the grain bag, that was all. Her body was frozen stiff when it was found, and the shoulders were so narrow and the body so slight that in death it looked like the body of some charming young girl.

Such things happened in towns of the Middle West, on farms near town, when I was a boy. A hunter out after rabbits found the old woman's body and did not touch it. Something, the beaten round path in the little snow-covered clearing, the silence of the place, the place where the dogs had worried the body trying to pull the grain bag away or tear it open—something startled the man and he hurried off to town.

I was in Main Street with one of my brothers who was town newsboy and who was taking the afternoon papers to the stores. It was almost night.

The hunter came into a grocery and told his story. Then he went to a hardware shop and into a drugstore. Men began to gather on the sidewalks. Then they started out along the road to the place in the woods.

My brother should have gone on about his business of distributing papers but he didn't. Everyone was going to the woods. The undertaker went and the town marshal. Several men got on a dray and rode out to where the path left the road and went into the woods, but the horses weren't very sharply shod and slid about on the slippery roads. They made no better time than those of us who walked.

The town marshal was a large man whose leg had been injured in the Civil War. He carried a heavy cane and limped rapidly along the road. My brother and I followed at his heels, and as we went other men and boys joined the crowd.

It had grown dark by the time we got to where the old woman had left the road but the moon had come out. The marshal was thinking there might have been a murder. He kept asking the hunter questions. The hunter went along with his gun across his shoulders, a dog following at his heels. It isn't often a rabbit hunter has a chance to be so conspicuous. He was taking full advantage of it, leading the procession with the town marshal. "I didn't see any wounds. She was a beautiful young girl. Her face was buried in the snow. No, I didn't know her." As a matter of fact, the hunter had not looked closely at the body. He had been frightened. She might have been murdered and someone might spring out from behind a tree and murder him. In a woods, in the late afternoon, when the trees are all bare and there is white snow on the ground, when all is silent, something creepy steals over the mind and body. If something strange or uncanny has happened in the neighborhood all you think about is getting away from there as fast as you can.

The crowd of men and boys had got to where the old woman had crossed the field and went, following the marshal and the hunter, up the slight incline and into the woods.

My brother and I were silent. He had his bundle of papers in a bag slung across his shoulder. When he got back to town he would have to go on distributing his papers before he went home to supper. If I went along, as he had no doubt already determined I should, we would both be late. Either mother or our older sister would have to warm our supper.

Well, we would have something to tell. A boy did not get such a chance very often. It was lucky we just happened to go into the grocery when the hunter came in. The hunter was a country fellow. Neither of us had ever seen him before.

Now the crowd of men and boys had got to the clearing. Darkness comes quickly on such winter nights, but the full moon made everything clear. My brother and I stood near the tree, beneath which the old woman had died.

She did not look old, lying there in that light, frozen and still. One of the men turned her over in the snow and I saw everything. My body trembled with some strange mystical feeling and so did my brother's. It might have been the cold.

Neither of us had ever seen a woman's body before. It may have been the snow, clinging to the frozen flesh, that made it look so white and lovely, so like marble. No woman had come with the party from town; but one of the men, he was the town blacksmith, took off his overcoat and spread it over her. Then he gathered her into his arms and started off to town, all the others following silently. At that time no one knew who she was.

V

I had seen everything, had seen the oval in the snow, like a miniature race track, where the dogs had run, had seen how the men were mystified, had seen the white bare young-looking shoulders, had heard the whispered comments of the men.

The men were simply mystified. They took the body to the undertaker's, and when the blacksmith, the hunter, the marshal and several others had got inside they closed the door. If father had been there perhaps he could have got in, but we boys couldn't.

I went with my brother to distribute the rest of his papers and when we got home it was my brother who told the story.

I kept silent and went to bed early. It may have been I was not satisfied with the way he told it.

Later, in the town, I must have heard other fragments of the old woman's story. She was recognized the next day and there was an investigation.

The husband and son were found somewhere and brought to town and there was an attempt to connect them with the woman's death, but it did not work. They had perfect enough alibis.

However, the town was against them. They had to get out. Where they went I never heard.

I remember only the picture there in the forest, the men standing about, the naked girlish-looking figure, face down in the snow, the tracks made by the running dogs and the clear cold winter sky above. White fragments of clouds were drifting across the sky. They went racing across the little open space among the trees.

The scene in the forest had become for me, without my knowing it, the foundation for the real story I am now trying to tell. The fragments, you see, had to be picked up slowly, long afterwards.

Things happened. When I was a young man I worked on the farm of a German. The hired-girl was afraid of her employer. The farmer's wife hated her.

I saw things at that place. Once later, I had a half-uncanny, mystical adventure with dogs in an Illinois forest on a clear, moonlit winter night. When I was a schoolboy, and on a summer day, I went with a boy friend out along a creek some miles from town and came to the house where the old woman had lived. No one had lived in the house since her death. The doors were broken from the hinges; the window lights were all broken. As the boy and I stood in the road outside, two dogs, just roving farm dogs no doubt, came running around the corner of the house. The dogs were tall, gaunt fellows and came down to the fence and glared through at us, standing in the road.

The whole thing, the story of the old woman's death, was to me as I grew older like music heard from far off. The notes had to be picked up slowly one at a time. Something had to be understood.

The woman who died was one destined to feed animal life. Anyway, that is all she ever did. She was feeding animal life before she was born, as a child, as a young woman working on the farm of the German, after she married, when she grew old and when she died. She fed animal life in cows, in chickens, in pigs, in horses, in dogs, in men. Her daughter had died in childhood and with her one son she had no articulate relations. On the night when she died she was hurrying homeward, bearing on her body food for animal life.

She died in the clearing in the woods and even after her death continued feeding animal life.

You see it is likely that, when my brother told the story, that night when we got home and my mother and sister sat listening, I did not think he got the point. He was too young and so was I. A thing so complete has its own beauty.

I shall not try to emphasize the point. I am only explaining why I was dissatisfied then and have been ever since. I speak of that only that you may understand why I have been impelled to try to tell the simple story over again.

MEN AND
WOMEN

————————————————

EDITOR'S NOTE

In *Horses and Men* and in *Sherwood Anderson's Notebook* there are brief lyrical portraits of writers. Dreiser, Gertrude Stein, Ring Lardner, Paul Rosenfeld, Sinclair Lewis. These portraits are, as he properly called them, "impressions"; and in his remarks on Ring Lardner what he has to say about Mark Twain very nearly overshadows the subject of the sketch. The "impressions" are his moments of glancing at his subjects, and in that glance perceiving something that he alone has the candor to express. In *Sherwood Anderson's Memoirs* there is another portrait, titled "The Death of D. H. Lawrence"—and again one receives a strange "shock of recognition." It also shows Anderson's courtesy to his fellow writers, and his chivalry—a chivalry, by the way, which he extended also to his treatment of women in his novels, stories, and autobiographies. It is almost an understatement to say that Anderson was no prude when he discussed and portrayed sexual relationships, an affinity which he held with George Moore and D. H. Lawrence, but it is equally significant that his candor never modified his chivalrous attitude in his personal relationships with men and women. It was that chivalrous quality in Anderson which Gertrude Stein in writing of him called "sweetness," a chivalry removed from all taint of hypocrisy.

Four American Impressions:

GERTRUDE STEIN, PAUL ROSENFELD, RING LARDNER, SINCLAIR LEWIS[1]

One who thinks a great deal about people and what they are up to in the world comes inevitably in time to relate them to experiences connected with his own life. The round hard apples in this old orchard are the breasts of my beloved. The curved round hill in the distance is the body of my beloved, lying asleep. I cannot avoid practicing this trick of lifting people out of the spots on which in actual life they stand and transferring them to what seems at the moment some more fitting sport in the fanciful world.

And I get also a kind of aroma from people. They are green healthy growing things or they have begun to decay. There is something in this man, to whom I have just talked, that has sent me away from him smiling and in an odd way pleased with myself. Why has this other man, although his words were kindly and his deeds apparently good, spread a cloud over my sky?

In my own boyhood in an Ohio town I went about delivering newspapers at kitchen doors, and there were certain houses to which I went—old brick houses with immense old-fashioned kitchens—in which I loved to linger. On Saturday mornings I sometimes managed to collect a fragrant cooky at such a place but there was something else that held me.

[1]These sketches were written in 1919 and published in *The New Republic*.

Something got into my mind connected with the great light kitchens and the women working in them that came sharply back when, last year, I went to visit an American woman, Miss Gertrude Stein, in her own large room in the house at 27 rue de Fleurus in Paris. In the great kitchen of my fanciful world in which, ever since that morning, I have seen Miss Stein standing there is a most sweet and gracious aroma. Along the walls are many shining pots and pans, and there are innumerable jars of fruits, jellies and preserves. Something is going on in the great room, for Miss Stein is a worker in words with the same loving touch in her strong fingers that was characteristic of the women of the kitchens of the brick houses in the town of my boyhood. She is an American woman of the old sort, one who cares for the handmade goodies and who scorns the factory-made foods, and in her own great kitchen she is making something with her materials, something sweet to the tongue and fragrant to the nostrils.

That her materials are the words of our English speech and that we do not, most of us, know or care too much what she is up to does not greatly matter to me. The impression I wish now to give you of her is of one very intent and earnest in a matter most of us have forgotten. She is laying word against word, relating sound to sound, feeling for the taste, the smell, the rhythm of the individual word. She is attempting to do something for the writers of our English speech that may be better understood after a time, and she is not in a hurry.

And I have always that picture of the woman in the great kitchen of words, standing there by a table, clean, strong, with red cheeks and sturdy legs, always quietly and smilingly at work. If her smile has in it something of the mystery, to the male at least, of the Mona Lisa, I remember that the women in the kitchens on the wintry mornings wore often that same smile.

She is making new, strange and to my ears sweet combinations of words. As an American writer I admire her because she, in her person, represents something sweet and healthy in our American life, and because I have a kind of undying faith that what she is up to in her word kitchen in Paris is of more importance to writers of English than the work of many of our more easily understood and more widely accepted word artists.

II

When it comes to our Mr. Ring Lardner, here is something else again. Here is another word fellow, one who cares about the words of our American speech and who is perhaps doing more than any other American to give new force to the words of our everyday life.

There is something I think I understand about Mr. Ring Lardner. The truth is that I believe there is something the matter with him and I have a fancy I know what it is. He is afraid of the highbrows. They scare him to death. I wonder why. For it is true that there is often, in a paragraph of his, more understanding of life, more human sympathy, more salty wisdom than in hundreds of pages of, say Mr. Sinclair Lewis's dreary prose—and I am sure Mr. Lewis would not hesitate to outface any highbrow in his lair.

I said that I thought I knew what was the matter with Mr. Ring Lardner. He comes from out in my country, from just such another town as the one in which I spent my own boyhood, and I remember certain shy lads of my own town who always made it a point to consort mostly with the town toughs—and for a reason. There was in them something extremely sensitive that did not want to be hurt. Even to mention the fact that there was in such a one a real love of life, a quick sharp stinging hunger for beauty, would have sent a blush of shame to his cheeks. He was intent upon covering up, concealing from everyone, at any cost, the shy hungry child he was carrying about within himself.

And I always see our Mr. Ring Lardner as such a fellow. He is covering up, sticking to the gang, keeping out of sight. And that is all right too, if in secret and in his suburban home he is really using his talent for sympathetic understanding of life, if in secret he is being another Mark Twain and working in secret on his own *Huckleberry Finn*. Mark Twain wrote and was proclaimed for writing his *Innocents Abroad, Following the Equator, Roughing It,* etc., etc., and was during his lifetime most widely recognized for such secondary work. And Mark Twain was just such another shy lad, bluffed by the highbrows—and even the glorious Mark had no more sensitive understanding of the fellow in the street, in the hooch joint, the ball-park and the city suburb than our Mr. Ring Lardner.

III

Which brings me to a man who, it seems to me, of all our American writers, is the one who is most unafraid, Mr. Paul Rosenfeld. Here is an American writer actually unashamed of being fine and sensitive in his work. To me it seems that he has really freed himself from both the high and the low brows and has made of himself a real aristocrat among writers of prose.

To be sure, to the man in the street, accustomed to the sloppiness of hurried newspaper writing, the Rosenfeld prose is sometimes difficult. His vocabulary is immense and he cares very, very much for just the shade of meaning he is striving to convey. Miss Jean Heap recently spoke of him as "our well-dressed writer of prose," and I should think Paul Rosenfeld would not too much resent the connotations of that. For, after all, Rosenfeld is our man of distinction, the American, it seems to me, who is unafraid and unashamed to live for the things of the spirit as expressed in the arts. I get him as the man walking cleanly and boldly and really accepting, daring to accept, the obligations of the civilized man. To my ears that acceptance has made his prose sound clearly and sweetly across many barren fields. To me it is often like soft bells heard ringing at evening across fields long let go to the weeds of carelessness and the general slam-it-through-ness of so much of our American writing.

IV

Of the four American writers concerning whose handling of our speech I have had the temerity to express my own feeling there is left Mr. Sinclair Lewis.

The texture of the prose written by Mr. Lewis gives me but faint joy and I cannot escape the conviction that for some reason Lewis has himself found but little joy, either in life among us or in his own effort to channel his reactions to our life into prose. There can be no doubt that this man, with his sharp journalistic nose for news of the outer surface of our lives, has found out a lot of things about us and the way we live in our towns and cities, but I am very sure that in the life of every man woman and child in the country there are forces at work that seem to have escaped the notice of Mr. Lewis. Mr. Ring Lardner has seen them and in his writing there is sometimes real laughter, but one has the feeling that Lewis never laughs at all, that he is in an odd way too serious about something to laugh.

For after all, even in Gopher Prairie or in Indianapolis, Indiana, boys go swimming in the creeks on summer afternoons, shadows play at evening on factory walls, old men dig angleworms and go fishing together, love comes to at least a few men and women, and everything else failing, the baseball club comes from a neighboring town and Tom Robinson gets a home run. That's something. There is an outlook on life across which even the cry of a child, choked to death by its own mother, would be something. Life in our American towns and cities is barren enough and there are enough people saying that with the growth of industrialism it has become continually more and more ugly, but Mr. Paul Rosenfeld and Mr. Ring Lardner apparently do not find it altogether barren and ugly. For them and for a growing number of men and women in America there is something like a dawn that Mr. Lewis has apparently sensed but little, for there is so little sense of it in the texture of his prose.

Reading Mr. Sinclair Lewis, one comes inevitably to the con-
clusion that here is a man writing who, wanting passionately
to love the life about him, cannot bring himself to do so, and
who, wanting perhaps to see beauty descend upon our lives
like a rainstorm, has become blind to the minor beauties our
lives hold.

And is it not just this sense of dreary spiritual death in
the man's work that is making it so widely read? To one
who is himself afraid to live there is, I am sure, a kind of
joy in seeing other men as dead. In my own feeling for the
man from whose pen has come all of this prose over which
there are so few lights and shades, I have come at last to
sense, most of all, the man fighting terrifically and ineffectually
for a thing about which he really does care. There is a kind
of fighter living inside Mr. Sinclair Lewis and there is, even
in this dull, unlighted prose of his, a kind of dawn coming.
In the dreary ocean of this prose, islands begin to appear.
In *Babbitt* there are moments when the people of whom he
writes, with such amazing attention to the outer details of
lives, begin to think and feel a little, and with the coming
of life into his people a kind of nervous, hurried beauty and
life flits, like a lantern carried by a night watchman past the
window of a factory as one stands waiting and watching in
a grim street on a night of December.

Dreiser

Heavy, heavy, hangs over thy head,
Fine, or superfine?

Theodore Dreiser is old—he is very, very old. I do not know how many years he has lived, perhaps forty, perhaps fifty, but he is very old. Something gray and bleak and hurtful, that has been in the world perhaps forever, is personified in him.

When Dreiser is gone men shall write books, many of them, and in the books they shall write there will be so many of the qualities Dreiser lacks. The new, the younger men shall have a sense of humor, and everyone knows Dreiser has no sense of humor. More than that, American prose writers shall have grace, lightness of touch, a dream of beauty breaking through the husks of life.

O, those who follow him shall have many things that Dreiser does not have. That is a part of the wonder and beauty of Theodore Dreiser, the things that others shall have, because of him.

Long ago, when he was editor of the *Delineator*, Dreiser went one day, with a woman friend, to visit an orphan asylum. The woman once told me the story of that afternoon in the big, ugly gray building, with Dreiser, looking heavy and lumpy and old, sitting on a platform, folding and refolding his pocket-handkerchief and watching the children—all in their little uniforms, trooping in.

"The tears ran down his cheeks and he shook his head," the woman said, and that is a real picture of Theodore Dreiser. He is old in spirit and he does not know what to do with life, so he tells about it as he sees it, simply and honestly. The tears run down his cheeks and he folds and refolds the pocket-handkerchief and shakes his head.

Heavy, heavy, the feet of Theodore. How easy to pick some of his books to pieces, to laugh at him for so much of his heavy prose.

The feet of Theodore are making a path, the heavy brutal feet. They are tramping through the wilderness of lies, making a path. Presently the path will be a street, with great arches overhead and delicately carved spires piercing the sky. Along the street will run children, shouting, "Look at me. See what I and my fellows of the new day have done"—forgetting the heavy feet of Dreiser.

The fellows of the ink-pots, the prose writers in America who follow Dreiser, will have much to do that he has never done. Their road is long but, because of him, those who follow will never have to face the road through the wilderness of Puritan denial, the road that Dreiser faced alone.

Heavy, heavy, hangs over thy head,
Fine, or superfine?

REPORTAGE
AND
EDITORIAL

The American County Fair

EDITOR'S NOTE

The American County Fair appeared in paper covers (a Limited edition of pamphlets) in 1930. Of impressionistic writers in America none has greater descriptive powers than Anderson at his best, particularly when he holds before the eyes of his readers the view of a racecourse, a Midwestern pastoral, an evening in New Orleans (as in "A Meeting South"), or a county fair. The scene in its descriptive detail takes on an unmistakable life of its own; it is not a "still life," but one with air and light between objects seen and heard— and between the very phrases of Anderson's prose.

It is an odd time in a town. The fair ground commonly is a deserted place. It stands on a hill.

The land rolls away. Now the fair is being held. From the grandstand, where you sit to watch the races, you can see, over a high board fence, into distant hills.

The fair is held sometimes at the end of August but sometimes not until late October or early November. It makes a difference in the color of the hills.

Hills are at their best when white farmhouses cling to their sides. Nature untouched by man is too terrible. It is too difficult of approach. You become terrorized. The pioneers, who go into lands where man has not been, must be very brave or very dull. Perhaps they are only dull.

You are always wanting man in nature—woman in nature. You can get it at the fair. What a place for pictures. You will do well, at the country fairs, not to draw too close.

What a scene it is. Suppose you go up into the high grandstand. There is the bright grandstand, yellow in the afternoon light. The hills in the distance are blue.

Thousands of cars are parked in a great field at the rear of the grandstand. A cloud of dust arises. Nowadays people come to a fair from two or three counties.

The shows are here—in the open space between the field where the cars are parked and the grandstand. There is the snake tamer, the fat woman, the hoochy-coochy girls, the woman buried alive, the man with the web feet and hands, a calf with two heads. The gamblers are out in force.

They have all sorts of little wheels. They are shrewd-looking, hard-faced young men and they have their women with them. The women whirl the wheels while the men implore the men in the crowd, begging them to come up and win money. Win money indeed. These men and women are young but already they know a thousand foxy tricks to get money.

The fair is something special in the county. In spite of all the talk about improving agriculture, etc., it is a pagan outbreak.

See the women going about, the girls from the towns and from the farms. They walk boldly. Now is the time to get yourself a man. They all feel that. It shows in the way they walk. It is in their eyes. They will stay at the fair all day and far into the night. They are tireless.

The men all act a little puzzled. They wander aimlessly about.

The state agricultural department has brought fine cattle to be shown. Some of the rich farmers have also brought fine fat cattle, huge horses, sheep and pigs.

The older men go down to the sheds to look. They stand about and talk, spitting on the ground. The young fellows do not go and the women do not go.

The older women go into the buildings and sheds where women's work is shown. An amazing number of the older women are fat. Fat bodies rubbing against each other, fat still faces.

The children are tired, become tired early in the day. They cry. The tears make little streaks in the tiny dusty faces. The mothers carry the children into the field where the cars are parked and lay them on the car seats. They sleep there. When they waken they again cry.

Now it is time for the races. A bell rings. The judges of the races are in the judges' stand that is directly in front of the grandstand. There is a race starter who has a voice like an auctioneer. He shouts through a megaphone.

It is difficult to clear the track for the races. Thousands of people have gathered there. The starter of the races, with his megaphone, shouts, the county sheriff, a large man, appears and shouts. The people move back slowly, reluctantly.

And now, here are the horses—the trotters and pacers. This is something to wait for.

The horses are moving down the tracks, swiftly and smoothly. What has man done more noble than this?

He has developed these fine beasts.

They have been taught to go at a certain gait, the trot or pace, faster, faster, faster. They are hitched to little carts, very delicately made, and the driver sits up close to the horse. The moving flanks of the horse are almost in the driver's lap.

The drivers are young and old men. Some of them, many of them in fact, are quiet respectable men at other times during the year, excepting only in the fall when the fairs are being held. Now they shout, they lean forward over their horses.

There is no money to be made racing horses at the fairs. The horses cost too much. It costs too much to train them.

Professional trainers must be employed. There is feed to be bought, harness, racing carts and other equipment. The trainer's salary must be paid and there are grooms, in our part of the country a black for each horse.

The owners are country bankers, farmers, doctors and merchants.

The horses race for a purse of say two hundred dollars. A hundred dollars is given the winner and the other hundred is distributed between the second, third, and fourth horse.

And now the doctors, bankers, merchants, prosperous farmers have become something other than doctors, bankers, merchants, farmers. They have put on little gaily colored caps and gaily colored coats. The horses are brought out hitched to their carts.

The respectable citizen, who has become a jockey, is on the track, before the grandstand walking up and down.

Now the crowd is all attention. The shows are deserted, the band stops playing.

People crowd into the grandstand, they crowd to the fences.

The jockeys have mounted the little sulkies with the delicate bicycle wheels and the horses are being warmed up.

They dash up and down. The horses also are excited and the drivers are tense.

The drivers try to appear cool. After all this is dangerous business. These horses, so highly bred, so finely trained, sometimes lose their heads.

The horses must score down past the grandstand and the judges' stand until the race starter decides it is a fair start. Each driver tries to crowd to the front, to give his horse an advantage.

If it is not a fair start a bell rings and they must try again.

In the Grand Circuit, to which the fastest of all the trotters and pacers go, where the purses are larger, nearly all driving is done by professional drivers but at these little fairs—here the owner himself has a chance.

What would Mr. Harry Sinclair give if he could himself ride one of his beautiful thoroughbreds, or Mr. Harry Payne Whitney, or Mr. Bradley?

It can't be done. The rider of the thoroughbred must weigh almost nothing. He must be a mere slip of a boy.

On the Grand Circuit where the fastest of all trotters and

pacers go the amount of money involved is large. They are racing for ten thousand dollars, not for two hundred.

But these men, these country bankers, doctors, lawyers, farmers, who are horse lovers, have also invested their money. The horses here are often but a few seconds slower than those on the Grand Circuit. Some of them are sons and daughters of great sires. At the stables, over there under that hill, you will hear names of kings bandied about "He is a son of Grayson Gravy 2.01½. All the sons of that fellow go fast."

There is talk too of the art of driving. There is a certain horse you must "tuck in" until you get to the head of the stretch. He is a stretch trotter. Wait. Wait. Wait. Then ask him for it.

Ask him softly or with a gentle tap of the whip.

"Now, now, now."

Or he may be one who will take his punishment like a soldier. Give it to him. Lay the whip to him. Shout.

"Ata boy. Ata boy." A wild cry.

You have to put your own excitement into the nerves of some of the horses, make them feel it, tell them what you want.

You want all they have got, every ounce. The horse to keep his head, not to lose the smooth rhythm of the trot or pace, not to leap into the air, to keep on trotting or pacing.

The stride to be lengthened more and more, the legs to reach, reach, reach.

All the very fast ones have that smooth long rhythmical stride. They have courage too. They know what they are doing.

It is something to be the driver of such a horse. Everything is in the driver. If he is timid or weak-hearted the horse will know it now.

The horse will lose confidence, he will never win.

Something like love between the man and the horse. You feel it when you go to the stables. Watch the way that man over there, that merchant, touches his horse. It is the touch of a lover.

Do you think he touches the goods in his store that way.

And what about his wife?

A wife is a wife but a horse is a horse.

Do you think there are many wives in America as beautiful as Mary Rose, who this afternoon, at our fair, won the 2.18 trot? Will they respond as courageously when you call on them?

Why Mary Rose will not cry, she will not sulk. She is what she is. Look at her.

This afternoon, in the 2.18 trot, after she had won two heats, in the third heat that great raw-looking gray there challenged her on the back stretch.

The gray came with a terrific burst of speed and passed Mary Rose.

She was tired, tired. Already she had gone, at top speed, to win two grueling heats.

But that man there, that not-too-slender merchant from a neighbouring town, who owns her, who was risking his precious neck driving her—he called upon her.

There was something pleading in his voice.

"Mary, Mary."

He touched her with the whip too.

Did you see how her ears lay back, did you hear how the breath whistled through her nostrils? Why you could hear it clear across the tracks, in the grandstand here, in the intense silence.

All these thousands of people silent, all staring.

Mary Rose seemed to get smaller. She flattened. Her body went down closer to earth. Her stride lengthened and quickened.

She went faster than she could go. That merchant sat up there and pled with her. He was like a determined, half-angry, hopeful boy.

She never went back on him though. She raced the gray through the stretch to the wire, neck and neck, and then, forty yards from the wire, she made him cough it up.

He broke his stride. Mary Rose won of course.

Can you imagine any wife doing that?

Is the man, that merchant, in love? Of course he is. He is a lover. What else?

And so the fair again. Every year a moment like that. Something pagan, everyone feeling it.

In the evenings, now-days, traveling musical comedy companies come, "Revue" they call them. Young girls come out and dance, and show their legs.

Fat comedians get off stale Broadway jokes. The people laugh, year after year, at the same jokes.

And then the fireworks.

It is best, in the evening, to go a little away, up the track. into the darkness.

See it from there, the moving lights, the moving pictures.

In the dark stables Mary Rose is resting now. It would be interesting to go there. You will find that man, that merchant, hanging about.

He is going home, to his store in another town, on the late train.

However he has come back for a last look. He goes into Mary Rose's stall, touches her once more in the darkness. She puts her head on his shoulder.

He is going away now, back to his store, but next week, at the next town where a fair is being held, and where there is racing, next Thursday he will be back again.

He will be driving Mary Rose in another race. She will not last long, three, four, five years, but perhaps she will drop a fast colt.

There is, after all, the uncertainty of this sort of thing. You have to take chances in life.

In Washington

EDITOR'S NOTE

In his lecture on "A Writer's Conception of Realism" Anderson spoke of "bad art—although it may possibly be very good journalism." Yet one side of Anderson's gift for writing was journalism of a kind that enabled him to own and write for two small-town papers, one Republican in politics, the other Democratic, both in Marion, Virginia, in 1925. The results of this adventure were published in *Hello Towns!* in 1929. In these writings Anderson became an elder version of his own George Willard of *Winesburg, Ohio*—it was his proof perhaps that, as Oscar Wilde once said, "life imitated art." In being owner of both papers he also showed an indifference to political names and slogans, a vehement indifference, overtones of which were heard in his lecture on Realism in 1939: "Since I have been here [he spoke at Olivet College in Michigan] I do not believe I have heard the word 'capitalist' or 'proletariat' used once. What a relief." But his books, *Perhaps Women* (1931), *No Swank* (1934), and *Puzzled America* (1935) were extended editorials on American life and culture.

As editor-reporter of his Marion, Virginia, newspapers, he visited Washington, D. C. and Mr. Herbert Hoover in 1927, and what he saw was not merely Mr. Hoover, a future

President, but areas of Washington, including the Freer Gallery and Whistler's Peacock Room. The piece is a burlesque of the usual "newspaper interview," yet it does not fail to contain its "editorial" commentary.

NEWS

In Washington, where I have been sent to interview the Secretary of Commerce, Mr. Hoover. I do not like the job much. Why did I take it?

I am always undertaking something the Lord never intended me to do.

I have arrived in the city in the early morning and am not to see the man until late afternoon. It is bitter cold. When I saw Washington last, some fifteen or twenty years ago, it was merely a great straggling town. Now it has become a modern city.

I have been at a big hotel and have left my bag. I begin wondering what I shall do with my day.

We who live in country towns miss certain things. The radio and the phonograph can bring us music by the best orchestras—if there are any bests—we can hear speakers talk, but there are things we cannot get.

We cannot see the best players on the stage and we cannot see paintings.

I decided to go to a museum.

There are days for everything. Was this a day to see paintings? I should, no doubt, have gone to talk to some politician, but I knew no politicians as politicians. No one ever talks politics to me. I went to the new Freer Gallery.

The Freer Gallery, named for its builder, was built by a rich man of Detroit and was intended primarily to house the paintings of the American painter Whistler. In it are housed, as well, many old and rare objects of Chinese and Japanese art.

I went to the gallery in the morning and it was quite empty

but for the attendants. There was a hushed quiet over the place. The walls and the attendants seemed crying out at me "be careful, walk quietly, this is a sacred place."

Sacred, indeed. What a strange thing is the life of the artist.

Standing in the gallery and looking at these paintings, conscious all the time of the uniformed attendants watching me, afraid perhaps I might steal some of these sacred objects, an odd feeling of annoyance creeping over me.

Such a man as Whistler lives. His work is condemned or praised by the men of his own time. It has been the fate of some men, who have produced the greatest art, made the greatest discoveries in science, the greatest contributions to scholarship, to live and die unknown. They are perhaps the lucky men.

Such a man as Whistler, fighting for fame. He was always a great fighter. Once he wrote a book called *The Gentle Art of Making Enemies*. He knew how to do that all right.

Much of his energy must have been spent in fighting for fame. Well, he has won. He has fame. Fame, in the end, does not always mean worth. If you keep insisting that you are a great man after a time people will believe. It doesn't necessarily mean you are great.

James McNeill Whistler was not one of the great painters of the world. His fighting and his personality got him somewhere. A rich patron of the arts, Mr. Freer, became devoted to him. He has spent hundreds of thousands of dollars, his time, his own energy, in making Mr. Whistler's fame secure. Mr. Freer, because of his devotion to another, may possible be a finer and a greater man than Mr. Whistler.

As for myself, I could not get over the feeling that much of Mr. Whistler's work is vastly overestimated. Many of these paintings, carefully guarded by paid attendants, housed in this great stone building, are commonplace enough.

I went out of the famous Peacock Room and into the room where the older art treasures are housed. There were the old Chinese and Japanese things.

Objects of art come out of a day when there is no such thing as publicity—paintings by reticent, devoted men.

Whistler has been rather widely advertised as having brought over into his own day much of the fineness of these older painters. He has not brought over so much.

Such a short time ago, some fifty years, and Whistler's house in London was being sold over his head. Many of these paintings, so sumptuously housed now, were sold then for a few shillings. Have they increased in value so much?

The value of the older Chinese and Japanese things is fixed. Money cannot express it. There is "The Waves at Matsushinea," painted by some unknown man called "Satatsu" in the seventeenth century. In another painting the Chinese Emperor Ming Huang is with his concubine Kuei-fei in a garden. What a charming lady! It is spring. She is singing to make the flowers bloom for her emperor.

And there is another painting. The Emperor Weu, of the Chow Dynasty, is meeting the sage, Chiang Tzu-ya. The two men are meeting on an island in a winding lake. All nature seems hushed and quiet. Clouds are standing still in the sky, as though intent on the scene below. There is a sense in the painting of infinite time, space, distance.

Mr. Hoover and I did not meet on an island in a winding lake. There were no fleecy clouds floating in the sky; no sense of infinite time, space, distance.

It may be that Mr. Hoover has in him the making of an emperor, but I am no sage.

If I had been a sage I would not have been where I was.

I was in a great office building in the modern city of Washington. Before me sat a well-dressed man of perhaps fifty. Like myself, he was a bit too fat. He had leaned too long over a desk, over figures and plans, and I had leaned too long over a typewriter. Besides that Mr. Hoover had just been to a dentist.

And he did not want to be interviewed.

"Are you an interviewer?" he asked. "Yes," I said doubtfully. I had never been such a thing before. I am a writer of books, sometimes a teller of tales. I run a country weekly. Country weeklies are not newspapers. We do not interview people. I am not a politically minded man. Always I am asking myself the question, "Why does any man want to be President? Why does any man want power?"

By my philosophy power is the forerunner of corruption.

To be a bright, intelligent newspaper interviewer, I should have asked Mr. Hoover some embarrassing questions. He was a member of the cabinet of Mr. Harding, sat cheek by jowl with Mr. Fall and Mr. Daugherty. A stench arose from that sitting. What about it?

The question trembled on my lips.

Other questions crowding into my mind. "What of the League of Nations, our attitude towards the small republics of Central America?"

Better that I should not ask such questions. The man would twist me about his little finger. "It is just possible he knows something about leagues of nations and all such things, but what do you know?" I was now asking myself.

A fragment of song floated up into my mind, even then, at that unfortunate moment. The song was like the clouds floating above that island when the Emperor Weu went to meet Chiang Tzu-ya.

My freedom sleeps in a mulberry bush.
My country is in the shivering legs of a little lost dog.

"I am not going to be interviewed," Mr. Hoover said again. "I don't care," I said. As a matter of fact, I did not care two straws. I had made a futile trip to Washington. Well, it was not futile. I had seen the Emperor Ming Huang with his concubine Kuei-fei walking in a garden.

The Emperor Ming Huang had walked in his garden with Kuei-fei in another age than my own. There were no factories in that age. Men did not rush through the streets in automobiles. There were no radios, no air-planes.

Just the same men fought wars, men were cruel and greedy, as in my own age.

My mind full of things far removed from Mr. Hoover and his age, I was going out the door, having got nothing from him, having failed as a modern newspaper correspondent—a task that no such man as myself should have undertaken—when Mr. Hoover called me back.

"I will not be interviewed, but we can talk," he said. Mr. Hoover was being kind. He must have felt my incompetence. I understood what he meant. He meant only that things were to be in his own hands. We were to speak only of those things that Mr. Hoover cared to discuss.

He began to talk now, first of the Mississippi problem. It was a huge problem, he said, but it could be met. There was a way out.

There was the river cutting down through the heart of the country, twisting and winding. Had I not spent days and weeks on the great river? I told him I had. "It is uncontrollable," I said. "The Mississippi is a thing in nature. It is nature." But did not Joshua make the sun stand still? I remembered a summer when I took the Mississippi as a god, became a river worshiper.

I was in a boat fishing on the Mississippi when a flood came. I felt its power, it put the fear of God into my heart.

But Mr. Hoover had been down there and was not afraid. He spoke of spillways. There was to be a new river bed creeping down westward of the Mississippi—all through the lower country.

Then when great floods came rampaging and tearing down and Mother Mississippi was on a spree, she was to be split in two. Two Mother Mississippis, gentled now, going down to the sea. "What a man," I said to myself.

And could he also handle like that the industrial age?

There was the question. That also had become to me like a thing in nature.

I had after all got down to the heart of what I wanted to ask Mr. Hoover.

The industrial age has been sweeping forward ever since I was a boy. I have seen the river of it swell and swell. It has swept over the entire land. The industrialists may not be Ming Huangs but they are in power.

They have raised this Mr. Hoover up out of the ranks of men as perhaps the finest Republican example of manhood and ability in present-day American political and industrial life. He is, apparently, a man very sure of himself. His career has been a notable one. From a small beginning he has risen steadily in power. There has never been any check. I felt, looking at him, that he has never known failure.

It is too bad never to have known that. Never to have known miserable nights of remorse, feeling the world too big and strange and difficult for you.

Well, power also, when it is sure of itself, can gentle a man. Mr. Hoover has nice eyes, a clear, cool voice. He gave me long rows of figures showing how the industrialists have improved things for the common man. We spoke of Mr. Ford and he was high in his praise of the man. "When I go to ride in an automobile," he said, "it does not matter to me that there are a million automobiles on the road just like mine. I am going somewhere and want to get there in what comfort I can and at the lowest cost."

That, it seemed to me, summed up Mr. Hoover's philosophy of life.

When you have a man's philosophy of life, why stay about? Why bother the man?

Mr. Hoover spoke of the farmers. It is quite true that, in the distribution of the good things the industrial age has brought, the industrialists and the financiers have got rather the best of it. Labor has been able to take good care of itself, Mr. Hoover thinks. The farmer is another problem. Here is one place where the modern system has not quite worked.

It is a matter, he said, of too much waste between the farmer and the consumer. I gathered that the whole system of merchandising would have to be brought up into the new age.

"Something like the systems of chain stores," I suggested. He fended me off there. I presume any man in political life has to be cautious. The merchant class is a large class. There are votes there. My mind flopped back to my own town. Voters gathered in the evening at the back of the drug store, the hardware store, the grocery store. The small, individual merchant, who is, I gather, at the bottom of the farmer's troubles, has power, too—in his own store.

There had been something hanging in my mind for a long time. I thought I would at least take a shot at it. All of this industrialism and standardization growing up in my day. I had seen it grow and grow. A whole nation riding in the same kind of cars, smoking the same kind of cigars, wearing the same kind of clothes, thinking the same thoughts.

Individualism, among the masses of the people, gradually dying.

You get a few men, drawn up and become powerful because they control the mass needs and the mass thought. No questions asked any more. All doubting men thrown aside.

Young men, buried yet down in the mass, squirming about. They not liking too well the harness of industrialism and standardization. Men coming into power, not as Lincoln came, nor yet as Napoleon came.

At the bottom of it all, a growing number of the younger men feeling hopeless boredom.

Is the heavy boredom of a standardized civilization true for Mr. Hoover as it is sometimes true for me? I asked Mr. Hoover that question and for the first time during our talk he did not seem comfortable.

But power is power. He fended off again. After all, the age and the system of the age that may destroy one man may make another. Mr. Hoover has been made by his age. Apparently, he is satisfied with it.

I got out of Mr. Hoover's presence feeling we had got nowhere. Surely it wasn't his fault. I went walking for a long time in the streets of Washington. The more I walked the more sure I was that Mr. Hoover is the ideal among Republican men to be the present-day President of the United States—if he can make them see it.

Other men feel that. I asked several men I had never seen before.

I asked a man who drove a streetcar, one who opened oysters, another who scrubbed the floor in the lobby of a hotel.

"He is the ideal man," they all said. They were afraid the politicians would not give him the chance. The reason given was that he has too much brains.

But these men's opinions have also been made by the standardized newspaper opinion of the age in which they live. Their expression of doubt was merely resentment. Mr. Hoover is the blameless man. In Mr. Hoover's head has developed the ideal brain for his time. Are the other leaders of his party afraid of him? Surely theirs are not the nameless fears of such men as myself.

It would be a little odd if, the age having produced a perfect thing, a man who does so very well and with such fine spirit just what everyone aparently believes they want done—should be thrown aside, being too perfect.

There is no doubt in my own mind. I am convinced Mr. Hoover would make the ideal Republican President.

No one will ever sing songs about Mr. Hoover after he is President—if they decide to give him the chance. There will be no paintings made of him walking at evening in a garden while a lovely lady sings to make the flowers bloom.

But it is not an age of painting, not an age of song.

And so there was I walking in the streets of Washington, having made a failure of my day. I had tried to be smart and had not been smart. I had got myself into a false position. What happens to the age in which a man lives is like the Mississippi, a thing in nature. It is no good quarreling with the age in which you live.

I had come to Washington, I think wanting to like Mr. Hoover, and had ended by admiring him. He had not warmed me. I went over past the White House and tried to think of Lincoln living there. Then I went back to the Freer Gallery for another look at Ming Huang walking in his garden and listening to the voice of Kueifei—but it was closed for the night.

A SELECTION
OF LETTERS

No selection of Sherwood Anderson's writings can be called complete without a selection from his letters, and through the courtesy of Mrs. Anderson, Miss Frances Steloff of The Gotham Book Mart in New York, and Mr. James Schevill of Berkeley, California, I have been able to gather together a group of letters that have not hitherto appeared between the covers of a book.

That air of personal candor which Anderson cultivated, and not always successfully, in many pages of his autobiographies has its best and, I believe, most enduring expression in this present selection of his letters. Here he is far less concerned with the problems of subjective and objective truths than in his other autobiographical writings, and throughout the letters one feels his strong temperamental affinity with his British contemporary, D. H. Lawrence. When Anderson wrote to Stieglitz of his own "display of unhealthy egotism" he was very close to what Lawrence felt when he spoke of "the world that is tainted with myself," and this likeness of feeling is not derived from any literary influences that Lawrence's writings may have had upon Anderson. Both Lawrence and Anderson, with totally different sources of experience, maintained a watchful distrust of merely political movements and motives; yet both frequently felt the need of writing manifestoes,

Lawrence in his *Pansies,* Anderson in his letters; and both contradicted their sanctions of large ideological movements in favor of thinking for themselves. Both writers were, of course, strongly Protestant in their convictions; they were "protesters" in favor of the arts, and they belonged to that branch of Protestantism that is commonly called heretical and is self-consciously unorthodox.

To the social as well as the literary historian these letters of Anderson's reflect the thinking and emotional reflexes of the period (1925-1940) through which he moved—most clearly perhaps the letters to John Anderson, to Theodore Dreiser, to John L. Lewis, to Edmund Wilson, and to Gilbert Wilson.

These letters are arranged, as nearly as possible, in chronological order. Where Anderson dated his letters the dates are given. Most times, however, Anderson did not date his letters. When it has been possible to assign dates, these are given in parentheses.

TO ALFRED STIEGLITZ[1]

New Orleans, La.,
July 10, 1925.

Dear Stieglitz:

I just got back from my trip on the river and found the two letters from you and one from Paul. I wish I could see and talk with you and did not have to try to say in a letter what your letter made me feel. The trip up the river was a sort of turning point. What has happened to me this year, has happened before. I turn in on myself, spend hours

Alfred Stieglitz (1864-1946) was a gifted photographer, and one of the most perceptive of American pioneers in introducing modern art in painting to the American public. In New York, his gallery "An American Place," in which the early paintings of Arthur B. Dove John Marin, Georgia O'Keeffe (Mrs. Alfred Stieglitz), and Marsdet Hartley were exhibited, became the center of a group which included Van Wyck Brooks, Paul Rosenfeld, Waldo Frank, Lewis Mumford, and the Stettheimer sisters.

analyzing myself and my attitude toward life and finally get myself into a state where I am half insane. Then something happens to clarify the atmosphere. I realize anew that if I do my job the best I can at the time, it isn't up to me to decide on its ultimate merit.

The whole thing is a display of unhealthy egotism on my part, and when I come out from under it, I am always intensely relieved. In this case I have probably been able to come out from under it because of E.

Naturally I wish that your own health might go on for twenty years yet without your body giving you pain or uneasiness. There is a way in which you are so like a father to many of us, that when you are depressed, it depresses us too.

Paul's letter, however, reports you as flying around and working again. I am so glad Georgia is working. Her work last year meant so much to me.

It has been very hot here and Elizabeth and I are going away to the country somewhere. I think we can probably find a place in the mountains of Virginia or North Carolina. Will write you as soon as we have an address.

Love to all of you.

Sincerely yours,

TO JOHN ANDERSON[1]

Hamburg-Amerika Line
(1927)

My dear John,

There were so many things I wanted to say to you while I was still in Paris and that I did not get said. It was really too bad that we had to be together at a time when I was a good deal upset in regard to any of my own work. If you go on with the arts—and I suspect you will—you will know such times.

[1] Son of Sherwood Anderson; a young painter.

There seems to be no escape. You would think that a greater command of your metier, what is called "fame," etc., would satisfy and quiet the thing inside but it doesn't. Sometimes I suspect that only dull people ever really are satisfied with themselves.

What I really wanted to say was how much I am pleased with you. I like your attitude toward life and work. You have all of my affection.

Naturally I hope you will find for yourself an outlet in painting. It is one of the most subtile and difficult of all the arts. A lifetime will not teach you half you want to know. It would indeed be pretty fine if during this year you could get a conviction, inside, that you know what you want to do in life. Perhaps it will turn out so. I hope so.

I think, John, you are a bit inclined to take your own health, etc., too seriously. I do it myself. Try not to think about illness.

You have also perhaps some inclination to stay too much away from people. Go about a good deal. Never hesitate to use the fact you are my son if it will help you to see some man in whose work you are interested. You have natural good taste—will not vulgarize opportunities. Do not hesitate to take them.

About money. I want you not merely to be careful about it, but, on the other hand, if something comes up you would like to do and that would take another $100, do not hesitate to ask for it.

The great thing I really want to say is that I am satisfied with you—and very proud to be your father.

As always,

S. A.

P.S. For three or four weeks I will be traveling and speaking almost every day. I may not write often. After I get to the farm I will. A good passage, so far. E. pretty well. However we are just out—long miles to go.

(1927)

Dear John,

I have been intending to write you for several days but have been absorbed in work. I just this morning got your note from the Seine boat. The movement of my story has stopped for a time. I will write you in the interval.

I've a notion that, in America, you will be less bothered with homosexually inclined men. However the arts have always been a refuge for such men.

They are, as I think you have guessed, the less vigorous men. There is some distinct challenge of life they do not want to meet, and can't meet.

However they can't escape sex. They seem to me to try to throw a kind of artificial glamor over it, plunge into fake mysticism, etc. Some of them have delicate minds.

On the other hand American men cannot understand love between man and man. We have all of the same types in America but—except in the big cities—they hide themselves away. All kinds of lonely queer figures here. We have them in the country as well as in the cities.

If you have, in life, such experiences as I have had, I think you will find that finding a few real companions is the most difficult thing on earth. You will have to take what you can get, here and there.

On the other hand it is a great mistake to draw away too much.

Paul Rosenfeld has been here for three weeks. He is a real man, vigorous, full of life but extremely delicate-minded. He is rather afraid of people. I've been watching him. Lord, how much he misses of association, little flashing things picked up, by not being able to meet people, quite frankly. Some men get their sensibilities hurt and hurt. They can't stand it any more. That's why I suppose real achievement in the arts calls for a reserve of physical power.

To heal hurt nerves—try again.

The brain both makes and destroys. I think you have to meet the challenge of the brain's development or sink into idiocracy. It's the challenge David Prall was talking about in his essay.

To the artist it means not to shrink from human life—no matter what its complications—a large order.

However a man doesn't make himself all at once—by a resolution.

Artists have a thing called style. It's what makes an artist distinctive. The style is himself. What is he?

He is, I dare say, what his relations with himself and others make him.

To keep my relationships—not to shrink from them and yet keep personal dignity.

Homosexuality dodges. It isn't in the main current.

Artists use the phrase—speaking of a certain man—"He is in the tradition."

The old tradition of the arts is really health. The artist man should really, I think, be the most masculine and manly of all men.

I have tried to get at that somewhat in *A Story-Teller's Story*. You'll get more out of that when you read it again.

If it's there. A man never quite knows whether or not he has got down the inner meaning he was going toward.

I think also, John, that manliness—maleness really—implies tenderness. Dreiser is perhaps the most important writer living—because, in spite of unspeakable prose crudeness, he has in him the most male tenderness.

If my own senses are as acute as I hope they are, I would not be surprised if you would find—if you live long and become an artist—you'll be an artist in spirit whether you are in fact or not—you'll find a decided drift toward a kind of decadence.

Hatred, cruelty—taking the place of tenderness and the attempt at understanding. It's easier.

A good many things may make it so. Industrialism, city life.

The growth of advertising and publicity.

Fake figures always being built up by publicity—in the arts—in government—everywhere.

Everyone really knowing.

The answer being cynicism.

That's the easy way out.

You'll come however to realize the arts are old and old and old. There is a kind of underlying brotherhood. The signs of it are pretty faint sometimes.

I suppose the only value of being in Europe—for a young American—is because you may feel old men through old work.

The true thing in some way stays.

The half men—all homos are that—at bottom avoid the whole challenge. They are likely to be clever, sensitive in certain directions.

Then they turn and muss everything up.

Such a one in life always goes to books, pictures, other men's work.

There is no relationship with life itself.

You could use the word "God" or "Nature." Sometimes I just call the central thing "it."

That thing for which all men of parts have always been willing to go any length.

To work and be modest and wait and work again.

Not too much talk in cafes, not too much association with second-rate men.

Not quitting while there is life left in the body.

I don't know what it's all about. I've not many real illusions about my own value to "the tradition." As far as I see, though, John, it's the only thing there is.

S. A.

Ripshin Farm
Grant, Virginia
(1927)

Dear John,

Something I should have said in my letter yesterday.

In relation to painting.

Don't be carried off your feet by anything because it is modern—the latest thing.

Go to the Louvre often and spend a good deal of time before the Rembrandts, the Delacroixs.

Learn to draw. Try to make your hand so unconsciously adept that it will put down what you feel without your having to think of your hands.

Then you can think of the thing before you.

Draw things that have some meaning to you. An apple, what does it mean?

The object drawn doesn't matter so much. It's what you feel about it, what it means to you.

A masterpiece could be made of a dish of turnips.

Draw, draw hundreds of drawings.

Try to remain humble. Smartness kills everything.

The object of art is not to make salable pictures. It is to save yourself.

Any clearness I have in my own life is due to my feeling for words.

The fools who write articles about me think that one morning I suddenly decided to write and began to produce masterpieces.

There is no special trick about writing or painting either. I wrote constantly for fifteen years before I produced anything with any solidity to it.

For days, weeks, and months now I can't do it.

You saw me in Paris this winter. I was in a dead blank time. You have to live through such times all your life.

The thing, of course, is to make yourself alive. Most people remain all of their lives in a stupor.

The point of being an artist is that you may live.

Such things as you suggested in your letter the other day. I said "Don't do what you would be ashamed to tell me about."

I was wrong.

You can't depend on me. Don't do what you would be ashamed of before a sheet of white paper—or a canvas.

The materials have to take the place of God.

About color. Be careful. Go to nature all you can. Instead of paint shops—other men's palettes—look at the sides of buildings in every light. Learn to observe little things—a red apple lying on a grey cloth.

Trees—trees against hills—everything. I know little enough. It seems to me that if I wanted to learn about color I would try always to make a separation. There is a plowed field here before me, below it a meadow, half decayed cornstalks in the meadow making yellow lines, stumps, sometimes like looking into an ink bottle, sometimes almost blue.

The same in nature is a composition.

You look at it thinking—what made up that color. I have walked over a piece of ground, after seeing it from a distance —trying to see what made the color I saw.

Light makes so much difference.

You won't arrive. It is an endless search.

I write as though you were a man. Well, you must know my heart is set on you.

It isn't your success I want. There is a possibility of your having a decent attitude toward people and work. That alone may make a man of you.

S. A.

P.S. Tell Church that David Prall finally got the Cezanne prints.

Also tell the man at the shop where you go for the Picasso book—or if you have been there, drop him a note—the shop I mean.

(1927)

Dear John,

Your letter outlining something of your hours—perhaps sometimes days and weeks—of hopelessness about yourself falls in strangely with what I am writing about just now.

First of all I do think that this growing sensitiveness to the danger of cleverness and prettiness is a big achievement in itself.

Whatever you do in life you are going to find people all around you faking and getting away with it apparently.

If you have time some day, read again the last section of

my *Story Teller's Story*—about the man who wrote football stories.

Fake men being acclaimed everywhere, fake furniture in houses, fake house building, city building.

Vast sums being acquired by men from fakiness.

That doesn't matter.

You can't fake raising corn in a field.

Life comes back to the substance in the sod.

The reason for being an artist is that it is the finest challenge there is.

It's a man's only possible approach to God.

I mean to humbleness, decency.

I suppose you can be an artist in your attitude no matter what you do. I don't know.

It depends on what you feel. I happen to have given myself the challenge of a prose writer. I am going to stick to it while I live.

And it isn't because of success or fame or anything else. I would chuck all that fast enough.

It's because that is my challenge to myself—what Mr. Prall meant in his article.

I think it would draw us a bit closer together if you really knew that I—at fifty—am much closer to your position than you know.

You have torn up some drawings. Within the last year I have torn up twenty-five starts at novels—some of them going to 20,000 words.

It's nothing.

I had faked as you had—was perhaps showing off.

Or I had listened to someone else. I hadn't found my own truth for the man I was writing about.

Something in your letter I think is wrong.

You say, "It is my world."

It isn't.

Your Uncle Earl who might have made a fine artist went wrong there. He got that idea fixed. It destroyed him.

What you felt, when you sat down to write me, a hundred,

say a thousand, say ten or five, other young men might at that very moment have been feeling—in Paris.

Men and women walking along the streets. What do you know of them? Study them—don't be afraid—go, man. Make drawings of their faces.

Don't listen too much to what people say. Try to think what they are thinking and feeling.

You are made ashamed by something in yourself when you go near people. You draw away—more and more.

Your Uncle Earl did that for fifteen years. He loved me and I loved him. He hid himself from me.

It was fifteen years lost. It brought about his death. I sat beside him before he died. I know what did it.

Refusing love because you won't pay the price of misunderstanding, your own confusion.

You have got to pay it all. What you were feeling when you wrote this letter you have got to pay over and over and over.

There's no dodging a damn thing.

In a book of mine *Many Marriages* I came somewhere near saying it.

Your life is like a filled cup you have got to carry in the midst of crowds.

I would go to school and I would try to get what they had to give. Any skill of any kind helps. I would go among people constantly and try to understand them.

Another person is as important as a tree or a mountain.

Don't dodge.

You are pretty young yet. So much to learn. For Christ's sake avoid intolerance.

For example, dear John, you write me, often constructing sentences in a slovenly way, putting in capitals at the wrong place, saying "are" when you mean "is." That's important too—something to learn.

If for nothing else—that my sense of words be not offended.

You see, John, I don't give a damn about your being just a painter. I want you to do whatever in the end gives you most happiness.

But I do want you to avoid intolerance, self-absorption —fear.

There's a hell of a lot more to say. I'll send your letter back. While you are there anyway draw.

Draw, draw, and draw.

See if you can't begin to find a bit of light on everything out through the end of your pencil. If you can I know you won't quit.

S. A.

TO BURTON EMMETT[1]

May 12, 1927

My Dear Burton Emmett,

It all makes me feel a little woozy. We had better talk of it some time. If you come here I could show you how I work. Much, nowadays all, of my work is done in longhand. When I actually write I get too excited for a typewriter.

I used to use it. Much of my stuff went down that way first.

The pen is more direct. I throw aside a terrific lot of stuff. Novels started that never get into the right key.

Everything is in the tone. Does it belong to me? Is it coming straight out of me?

Often things break dead off. I might go on but would have to force my stroke.

I start again.

I get ideas. An idea is not a theme.

Theme and the prose surface to fit.

I am thinking of all this MS. that never gets anywhere.

Has that sort of stuff value?

We ought to think of real values.

I can't quite think you haven't the artist's impulse. I value you because you respond. Frankly I'm a bit afraid of the collector's impulse. I don't understand.

Let's forget the money matter, for the time anyway. Money

[1]Burton Emmett and his wife, Mary, were close friends of the Andersons, well known as art collectors and patrons.

is an odd thing. I hardly understand that either. When I have a few hundred dollars in hand I feel rich until it is spent. Then, I admit, I worry.

What a little frightens me about the collector's impulse is that it must have in it at bottom possessiveness. I may be wrong. Some day we will talk it out.

And then the gamble. There is no proof anything of mine will have permanent value. I'm not working for that. Oblivion doesn't scare me. Often it seems the sweetest of all ideas.

I am driving at some indefinite thing—the "it." The mystic in me arises there.

Don't bother to think of it now. What I have in the way of MS. will be here.

Do try sometime this summer to drive down for a few days. We'll go into the woods, sit on a log and talk.

Sincerely,

TO FERDINAND SCHEVILL [1]

Marion, Virginia, December, 1930.

It has been an odd year. I am at any rate a good deal amused at myself. This winter I have had opportunity to make three or four thousand dollars but can't make any of it. I'm becoming a nut. When I am offered money for anything it becomes spoiled for me. It doesn't matter so much as I spend little.

I've about concluded that it is wrong for me to go on thinking of myself as an artist at all. I can't be professional, it seems. On the other hand I can't quite go to work at some commercial thing.

Perhaps it will work. I think I will try to get someone to back me in devoting myself to the country press. It seems I do believe, after three years down here, that the country press offers the biggest opportunity in America for educational work in a real sense. All the big universities now have journalistic

[1] American historian and contemporary of Anderson.

schools. Why could I not do a good thing toward directing some of the younger talent and energy away from the cities and to the little weeklies? I would like to go into propaganda work for something of this sort. The country press was once quite a powerful thing but it has gone to seed. It has got into the hands of the petty bourgeoisie. In a way I think we have proved down here that it doesn't need to be quite that. I believe that I am enough of a figure to attract attention to the idea. I might take it up as a work I could do. If I do I should get someone with money to put up a fund. It wouldn't need be so much. The money would not need to be given, just the interest, for it to keep me going at it, pay a secretary, etc. If I went into it I would write and lecture on the subject. I wouldn't mind doing that. What I hated about the other kind of lecturing I did was that it had to be devoted to the arts and indirectly to myself, a kind of exhibitionism. I have a kind of growing conviction that these little country papers, once they got into the hands of live young men and women, could do rather wonders. I believe we all believe now that there must come a kind of change in our civilization. The alert, well-educated young men, or women, with a kind of flair—and there must be many such—could get a feeling on a country paper they can never get buried on the big dailies. Twenty or thirty such people in a state, say like Illinois or Virginia, could do a lot in ten years. They could check a lot of brutality, wipe out a lot of ignorance, and the young men and women doing it might well feel they were going somewhere. At that they could make a living doing it.

I believe it wants but someone of some little prominence pushing the idea. What do you think?

TO EDMUND WILSON[1]

(Summer, 1931)

Dear Wilson,

I got a wire from Tom Tippitt at Charleston—I guess it was after you left there—wanting me to come over and address the strikers from the courthouse steps. I didn't go. I had engaged to go down South.

I might have gone just the same but was uncertain. I have a queer guilty feeling just now about taking any part in pulling people out on strike, We go and stir them up. Out they come and presently get licked. Then we go comfortably off. It seems to me that if we, of what I presume you might call the intelligentsia, are to go in at all with the workers perhaps we should be ready to go all the way. I mean that we should be willing to go live with them in their way and take it in the neck with them.

I suppose the Negroes are good communist material but they will be making a mistake, won't they, if they take the material just because it is easy.

There are no *New Republics* sold here. I have sent a subscription and have asked for the number containing your article on West Virginia.

I sent for the books on Lenin, Stalin, etc. They are interesting but certainly impersonal. The books make them seem hardly human.

I have had a bad week's slump but am feeling more like writing again. It was great fun seeing you. I hope you will come this way again. Some of these days we'll do that stunt,

---

[1]This letter to Edmund Wilson was written during the period (1926-1931) when Wilson, as literary editor of *The New Republic*, made that publication the most highly respected and influential critical journal in the United States; not a little of its influence was due to the essays contributed by Wilson himself, which were later collected and published in his three volumes of criticism, *Axel's Castle*, *The Triple Thinkers*, *The Wound and the Bow*.

get in the car and go off bumming together. Love to Mrs. Wilson.

As always,
Sherwood

TO———¹

I will not try to answer the questions in your recent letter in detail. To an observer, who stands a little aside in such a civilization as has been built up in America—a part of it and yet not wholly a part—an artist—the American culture does not seem a thing made yet. Everything here is as yet in flux, in movement.

There has been and is this tremendous energy here. It has taken and still takes the form of mechanical development of life. This has been carried to ridiculous lengths. Life has got out of gear. The production of goods has been carried to extreme lengths and every conceivable method used to foist the goods upon the people. The plan has largely succeeded. We Americans are flooded with goods, we are drowned in goods. . . . The idea seemed to be that things could go on so forever. We could make cheap cars, mechanical clothes, washing machines, iceless refrigerators, etc., for all the world while we stayed at home and rode about in somewhat better cars—something of that sort. We have clung to the idea until we have got ourselves disliked over much of the world. The truth is that we are people like all other people. Do not judge us by the rich boaster you see taking his vacation in Paris, throwing his money about there.

The thing draws to its logical end. A part of the mechanical development here has been the automatic machines. This is constantly throwing men out of work. We stand idly by, our hands useless, while the goods still pour out of the machines. There is little growth of socialistic feeling here yet. We cannot yet quite face the fact that the American scheme isn't going to work. A curious part of the situation is this—it is an

¹Addressee and date are unknown.

undoubtable fact that a man's hands, having been separated from materials in his work, become ineffective.

Men, more than they yet realize, live through their hands. When the hands become useless something happens also to the mind. The real danger in modern automatic machinery lies in the fact that it produces impotence.

But the American people are not impotent, not yet. If we can avoid war, that so burns up young energy without results, I expect the readjustment to take place. I expect new impulses in art and literature, new political leadership, new facing of the problems that are becoming real in America as in the rest of the world. I expect America to draw nearer Europe, nearer all the rest of the world. I expect youth to be heard over here.

Sherwood Anderson

TO DOROTHY DUDLEY[1]

(Early spring, 1933)

Dear Dorothy Dudley:

I am in the mood to answer your letter at once but you will have to put up with the job of untangling my script. There are many provocative things in your letter.

In the first place don't tell me you are poor. I thought you Dudleys were well heeled. You amaze and shock me. You can't buy my book and I have no money to buy and send it. I never made any money out of writing except once. *Dark Laughter*. That I took and with it built a grand stone house in the Blue Ridge mountains of Virginia—spending it all in one grand, gorgeous building splurge and I haven't been able to afford to live there since.

I'm going to try again this summer. The place is big enough for ten or twelve people to live and I'm going to get a cook, plant a big garden and try some kind of co-operative scheme. A number of us could go there summers and live, I believe,

[1] A close friend of Theodore Dreiser and the author of a study of his writings, *Forgotten Frontiers*.

for a few dollars a week. Better get you a blanket, sheets and cat and come there and start that book.

And as regards Sandburg, Dreiser, etc. First of all you should know what damn crazy egotists all poets seem to be and you were making Dreiser bigger and more significant than any of the rest of us—which he probably was and is— but I fancy old Carl didn't like it.

And I do think you are mistaken in thinking that Dreiser has gone over to externals. I think he is like the rest of us in America now—confused and baffled. My dear woman, when you see at first hand what is going on here it's hard not to become a rampant red and cry "anything but this."

You know, my dear, it is not only the hunger and destitution—it's something gone out of America—an old faith lost and no new one got. It's youth not given a break—youth licked before it starts.

Well Dorothy Dudley—if you haven't any money go somewhere and get some and get at that book. You can't ask whether or not they want it. I think that—in the Dreiser book—you did show a detached attitude and a real ability to grasp things. And as regards this other thing, you brought it out clearly in your book— the place in which we Americans have failed most dismally—suspicion of one another—lack of any real belief in comradeship—failure to say a word to one another. My dear, it is a common experience of my own. How many times it has happened to me. I write a book—tear it out of my very guts, and there is the same old patronizing senseless patter about it in public. Often the same men who chatter in public about my "groping" "vagueness" etc etc etc will write me a private letter saying just the opposite.

As though if we dared love and help each other we had in some way sinned. Is that Puritanism, I dunno.

Anyway we have to begin and again begin and again to try to help each other, and work together, and make if we can a few little cells of good feeling and hope.

                                        Sherwood Anderson

TO BURTON AND MARY EMMETT[1]

Chicago,
September 15, 1933

Dear Burt and Mary:

I came up here to Chicago with Eleanor who had to come to a meeting of government officials—to discuss means of enforcing the minimum wage. I tell her she ought to bring up the matter of author's wage, but she won't. We are going home tomorrow, pack up and go on to New York.

We went for an evening to the Fair and it rained but I thought it rather wonderful, and oddly cheap and gaudy too —a mixture, like everything now—some kind of old life among us gone and the new life not born.

It is marvelous to think of being in your house but I can't help wishing you were there, we dropping in on you, doing things together, talking, etc. Perhaps you don't know what it means to us but you will know when I tell you I haven't made a cent this year.

It's because everything I've done this year has been for the future—the play on which there must still be work done and then this new book.

I want to tell—in story form—half story and half reflection —the tale of what happened to a young American business man that reversed everything in him—attitude toward his fellows, toward sex, toward the arts and his adventuring in the American field of intellectuals and artists, and have got nearly 40,000 words of it done. I am calling it "I Build my House," the house being not necessarily a physical house but rather the house of a man's self—with all the good and bad, kindness and hard selfishness that he is.

All of them requiring great frankness and work in trying to see a little clearly.

The hardest thing of all to see—a man's self.

Chicago itself is much more exciting to me than its World's

[1] See note, p. 468.

Fair. What a city it is, folks—how amazing, changing, un-disciplined, odd flashes of a new world, remnants of an old.

I took Eleanor with me and we went pretending we were a couple seeking rooms—I think the landlady was Suspicious. She may have thought I had made a pick-up on the street.

We went to the old rooming house and to the room where I wrote *Winesburg*.

Afterwards we wanted to go there—sleep there while we were here, but I wouldn't. Our going was such a success—old dreams coming back—faces popping up.

"No," I said, "let me have it just as it is."

How I'd like to talk with you both, be with you both, here in Chicago, where you two also had a life.

Dear people, you can't imagine all it means your offering the house to us for the winter.

Love,
Sherwood

TO THEODORE DREISER[1]

Marion, Virginia
January 2, 1936

Dear Teddy:

For the last year or two I have had something in my mind that you and I should have spoken about and during the last year or two it has been sharpened in my mind by the suicide of fellows like Hart Crane, Vachel Lindsay, and others, to say nothing of the bitterness of a Masters. In your play, *American Tragedy*, the play ends by the pronouncement that we can forgive a murderer but that society cannot be forgiven. To tell the truth, Ted, I think it nonsense to talk this way about society. I doubt if there is any such thing. If there has been a betrayal in America I think it is our betrayal of each other.

I do not believe that we—and by the word "we" I mean artists, writers, singers, etc.—have really stood by each other.

[1]The novelist.

There is a curious thing in America. The land is very vast. I think for example that French society has been able to attain to a real culture because we can say that Paris is France... as we could say London is England.

Now we know that New York is not America, Chicago is not America, San Francisco is not America. We have a curious situation. We are too much separated. I have hinted at this matter to you before and I take it to you because you are one of the least guilty, in the way I mean, of any of us. I know of no one more willing than you to put out a hand to others, more ready to give yourself. I know of no man among us with less bitterness in his nature. One of the reasons I love you is because in your presence I never do feel this bitterness.

Now what I have been thinking is that we need here among us some kind of new building up of a relationship between man and man. I feel so strongly on this matter that I am thinking of trying to get my thoughts and those of others who also feel this thing into form. I think even of a general letter or pamphlet that I might call "American Man to American Man." I think it is our loneliness for each other that has made most of us throw too much on woman and I also think that this is so much true that we are habitually making women carry more than their load.

I do not think that it is necessarily unfair to women to say frankly that the imaginative world is naturally the male province, but look what we do. We try to compensate for our loneliness for each other by throwing ourselves into the arms of woman. I believe it is in the nature of things that this is not sound. Instead of demanding of women we should be giving. Woman really wants personal beauty, one might almost say showered down upon her, that can only come out of the imaginative life. We have all been shirking our jobs but I do not believe that our shirking is due primarily to our own weakness but to our confusion and that our confusion comes partly from the tremendous size of the country. I even think that our Civil War was brought on by the impossibility or seeming impossibility of man finding man.

I have written you something about this before but have

not amplified my idea as I am trying to do in this letter. I have been trying to think my way through this problem and the thought has occurred to me that in a country like this where personal relations in any sustained way between men working in the imaginative field are almost impossible, that it would help for all of us to return to the old habit of letter writing between man and man that has at certain periods existed in the world.

For example, Ted, suppose that every morning when you go to your desk to work you would begin your day's work by writing, let's say, one letter to one other man working in the same field as you are. Suppose we did, by this effort, produce less as writers. There is probably too much being produced. I am suggesting this as the only way out I can see in the situation. It isn't that I want you to write to me. I could give you names and addresses of others who need you and whom you need. I think it possible to build up a kind of network of relationships, something closer say between writers and painters, painters and song makers, etc., etc.

I think now that we are too much confused by the political. I think this need of man for man in the imaginative world is more important. I think that if it had existed, men like Crane and Lindsay would not have committed suicide. I would like to issue a pamphlet, or a general letter, on this subject, not for publication in some magazine where the idea might be muddled by all sorts of sentimentality, but where it might reach out to all sorts of men needing what I am talking about here.

Teddy, the truth is that although I am addressing this letter to you, I am only doing it because you may possibly be the most distinguished man among us and I tell you frankly that I may use this letter as the basis of what I want to say to many others.

If I do this, I will ask you and several others to whom I may send copies of this letter to send me letters expressing their feelings in the matter to be included in the pamphlet.

I will say no more about all this today. I am writing of this on New Year's day. The project is very close to me. I think it may be to you.

Sincerely yours,
Sherwood Anderson

Notes : I am holding the above letter. It is interesting to me that on the day after I wrote the above I had two letters, one from Edgar Lee Masters, rather blaming the East and its attitude toward the West for the very thing I have tried to express above, and one from Malcolm Cowley[1] blaming the small bickerings, jealousies and cowardice of our little literary and intellectual groups in our cities.

Jasper Deeter of Hedgerow Theatre passed through our Virginia country and spent a night at a neighboring town. We gathered in a room and talked until late. Jap laughed and said that the great crime in this country was to be serious about anything.

I do know that he is persistently, and I believe in a fine impersonal way, serious about the theatre.

He objected that such a plan would bring down upon any one of us a flood of letters.

Well we all know about such letters. They come, in ninety-five per cent of cases, from young men and women who want to push themselves forward by crawling into bed with some man, or men, who they think has, as the saying is, arrived.

It's pretty grubby, most of it.

At the same time, tremendously needed.

I think it may be possible that the above idea, if it amounts to anything, may have to be a matter for each man to handle for himself, that the best that can be done is a general recognition of the need.

This we all know. We have very little real and sharply sustained criticism. How many of you constantly get letters

[1]Former literary editor of The New Republic, critic, poet, and author of *Exile's Return.*

asking you to go to bat for some book. What really basic cheapness in this whole idea.

One wonders sometimes if maleness is going out of our American life. It is amusing, is it not, that our most distinguished critic is a woman — Mary Colum.[1]

Something is constantly happening here. New men of talent come along. The critics are constantly trying to use the new man of talent to kill off the old—as though the minds of the critics could not hold the thought that two talented men, in the same art, could exist within the same country.

Today, for example, Hemingway is the new man. What praise lavished on him. Look out, Hemmy, they'll be trying to kill you off tomorrow.

Or it is Bill Faulkner, or Thomas Wolfe.

This I believe to be true—that any man of talent, whose talent has come to life and form in any sound piece of work, is never dead again until he is completely and finally physically dead. We all have lapses, go off into the political, get Hollywood-caught, money hunger comes.

We lose touch, do bad, rotten work.

O.K. We live in difficult times.

Can you believe that Vachel Lindsay would have taken . . if on that day he had got even two or three letters from some of the rest of us?

"Keep shooting, lad. Do not let them put the bee on you. You have done good work and will do good work again. We need you." You all know what I mean.

I am a little afraid, writing all of the above. Will my fellows be saying, "Well, well, Sherwood is down"?

No, I am not. I do not believe any man in American letters has been as well treated by his contemporaries as I have. It just happens that I know so many others who, because of some shyness, resentment over past treatment, too much crowing by the destroyers over some not quite up to snuff piece

[1]Author of *From These Roots* and *Life and the Dream*.

of work done, have this terrible feeling of isolation that the rest of us too often do nothing to buck.

The question in my own mind is this—is it possible to do anything about all this? Do you think—my general notion—that intellectuals, artists, etc., in this country lead peculiarly lonely lives? Would it only lead to a lot of sentimental gush to try to do anything about it?

S. A.

Note. How insulting women are sometimes in their day of triumph. "The way to a man's heart is through his belly." There's a sample of it for you.

TO JOHN L. LEWIS[1]

(1936)

John L. Lewis:

I have been wondering why something is not being done to draw the American intellectuals closer to American labor. Here we have "The friends of Soviet Russia," "Friends of New Spain," etc., etc., more or less organized groups of intellectuals, and united, trying, let's say, to give people a clearer view of what is going on in other countries.

Why not an organization here, let's say "Friends of American Workers"

To be sure there is the Author's League, more or less a trade union, but rather too conservative even for the A. F. of L.

And then there are some smaller, probably communist controlled groups.

Writers, for example, like Sinclair Lewis, Theodore Dreiser and a whole host of other men and women are not communists, nor are they conservatives. They are probably sincere believers in democracy and if it is true that labor is now at

[1] John L. Lewis of the United Mine Workers of America. There is some doubt that this letter was ever mailed.

the parting of the roads, labor more and more to be felt as a real power in national affairs, wouldn't it be a smart move for your organization to attempt an organization of writers?

Get some man who knows how to organize such a group. Get a few big names among writers to serve as a sort of advisory board. None of the real writers would probably be worth a damn at building such an organization.

The idea, however, being for some of your fellows, in the midst of the struggle, to meet occasionally with groups of writers having real power, letting them in on what you are doing, getting acquainted with them personally, etc.

The idea being a more or less loose organization of the writers in closer touch with labor, the idea itself sponsored by your group.

TO HENRY GODDARD LEACH[1]

(June 1936)

Dear Leach,

I have read with interest the discussion between Drs. Harry Laidler and Eustace Seligman. I am afraid it only adds to my confusion. The difficulty with me is that when I hear anything that seems like a defense of capitalism. I become communistic and when I hear communistic arguments, I become somewhat tender toward capitalism.

I don't believe anyone quite knows what makes wars.

I don't believe anyone can really think clearly on any subject involving whole peoples.

I do think that our present passion for getting at everything through economics is a little insane. When again, if ever, we can all begin to at least try to think small, if ever, we can all begin to at least try to think small, in little circles, a family, a few acquaintances, getting at what makes wars

[1]Editor of *The Forum* (1923-1940); Anderson's letter is obviously a reply to a series of questions sent to him by that journal of controversial opinions.

there, not forever jumping off into these huge pronouncements
...God help me, I'm always doing it too....

When as individuals we can learn more of the ways of
peace, we will have taken a great step toward universal peace.

TO MARY BLAIR[1]

New York
Friday
(Oct. 30, 1936)

Dear Mary Blair,

I think you are entirely justified, entirely right. How it
happened I don't know because I remember so vividly your
work.

I think it must be just one of those things that happen to
us—in American life. You are not now in the public eye.
Past work, no matter how fine, is forgotten. Apparently we'll
all fall into the pattern—the immediate.

I hope you can find it in your heart to forgive me. I feel
very humble and ashamed.

Sherwood Anderson

TO JAMES BOYD[2]

(1937)

Dear Jim,

All sorts of things in the head, dancing about. A man
becomes, outwardly, stolid, middle-aged, and remains a colt
inside. I'm thinking of things I wish I had talked over with
you but, as suggested, too many ideas. Sometimes I wish I
were like a Brisbane, talking, talking, all sorts of wisdom, into
a graphophone.

[1] Mary Blair (1895-1947) was a highly gifted actress, whose career
was associated with the Provincetown Playhouse in New York; she
was also the wife of Edmund Wilson.

[2] James Boyd (1888-1944) was a historical novelist whose best-known
books were *Drums* and *Marching On*.

It was rather a longer drive than I thought but we got into New Orleans at four Sunday, all hotel rooms taken, prices up, the outlook for any prolonged stay here thin. We get off tomorrow morning (Wednesday) for Corpus Christi, Texas.

Tom Wolfe had just been here, evidently being made much a hero and social lion. Wish I had seen him. I tried to call him, hearing he had holed-up at Pass Christian but he had left there, they said, for N. C. From all my friends here say, he is evidently troubled, rather distraught and upset. Aint it hell? You keep thinking of the other fellow as going on, eating, drinking, perpetually working and happy. I have been having a grand time thinking of Wolfe in that way, a kind of "roll river" man and now to find that he also gets upset, perhaps even discouraged. . .it's disillusioning. Perhaps you'd better write him. If I had found him here I'd have taken him off to Texas where, as far as I know, no one is literary.

After tonight we will have had three evenings here. . .too much drinking, talk until two or three, etc., and will be glad to consort with Kansas wheat farmers, down on the coast in their trailers. Wish you and Mrs. Boyd (am tempted to write "Kate") were along.

We had such a good and satisfying time there.

I took Paul's[1] *Rising Sun* play as well as the Virginia Woolf and will return them in one package.

My idea of the letters I wrote you and Paul and didn't send, after my first visit, was I guess a kind of confessional letter writing, as between several of us, working now, trying each in his own way to outline to the others his own difficulties, always of course in respect to work and living.

The two being so damned inseparable.

Such ideas seem so far-reaching and all right often until you try to explain definitely to another just what you mean. I presume I seek a feeling of some sort of more or less compact body of us, with some sense not only of working together to hold on to something, but also of keeping each other alive.

It may all be silly. If you do see Wolfe and if I have

[1]Paul Green, playwright, author of *Johnny Johnson*.

suggested anything at all to you by these words, talk it over with him.

You are very very fine people. It seems so foolish that I have not known you both longer. Anyway I'm grateful to you for being.

Sherwood Anderson

2700 Rincon St.
Corpus Christi, Texas
Feb. 21, 1937

Dear Jim,

I am writing you at Eleanor's hand because I just came out the hospital here after a two weeks' illness.

I was pretty sick beginning with a bad flu that upset my guts. There are too many yards of guts. It is one of God's mistakes, and every inch of mine sore as an ulcerated tooth.

I was terribly sorry to miss Wolfe as I believe so much in his basic soundness and sweetness. I think he will be more and more perhaps our great novelist. This tremendous fertility and richness of his has glorious value.

I wish we had gone to the Bahamas. Does it cost much there? I always have to think of that as I make so little money. Here we live really in a little auto camp at the water's edge having kitchen, sitting room, dining room and bedroom all miraculously crowded into one room. Can walk straight down along a little pier from the door and catch fish to eat. Eleanor does the cooking. The whole thing costing sixteen a week. (E. says this is a lie.)

Got both your Brownsville letters and the one here but, alas, your script is as hard to read as my own although yours seems somewhat more distinguished.

Glad you are reading Borrow, as I love his gusto, and don't mind his prejudice.

What I think hurt me a little about Green[1] was his bunking himself about Hollywood. After all an artist should be an artist in the sense that he accepts the artist's morality. I some-

[1] Paul Green.

times think it is the only true morality and that it is closely allied with what should be the morality of the craftsman or worker.

Jim, I do not believe that a man will come to save us. We must in some way save ourselves and others through brotherhood. You see, this terrible spiritual poverty comes back to men's breaking faith as it were with their own hands and bodies—as a woman may find God through her body in children so man must sometime come to realize again that he can only find God through his own body as expressed in work.

Does this seem far-fetched? It isn't. It is one thing I know with my whole soul.

And I do not feel proud that I also have never gone for something like the Hollywood thing—that is to say cheapening of my attitude toward figures in an imaginative world for money. I have never been greatly tempted. No one ever offered me big money. So I cannot, too much, condemn Green, for example, for going back to that trash.

I guess you know that I say all this loving very much something fine in Green.

Oh, keep clinging to this idea of a possible group of men who might help each other in this matter. I was full of it after the first evening with you and Paul and wrote many pages that I didn't send. One grows skeptical and even afraid. It seems an impertinence to be warning others although I kept wanting to shout at Green as though following him along the street and shouting, "Don't, don't!"

It is so hard on the other hand to accept poverty. How much more work I could do if I could afford, for example, a paid secretary. One places such horrible limitations on him- self by poverty, too. I keep saying to myself, for example, that will live only for the week or month, but occasional fears come to paralyze me, the fear, for example, of old age and dependence. And it seems so simple to settle it all by going for a time to some place like Hollywood and raking in some cash.

What is not realized is that the artist's obligation to people in the imaginative world is the same as a man's obligation to real people in a real world. You see the demand always made is to sell out these imaginative people. Of course all this is a deep subject, but to us at least, who are artists, the spiritual wreck we are in in some way has its basis here.

I wonder, Jim, can we help each other? Could you and I make Paul see and understand this? Is some sort of male grouping of American artists in our own age and time possible? Can we give this kind of love? It is thinking of it that continually half paralyzes me. I so much want it to begin to happen.

When will you be back in Southern Pines? I hope it may be possible for us to see each other this spring.

Give my best to Kate. It may sound impertinent calling her Kate but I think of her so. I was much charmed by a fine quality I felt in her.

I think I shall be better now and hope I shall do some work. Write me often.

> Sherwood
> by EA

> Saturday
> (1937)

Dear Jim:

It is uncertain how long we will be here. It depends largely upon Eleanor, who seems to have got herself tied up here.

How have you escaped? I seem to have become a kind of stuffed shirt for all sorts of things. People keep coming to me, wanting me to sign this or that manifesto for Cultural Freedom, for Peace and Democracy, for this and that. I do it and find myself involved.

From time to time an impulse comes to me. I would like to write the story of a man during an hour of his life, without physical action, the man sitting, or standing, or just walking about. All that he is that made him what he is. I have this temptation and at the same time realize that man is best understood by his actions.

Sometimes my feeling about inanimate objects goes, I'm afraid, to too great lengths. I remember a room in which I once lived in Chicago. Some men came to see me one evening and something vile happened. It was largely stuff going on in the men. It seemed to me to make the room vile. I had worked pretty well there but after it happened couldn't work. I got the notion they had put something into the very furniture of the room, into the walls and the wall paper. I carry it too far I think sometimes.

Your letter was something fine to me, the quality of the mind back of it so finely shown. We are working in a tough time, Jim. There are so many forces pulling away from the real point. It is good to have you thus unload your mind to me. I am grateful.

Sherwood A

TO PAUL APPEL[1]

The Miller Hotel
Brownsville, Texas
April 1, 1938

Dear Paul Appel,

Your letter of March 10, with enclosure, just caught up with me. I'd say that it is pretty hard to answer most of the questions you are putting up to yourselves. I'd say that the central difficulty, in all publishing, in all of its forms, is that there is a pretense of an interest, say in literature, or science, or in truth, while there is, at the same time, the fact that the whole set-up is a business set-up.

But how are you going to avoid this in the modern world? You have the same thing in the churches, in politics, in the colleges. It all seems to me to go with our kind of civilization. We have to thread our way through it as best we can. What we have got is an almost universal control of all of the channels of public expression by business and the central idea of business is profits.

I think that the whole set-up, from the writer's point of view, is hardest on the young, on the new writers as they

A young novelist and short story writer.

come on. It is pretty hard for them to realize how hard-boiled it all is. It confuses, puzzles and defeats them.

But how are you going to change it without changing the whole civilization? That is what you are up against.

Sherwood Anderson

TO ALFRED STIEGLITZ

August Sixth
1938

Dear Stieglitz,

I have written asking for the photograph. It is a way to remind myself how rich I am. Already I have some twelve or fifteen men looking down from the wall of the room. It is just possible that the whole thing will be too much for many people. There is such a richness of life, of character.

I was shocked to hear of your illness. It doesn't seem right. Illness in you is too much like a mountain running from the moon.

But I know this—that the life in you is real life. I have made an epitaph for my own grave—"Life not Death is the Adventure."

You shall always mean sweet life to me.

As always,

TO MAXWELL PERKINS[1]

(September 20, 1938)

Dear Max,

I was terribly upset by Tom's illness and death. Such a grand young talent gone. Eleanor thought I should go down to Asheville, to his funeral, but hating funerals, I didn't. I did however send his mother a wire. It's bad business. Tom had so much of the thing needed—vitality—great and rich talent.

Friend and editor of Thomas Wolfe.

To tell the truth however, Max, when he separated himself from you, I was afraid for him. I had a friend once, strangely like Tom, who, after years of tearing himself to pieces, much as Tom did, ended by drinking himself insane. Naturally, Max, I never mentioned this to anyone—a curious likeness in the two men—the same violence—talent—Mississippi River kind of force—and I speak of it to you only because, in spite of everything, you remained, to the end, closer to Tom than anyone else. I was often frankly afraid Tom would drive himself into the black hole of insanity as my other friend did, but my saying this is just for you.

The loss to literature is just a bitter fact. It hurts. We don't get many in Tom's class.

As regards the book on writing . . . Max, it is true that an amazing number of the younger writers have gone out of their way to say practically that I have shown them the way. They have written to tell me so. If it would be in decent taste to use some of the things said for the book on writing to introduce it, it ought to count—whether or not it would be in good taste to use these expressions of esteem, in private letters, for example from such men as Tom, I a good deal doubt. It is something we could talk about anyway.

I keep going on with the other book—I have now given the title "Men and Their Women"—in the loose form I have told you about. Anyway, Max, it is the form that seems best fitted to what talent I have.

I wish we had got you down here this summer. I'll not be satisfied until you know this beautiful country. I'm sure, if you come once, you would come again.

I'll be in New York sometime in October.

As always,

TO JAMES BOYD

April 10, 1939

Dear Jim:

I just got your letter yesterday. I was mighty sorry not to see you and Katherine when I was on my way South. Southern Pines and particularly your place were so lovely that spring morning. A colored girl came to the door and I asked her for a little slip of paper. I wrote my name on the paper leaning against the nose of my car. Filled with sadness that you weren't there. I knew there were a lot of trotting horses in training over at that track where we once went together. I thought we might have a morning together over there watching them step.

In your letter I like particularly your saying that about the business of writing—that it is the highest business there is, although I wasn't so hot, Jim, on your using the word "business" to get at your meaning and between us, Jim, I don't think that talent has a great deal to do with it either.

The country and our civilization has lost its morality and what is man without morality?

You see, Jim, it is my notion that we American writers, all of us, are pretty lousy. Who among us really takes upon his shoulders the responsibility of what you speak of as the business of writing? We do make a business of it.

I guess it is pretty much my notion that man's real life is lived out there in the imaginative world and that is where we sell him out. That's what we writers haven't found out. That is what we will some day have to find out if we are really ever to take on the responsibility implied in your saying that writing is the highest business there is.

I know you agree with me, Jim. I am mighty sorry I did not see you. I haven't yet read your new book. Tell Max to send me a copy.

With my best wishes to you both,
Sherwood

TO ETTIE STETTHEIMER[1]

Marion, Virginia
August 14, 1939

Dear Ettie Stettheimer:

I am sorry I did not get in to see you before I left New York. I wasn't well, wasn't working and came home here expecting to return to New York before finally coming for the summer but simply stayed here, Mrs. Anderson coming later.

We have been having guests. There is held here annually what they call a musical festival. It is held on one of the highest mountains east of the Mississippi, a mountain only some twenty miles from here. The idea is that the mountaineers, men and women, will come trooping up into the mountain. They will burst into song. There is a kind of man or woman who goes in for heavy FOLK . . . Percy MacKaye[2] and others. They all come.

They have had a good deal of trouble. Young men from New York's eastside put on faded overalls, tie red handkerchiefs about their necks and get all the prizes. Some of these New York eastsiders are wonderful in FOLK.

A good many Folk seekers usually get washed up on our doorsteps. It is wonderful. Two or three years ago Mrs. Roosevelt was here. There must have been at least ten thousand people that year all seeking the lonely mountain singer. You should come down and see us here. Really the country is very beautiful.

I hear from Paul Rosenfeld that you have moved. Lewis Galantière[3] was here with his tall beautiful wife. Ferdinand Schevill is coming in September and perhaps if he can get away from his Virgin Islands, Robert Lovett will come.

---

[1] Author of the novel *Love-Days*, written under the pseudonym of Henrie Waste.
[2] Poet and dramatist, author of *Kentucky Mountain Fantasies, etc.*
[3] Author, translator of modern French and German works.

I am writing only short stories. I have a lot I want to tell you if I can. I would like to have news of you.

Sherwood Anderson

TO GILBERT WILSON[1]

Denver, Colorado
October 26, 1939

Dear Gilbert Wilson:

Your letter reached me only yesterday at Denver, Colorado. I have been wandering around since you left our place and mail has been following me from place to place in the meantime. Your letter puzzles me, and of course I do not know how to answer it nor can I tell you what to do. In the first place, however, let me say that the letter from Alexander seems to me very fair and sympathetic. It seems a shame to let them down, and the first thought that occurred to me when I read that you were out living with Art and going off by yourself was to wonder why instead you didn't go to Antioch and sit down before that mural and do your thinking about it rather than about yourself.

Of course I know that you are terribly puzzled and it seems to me also that all of those who accepted as a kind of mission the changing of human beings through some big national movement have been let down most terribly by recent events.

I expect this has upset you. My own theory as to the position of the working artist that I expounded to you when you were with me may be also a dodging of the issue, but at least in the absorption in other individuals you are not let down so terribly as you are in these big attempts that take in great masses of people.

I do not know whether or not, when you were at my place, you took much note of the man who runs my farm and who, with his son, was building the barn. He is a simple country man and can barely read and write, but I must say gives me more satisfaction as a companion and friend than most of the

[1] A painter, best known for his murals.

artists who come to me and who are so terribly concerned about their genius and their missions.

Frankly, I do not believe this sort of thing concerns me at all. I have no feeling of being a public figure and do not want to be one, and often I think that my own interest in the lives of people about me has at bottom more integrity than this ambitious effort to think of masses of people, where they are going and what is best for them. . . .

You have talked to me a great deal of what Art means to you. You come to me and to Dreiser. I do not think we can really help. The truth is that we are probably wanting what you say you want, but have had experience enough to know that few men get it. I really think there is some danger of surrender to self-pity and also perhaps too much clutching at others. There is too much emphasis on what you can get from others and not enough on giving. This may sound like preaching, but it is pretty sound.

The truth is, all I can see for you, if you play fair, is to return to Antioch and face your problem there.

I am sorry not to be more helpful. I do not know what else to say.

As always,
Sherwood Anderson

New York,
March 20, 1940

Dear Gilbert Wilson:[1]

The other day I received a copy of the little magazine *Unquote* containing the correspondence between you and White. It is certainly revealing.

However, I do not wonder that the man is puzzled. Who isn't nowadays? Have the Communists really hooked up with the Fascists? It makes a sick-looking picture.

Am I right in thinking that every effort we make to think our way through these big world movements is bound to

[1] At the time of this letter, Wilson had returned to Antioch College.

come to nothing just now, so that a man must work in his own back yard, hoping that these big power-hungry ones will kill each other off and a little sanity come back into life?

Anyway you know what I mean when we talked of a man working in the small, trying to save a little of the feeling of man for man.

Sincerely,
Sherwood Anderson

TO ANITA LOOS[1]

The Royalton
December 1, 1940

Dear Anita:

. . . Eleanor and I will be here, at least by present plans, until the 15th or 20th of December. We will then, I presume, go home for the holidays. And I expect we will be off to South America about the middle of January. There was some talk of my going down there, with Rockefeller money, on a kind of cultural mission, to get in touch with South American writers, but now I believe I will probably be sent by one of the magazines. This kind of a trip would be much less official and would be more in my line. Eleanor will go with me if we pull it off and I think we will.

I am glad to hear that you were out for Roosevelt. I did not do much but Eleanor was hot on the job. She even made several street-corner speeches here in New York, and had some good stories to tell of her experiences.

Naturally, Anita, I am keenly interested in what you say of Hakim, the producer of *Baker's Wife*. I may have told you that when *The Baker's Wife* opened in New York two or three of the critics said something to the effect that it was the kind of movie that Sherwood Anderson could do, and when I saw it I felt a little bit that way myself. As regards the material, I think I would suggest, first of all, two stories.

[1] The author of the famous *Gentlemen Prefer Blondes;* "John" refers to her husband, John Emerson.

In *Winesburg, Ohio* there is the story called "A Man of Ideas." I am pretty sure that a figure of this story, Jo Welling, could be worked up into something both very amusing and very human. It would have to be built up, to be sure, but the story in *Winesburg* could, I am also sure, give the key to how to work it up.

And then there is the title story to the book called *The Triumph of the Egg*. With another fellow helping me I once made a little play out of this story that was produced by the old Provincetown theatre. Gene O'Neill had a two-act play, *Different*, and we filled out the evening with the *Egg*. I think the figure here of the poor little restaurant keeper trying to be a public entertainer could also be made into something rather grand if handled right.

I think these two stories are the ones I would tell Mr. Hakim to look at. *Winesburg, Ohio* is in the Modern Library and therefore could be got in any bookstore. I believe *Triumph of the Egg* is now out of print but under other cover today I am sending you one.

I just made a change of publishers, leaving Scribner's and going to Harcourt Brace. I am doing a book of memoirs, in which by the way I hope to do John justice, and Harcourt Brace were so enthusiastic about the project and made such a good offer on it that I am going over to them.

Some time ago a friend of mine here recommended to me a Hollywood agent named Ned Brown. I know very little about him but he seems to write intelligent letters and to be anxious to get to work on my material, so I may ask him to go to see Mr. Hakim, but before he does so I am going to take the liberty of asking him to first call you on the telephone as I think it would be much nicer if the first suggestions to Hakim in regard to the stories came from you.

I wish, Anita, that it were possible for you and John to take the trip to South America with us for this winter. Perhaps we can do it together next winter.

Sincerely yours,
Sherwood

P.S. Both Eleanor and myself are struggling with the Spanish language. I bought an outfit called "Linguaphone." I put the records on the phonograph so that I may hear the actual spoken language. I think the outfit would be a big help to you.

THE VIKING PORTABLE LIBRARY

VIKING CRITICAL LIBRARY

Malcolm Cowley, *General Editor*

Sherwood Anderson

WINESBURG, OHIO: TEXT AND CRITICISM

Edited by John H. Ferres

This volume contains the complete text of *Winesburg, Ohio*, including Anderson's comments; six contemporary reviews; twenty critical essays; a chronology of Anderson's life; topics for discussion and papers; and a bibliography.

Jack Kerouac

ON THE ROAD: TEXT AND CRITICISM

Edited by Scott Donaldson

In addition to the complete text, this volume contains four essays on the Beat Generation, including Kerouac's own essay on its origins; nine critical commentaries; four pieces on Kerouac and his art; a chronology; a biography; topics for discussion and papers; and a selected bibliography.

John Steinbeck

THE GRAPES OF WRATH: TEXT AND CRITICISM

Edited by Peter Lisca

This Critical Edition contains the complete text of the novel; sixteen critical essays; a chronology of Steinbeck's life; a bibliography; and topics for discussion and papers.

Ken Kesey

ONE FLEW OVER THE CUCKOO'S NEST: TEXT AND CRITICISM

Edited by John C. Pratt

This volume contains the complete text; an early draft of the opening scene of the novel; two letters from, and two interviews with, the author; eleven critical essays; seven analogies and perspectives, including selections from Ralph Ellison's *Invisible Man*, Robert Penn Warren's *All the King's Men*, and Jack Kerouac's *On the Road;* topics for discussion and papers; a chronology; and selected bibliography.

Other important titles in the Viking Critical Library:

THE CRUCIBLE, *Arthur Miller, Edited by Gerald Weales*

DEATH OF A SALESMAN, *Arthur Miller, Edited by Gerald Weales*

HERZOG, *Saul Bellow, Edited by Irving Howe*